J. B. Mackie

The Life and Work of Duncan McLaren

Vol. I

J. B. Mackie

The Life and Work of Duncan McLaren
Vol. I

ISBN/EAN: 9783337062699

Printed in Europe, USA, Canada, Australia, Japan

Cover: Foto ©Raphael Reischuk / pixelio.de

More available books at **www.hansebooks.com**

McLaren
1862

THE
LIFE AND WORK
OF
DUNCAN M^cLAREN

BY

J. B. MACKIE

Vol. I.

THOMAS NELSON AND SONS
London, Edinburgh, and New York

1888

DEDICATED

TO

The Citizens of Edinburgh.

PREFACE.

Tᴜɪs biography has been written in the belief that the life
of Duncan McLaren exalted individual public service as at
once the privilege and glory of a free people—the foundation of the well-being and safety of the commonwealth ; and
that a faithful record of his long and arduous career, as
merchant, citizen, councillor, and statesman, illustrating the
chivalrousness of spirit in which his public work was undertaken, the heroism and fidelity with which it was carried on,
and the substantial public benefits it secured, may not only
stimulate public-spirited men to self-sacrificing efforts for
the common good, but, in these days when the principle of
self-government is being universally applied, in county as
well as in municipal and national administration, be read
with a sense of encouragement as well as gratitude. The
best guarantee for the future prosperity of the country,
under the extension of the conditions of national life established in 1832, is to be found in the increased purity and
efficiency of administration and the more actively beneficent
tendency of legislation which were introduced with the first
Reform Act.

Duncan McLaren's public work began with the Reformed
Town Council, and it extended over a period of upwards
of fifty years. Its record is writ large in the civic annals
of Edinburgh and in the political history of Scotland. For

his service was at once continuous and multiform ;—educational, municipal, ecclesiastical, and political. There were distinct epochs in his career, when exceptionally onerous duties or strikingly successful achievements gave evidence of his remarkable powers of resource, and won for him special expressions of public gratitude. His establishment of the Heriot Free Schools; his settlement of the City affairs; his championship of the cause of Free Trade; his controversy with Mr. Macaulay; the social reform inaugurated during his Lord Provostship, which resulted in the Forbes Mackenzie Act; his sixteen years of parliamentary work as senior Member for Edinburgh, are in themselves distinct and prominent features capable of presentation in chronological order. But they were only incidents in struggles and controversies which lasted the greater part of his public life, and in which, so long as they were public questions, he bore always an active and generally a leading part. His establishment of the Heriot Free Schools was only the starting-point of labours as national educational reformer which never ceased until the adoption of Lord Advocate Young's Act in 1872. He was an advocate of penny postage, free tolls, and the abolition of petty customs long before the agitation for the abolition of the Corn-laws was set on foot; and after his friend Richard Cobden had been withdrawn from the field of battle, he contended in the House of Commons as well as in the Chamber of Commerce for the development of Free Trade policy. His superintendence of every department of municipal life in Edinburgh, for years after he had left the Council, was as vigilant as his participation in every new public movement for the good of the people was prompt and energetic. His resistance to Church aggression, his battle for religious equality, his advocacy of franchise reform as the right of every householder, were carried on simultaneously and persistently alike in local and national affairs, from the day on which he entered public life till his death.

To portray a public career so prolonged and many-sided, so full of activity and so crowded with details, so well ordered and so complete, is necessarily a work of great difficulty. Where the interest of a life centres in personal narrative, it is easy for the biographer to give its history in chronological order. Where, as in Mr. McLaren's case, his life expressed itself in the widely varied public questions which engrossed him, the subject classifies itself naturally according to work. The reader of the following pages will therefore find that sometimes at the end of a chapter he is brought almost to the close of Mr. McLaren's life, while in the next chapter he again sees him at the beginning of his career. But while sequence in time is necessarily excluded from the plan of this biography, no other mode of treatment could do justice to a life so impersonal as Mr. McLaren's, and so intimately associated with all the leading political and local questions of his day.

In the execution of his task the author has had many encouragements and advantages. He was invited to undertake it by Duncan McLaren himself, from whom he received some specially prepared memoranda. The stores of papers and documents collected at Newington House were placed at his disposal. The aid of the various members of the family was always within his reach, and was rendered with a filial devotion and a loyalty to truth in themselves beautiful and inspiring. Mrs. McLaren's stimulating sympathy and help never failed, and are exhibited more particularly in the introductory chapters, dealing with her husband's personal and domestic life, and in the concluding chapter, describing his last illness.

This work has been, from first to last, a labour of love; and if the reader's appreciation of the character of Duncan McLaren increase during the perusal of this memoir in anything like the proportion with which it has increased in the mind of the author during its compilation, he will feel that his efforts to do justice to a great and noble life, and to attract by Duncan McLaren's example pure-hearted patriotic men to public service, cannot have wholly failed.

> " Thy pardon for this long and tedious case,
>   Which, now that I review it, needs must seem
>   Unduly dwelt on, prolixly set forth.
>   Yet I discern in what is writ
>   Good cause for the peculiar interest
>   And awe, indeed, this man has touched me with."

NEWCASTLE-ON-TYNE, *December* 1888.

CONTENTS.

CHAPTER I.

PARENTAGE AND EARLY LIFE.

CHAPTER II.

PERSONAL HISTORY, 1824-48.

CHAPTER III.

MARRIAGE WITH MISS BRIGHT AND SUBSEQUENT FAMILY LIFE, 1848-1885.

CHAPTER IV.

THE REFORMED TOWN COUNCIL.

CHAPTER V.

SETTLEMENT OF THE CITY AFFAIRS.

CHAPTER VI.

ESTABLISHMENT OF HERIOT FREE SCHOOLS.

CHAPTER VII.

JOURNALISTIC WORK.

CHAPTER VIII.

THE VOLUNTARY CONTROVERSY.

CHAPTER IX.

THE ANNUITY-TAX.

CHAPTER X.

EARLY CORRESPONDENCE WITH MR. MACAULAY.

CHAPTER XI.

THE CORN-LAWS.

CHAPTER XIV.

THE CIVIC REIGN.

THE LIFE AND WORK

OF

DUNCAN M^cLAREN.

CHAPTER I.

PARENTAGE AND EARLY LIFE.

THE Braes of Balquhidder, the country lying between the head of Loch Lomond and Loch Earn, under the shadow of Ben More, is the recognised home of the McLarens. But the clan had a history before they settled in "the town at the back of the country." Students of Gaelic traditions and history assign to the clan an ancient descent. Setting aside a legend, conveniently shrouded in the mists of antiquity, associating the origin of the family with a "Mermaid's love," Logan, in his work on the "Clans of the Scottish Highlands," makes the authentic history of the McLarens commence with the sixth century.[1] According to this authority, Laren or Laurin, one of the sons of Eric, who settled in Argyle in 503, acquired the district of Lorne, which from him is said to have obtained its name. This appellation, however spelt, is invariably pronounced *Lawren* by the Gael; and there can be no reasonable doubt that it is a modification of Lawrence, the name of the saint who suffered martyrdom under Valerian, A.D. 261. Its Gaelic orthography is *Labhrauin*, the *bh* being quiescent. In 843 Kenneth McAlpin, chief of the descendants of Eric's sons, overthrew the Southern Picts, took possession of their ter-

The High-
land home
of the
McLarens.

---

[1] This legend is recognised by the Heralds of 1781 in the armorial bearings of Lord Dreghorn, son of the famous mathematician, Professor Colin McLaurin, who claimed the chiefship.

ritories, and transferred the seat of government to their capital, Abernethie in Strathearn, in Perthshire, where Kenneth was crowned king of all Scotland. It was the established custom that conquerors should apportion the lands acquired among their victorious followers; and it is somewhat more than assumption to say that the chief of the tribe of Laurin of Argyle received a due share.[1]

The country of the clan.

Balquhidder and Strathearn have ever been known as "the country of the Clan Laurin," and the identity of the appellation, as demonstration of a common origin, is corroborated by the tradition that three brothers from Argyle had this territory assigned to them—the eldest occupying the centre, the second the Bruach at the west, and the third the extreme east of the district. This tradition is borne out by an observance jealously regarded to the present day, in accordance with which the burial-places of the three branches of the clan are marked out in the kirkyard according to the location described.

Romantic history.

This is not the place, however, to write the history of the clan, interesting though it be. Suffice it to say, that it is as full of romance, appeals as strongly to the love of adventure, and is as typical of Highland chivalry and as illustrative of the vicissitudes of cateran life, as the history of other more prominent Highland families. For the Laurins were a brave, resolute race of men; on one side of their nature, like the Highlanders, generous and loyal-hearted; on the other, resentful and pugnacious, gentle friends but terrible enemies, "faithful in love " and " dauntless in war." They bore a conspicuous part in the early national struggles,

---

[1] See " The Highlands of Scotland," by Skene ; Logan's " Clans of the Scottish Highlands ; " " History of the Highlands," by James Brown ; " Historical Geography of the Clans of Scotland," by T. B. Johnston and Colin Robertson ; or, " The Stewarts of Appin," by H. T. Stewart.

and they frequently, too, displayed their valour in conflict with neighbours like the Buchanans, the McDonalds, the McGregors, and the Campbells. The persistency, indeed, with which they carried on their tribal feuds was the chief cause of their decay. It gradually wasted their strength, caused their dispersion, and led them to re-mingle with the Argyleshire branches of the family. Few of the descendants of the ancient clan are to be found in the old Balquhidder country; and the traditions of the Stewarts of Appin and of the McLarens are to a large extent identical. Dr. Mitchell assigns the chiefship to Donald McLaren of Ardeveich, Loch Earn Head, and mentions that one of his distant progenitors signed the Ragman's Roll in 1296.

Among the many distinguished men who, in compara-tively recent times, owned kinship with the clan, may be mentioned the Rev. John McLaurin, son of the parish minister of Glendarrich in Argyleshire, born in 1693, for many years minister of Ram's Horn or St. David's parish church in Glasgow, one of the most eminent preachers of his time, and the author of sermons described by the late Dr. John Eadie as " grand and massive, abounding in original, profound, and suggestive thought, and yet very spiritual in force." He had a younger and more famous brother, Colin, who, as professor of mathematics, first in Aberdeen, and afterwards in Edinburgh, honourably main-tained the national reputation for learning. John, the son of the Professor, attained the dignity of a Senator of the College of Justice under the title of Lord Dreghorn; and among other distinguished representatives of the clan was Ewen McLaurin, who, during the first American war, raised at his own charge the South Carolina Loyalists. But of the members of the clan who have signalised themselves in the church, the army, medicine, and law, none has rendered more conspicuous service to his country than Duncan McLaren, the citizen-patriot, who for upwards of half a century led the van of political progress in Scotland, and whose more than fifty years of public work supply a record of devotion to social and national well-being as honourable as is to be found in the range of Scotland's political annals.

Duncan McLaren did not concern himself with those claims of long descent which exercised the imagination and gratified the pride of other members of the clan. He was born poor, and he never forgot or strove to conceal the fact. But he had an honourable parentage, and of that heritage he was justly proud. To his mind the home of his family never was Balquhidder, but always the sea-swept shores of Argyle, at the entrance of the Linnhe Loch, whose waters pour into the Firth of Lorne, where the green island of Lismore guards the entrance of the great water-way into the Inverness-shire Highlands. On the one side stretches to the Atlantic the Sound of Mull, while towards the mainland the peaks of Ben Cruachan rise behind the mouth of Loch Etive. In ancient days the Bishops of Argyle made Lismore their fertile and peaceful abode, and there the forefathers of Duncan McLaren lived for generations. John McLaren, his grandfather, was a man of some substance. He occupied the farm of Ballymachelichan, and as evidence of his appreciation of learning it may be mentioned, that he joined with other three heads of families of the district for the maintenance of a teacher for the education of their children. The school where the pupils met was as nearly as possible equidistant from the four homesteads, and the teacher boarded successively with each family for three months. The household at Ballymachelichan, in its happiest days, consisted of John McLaren, the farmer, his wife, his sister Effie, and three sons, John, Neil, and Duncan. The

(marginal note:) Duncan McLaren's Highland home.

(marginal note:) His parentage.

memory of John M‘Laren's wife (whose maiden name was Mary M‘Coll) was lovingly cherished in the family. She was a fair-haired, beautiful woman, and ruled her family by the power of love. Her sons were devoted to her; and Effie, her sister-in-law, regarded her with feelings of warmest respect and esteem. A pathetic story illustrates the strength of her attachment to her husband. One day when he was absent on the mainland, a wild storm arose and lashed the waters of Loch Linnhe with fury. Concerned for the safety of her husband, she went to an exposed spot, commanding a view of the course which the returning boat was likely to take. Regardless of the pitiless rain and the biting wind as she was of her own welfare, she remained too long at her post of observation, straining her eyes seawards, hoping to catch a sight through the mist of what she held so dear. Her husband landed in safety, but the anxious wife never recovered from the effects of this exposure to the storm, and all too soon the once happy homestead became a place of mourning. Oppressed by the gloom that had settled over his household, the father introduced, perhaps too quickly, a young wife, and the sorrowing sons were bitterly resentful. Their aunt Effie took their part, and it was soon found that the old family concord could not be restored. John and Neil, the two elder sons, left Lismore for ever, and Aunt Effie with them, leaving behind Duncan, the youngest son, who soon afterwards died.

The wayfarers had no certain place of abode in view when they left their father's roof. They established themselves for some time in the old country of their clan at Bridge of Earn in Perthshire, but subsequently they drew nearer to their native district, and made their abode in Glenorchy at the head of Loch Awe. Thence Neil went to Appin to stay with relatives named McMarrich, who treated him as a member of the household. Here he found a new home, and, acting the part of an adopted son, he became known as Neil McMarrich. He possessed much of his mother's beauty; and possibly his comely appearance helped him to win the favour and affection of the elder McMarrich. He prospered in business, and soon finding himself able to rent and stock a farm, he asked his brother John, then just married, to leave Dalmally and join him. This arrangement was agreed to, but the untimely and tragic death of Neil prevented its fulfilment. The sad occurrence was the result of misplaced affection, not however on the victim's part, and the incident well illustrates the yet unsettled state in which the Scottish Highlands remained at the end of the eighteenth century. Then, as now, the country was thinly peopled. Farming, it is true, was just emerging from its primitive and uneconomical methods, but roads were still bad and transport difficult, and the markets were too distant to justify the expenditure which alone could render farming really profitable, even if the crofters in general had been as well able as was Neil McLaren to stock their farms. Law was dispensed also by methods much less satisfactory and much less certain than those which obtain to-day; while the order that was maintained was achieved rather by the action of the well-disposed among the population than by the strength or vigilance of the central authority. In communities so placed, the passions, by which in all times humanity is actuated, have freer play, and the fear of punishment, which in more settled states frequently acts as a deterrent from crime, is much less powerful than where law is strong and the pursuing feet of justice swift and certain. In all conditions of society, settled and unsettled, jealousy and the desire to escape from inconvenient pecuniary obligations have acted as powerful motives in the human heart, and they did not fail of their influence in this family tragedy. Neil had a friend called McIntyre, to whom he had been able to render pecuniary assistance, and McIntyre in turn felt himself bound to repay his obligations, either in similar form, or, as was more common at the time, in kind. Nor is there any reason to think he would have attempted to repudiate his liabilities had not jealousy entered his breast. McIntyre was engaged to a young woman who was also acquainted with Neil McLaren or McMarrich, and over her heart Neil's handsome face and figure, together with his prosperous career, had obtained considerable influence. Neil himself, it is believed, did not at all reciprocate her admiration; but the fact of its existence, which she was unable to conceal from McIntyre, was sufficient to madden him against his friend. He made a pretext that he wished to repay Neil the advances he had made him, and invited him to meet him at a lonely spot in the country for this purpose. There was nothing unusual in this proceeding. It was generally considered a wise thing, when considerable sums or articles of value were in the possession of any one, that the fact should be concealed. Accordingly Neil made his way to the place without any misgiving, and was attacked by McIntyre from behind and brutally murdered before he could have had time to suspect foul play. Leaving the body by the ford where the deed was committed, McIntyre fled and disappeared. Alarmed at the prolonged absence of his brother, John went off into the Appin country to search for him. His horror at finding his brother's body lying by the ford wrapped in his plaid was such that he was never the same man afterwards. He assembled twenty men, who raised the hue and cry and set off in pursuit of the murderer, with the intention that his blood should expiate his crime. The search was long and minute, but fruitless. M‘Intyre had a long start of his pursuers, and knowing that it would never be possible for him to return to the district, as his crime would sooner or later be traced to him, he made his way south and enlisted in the army. He was sent to Jamaica, where he was convicted of another capital offence and condemned to be shot.

On John M‘Laren, besides the mental suffering he endured, the sad event had disastrous consequences. Not only did it dash to the ground all the hopes of the brotherly reunion to which he was looking forward, but in addition to this Neil's debtors for the most part seized the opportunity to repudiate the debts they owed him. It was with these moneys that John had hoped to stock the farm. Besides this, John felt himself not only bound in honour to pay his brother's debts, but also to fee the twenty men who had assisted him to pursue the murderer; and in doing so he completely impoverished himself. In his wife, Cathe-

The M‘Lel- rine M‘Lellan, however, he found a brave and competent
lans. helpmeet. She too came of a good and honourable stock. Though bearing a Stewartry name, her family considered themselves Highland in blood as well as by birth. She was the youngest daughter of John M‘Lellan and Sarah M‘Intyre, who occupied the farm of Edandonich in Glenorchy, between Dalmally and the boundary line of Argyleshire and Perthshire. John M‘Lellan was a leading man among the farmers and crofters of the district, their representative in any dispute with the factor, and their spokesman in consultations or communications with a man of even greater authority than the factor—the minister. John possessed the confidence of the landlord as well as of the tenantry.

His probity and discreetness caused him to be selected by
the factor for the conveyance of the rent-money to Edinburgh, and in these missions he was generally accompanied
by an escort of not less than ten men. Sarah McIntyre,
his wife, was a woman of the strongest type of character.
Industrious herself, she meant that her children should be
industrious also, and she ruled them with an iron will. She
allotted tasks to her daughters and servants proportionate
to their skill and attainments, requiring each of them to
spin a certain amount of wool or flax daily in addition to
her share of household work; and she also found evening
occupation for her sons. All the wearing apparel was home-
made and home-dyed, for the good woman was skilful in
all housewifely accomplishments. She had a fondness for
colour, and was constantly experimenting and planning to
discover a way of getting brighter tints. Her husband so
far sympathised with this hobby as to bring home from
Edinburgh, on one of his visits there (carrying it, it is said,
all the way in his hand), a large brass pan to supersede the
ordinary thick black pot of the Highland farm, in the hope
that the nobler metal might not, like its iron predecessor,
interfere with the bright scarlet and other vivid colours she
liked. In her old age—she lived for ninety years—she did
not let her authority depart from her. Even when confined
to bed, she kept a vigilant eye on the household, and negli-
gent wrong-doers were frequently surprised by strokes from
a long stick she kept by her side.

The McLellan family consisted of five sons and two
daughters. The youngest of these was named Catherine.
At the age of seventeen years she married John McLaren,
then established with his aunt Effie at Dalmally. Twelve
children were born of the marriage. Of these, seven died
in early life, leaving no descendants now alive. Margaret

married a McKay, and left a son and grandchildren, now settled in Canada. John left descendants, amongst whom is William Ralston, his grandson, distinguished amongst journalists for his contributions to the *Graphic*, **Punch**, and other illustrated periodicals and books. The three youngest children of the twelve alone survived the first half of the century, and they all reached a great age. These were Janet, who died in her ninetieth year; Euphemia, who died in her eighty-eighth year; and Duncan, the subject of this memoir, who was born 12th January 1800, the first day of the century, reckoned according to the old style, which still obtained in Scotland.

Scotland at the end of last century.

In 1799 John McLaren with his large family had removed from Glenorchy to Renton, a small industrial town in Dumbartonshire, on the banks of the Leven, at the foot of Loch Lomond. Times were bad in the country; and though that primitive condition of society which compelled a private individual to raise a force of twenty men to pursue a murderer, and made it necessary to send ten men as escort when a messenger travelled to Edinburgh with rent-money, was passing away, the condition of the humbler classes was nevertheless one of deep poverty.

National Debt.

The French war, disastrous to the interests of all concerned, was drawing to a close. The National Debt, which rose in 1815 to over £900,000,000 sterling, was then already pressing heavily on the nation, and every rank of society was suffering throughout the country. A few, indeed, had benefited by the fictitious demand which the war had created, but even this temporary inflation of prosperity had to a great extent disappeared. All commodities had become much enhanced in price, and wages, though they had risen, had not increased in proportion to the rise in the price of commodities. Wheat was more than double what it had

been a few years before, and actually stood in 1801 at
£5, 19s. 6d. a quarter. The depressed state of the United
Kingdom was unmistakably seen in the increased expenditure on the relief of the poor, which, standing at an average
of about £2,000,000 sterling for England and Wales in the
three years ending 1785, had risen to about £4,000,000 in
1800, and rose steadily during subsequent years till, in 1818,
it reached nearly eight millions sterling, equal to a rate of
no less than thirteen shillings and fourpence on every man,
woman and child in the country. In the meantime, the
population had not increased above one-eighth, and the drain
on the strength of the country was such that it was doubtful if at that time any particular increase was taking place.
The increased cost of provisions supplied to the paupers
could not, on the most free computation, account for more
than fifty per cent. of the increased expenditure on the
relief of the poor, so that fifty per cent. still remained
as a fair allowance for the increase of pauperism that
had taken place. Still, manufactures were slowly developing themselves. During the years immediately preceding
this time a few power-looms had been erected in Glasgow
and the neighbouring country, chiefly for weaving calicoes.
Some of the people connected with this industry had prospered. The schools in the manufacturing districts were
better than those in the country parts, and when John
McLaren came to look at his large and still increasing
family, it is no matter for wonder that he should conclude
that they would have a better chance in industrial life there
than in the Highlands.

John McLaren was essentially " a staid God-fearing man," Duncan
chastened but not soured by trial, and enjoyed, like his son McLaren's
Duncan, a remarkable evenness and placidity of temper. That parents.
son and his two sisters, in the evening of their own lives,

casting their memories back across an intervening space of
more than half a century, could say with perfect truthfulness
that they **had never seen him give** way to anger. **In the**
household of such a man, living at such a time and brought
up in the traditions of piety which have always been characteristic of the Scottish peasantry, **it** will be readily believed
that religion had no secondary place. The study of the Bible
was carried **on** after **the** reverent manner with which the
national poet has familiarised **all the world** in the " Cottar's
Saturday Night ;" and the father was above all things anxious
that his children should be brought up in the faith which,
amid his many disappointments, had proved **to him so** effec-
tual a support. **But the life of the family, although the**
religious sentiment was dominant, was **not** gloomy or ascetic.
Considering their limited means, John and Catherine McLaren
dispensed a liberal and cheerful hospitality. They were good
and friendly neighbours; and all family friends and con-
nections passing by Loch Lomond between the Argyleshire
or Perthshire Highlands **and Glasgow were** entertained
freely by the bright, energetic, and practical housewife **in**
the Renton **home. Catherine** McLaren **was possessed of a**
strongly marked individuality. **Her** daughter Janet, writing of her in her **own old** age, furnishes the following beautiful portraiture of her mother for the grandchildren who were
taught **to** admire and love her memory :—" **I do** not know
what to say about my mother, for she was perfect in the eyes
of her family, and everything she did was right. This opinion
was shared by others also who knew her well. **Mr.** Patrick
Mitchell, the manager of the large printworks at Renton,
met my brother John one **day, and** asked him **where** my
mother had **gone to** live. He said, ' **To Glasgow.'** Mr.
Mitchell replied, ' Well, she has **not** left her equal in **worth**
and industry in the county of Dumbarton.' She was indus-

MOTHER OF DUNCAN McLAREN
AT 80

trious to the end of her life, and as long as she was able to sit up, she was either knitting or sewing. She was skilful with the spinning-wheel, and could show many a piece of linen woven of the yarn which she had spun in her Highland home. In her old age she often referred with regret to the disappearance of the domestic spinning-wheel. Notable for her frugality, her horror of debt—the chief surely of the minor domestic virtues—enabled her to live within her income under all emergencies." Her pre-eminent housewifely qualities, her unfailing courage and tireless energy and happy temperament, long had scope for their exercise. Her husband was struck down by paralysis, and after a protracted illness, during which the future welfare of the family was his chief care, he died in his seventy-fourth year. It was then his widow removed to Glasgow, to be near her children and grandchildren there ; but afterwards, yielding to the request of her youngest son, the subject of this memoir, she went to Portobello, where she died at an advanced age. Her portrait, painted when she was over eighty years of age, shows a handsome old lady, whose features express much firmness and uprightness of character.

In her successive removals she was accompanied by her two daughters, Janet and Euphemia, the latter named after the brave Aunt Effie of old Lismore and Dalmally times, who lived helpful and honoured till she attained the ripe age of one hundred and two years. Janet and Euphemia reproduced in their characters all the piety, fidelity, and independence which characterised the parents. Janet was a woman of very superior intelligence. Her love of books, which began in childhood, continued throughout her long life, and rendered her a most interesting companion. She followed the developments of public life, and especially her brother's share in them, with keen interest.

Besides being practical and sensible, she also had her grand-mother's artistic sense and love of colour. "Greatly she surprised us," writes Mrs. Duncan McLaren, "when in 1851 we took her to the first Exhibition in London, by her partiality for the goldsmiths' department, and her knowledge of all famous and national jewels. She had, too, a heroic love for all that was truly good and noble in the history of her country, and her demeanour was courteous and digni-fied towards all. Aunt Phemie," her sister-in-law con-tinues, "was a domestic character. It would not be easy to describe her worth, her devotion to those she loved, her nursing power, which was often called into use in her brother's family. She was like the goddess of the sick-room, and there was a tradition in the family that any patient, however ill, who came under her care, was sure to recover. She was one of those unmarried women whose self-denying love has proved so great a blessing to many a family circle." "Aunt Janet" died in 1883, in her ninetieth year, her younger sister surviving her little more than a twelvemonth; and their niece Henrietta, the only daughter of a long-deceased brother, who had been their companion and devoted nurse for many years, died soon afterwards.

His child-hood.

The traits which distinguished the manhood of Duncan McLaren displayed themselves in the child. Patience, calm-ness, pertinacity of purpose, the resolve to test everything for himself, and not least, the readiness to learn from ex-perience, all were part of his character from his earliest years. An incident illustrative of this used to be related of him. One Sunday, when he was about four years of age, he was left in the charge of his sister Janet while the family were at church. To console him for her absence his mother had given him a penny "to himself." The child wished to spend it on a cake, and though his sister told him it was the Sabbath and that the baker's shop would be shut, nothing would satisfy him but to try. She led him at last to the baker across the road and knocked. A woman came to the door, and, on hearing the request, abruptly shut the door, saying indignantly that nobody sold cakes on the Sabbath. Janet expected some sign of disappointment, but the boy walked away apparently quite satisfied at having made the attempt, and having had a reasonable answer. This was in keeping with his conduct all through life. He used to say that the word "cannot" was not in his vocabulary; he never believed that anything was impossible until he had proved for himself that it was so. "Try" was his motto, and if he tried and failed, he was contented, so long as he had done his best and could do no more.

In those days luxuries were rare in Scotland, and for the simple Highland family on the Leven a comfortable lot was only to be won by work; and no time was lost in developing the capacities of the children, industrial, mental, and moral. At ten years of age Duncan was better prepared for the battle of life than many a lad of modern times when well into his teens. In 1810 he was sent to live with a kinsman at Dalmally who had no children of his own. The parting with his mother was not easy either for him or her; but he was going to live with his mother's nephew, Hugh M°Lellan, and the separation might have been worse. His cousin lived at the farm of Tulloch. The house stood on a hill where Glenorchy joins the lesser valley of Glen Strae. Below lay Kilchurn Castle, mirrored in the placid waters of Loch Awe, while the blue ridges and misty corries of Ben Vurie bounded the valley on the right, and supported the mighty buttresses of Ben Cruachan, which rose

1804

Leaves home for Dalmally.

beyond. Such was the spot in which Duncan passed the next two years of his boyhood; and the picture of the scene, painted by the brush of Arthur Perigal, was one of the best-prized possessions of his later days. Not two miles from Tulloch lay Edandonich, where his parents dwelt eleven years before. But while the house at Edandonich stands now as it did then, the only remains of the cottage at Tulloch are the few stones that mark its boundary. It has shared the fate of many another crofter's homestead in the Highlands, where green patches in the heather are the only vestige of the dwellings of the honest, frugal peasants of those days. But in the Dalmally country the crofters are not extinct, and the fertile oat-fields on the river-side still testify to the worth of peasant-farming.

Boyhood.

Though small for his age, the boy had considerable activity and muscular strength, and his quick eye and steady nerve enabled him to bear his part well in country sports. He used to tell how on one occasion a great shinty or hockey match, in which the best talent of the country-side was engaged, was played at Dalmally, and how he was one of the Dalmally players. His side was sorely pressed, and a big Highlander, secure of victory, was taking his aim for the final drive, when, to his amazement, he saw the ball disappear. Little Duncan McLaren, whom he had despised as a rival, had slipped up behind the Highland giant, and placing his club between the man's legs, had nimbly drawn off the ball, and before the champion could recover from his surprise, the ball, smartly hit by Duncan, was bounding towards the opposite goal, amidst the applause of the bystanders. But the attractions of outdoor sports were not allowed to interfere with his school-work. An old man who had been his schoolfellow said to Mr. Bright, on one of his visits to Dalmally, "Duncan wasn't much for play;

he loved his books better." He proved himself an apt scholar at the little school above Strae Bridge, and made such progress that in a short time the old teacher began to use him as an assistant, and to talk of his succeeding him in the onerous duties and scanty emoluments of the Highland school.

But when he was in his twelfth year, an opening occurred possessing stronger attractions for his relatives than the prospect of the reversion of the mastership of Glen Strae school. Mrs. McLellan's brother, Nicol McIntyre, was in business as a merchant at Dunbar, and it was arranged that Duncan should go to him as an apprentice. Accordingly in the spring of 1812 the young lad quitted Dalmally for Dunbar. Across the valley and above Kilchurn Castle stands on a hill a monument to the Gaelic poet Duncan Ban McIntyre. An easy carriage-road from Dalmally now ascends this hill, and winds along the loch to Cladich, and thence to Inverary. But in those days a hill-path scarcely indicated the way, and the boy had before him a weary and lonesome journey on foot. In the sixteen miles of mountain-track before reaching Inverary, he scarcely saw a sign of human life, and the way was to him entirely unknown; but he had been told to keep by the stream, and so he followed the Aray, from which the little town takes its name. Thus guided, he arrived in safety at his night's resting-place on the shore of Loch Fyne, and slept within sight of the castle of the great magnate of the district—The McCallum More. Thence he proceeded to Dunbar; and a few days afterwards his father was apprised by the following letter of the wayfarer's safety :—

DUNBAR, May 2, 1812.

DEAR SIR,—According to your request, I hand you this line to acquaint you of Duncan your son's arrival in this place, Thursday evening last, with the Dunbar carrier; and he is going to do well seemingly, but his trial is but short yet. He is not so big as Hugh McLellan described him to me. If I had known him to be so young, I would have had him for four years in place of three, as he will be of very little use to me for twelve months upon account of his being so short. He cannot take down the goods nor put them up again for some time. You can consider if you think what I say to be reasonable, and also whether I am to keep him in clothes, school, &c. Let me hear from you soon, and I'll write you occasionally now and then, informing you of Duncan's welfare.—Yours sincerely,   N. McIntyre.

This letter reflects much better than any lengthy description could the character of Mr. McIntyre. The shrewd and self-regarding but not discourteous country merchant stands out friendly and kindly as representative of the Scottish *bourgeoisie* of his day. The apprenticeship seems to have been extended from three to four years, but it does not appear that any further schooling was obtained for the boy, who was left pretty much to his own resources in picking up information by miscellaneous reading. At Dunbar, which was described by Smollett about fifty years before this time as "a neat little town situated on the seaside, where in the country-inn their entertainment far exceeded their expectations," though he gives no credit to the Scotch for that, because, as he says, "the landlord was an Englishman," Duncan was scrupulous in his attention to business, and soon so ingratiated himself both with his master and his customers, that long before the apprenticeship was over he had practically gained complete control over the business. He has himself, in a public lecture delivered in Edinburgh in 1868, given an account of the way in which his leisure-time was spent during this critical and formative period of his life and character. "As you may suppose," he said, "at that early age my education was not very

extensive. I could do what in England they call the three
R's pretty well; and that was about the bulk of it. But
I was fortunate in having a good deal of leisure, and,
through the kindness of my employer, I was allowed to
use that leisure in the way of reading or doing anything
else I liked. I became a voracious reader, and all the
books in the house I soon got through. Then my friend
begged and borrowed for me, and as it became known I
was fond of reading, a relation of his said he would send
me something that would give me plenty to do. He sent
two large quarto volumes of Gregory's Encyclopædia. I
was not daunted, but began at the beginning and read them
through, except the articles on Mathematics and Algebra,
and matters of that kind, in which I was not sufficiently
instructed. But although that may seem an absurd kind
of educational process, and one I should not recommend
any one else to follow, because they might get much more
useful books, I feel bound to say I got more benefit from
the reading of that work than from any reading I ever had.
At that early age things got impressed upon my mind. I
got a smattering of everything; whether gunnery, fortifica-
tions, shipbuilding, cannon-founding, or anything whatever,
I went on and read it out and out; and in this way I
got a good deal of information. At this time the *Scotsman*
newspaper was first published. One of my friends took in
that paper, and was so kind as to give me a reading of it,
from which I derived great advantage. The foundation of
all the political knowledge I ever had was derived from that
paper, which was most ably conducted at that time." [1]

---

[1] The first number of the *Scotsman*, price fourpence, was published 25th
January 1817, and the reference in the extract must therefore be, at the
earliest, to the year during which Mr. McLaren remained in Dunbar after
the apprenticeship was ended.

It may here be mentioned, that after this lecture had been delivered, the son of the old Dunbar friend referred to sent him a number of early volumes of the *Scotsman*, thinking that it would interest him to see again the very numbers of the paper he had read over half a century before.

Engagement in Haddington.

In 1816 the apprenticeship ended, and he remained with his employer at what now seems the very small salary of £14 a year, with board and lodging. In 1817 he was engaged by Mr. M‘Intyre's brother in Haddington, the county town of East Lothian, for £16 a year, with board and lodging; and in the following year, tempted by a salary of £40 and the attractions of a wider field for work, with the better opportunities of advancement it offered, he passed into the employment of Messrs. John Lauder & Co. in the High Street of Edinburgh. This firm was then carrying on a large retail business in the city, and a wholesale business in addition in various parts of Scotland, and were in high repute as merchants of standing and honour.

Removal to Edinburgh.

Few young men entering on the business of life in Edinburgh or any other large town, free from the personal supervision of parents or of friends, ever voluntarily subjected themselves to a severer discipline than did this country youth of eighteen years of age. His early religious training made it impossible for him to be satisfied with the gay frivolities sought by many youths, and conspired with his thirst for knowledge to point out a more excellent way. In

Life in Edinburgh.

summer the day began by a three-mile walk before breakfast to Newhaven for a bathe in the Firth of Forth, and then back to breakfast in time to open the shop at eight. The whole day was spent at business, the hours for which were at that time considerably longer than they are now. Immediately on his arrival in Edinburgh he had joined the

Select Subscription Library, and there, or at the School of Arts, most of his evenings were spent. To the former institution indeed he was happily able to afford material assistance as well as to receive benefit from its books, for he actively helped in the management, bringing to its service that talent for accounts which was destined afterwards to play so important a part in affairs of much greater consequence. For a series of years after this time he prepared for the benefit of the members statistical statements of the affairs of the Society, showing the membership, classifying the books, and setting forth the state of the accounts. At the School of Arts courses of lectures were given in the various branches of general education, and young McLaren availed himself of the advantages of many of these. In the lecture from which extracts have already been made he thus refers to some of the experiences of this time :—" During the period I was with Messrs. John Lauder & Co., and for some years afterwards, I took every opportunity of improving my education by attending lectures, and by cultivating reading of a more elevated kind from a better selection of books, for I became a member of the Select Subscription Library and had access to all kinds of books; and I may state that I mastered Adam Smith at an early period of my life, to my great advantage. One of my employers had a nephew [1] who took the first prize in mathematics in Professor Leslie's class. This was a day-class at the university; no young man who was engaged in business could attend it, and he offered to instruct me gratuitously in the evenings. I gladly accepted his offer, and went through Euclid with him, feeling greatly obliged and greatly benefited by the instruction I then

---

[1] Afterwards known as Dr. John Taylor of Busby, one of the most accomplished scholars in the ministry of the United Presbyterian Church.

received.   I also attended lectures on various subjects, including chemistry, and before the dreadful Burke and Hare murders I attended a full course of lectures on anatomy by Dr. Knox, who figured so conspicuously in that affair.   I also attended some lectures at the School of Arts."

A life-long friend.

Among the very few intimate friendships which Duncan McLaren formed during his early life was one with Charles Leopold Robertson, a companion of his own age, who also attended these lectures.   Alike in many of their circumstances, their lives diverged into very different courses, but were marked by the same sense of duty and principle.   Mr. Robertson's narrower life, first as a clerk in an Edinburgh bank, and subsequently as manager of the Wilts and Dorset Banking Company at Frome, proved no barrier to the deep interest which the friends took in each other to the last. On his death in 1875, Mr. Robertson left, as a portion of his small savings, the sum of £400 to the friend of his youth.   It seemed only right to use this money to preserve the memory of so good a man in his native city which he loved so well; and Duncan McLaren therefore, at a meeting of the Watt Institute and School of Arts, now known as the Heriot-Watt College, explaining these circumstances, offered the money to establish some small annual prizes bearing Charles Robertson's name.   Lord Shand, however, who presided, proposed that they should bear the double name of the McLaren-Robertson prizes, in remembrance of the early friendship which had been formed in that institution, and this suggestion the meeting heartily endorsed.   Wishing that more particulars of the self-sacrificing life of Charles Robertson should be known to the recipients of these prizes, Mrs. McLaren wrote a touching little account of the story in the form of a letter, headed " A Quiet Heroic Life," a copy of which, it is provided, shall be given every year to each prize-winner.[1]

1818

Another book which young McLaren mastered as thoroughly as the " Wealth of Nations " was Paley's " Principles of Moral and Political Philosophy." The distinguished author of the " Evidences of Christianity " died in 1805, and his works were at this time at the zenith of a fame which they maintained undiminished for many years thereafter. To his latest days the impression made on Duncan McLaren by the study of the " Principles of Moral and Political Philosophy " was never effaced. Thus it was that, in a newspaper letter written about three months before his death, he very happily applied an extract from Paley in explanation of the moral law that promises are binding " in the sense in which the promiser believed the promisee accepted the promise ; " that it is the expectation on either side that constitutes the promise, and, " consequently, any action or conduct towards another, which we are sensible excites expectation in that other, is as much a promise and creates as strict an obligation as the most express assurance." And with characteristic adherence to principle, he goes on to say: " As the moral law cannot be altered, why should not the law of the land be altered in conformity thereto by an Act of Parliament to apply in future cases ?" A writer who claimed personal acquaintance with the late Lord Iddesleigh said

Moral training.

---

[1] The conditions of eligibility attached by the College to these prizes are as follows :—(1.) Men and boys employed in any trade or other manual labour or occupation as ordinary workmen, and as such earning daily or weekly wages, or apprentices in the same occupations ; (2.) Young women employed in shops or warehouses, or in any kind of mechanical or trading occupation, and as such earning daily, weekly, or monthly wages ; and (3.) Young men under twenty years of age employed in shops or warehouses as salesmen, clerks, or porters, and as such earning daily, weekly, or monthly wages, and also apprentices in shops or warehouses.

See Appendix.

some time ago, that he also recognised this interpretation of the bearings of the moral law as stated by Paley, and, like Mr. McLaren, strove to give effect to it as a rule of conduct and life.

Liberal sympathies.

Born at the commencement of this century, Duncan McLaren naturally participated in the liberal spirit which marked the growth of the new age. His early years were spent amidst the excitements and alarms of war, but now that these critical times had passed away, it was seen that the spirit of modern thought and liberal opinion had lived and gained strength notwithstanding all the efforts of bitter Tory opposition to crush it. Edinburgh had played her part nobly in the struggle for liberty, and no adopted home could have provided better soil on which to nourish and strengthen a mind of the quality of young McLaren's. Within a few years there had passed through the University of Edinburgh, in preparation for the distinction which in different spheres awaited them, such men as Brougham, Jeffrey, Cockburn, Lord Henry Petty, Lord John Russell and Francis Horner. These and many others were penetrated with the new spirit, and through them the seat of learning, founded by James VI. for the people, was to wield her just influence, and to give philosophic sanction to the movements which were destined to result from the changed standpoint of the time.

The Pantheon meeting.

In 1814 was held the first assemblage of the people of Edinburgh for a public object, when a petition was adopted in favour of the abolition of West Indian Slavery; a most significant meeting to those with insight to read the signs of the times. In 1820 a great demonstration was held in the Pantheon in favour of Reform, at which Duncan McLaren, just come as a youth to the city, first held up his hand for freedom; and in after years he often referred to this as

evidence of his early zeal as a Reformer.   Jeffrey, Cockburn, 1820
and their companions were at this time the leaders of Edinburgh Liberalism, and they, along with the men who founded
the *Scotsman*, sympathising with the movement they saw
going on in their midst, were not wanting in courage or
wisdom to direct it.

Such were the circumstances amidst which young McLaren
took up his residence and entered on his life-work in Edinburgh. Though no university training had bestowed on him
the power of giving expression to his youthful aims and
impulses, he had at least been born amid the very changes
whose onward movement was to bring to vigorous maturity
that modern spirit the infancy and early childhood of which
had been coincident with his own. There was thus the
less reason for any verbal or literary expression of the hopes
and aspirations which were silently working within him.
But such success as might lie before him could be achieved A rigid self-dis-cipline.
only in one way. Indeed there is much reason to believe
that the success which did in fact so richly reward his
patient endeavour was for a long time entirely out of the
reach both of his ambition and his desire. Nothing seems
to have been in his mind beyond the determination indus-
triously to do his duty towards those into whose service
he had entered and whose interests he had at heart, while
he was equally resolved to omit no opportunity for self-
culture, in order to fit himself for whatever path the future
might open up to him. These aims, he knew, could be
attained only by the exercise of virtues which, if laudable
to the onlooker, are very apt to appear to the performer of
them rather commonplace and repellent. But a mind trained
in the old Scottish Covenanting spirit was accustomed to
make little account of liking or disliking. He determined
at once to base his future life on the patient performance

of duty, and on the practice of the rigid economy which his own clear perception recommended and his limited income rendered inevitable. Forty pounds a year is not much in these days of cheap food and cheap clothing; but it was a good deal less in 1818, when wheat was worth eighty-six shillings a quarter, and when oatmeal was nearly twice as dear as it is to-day. Withal, he was not unmindful of the claims of kindred and hospitality. His mother, then a widow, was living in Glasgow with her two daughters, and on one occasion when Duncan went there on business, he brought his sister Janet back with him to his lodgings in St. Patrick Square, to show her the beauties of the capital. They travelled by canal-boat, as being cheaper than the coach. Janet was surprised to see how well her brother lived, for tea, which was then a costly luxury to the ordinary householder, appeared regularly with other good things on the breakfast-table. But the reason of this good fare was revealed to her when, on the morning of her departure, she chanced to overhear her brother say to the servant, "Jessie, you'll bring porridge to-morrow again as usual."

His religious convictions were shown by the step which he soon took of connecting himself with Bristo Street United Presbyterian Church, then under the ministry of Dr. James Peddie, and the chief centre of Liberal Dissent in Scotland. It does not appear that the rising scientific scepticism of the time had exerted any influence on his mind at eighteen years of age, or that his knowledge of books and culture, such as it was, had in the least dimmed the clearness or imparted any hesitancy to the fulness of his assent to the simple faith in which he had been brought up, and in which those around whom centred his most loved and honoured recollections had lived. His mind was thus well

prepared, like a soil carefully tilled, for the acceptance of the
teaching of the venerable and public-spirited minister, into
whose Christian work and denominational activity he threw
himself thoroughly and without reservation. For Dr. James
Peddie he entertained a high respect and admiration; and
in after years he frequently referred in terms of grateful
appreciation to the advantages he was conscious of having
derived from association with him. There can be little doubt
that to the influence of that association must be in large
part attributed the determined attitude which he afterwards
assumed in reference to the Established Church, and the
efforts he made towards the organisation of the Scottish
Voluntaries in defence of their rights and privileges. In a
note written by the Rev. Dr. William Peddie, son and successor in the Bristo Street ministry of Dr. James Peddie, it
is said, "Mr. McLaren was admitted a member of the congregation soon after he came to Edinburgh. In the year
1838 he was elected to the eldership, but he saw it meet to
decline acceptance of that office. He continued, however, a
steady and attached worshipper in Bristo Street Church for
a long series of years, and manifested not a little active
interest in its concerns, even up to the period when his time
became more engrossed with civic and political affairs. He
was always ready to give his valuable service in any case of
difficulty, and took his share in all the pecuniary responsibilities of the congregation with exemplary liberality. He
and his family occupied the same pew with Mr. John Ritchie,
the proprietor of the *Scotsman*, and this circumstance may
be noted as marking the period of his first indirect connection with that powerful newspaper."

1820

Connection
with Bristo
Church.

CHAPTER II.

PERSONAL HISTORY.

Duncan McLaren remained in the service of Messrs. John Lauder & Co. from 1818 to 1824, at a salary which increased every year. But his duties and responsibilities increased far more rapidly. He attended closely to business, and his employers' interests were considered his own. An illustration of his scrupulous fidelity was given soon after his arrival in Edinburgh. An East Lothian banker had been accused of forgery. Mr. McLaren was requested by the police authorities to go to Glasgow to identify him. His evidence proved the prisoner not to be the real culprit. When offered some remuneration for his services, he refused to take anything beyond the coach-fare, saying that he had been put to no further expense, as he stayed with his mother. "At least," said the procurator-fiscal, "you will accept some acknowledgment for the time you have spent." "No; my time is my employer's, not my own," was the response. The incident reached the ears of Mr. Lauder, and confirmed him in the opinion he already held of the young man's unbending integrity, and he soon intrusted him with the confidential business of the firm, occasionally sending him to London to buy goods, a mission at that time generally reserved for principals. The confidence he inspired among the business men with whom he was brought into relation resulted in an offer which came from a large wholesale house that he should go as their representative to South America. This offer was accompanied by the promise of what was considered at that time the handsome salary of £200 a year. He had resolved to accept the offer, when the firm got into difficulties, and the negotiations were dropped. He was much disappointed, and in after days has been heard to say that had he at that time been offered a post for life worth £200 a year, he would have accepted the offer gladly, and would have thought himself a fortunate man.

A much more substantial proof of confidence in his business talents and uprightness was soon afterwards afforded to him. In 1824 Mr. Lauder wished to retire from business. Duncan McLaren in the following autobiographical note, penned late in life, gives an interesting account of the change in his position which resulted from this decision :—" During the last three years of my engagement with Messrs. Lauder and Co., I was intrusted with the confidential work of going to the market to buy goods. During this period I became acquainted with Mr. White, of White, Urquhart, & Co., Glasgow, an excellent man in all respects, who took a fancy in a certain sense to me, and thought, from what he had seen and heard of my talents and industry and my desire to promote the interests of my employers, that I would be certain to succeed if I began business on my own account. He knew that I had no money of my own excepting a trifling amount from savings on my salary, after assisting near relatives who were poorer than myself; and, to my surprise, he one day told me that he had formed such an opinion of me, that, if I desired to begin business, he would lend me whatever money I required, at a low rate of interest, and without any security. I thanked him very sincerely, and said I would take six months to consider the matter, and then inform him what decision I should come to. One difficulty with me was—what if I should not succeed and should lose my friend's money? And how could I ever repay him if such should be the case?

"Eventually I felt satisfied in my own mind that I should succeed, and resolved to accept my kind friend's offer. When I told him this with overflowing expressions of gratitude and thanks, he asked me how much money I should require. I said I had carefully considered the matter, and thought that £800 would be the requisite sum. My friend thought this was rather a small sum, but said when I had occasion to go to the markets (London and Manchester), as was then customary in spring and autumn, he would give such additional temporary loans as I might require. He gave me a draft for £800, for which I gave him my promissory note, and I took a shop in what was then an excellent central situation, and succeeded beyond my most sanguine expectations. My friend often made me additional temporary loans on going to market, and in a few years I repaid him in full, principal and interest, and up to the present day never think of him without the deepest feelings of gratitude." The correspondence relating to this generous offer was carefully preserved, the packet being labelled "From my great benefactor."

Begins
business
on his own
account.

The small shop in the High Street in which Duncan McLaren commenced business on his own account in 1824 was opposite St. Giles's Church, a few doors above the Royal Exchange. It now forms part of the extensive premises occupied by the firm of McLaren, Son, & Co. It was then the property of Sir John Marjoribanks of Lees, father of the present Lord Tweedmouth. To show the principles on which he commenced business, we again quote from his public lecture :—"At that time the profits were

large—considerably larger than they are now. And there
was a curious system in Edinburgh, then almost universal,
of naming a higher price for an article than that which
people were really willing to give. It used to be called
'prigging,' and in certain districts of the city, particularly
the South Bridge, it was carried on to an extent really quite
disreputable. With the exception of Alexander Cruickshank,
a Quaker, opposite the Surgeons' Hall, I believe there was
hardly a shopkeeper who would not make an abatement on
the total of the account, or on the price of a single article.
I did not like that system, and I resolved, when I began
business, that I would make no abatement in any shape or
way, directly or indirectly—that I would take shillings as
well as pounds, and pence as well as shillings. I was
warned that this plan would never do; people would be
offended, as it had been tried before; but I said I would
try, for I was satisfied that it was the right way. I did
try, and it succeeded, and the practice I began is now all
but universal in this city."

In those days the New Town of Edinburgh was becoming
an important part of the city, but as it was wholly used
for residential purposes, business was done almost entirely
on the South and North Bridges and in the High Street.
Princes Street was a terrace of dwelling-houses, and those
who know it now as one of the finest promenades in Europe,
consisting entirely of magnificent hotels, shops, offices, and
clubs, will find it difficult to imagine it as the quiet side of
Old Edinburgh. The Mound was then hardly completed,
and the North Bridge was the main access to the New
Town. Railways and omnibuses there were none, and
coaches were few in number. Hackney-carriages were
rarely used, and the street-porters, of whom a few still
remain, did most of the work of carrying goods and

 passengers from street to street. At the corners of the streets frequented by these useful functionaries there were usually to be found two or three sedan-chairs, in which ladies at all times, and gentlemen when in evening-dress, were carried by two stout Highlanders, often at a brisk trot. The character of the streets and closes of the Old Town of Edinburgh, caused this mode of locomotion to survive in its precincts long after it had fallen into disuse in other towns. By this time, however, the fashionable and professional world had deserted their former residences in the Old Town, with the exception of George Square. One of the last survivors of the Edinburgh society which peopled the once aristocratic High Street was an ex-governor of a West India island, who occupied a flat above McLaren's shop, and there entertained his friends in the style of the previous half-century. But, lying as it did between the Law Courts and public offices in and about the Parliament House, the Council Chambers, and the University on the one side, and the streets and squares of the New Town on the other, the High Street was particularly well situated for the purposes of trade.

Business prospers. The business prospered, and soon gained a reputation beyond the bounds of the city. Mr. McLaren had the power, which does not always accompany personal capacity, of choosing the right men to assist him. Having chosen them, he always trusted them implicitly, and the consequence was perfect confidence between employer and employed; and changes seldom occurred, except such as were caused by promotion and the extension of the business. He interested himself also in the welfare of all who served him, and, at a time when long hours of service were exacted, he heartily supported the short-hours movement—a service which in 1832 unexpectedly obtained for him a cordial vote of thanks, as expressed in the following letter :—

EDINBURGH, *October* 20, 1832.

SIR,—The Committee of the shopmen and mercantile clerks having understood, through a quarter on which they place the greatest reliance, that you have rendered them most valuable service in aiding their efforts to induce some of the most influential merchants in the Lawnmarket to shut their shops, in accordance with their memorial, they have deputed me to return you their most sincere thanks for your kindness, as they feel assured, from the denials they received in your neighbourhood, that without your aid they would not have succeeded in their object.

They are the more grateful for your unlooked-for exertions when they contrast it with the selfish feeling displayed by some merchants.

The Committee have charged me to express a hope that the young men you employ will, after this mark of attention to their interest, feel it a duty as well as a pleasure to redouble their exertions. (Signed) THOS. MOFFAT.

As the business increased and additional premises were required, Don's Close and adjoining property were annexed, and by an arrangement with the Town Council, Warriston's Close was made double its former width, as compensation and substitute for Don's.

In 1829 Duncan McLaren married Grant, youngest daughter of William Aitken, formerly a merchant at Dunbar, but who at the period of young McLaren's apprenticeship had retired from business, and had built himself a house at Haddington called "The Retreat." Grant Aitken's sister was the wife of Nicol McIntyre, with whom Duncan had served his apprenticeship. In these circumstances, and during his residence at Haddington, the friendship which had been formed between the young people laid the best foundation for the happiness which was so fully realised in their too short married life. Mrs. McLaren was of a cheerful and vivacious disposition. A portrait painted soon after her marriage represents her as possessing much sweetness and intelligence, with great delicacy of feature. She took a deep and loving interest in all her husband's pursuits, and in matters beyond the joys and cares of her own household, as we find in a playful letter written to him when he was on one of his London journeys, in which she threatens him with a scolding on his return home for having sent her only a Scotch paper when she was longing for an English one.

They began their married life in a house in Princes Street at the corner of Castle Street, looking over the well-known gardens to the Castle beyond; but after a while they removed to a house in Ramsay Gardens on the Castle Hill. The locality was named after the author of the "Gentle Shepherd." In addition to its associations, it commanded a magnificent view of the New Town and north side of Edinburgh, with the Firth of Forth and the Fife-shire hills on the north side of the estuary.

Heavy bereavements.

Of the three children born of the marriage, two still survive, one now Lord McLaren, a judge of the Court of Session, the other Mrs. Millar of Sheardale. But this happy married life was of short duration. Grant McLaren died in 1833, in the twenty-ninth year of her age. With much to live for, the young wife and mother met the blow which was to remove her from earthly happiness with Christian fortitude. The grief caused by this sad event was intensified by the death soon after from croup of Anne, the eldest daughter, a child of great promise, when less than five years old. Her innocent and intelligent companionship had been her father's solace after his bereavement. For the first trial he had been prepared by

a suffering illness, but the shock which he sustained by
the sudden death of this beloved child cost him more, he
has been heard to say, than all the troubles of his life
put together.

But private grief cannot stay the march of public events,
though it often leads those who suffer from it to take a
part in them. The echoes of the conflict connected with
the passing of the great Reform Act had just died away,
and the changes introduced by the reformed Parliament
were beginning to be felt. The Municipal Corporations
Bill passed into law in 1835, the year after his second bereavement, and he threw himself into public life and entered
the Town Council. In ecclesiastical affairs also the times
were full of interest. The Non-Intrusion controversy had
been raging for some years, with an interest for Scotchmen
which perhaps only Scotchmen are capable of understanding.
His judgment and sympathies were generally on the side of
the Dissentient Evangelical party, with the exception of
those episodes in their history in which they sought to
place the resolutions of the Church above the law of the
land. Their ultimate heroic secession from the endowments
of the Church, at what they believed to be the call of duty,
commanded his appreciation and even reverence, and led
to the close alliance which so long subsisted between the
leading politicians of the Free Church of Scotland and
himself.

To return to the more strictly private side of Duncan
McLaren's history. The three years which intervened between the death of his first wife and his second marriage
were perhaps less eventful as regards public work than
those which immediately followed. In subsequent chapters
his introduction to the reformed Town Council and his
efforts for the extrication of the city's affairs from finan-

cial embarrassment are fully reviewed, and it would serve no useful purpose to go over the same ground here. It will readily be understood that the political and municipal work of the young city merchant laid the foundation of private friendships and intimacies which subsisted through life. It was in the course of his labours in municipal affairs under the reformed Town Council that he was intro-

The Ren-
ton family.

duced to the house of William Renton in Buccleuch Place, at that time a centre of Liberal thought in Edinburgh.

Mrs. Renton [1] was a woman of strong character and untiring benevolence, the mother of a large family, of whom more than one member attained positions of distinction and usefulness in the Church, in politics, and in finance. She was an example of the influence of the teaching and training of Evangelical Dissent on the minds and lives of the women of Scotland. Her piety was deep-seated and eminently practical, and the extent of her beneficent ministry made her name a household word among the poor and suffering. Few of her contemporaries were better versed in current political and ecclesiastical questions, and all her convictions and sympathies were with the Protestant democracy that asserted the duty of self-government along with the sacredness of personal freedom and responsibility both in Church and State. When the political martyrs, whose monument is the chief attraction in Calton Cemetery, were lying in the Calton Prison, she and her mother personally ministered to their wants; and from that time she was ever in the forefront of political thought and activity. With so much in common to draw him into near sympathy with this family, Duncan McLaren was led to form a closer

---

[1] A beautiful memoir of Mrs. Renton was written many years ago by her son, the Rev. Henry Renton of Kelso, and printed for private circulation only.

union with it by his marriage with the youngest daughter, Christina Gordon Renton.

Like the first, the second period of married life was of short duration. The marriage took place in 1836. Unfortunately, the delicacy which had given Christina Renton's parents anxiety from her girlhood increased after marriage ; and although she bore her sufferings without complaint, it was impossible that her husband should not feel a good deal of anxiety on her account. He would fain have given up public life, but by this time he had been elected City Treasurer, and had got deeply into the business of unravelling the complications and confusions into which the Edinburgh city finances had fallen. His wife, moreover, had a chivalric love for the public work in which her husband was engaged, and encouraged him in the course which her own judgment told her was the path of duty. He felt himself, what was even more fully realised by his friends, that to withdraw at that stage would involve a disastrous surrender of public interests, which no one else at the moment was so competent to deal with. In 1838 the bill before Parliament for the settlement of the City affairs was being examined and criticised, and Duncan McLaren was obliged to remain in London in charge of it until it finally became law.[1]

During his stay in London he wrote long and numerous letters to his wife, in which he gave full and detailed accounts of the negotiations which finally culminated in the passing of the bill.

[Marginal notes: 1836 — Marriage with Miss Renton. Home claims and ties. Letters from London.]

---

[1] The issue of the business is now matter of history, a curious reference to which was made in the hearing of the writer of this note, showing how widely that history has become known. The editor of one of the newspapers in a Yorkshire borough was talking of the condition of the municipal accounts, and after stating that in his opinion they were by no means in a satisfactory state, and regretting that there was no one of leisure in the town competent and willing to attempt to set them straight, he ended with the declaration, "We want a Duncan McLaren here!"

The following interesting letter gives an account of his visit to Westminster Abbey to witness the coronation of Queen Victoria in June 1838 :—

" I found," he writes, " a letter from the London agents for the city, Spottiswoode & Robertson, saying that one of the city Members, Sir John Campbell,[1] had a coronation-ticket for me, and requesting me to call soon in case I needed court-dress. I of course called early, and was presented with the ticket by Lady Stratheden (Sir John Campbell's wife), who came into the room for the purpose. I asked her about dress, and she said, to my great relief, a dinner-dress was all that was required. She said, too, I had better be at Westminster Abbey at five o'clock in the morning to get a good place ! This was rather early for me, but I accepted the ticket. Lady Stratheden is a peeress in her own right, and as such, I presume, she got a few tickets. I had no doubt this was the way it came, else *you know* I would not have taken it from her or any one else if it had been purchased, for they were selling as high as £25. I got up at half-past four this morning, and was in the Abbey by half-past five, and remained there till four in the afternoon. I had a delightful view of the Queen and all the company as they arrived for several hours before her. They passed in review before me, and it was a splendid sight,—the whole nobility of the land passing before one leisurely from six to ten o'clock. I only wished you had been with me to make my enjoyment greater. There was nothing struck me so much in seeing the peeresses walk along before me in procession as the fact that, with very few exceptions, they were all very stout women. I really never saw so many stout ladies, or women of any rank or class. I remarked, too, that when any one about fifteen stone weight appeared who was well made, the whisper among the gentlemen near me was, ' She is a very fine woman.' All those of a more slender form were allowed to pass without notice. It was very beautiful to see them in their crimson velvet robes, with trains three or four yards long, sailing

---

[1] Afterwards Lord Chancellor.

along the ground like peacocks. The Queen is rather little as
compared with those whom I have been describing. I saw her
for at least ten minutes, as there was a stoppage in the procession,
or at least a very slow movement, when she was near me ; and
I saw the Duchess of Kent for a much longer time. The Queen
is decidedly what would be called good-looking anywhere. The
whole thing was worth going a thousand miles to see."

1838

On his return home, he found the state of his wife's
health had not improved, and owing to this domestic
anxiety, he began to extricate himself from the burden of
municipal duties. But all his loving care, combined with
the efforts of the best medical skill, were unavailing to
restore the lost health. The weakness steadily increased,
and the winter of 1841 found his home again darkened by
bereavement. The second family consisted of three children,
the eldest, Agnes, now Dr. Agnes McLaren ; Duncan, named
after his father, and his successor in the business ; and
Catherine, who became the wife of John S. Oliver, his
partner in business. She, like her mother, died in early
married life, leaving two sons.

Heavy
sorrow.

Lord McLaren has kindly placed at the disposal of the
biographer the following reminiscences of the family life
between 1836 and 1845 :—

" My earliest impressions of home life belong to the
period of my father's second marriage. He was then living
in No. 2 Ramsay Gardens, a little terraced street on the
Castle bank, which overlooked Princes Street, then almost
entirely a residential street. I think the New Club (which
I remember being built) was the first break in the dull
and decorous uniformity of this now picturesque and
lively thoroughfare. Railways had not then been thought
of, and the Princes Street Gardens, through which we were
accustomed to walk to the New Town, had the aspect of

Lord McLa-
ren's remi-
niscences.

a suburban park, stretching away towards the fields and woodlands on which the West End of Edinburgh has since been built. In these days my father doubtless found his corner in the Castle rock a very convenient abode, being, as it was, within five minutes' walk of his business and of the Council Chambers, between which he spent the chief part of his time. He gave me the impression of being always occupied. He was in the habit of dining at four o'clock, and after dinner he went back to business, for at that time a great deal of shopping was done in the evening, and the introduction of gas, which I remember being talked of as a new thing, no doubt made the streets appear most brilliant to a generation which had been accustomed to the dismal lantern and the link-boy's torch.

" In the summer months we lived a good deal at New Gardens, a quaint little house near Queensferry with a walled garden, almost on the site now occupied by the works of the Forth Bridge contractors. My father generally came out in the afternoons, returning to business in the mornings ; but excepting occasional country drives and walks in Dalmeny Woods, I cannot recall any particular incidents of our life.

" During this period he was successively Bailie and Treasurer in the Corporation of Edinburgh, and I remember that his friends used to speak of the Provostship as a thing in store for him, though at that time I do not think he desired it. I am speaking still of the period of his second marriage, 1836–1841 ; and during a great part of this time his wife's health was a cause of great anxiety to him, though I was then too young to realise this fully. I recollect more than one journey with her, undertaken for the benefit of her health. This was before the establishment of the main lines of railway through England. My second mother never regained her health, and her death, which occurred on the 1st November

1841, was a great grief to my father.   I think that for some
years afterwards he took less part in local politics than he had
been accustomed to do, and did not see much company.

"From 1841 to 1844, being unable to attend school or
leave the house in the winter months on account of illness, I
was a good deal with my father in the evenings.   He wrote
much for the press, writing with great rapidity in the same
bold, clear-cut character which has become so familiar to
a large circle of correspondents.   He was accustomed to
hand me the sheets of MS. to look over as he wrote them,
and in this way I came to know about Edinburgh politics
and finance, the management of the Police and of the Infirmary, National Education, and the various notes of the
'drum ecclesiastic,' which in those days conspired to distract
the public attention from the real and pressing necessities
of the illiterate poor.   I think the Free Trade movement
was the mainspring which drew my father back into public
life.   But there his action was viewed with jealousy by
that school of Whigs who take the epithet 'old' as part of
their proper designation.   Liberalism had just received a
severe check by the return of Sir Robert Peel to power at
the head of a large majority, and was also suffering from
internal dissension and the inability of its leaders to appeal
to the popular imagination, or to sympathise with the wants
of the commercial and industrial classes.

"My father was one of the first in Scotland to realise the
absolute necessity of the 'total and immediate' repeal of
the corn-laws, and he received little support from his former
allies in the Council and the city.   Lord John Russell had
declared for a 'fixed duty' of five shillings on corn, I presume
with the view of conciliating that considerable section of the
Liberal party whose interests were bound up with the land,
and the Edinburgh Whigs were very angry with any one

who presumed to be more advanced than their chief. They used to come to the Free Trade committee meetings with their ' one-horse ' affair, the moderate fixed duty ; but were, as I understand, invariably beaten by my father and the Free Trade party, who held fast to the principle that the taxation on food was public plunder for the benefit of the landowners. My father worked incessantly at this question, carrying on a large correspondence with all parts of Scotland and organising meetings ; but at this distance of time I cannot give details. There was a great Anti-Corn-Law meeting in the Music Hall, I think the first public meeting held in that building. I was present, and heard speeches by Cobden, Bright, and (I think) Colonel Perronet Thompson, well known as a vigorous writer and speaker on this subject. Cobden was my father's guest on this occasion, and his visit was the foundation of an intimacy which lasted through life, and which I need not say my father highly valued.

" I now pass to some purely personal matters. One marked characteristic of my father was his great sensibility to the sufferings of others, and sympathetic kindness on all occasions of illness or failing health in his family circle. My own health, which had been much shattered in these years of early boyhood, had so far improved that in 1844 a very competent adviser, the famous physician Andrew Combe (brother of George), predicted my complete recovery if I could be removed for a term of years to a milder climate.

" There was no lady friend to whose care I could be intrusted, and my father resolved to accompany me to Madeira, which was at that time considered the most suitable invalid resort for such patients as myself. During the summer I had travelled with him round the West Coast of Scotland and through the central districts of the Highlands, and in October 1844 we sailed together from Liverpool for

Funchal, Madeira. We had a rough passage, and the view of the terraced and vine-clad slopes of this most lovely bay might be compared to the gardens of Armida, if you substitute the figures of sunburnt fishermen for the nymphs of the Italian poet. We spent four or five months here, residing in a villa boarding-house, enclosed in a semi-tropical garden, where geraniums and fuschias bloomed through the winter.

"My father and I spent a great part of our time on horseback, generally riding out some miles into the country in the morning, and again in the afternoon after an early dinner. Sometimes we went an excursion of three or four days. At that time he was very much interested in geology, a study which he had taken to through association with his early friend, Charles Maclaren, then editor of the *Scotsman*, and author of 'Geology of Fife and the Lothians.' The volcanic scenery of the Madeira Isles was a subject of fresh interest to my father, being of course entirely different from anything to be seen in the United Kingdom, and he would often call my attention to the phenomena indicative of the order of succession of the volcanic outbursts, while I endeavoured to interest him in the flora and ferns, which I cultivated with, I suspect, a very slender foundation of scientific acquirement. He was never a great reader of library books, but was insatiable in his search for information, and he had not been long in the island before he set to work to find out all about the laws, local customs, trade, and finance of this dependency of Portugal. From official documents which he had translated to him, from intercourse with English and native residents, and from his own observation, he wrote an interesting series of letters on Madeira, which appeared at the time in one of the Edinburgh newspapers, and were afterwards published by Messrs. W. & R. Chambers as one of their series of popular tracts.

" He did not enter much into the gaieties of the English society here, but was nevertheless a popular member of it, knowing almost every one, and entering more or less into their different interests. During his stay in Madeira he made the acquaintance of John Scott Oliver, who was in business there, and who some years afterwards became my father's partner, and in 1862 entered into a nearer relationship by marrying my sister Catherine.

" Instead of coming home direct from Madeira, my father joined a party who engaged a coasting steamer for a trip to Gibraltar. Thence we travelled through Spain, the North of Italy, Switzerland, and Germany to England. I do not enter into particulars of this journey, because I daresay there is not much in it of the material from which biographies are made. But some of my recollections contrast curiously with the present order of things. For example, there was not a mile of railway in any part of our continental route, and in crossing Spain we were drawn by a dozen or more mules along roads which were generally execrable. The top of the diligence (which carried the mails) was occupied by carabineers with loaded muskets, but they did not in our journey find any occasion to use them.

" Here I think I may break off my memorandum, because, after spending a brief summer at home, I was abroad again for two years and a half. I returned about the time of my father's marriage to Miss Bright, which may be considered a new epoch in his life and that of his family. There is no doubt as to the powerful influence which my present mother exerted in strengthening and refining the intellectual character of my father, an influence which was not less beneficent towards the members of his family. But it is not possible for me to enter more fully on these topics in the present volume."

CHAPTER III.

MARRIAGE WITH MISS BRIGHT AND SUBSEQUENT FAMILY LIFE.

THE Anti-Corn-Law agitation was the connecting link between Duncan McLaren and his future domestic life. It was at the Conference held in London during the Parliamentary session of 1842, when, as chairman, he rendered great service to the Anti-Corn-Law League, that he first became acquainted with John Bright. A warm friendship ensued, and he agreed to visit Rochdale during the meeting of the British Association for the Advancement of Science at Manchester, which he had arranged to attend. John Bright, on his return home, spoke of his new friend as one of the most remarkable men he had ever met, and the prospect of his visit accordingly excited pleasurable anticipations.

The following letter, written by Mrs. McLaren some time after her marriage, gives an interesting account of this visit, and the important results to which it gave rise :—

November 30, 1853.

MY DEAR FRIEND,—I am thankful that our Blackpool journey had such good results, and that my husband's efforts on your behalf have been successful, and that you find yourself happy and comfortable after so much that has been trying to you. He certainly has a wonderful power in arranging difficult matters, but people see how just his views are, so he succeeds with them.

You ask me to tell you how I first became acquainted with

him. To answer your question, I think I must, as children say, begin at the beginning. You know I lived at One Ash with my brother John Bright, after the sad loss of his wife, during all the Anti-Corn-Law agitation. When he returned from the great Anti-Corn-Law Conference in 1842, he told me he had met one of the most extraordinary men he had ever seen, and his name was Duncan McLaren. He described how the Conference was likely to end in nothing owing to so much difference of opinion, when that good man, Joseph Sturge, proposed that Duncan McLaren should take the chair. Many looked surprised, as few knew him. He took the chair, and made such a wonderful *résumé* of the opinions that had been expressed, deducing from them what the Conference ought to decide upon, that the meeting soon found itself brought into harmonious conditions. " But," my brother added, " the very appearance of the chairman, with his large head, clear open brow, and gentle voice, albeit with his Scottish accent, made a powerful impression upon the whole audience." He presided over that great meeting during tho first two days. My brother spoke of his chairmanship with the greatest admiration. He dwelt also with much pleasure and interest on the acquaintance both he and Mr. McLaren had made of a gentleman there, Mr. Hamer Stansfeld, which afterwards ripened into a warm friendship. It was the same Mr. Stansfeld who introduced hydropathy into England, and by whose efforts the Ben Rhydding Hydropathic Establishment was built. You will smile when I give you a proof of the deep impression these descriptions of men my brother had so much admired made upon me, for our minds were then full of hero-worship for all who worked prominently on that great Anti-Corn-Law question. Some little time afterwards, being at Malvern with my brother Benjamin, we ascended the beautiful Malvern Hills. I shall never forget the music of the Hereford Cathedral bells which broke upon our ears as we gained the summit. A gentleman and lady were there before us, with whom we entered into conversation. I hardly know how it possessed me, but I said, " Pray excuse this question. Is your name Hamer Stansfeld ?' He replied, " Yes ; but how do you know me ?" I said, " Because

you exactly answer the description my brother John Bright gave
of the Hamer Stansfeld he met at the Anti-Corn-Law Conference in London in 1842." I hardly need add this was the beginning of a pleasant friendship. Shortly afterwards the British
Association Meeting was held in Manchester. Mr. McLaren, in
accordance with an invitation which my brother had given him,
wrote to say he hoped to be there. A little proud of the incident
on the Malvern Hills, I playfully said, on leaving home to attend
the meetings of the Association (my brother being detained at
home by a cold), "I shall be sure to find Duncan McLaren at one
of the meetings, and shall bring him back with me." However,
I found no one who answered to his description. On my return,
my brother met me at the door, and I said, "You will be disappointed to see me come home alone, but Mr. McLaren was not
there." "No," my brother said, "he preferred coming here, and
has been with me all the afternoon." This was my first introduction to Mr. McLaren. He looked older than I expected, but
he was under the influence of a great sorrow. Next day, Sunday,
we went down to Green Bank to dine with my father. Two
ladies were staying there, Mrs. Richardson and her daughter
from Belfast. They were to sail for Dublin the following day,
and were to accompany us next morning to Manchester *en route*
for Liverpool. We were to drive to Manchester, as we always
preferred this to going by train. Mr. McLaren asked us if this
was wise, and urged us very much to go by train, as these ladies
were bound to go by a certain train to Liverpool in order to
catch the Dublin steamer. We said there was no danger of our
not being in time, and we preferred driving as usual. We were
surprised, to say the least of it, to find a comparative stranger
press his views so much upon us as to the risk there was in
driving. We started as agreed upon next morning, when, to our
dismay, after going about four miles on the road, one of the
horses fell down in a fit. Judge of our humiliation! Not a
word escaped Mr. McLaren about his superior wisdom; he was
full of sympathy and full of help. We happened to be near a
small station, so we waited for the next train and proceeded to
Manchester, but our friends were too late for the Liverpool train

and missed the boat for Ireland.　As you may suppose, this laid the foundation for an almost superstitious regard for Mr. McLaren's judgment, which feeling has often been called forth during our married life, and the children share it with me. When I tell him if he had lived a couple of hundred years ago, he would have been thought to have second-sight, he quietly replies, "Then second-sight comes from the power and habit of observation and the possession of common sense."　This is too long a letter, but I thought you would like to hear the whole story.—Yours ever affectionately,　　　Priscilla McLaren.

It was not, however, till 1848 that the friendship thus begun resulted in marriage.　A second letter from Mrs. McLaren's pen describing this event forms a fitting sequel to the one just given describing their first meeting.

Newington House, *December* 16, 1853.

My dear Friend,— . . . You know the close tie which bound me to my brother John from my girlhood, and his motherless little girl, Helen,[1] was like my very own.　What I felt in giving up this child of my affections to another mother when my brother married again was a good preparation of heart for the duties which had been pressed upon me, and which in future were to be mine. . . . The outward separation from the "Society of Friends," to which I was deeply attached, and which was a consequence of marriage with one not united in membership to it, was a great burden to me; but I felt that the deepest feelings of the heart ought not to be set aside for the sake of a rule that was not only impolitic but unjust.[2] . . . Amongst the "Friends" no minister is employed in the marriage-service; the bride and bridegroom "do themselves the solemn rite perform."

---

[1] Now Mrs. Helen Bright Clark, of Street, Somerset.

[2] At that time members of the "Society of Friends" marrying those of another denomination forfeited their membership.　This rule is now dispensed with, and "Friends" have opened their meeting-houses for marriages with those not in membership with them.

McLaren, in order to meet my views on this point, consented that
we should be married at the Registrar's office. This was objected
to as not being respectable. "Then," I said, "this is an opportunity for making it respectable."

My husband had seen very little of English scenery; so after
our marriage we visited Derbyshire and Nottinghamshire. He
was charmed with Haddon Hall and other houses of historic
interest, and in visiting the Dukeries he enjoyed the splendid
trees, which gave him a good idea of the woodland beauty of the
ancient forest of Sherwood.

We saw Newstead Abbey, and were much interested in visiting
Annesley Hall, the home of Miss Chaworth's girlhood as well
as that of her married life. It was to the unrequited love which
Byron had for her that we owe that touching poem of unsur-
passed beauty, "The Dream." We went afterwards into Wales,
where I must say McLaren found a pleasure quite as congenial
in watching the riveting of plates and other operations in the
construction of the Tubular Bridge across the Menai Straits.[1]
We then proceeded to the English Lakes, and Rydal and the
beautiful surroundings of Wordsworth's home life concluded what
is called the " wedding journey ; " and when my husband, after his
long and patient waiting, landed me at the home which was to
be *ours*, the door opened upon a group of three little girls in
pretty white frocks, each holding a lovely bouquet to present to
me as a love-offering, whilst two dear boys and the grandparents
met us with an equally affectionate welcome. . . .

This is an egotistical letter ; but as you asked for it and I promised it, I feel bound to send it.—Yours always lovingly,

P. M^cL.

It was to his house 24 Rutland Street that Duncan McLaren
brought the wife who for thirty-eight years helped, loved,

---

[1] Though this bridge was considered a great wonder at that time, it
appears almost insignificant compared with the more recent efforts of
scientific skill. Mr. McLaren, on visiting the scene of the Forth Bridge,
said it was so great a wonder, that if he were living when it was completed,
he should like to be taken to see it, even if he died half an hour afterwards.

and encouraged him with unceasing devotion. His home
became a place of sunshine, sustained by a warm all-per-
vading affection; and its owner, conscious of a new impulse
and inspiration influencing the highest and noblest qualities
of his mind, devoted himself to public work with redoubled
ardour. Here two of his younger children were born,
Charles Benjamin Bright, now a barrister at the English
bar, and Member for Stafford from 1880 to 1886, and Helen
Priscilla, now wife of Dr. Rabagliati. In 1852 he bought
Newington House, where he resided for the remainder of
his life, and which is associated with all his important
public labours, both as Lord Provost and Member for the
city. In this house was born his youngest son, Walter
Stowe Bright, now in business in Keighley, Yorkshire, and
Member for the Crewe Division of Cheshire.

Duncan McLaren's reputation as a man of business, and
his mastery of the science of accounts, brought him many
opportunities of occupation wider and more varied than that
which he had chosen at the outset of life; but his time and
energies were devoted, as a rule, rather to the public advantage than to his own. Some of the public services outside
the sphere of politics, which later in life he was in the habit
of recalling with pardonable pride, were connected with
railway management. He assisted in the dethronement of
Mr. Hudson, "the Railway King," so called because of the
magnificence of his railway building enterprises. Certainly
never was monarch less regardful of the interests of his
subjects than was Mr. Hudson of the infant struggles of
the English railway companies, or more reckless in the use
he made of his supremacy in the direction of railway policy.
In May 1849 the shareholders of the York, Newcastle, and
Berwick (now part of the North-Eastern) Railway Company
appointed a special committee of investigation into the

affairs of the line, and Duncan McLaren was asked to serve on it, his colleagues being Messrs. James Meek, Horatio Law, James Leechman, and John Ripling, with Mr. George Leeman (afterwards Member for York) as secretary. The committee issued a series of reports as the result of their searching and elaborate investigations, which ended the reign of Mr. Hudson, marked out a safer and sounder policy and system of management, and restored the control of their property to the shareholders. In the financial part of the investigation Duncan McLaren took a prominent part, and a handsome piece of plate which each member of the committee received from the shareholders testified their appreciation of the services rendered. While still acting as a member of this committee, he was appointed a director of the company at the half-yearly meeting of the shareholders held on 23rd August 1849; and he remained a member of the Board for six years.

Previous to his appointment as a member of the investigation committee of the affairs of this company, he had acted for some time as auditor of the Edinburgh and Glasgow Railway Company, but on his appointment to the former position he felt compelled to withdraw from the latter. His resignation caused much regret. The chairman of the Edinburgh and Glasgow Company personally urged him to reconsider his decision, saying, on behalf of himself and his colleagues, that they felt clearly " that it is impossible to find a successor so well qualified to act, and who would be satisfactory to the shareholders," and suggesting that his name might at least be retained as co-auditor, while the work was done by his colleague. He, however, was then, as ever during his life, steadfast in his resolve to undertake no responsibility which he was not able to discharge by his own personal efforts. He had never made a special study of accounts beyond what was necessary for an ordinary private business, but his power of unravelling intricate masses of figures and drawing conclusions from them seemed to be intuitive; and the financial part of any new undertaking in which he was from time to time engaged was immediately seen through and carefully watched.

At the time of his joining the Committee of Investigation, he was engaged in winding up the affairs of the Exchange Bank of Scotland, of which he had acted as manager from its origin in 1845; and in anticipation of the close of this work, attempts were made to engage him professionally in railway administration. Mr. H. G. Thompson of Moat Hall, York, then acting as general manager of the York and North Midland and the East and West Yorkshire Railways, conceived a great regard for him, and earnestly endeavoured to induce him to become his successor in that post. In the summer of 1850 Mr. Thompson wrote: "Would you, after your Exchange Company's affairs are wound up, accept any place connected with the management of a railway company, with an adequate salary?" After some further correspondence, the offer was conditionally accepted. But the ties which bound him to Edinburgh and to independent public life were stronger than he at first thought; and, supported by Mrs. McLaren, who shared his interest in public work, he eventually resolved to remain a citizen of Edinburgh, and accordingly wrote to Mr. Thompson withdrawing his acceptance of the proposed engagement. "It is the only instance," he said, "in the course of my public life in which I have halted between two opinions. I hope most sincerely you will find some person better qualified in all respects than I am to fill the office." Mr. Thompson sent a kind letter in reply, asking for a reconsideration of the decision, and expressing his own willingness to continue in office for a time, if the delay would help to clear the way for his friend's removal southwards.

Meanwhile another offer came from Manchester. Mr. Bannerman, Mr. Houldsworth, and other prominent Lancashire merchants invited him to accept the managership of the Lancashire and Yorkshire Railway Company. With less hesitation, he declined this second offer, and again asked Mr. Thompson to liberate him from his conditional acceptance of the York appointment. By these decisions York and the railway companies may have lost, but Edinburgh and himself were certainly the gainers. The following letter, written by Mrs. McLaren, throws further light on the motives that led to the refusal of these offers :—

. . . Now that it is all over, I am going to tell you of a temptation we have been under, which might greatly have altered our future life. McLaren's services connected with railway matters, in which you know he has been for some time engaged, have caused quite a sort of love affair between him and Mr. Thompson of York, which has had a painful as well as a pleasant side to it, as I suppose all unsuccessful love affairs have. Mr. Thompson was most anxious that McLaren should succeed him as general manager of the York and North Midland Railways. The offer was most urgently made, with every inducement to tempt us to accept it. The idea to me of living at York was delightful, for besides bringing me nearer to my old home and you all, McLaren knew how fond I was of York and its surroundings, with all their dear old associations; and this, with a strongly reciprocated regard for Mr. Thompson, caused him half to accept the offer so persistently made by his friend. Whilst we saw much that was pleasant in the prospect placed before us, we could not but feel there was another side to the picture—that there was much to look back upon as well as to look forward to. I thought of all McLaren had done for Edinburgh, and felt

1850

Another offer of railway management.

Motives which led to refusal of these offers.

that, with such a past, there must be much in the future that might call for talents such as he possessed.

Though great ability was needed, there were others who could manage railway business, whilst McLaren's mind was adapted for political work. With his strong sense of justice, and great moral courage and force of character to act upon it, there could not fail to open for him in his own city a more distinguished and congenial career of usefulness, from which it was his duty not to turn aside. As this consciousness grew upon us, we felt we must give up the thought of living at York, but it cost McLaren a good deal to disappoint his friend. I hope the future may justify the decision he has arrived at. I feel sure J. will approve of it.

From this time Duncan McLaren abandoned all connection with railway management, while his experience in the conduct of the affairs of the Exchange Bank had caused him so much mental worry, that he resolved never again to endanger his happiness by connection with joint-stock companies. So thoroughly did he carry out this resolution, that when the company for the establishment of the Edinburgh Literary Institute was formed in 1870, he refused to take shares in the concern, although his son Duncan was one of the founders. He, however, cordially approved of the object of the company, and gave a handsome donation to the funds. In 1885, referring to a suggestion that he should take some shares as security for a loan, he wrote to say that he would lend the money, but would rather not have the shares. And about this time, in a private conversation, he said, " I daresay I might have been a rich man if I had directed my efforts to make wealth, and had invested in stocks and shares, because, with my knowledge of the world of business and my general power of judgment, I could probably have made good investments, but I did not care to be troubled with it. I did not wish my peace of

mind to be disturbed by fluctuations of the market. I
valued my freedom from worry of that sort more than
money."

An imperfect view of Duncan McLaren's character would
be given if no reference were here made to his family life.
Known as he was to the outside world, devoting his energies
to the public service, sparing neither himself nor any one else
in his efforts to further what he believed to be right, it might
have been supposed that he had little time for domestic
and family duties, and that he was as stern and unbending
in private as he was in public life. Few estimates of his
character could be more inaccurate. There probably never
was a man who more strongly felt that his first duty was
to his family. We do not always see that men who have
actively engaged in public work find that their children
follow in their father's footsteps. It may be that the principles which many men labour to promote are not made sufficiently interesting to their children. But Duncan McLaren's
religious, moral, and political principles were carried into
the home life, and were made the subject of daily conversation and of "table-talk," so that his children were imbued
with his principles from their earliest years, though no
attempt was made to force their minds into a particular
groove. To this his wife gave every encouragement.
Family interest in highest principles cannot be maintained
where both parents are not alike interested in them.

A lady intimately acquainted with the home life at
Newington House writes: "I think a few touches even
of nursery life may tell as much of character as some of the
more important details of a man's public career, and thus I
send you a few recollections of Mr. McLaren connected with
the child life of his home. One of his boys had rheumatic
fever, and on one occasion, when it was needful to attend to

1850

Family
training.

1850

s chil-
en's faith
him.

a complete change of toilet, the child, dreading the pain, persistently refused the ministrations of his mother and the nurse. His father being appealed to, came to the rescue, and requested the nurses to leave the room, saying 'Just leave the boy to me.' They heard outside the gentle tones of the father soothing the child, and were shortly called back to find the bed and the little invalid made, as the saying is, all over again. The confidence in his father was exemplified by this boy on another occasion. Visiting a family near, a small box was laid aside after resisting every effort to open it. The little fellow timidly asked if he might take it home, as he was quite sure his father could open it. Mr. McLaren, spurred on by his child's faith in him, spent some time in mastering the difficulty, and at last opened the box, which the boy carried back in triumph. The Rev. Dr. Robson of Glasgow, who was staying at Newington House, was so touched by this little incident, that he used it in his next sermon to illustrate the need of a more implicit faith in the power and love of our Heavenly Father.

"I must not omit another result of the faith felt in him by his children. One of them used to stammer, which gave his father much concern. One day he called the child to him, and said, 'Now, my boy, I am going to cure you of stammering; open your mouth;' and taking a pencil-case from his pocket, laid it upon his tongue with some pressure, saying, 'Now, go away; you will never stammer again.' His faith cured him, and he never stammered afterwards.

"I remember one of the pictures in the children's nursery was that of 'William Penn's Treaty with the North American Indians,' the only picture which, in the more rigid days of Quakerism, was allowed to hang on the walls of the houses of the 'Friends,' and the children were told that was 'the only

treaty ever made without an oath, and the only treaty which
was never broken.' So Voltaire said. That picture taught
the lesson of justice, whilst in that of Fisch representing
Charles V. in the studio of Titian stooping to pick up the
brush which the artist had let fall, they were taught by an
Emperor the same truth as that taught in the lines of the
peasant-poet of Scotland,

> 'The rank is but the guinea stamp,
> The man's the gowd for a' that.'

"And the following anecdotes were perhaps the result
of such teaching. Mrs. McLaren went one Sunday evening
into the children's bedroom to tell them of a revival of religion in America, about which their minister, Mr. Robertson,
had been telling his people. She did not think the youngest
boy could understand much about it, and was not a little
surprised when he rose up in bed and said, ' But, mamma,
did he say it had reached the hearts of the slave-owners?
for if he did not, I don't think much of it.' When the
Prince Consort came to Edinburgh to lay the foundation-
stone of the Post Office, this boy refused to go to see the
ceremony, saying a prince was no better than any other
man. When told it would be disrespectful to his father not
to go, as he had got a ticket for him, he went. The reverential attitude of the Prince during the long prayer offered
in the cold east wind which prevailed on that morning, and
his pure and noble countenance, struck the child with so
much awe and admiration, that when all was over he said
almost breathlessly, ' Oh, papa, when I'm a man I hope I
may be like Prince Albert.' "

During the earlier portion of his life, Duncan McLaren,
no doubt, was imbued with a considerable share of the old
Scotch disciplinarian feeling in educating his children, but
gradually this passed away, and his habit was to appeal

to their reason, and not to rest upon his own authority. Though the parental tie was very strong, and respect for his wishes and judgment was always shown, he was anxious not to carry this deference too far ; and while he was ever ready to advise and help his children, he would always add that he wished their decision in thought and action to be entirely their own, and not to be merely the echo of his opinions. His judgment was, however, so sound as to inspire in his family almost unbounded confidence, which led them to consult him on all occasions, even up to the latest period of his life. The veneration with which he was regarded by those in every part of Scotland with whom he was associated in public questions was shared to the fullest extent by the inmates of his own home.

The Sunday evenings were always interesting, when he instructed his children in Scripture history, deducing therefrom lessons for practical everyday life. Neither in politics nor in business would he tolerate any deviation from the moral law, and public rectitude he regarded as of equal moment with private morality. Such was the teaching of his own life. He held no principle more strongly than love of peace and horror of war, and in these Sunday evenings he would dwell often on this topic, insisting on the duty of peace both from a religious and a political point of view. So deep were his feelings on this subject, that his children remember that at the dinner-table during his Lord Provostship, after the first engagement in the Crimean War, when the list of the killed and wounded was handed to him, he broke down, and was unable to read the contents aloud to his family. Long afterwards, in 1870, when the Franco-German war was declared, a German lady, who was a guest in the house, relates that when he told her the tidings, his eyes were full of tears and his voice trembled with emotion.

In the subordinate details of life he constantly impressed upon his children the time-honoured and familiar maxims, " Whatever is worth doing is worth doing well," and " If at first you don't succeed, try, try, try again," which had been of so much service to him in his own career. Slip-shod work and untidiness he could not endure. Even in the cutting and folding of a newspaper he was scrupulously neat, and was annoyed if any one were not the same. As a newspaper-reader, he was omnivorous, and when he was absent from his children, he seemed constantly to have them in his mind even during this his favourite occupation ; for if he came upon any paragraph which he thought would interest any one of them, he would at once cut it out, write his or her name on it, and send it off by post. The scrap-books containing these cuttings, which are still pre-served, show how much his thoughts must have centred on the instruction and welfare of his children.

His letters show how much he sympathised with them in their juvenile pursuits. The following are examples of many :—

BEN RHYDDING, *October* 17, 1857.

MY DEAR WALTER, HELEN, AND CHARLES,—I am longing very much to see you all ; I hope to have this pleasure some day next week. I am glad to hear you are all well. Mamma and I are much better, and she thinks I am growing younger, but I think this must be a mistake. We have a pretty little lake here, and there are six white ducks which always swim on it, or rest on a little island in the middle of it. The lake is about the size of our lawn. To-day I threw in some small bits of gingerbread to them, and they dived for them, and caught them very cleverly before the bits had sunk to the bottom. I daresay they thought the gingerbread very nice. I threw the gingerbread so near the different ducks that I think every one of them got a taste, for the one nearest to where the bit of gingerbread fell was always sure to get it, though they all tried.   You know this is the way I like little children to be treated—just as the ducks were—that they should all get the very same kindness, and no one should be greedy or try to get more than his just share.—I am your affectionate father,   D. McLaren.

EDINBURGH, *May* 22, 1859.

MY DEAR CHARLES,—Yesterday I remained in the garden all day working, and your rabbit-house was the better for it.   The buck killed one of the young ones, which was taken away and buried, and the place was all cleaned out.   I then sent one of Currie's men inside the inner house, and with a hatchet and pieces of wood he filled up the passage through which the rabbits passed from one end to the other.   When the man was in, you could not see a bit of him, even the feet.   It was large enough to hold him, although your mamma thinks it is hardly large enough to hold rabbits.   The buck is now shut up at one end.   I gave them a large quantity of dandelions, for which they looked very thankful, but the buck looks rather solitary in his separate dwelling.

I got the earth all delved up in the north end of the henhouse-yard, so as to let the hens scrape and work in it, as they do in the wood.   It was very hard, and the man had to take a pick to break up the earth.   We have brought back the cock and hen from the stable-yard, and the dogs will now have it to play in. The hens have dug up your gardens very much, and they don't look well.   I took out all the weeds from the border yesterday.

There are a great number of dandelions in the wood, for the gardener allowed them to run to seed without cutting them; so I began to pull them up for the rabbits.   When the potatoes were planted, and when this ground was cleared, I then pulled them regularly upwards, taking *all* of them out as I went up, so that the ground is now cleared up to the ring-swing.   This is the way to do anything *well*;—to make a portion of it, however small, quite perfect and complete, and then another and another, and in course of time the whole will be done by perseverance. The way little boys and careless people do is to pull one here and another there, and in this way their work is of no real

advantage. When the people of this country go to the backwoods
of America to plant corn, they find the whole country covered
with trees, and they begin, as I did with the dandelions, to
uproot *all* the trees *within a small space*, and then they build a
wood house for themselves with the trees. When this is done,
they cut down *all* those within a *small* circle (as great as they
can overtake), and on it they plant potatoes, corn, and other
things to live on during the winter. In spring they begin to
cut more and plant the ground, and so on year by year, until
many miles of country—as great as from Edinburgh to where
you now are at Southport—which were all forests are now corn-
fields; but if they had cut one tree here and there, they would
never have succeeded as they have done.

You know when George was here he always talked about the
rabbit-house not being "right made," and that the passage ought
to be filled up; but he was a man who liked to talk rather than
work, and therefore he did not fill up the place himself. When
Currie's man told me the rabbit was killed, I told him to bring
the hatchet and cut some pieces of wood, and go inside and fill
them up, and I was there and saw it done. It was finished in
less than half an hour altogether, and I am sure George talked
far more than half an hour about it, but never worked to put it
right. Now, when you and Walter grow up, I want you to learn
that the right way is not to go on talking about evils, but to try
to remove them by *doing something*, in place of speaking about
what ought to be done.

Mrs. Robson was here a short time yesterday. Grandmamma
is rather better. She was out in the garden yesterday. We are
all well. Much love to all.—Ever your affectionate father,

D. McLaren.

Edinburgh, *May* 11, 1862.

My dear Charles,—I believe to-morrow will be your birthday,
and that you will then be twelve years of age. I affectionately
congratulate you on the event, and wish you every measure of
happiness which any one can enjoy. Before I left Ventnor I told
you that within three months of your age I went to be an apprentice about a hundred miles away from my friends, and in a town

which did not contain a person that I had ever seen before. You will have great advantages as compared with this experience of mine, and I hope you will so improve them that you may be so much more happy, distinguished, and good than I was, as your superior advantages seem to render possible. For you know the Bible strongly enforces the principle in many forms, that according as our advantages and opportunities of doing good to others and ourselves increase, so do our responsibilities increase, and that all these considerations should constantly be present to our minds. . . . . .

I got safe home about eight o'clock last night, having left London at nine in the morning. Duncan met me at the train. I found him, and Grant, and Agnes quite well. John's book is hard work for him. He has got 450 pages printed, and there are other 600 to print, and of them about 100 pages are still to write. I mean *printed* pages. There would be about two written pages to each printed page.

I hope you, as being the oldest boy at Ventnor, will take good care of your mamma, and get her either to ride out on Helen's horse or to drive out in a carriage, for her health requires that she should do either the one or the other. Give my love to her, and to Catherine, Helen, and Walter. I hope you all agree well together and are kind to one another.

At Portsmouth Dockyard I was in a room 1092 feet long. Our premises in the High Street are only 193 feet. In that room I saw boys, not bigger or stronger-looking than you are, who had to earn their living by carrying the small cords out of which ropes are made from one end of that room to the other, and in doing this they walk as much as twenty-five miles a day. It was a room for spinning ropes for ships of war. Now tell me how many times the boys would have to walk from end to end of the room to make up the twenty-five miles, which is equal to walking to Ryde from Ventnor and back again.

I am, my dear Charles, your affectionate father,

D. M^cLAREN.

Duncan McLaren did not always get credit for the deeply sympathetic nature which he possessed. It is true he did not form friendships easily, and had little of that *bonhommie* of character which leads to a certain kind of popularity. Ordinary society had not that attraction for him which he found in the companionship of men whose lives were devoted to intellectual or public work. Thus at one time he took great interest in attending the annual meetings of the Association for the Promotion of Social Science and of the British Association; but he was attracted to them more by the men he met there and the friendships he formed than by the discussions, in which he took but a small part. It was at the meeting of the former in Glasgow in the year 1860 that he first met Henry Fawcett, who was there with his sister. In a memorandum, written at the time of Professor Fawcett's death, Mrs. McLaren says :—

"*Nov.* 7, 1884.—This morning has brought the sad intelligence of the death of Henry Fawcett. What a loss to us women and to the world! I don't know when I have seen McLaren so much affected. It was at the Social Science Meeting in Glasgow we first met Mr. Fawcett and his sister, Maria, who was devoted to him. I never before realised how much affectionate feeling could be expressed in one word. She told us the touching story of her brother's blindness, and whenever she spoke of ' Harry,' she threw into the word such a depth of love and tenderness of feeling as it would not be easy to describe ; and yet there was mingled with it a cheerfulness of tone which in the circumstances only his own indomitable spirit could have imparted to hers. After the meetings were over, they paid us a visit at Newington House, which we much enjoyed. In February 1860, when Mr. Fawcett first came out as a candidate for parliamentary honours by offering to contest Southwark, McLaren appeared unexpectedly on the platform and addressed a meeting in his favour, speaking of his intellectual claims in the highest terms. Subsequently, after Mr. Fawcett's first contest in Brighton in 1864, my husband wrote me, ' You will see with regret Fawcett is beaten, because the Whig candidate would not give in. I am rather glad a Tory got in since Fawcett did not.' On the occasion of a pleasant journey into Cornwall, we returned by Salisbury and visited the Fawcetts, who gave us a warm welcome in their pretty home in the country. They seemed very grateful to McLaren for having endeavoured to help their son at his election contest. It gave them as much pleasure to talk of 'Harry' as it gave us to hear about him. They told us how, when he was a boy, he one day gave them some concern by not returning home in time for dinner. When he made his appearance, and was questioned as to the cause of his absence, he said he had always pitied a poor apple-woman who sate at a stall and never seemed to get any dinner, so he had told her if she would go home and get her dinner, he would keep her stall till she came back. 'As the woman accepted my offer,' he said, 'it kept me from my own dinner, but now I am ready for it.'

"'This first story we heard of his boyhood's life had its fitting and consistent sequel in almost the last act of his manhood. He had declined, along with Mr. Leonard Courtney, to follow the Liberal Ministry, of which they were both members, in voting against Mr. Woodall's amendment to the Reform Bill of 1884 to extend the franchise to women. When addressing his constituents at Hackney, he faced with a brave denial the assertion that to have passed that amendment would have overweighted the bill, adding, ' Depend upon it, the claims of women householders to vote will be so irresistible, that when the suffrage has been conferred on every man who is a householder, however poor and uneducated he may be, the demand of women householders to be enfranchised will not rest till it is conceded;' and with these last words he left us. His life seems to me like a grand poem, and he died as such a warrior should die, with the sword of truth unsheathed." [1]

---

[1] When one or two amongst those who were opposed to justice to women had, in the House of Commons in 1876, traduced some who worked in that cause, Mr. Fawcett in a noble speech defended the ladies from such " vile aspersions," saying they were women of whose friendship any man who knows them, on whatever side of the House he may sit, "must feel proud."

In 1864 Mr. and Mrs. McLaren attended the British Association Meetings at Bath, and thence proceeded to Dunford on a visit to Mr. Cobden. Greatly he enjoyed this intercourse with his old political friend, and their daily drives in the neighbourhood of Midhurst. This was the last occasion on which these two friends were to meet, for on the 2nd of April on the following year the whole country mourned the death of Richard Cobden. A month later Mr. McLaren in a letter to his wife wrote: "To-morrow is our Chamber of Commerce meeting. I suggested that we should get up a Chamber of Commerce subscription for a marble bust of Cobden to be placed in the chamber. The idea has taken well, and it is to be proposed formally to-morrow by Mr. David McLaren, and I have no doubt will be carried and will succeed." Next day he wrote: "I brought forward the resolution regarding Cobden's death, but said nothing that I intended to say. I felt very sad and broken down, but what I did say seemed to please the people. Mr. R. M. Smith seconded the resolution, but said little. Then Mr. David McLaren moved the resolution about the bust, and made a most beautiful speech, and Mr. Todd seconded it. We commenced the subscription at once."

The same winter (1864), owing to the severe illness of one of his children, he took a house at Clifton, and while there, in addition to the sadness caused by the loss of his dear friend Mr. Cobden, he had also to lament the death of his brother-in-law, Samuel Lucas, the editor of the *Morning Star*,[1] which occurred just as the nation received the shock of the news of the assassination of President Lincoln. It was under these depressing circumstances that

---

[1] Then the only Advanced Liberal daily paper in London, and since merged in the *Daily News.*

he received a requisition asking him to become a candidate
for the representation of Edinburgh. This caused him to
abandon the idea which he then entertained of removing
for a time to the South of England, and he returned to
Edinburgh.

In September 1865 Mrs. McLaren writes :—

"McLaren wrote for tickets for the British Association at
Birmingham, and received a most kind letter from our friend
Mrs. Joseph Sturge, asking us and our children to be her guests.
. . . It is delightful to be in a real Quaker home, there is such
a charming simplicity and truthfulness about everything. We
enjoyed our visit immensely, and McLaren was in his element
in this atmosphere of benevolent thought and action. Joseph
Sturge [1] took us to see the Reformatory for boys at Stoke, which
his father had established many years before."

Later, in 1873, Mrs. McLaren again writes :—

"We have again been to Birmingham, and have had a time of
great pleasure mingled with thankfulness over the occasion of
the great meeting to welcome my brother, John Bright, on his
reappearance in public life after his long illness. What a treat
it was to hear his beautiful voice once more raised in the cause
of truth ! We were the guests of Mr. and Mrs. Middlemore,
and were much interested in the work carried on by their son
in rescuing gutter children. He takes them out himself in de-
tachments to Canada, after a preparatory training in his admirable Homes."

Mrs. McLaren adds :—

"My husband's last visit to Birmingham, and to his dear
friends the Sturges, was at the demonstration to celebrate the
twenty-fifth anniversary of my brother's connection with the
borough as its parliamentary representative—a wonderful manifestation of enthusiastic esteem for their long-tried Member !"

---

[1] The son of the Birmingham philanthropist.

The last meeting of the British Association which Mr. McLaren attended with his wife and children was that held at Bradford in 1873, where they were the guests of Mr. Robert Kell, one of the leaders of the Radical party in the West Riding of Yorkshire. It would not be easy to describe the pleasure he felt in the friendship of Mr. and Mrs. Kell, nor the grateful sense he had of their unvarying kindness to his family.

Among the personal friends who contributed to the relaxation of his parliamentary life were Mr. and Mrs. Frederick Pennington, at whose beautiful home amid the Surrey hills he and Mrs. McLaren were frequent visitors. The Saturday to Monday parties at Broome Hall included many guests of eminence in politics, art, or letters, and longer visits during parliamentary recesses afforded opportunities of ripening House of Commons acquaintances into personal friendships. Mr. Pennington himself sat for the borough of Stockport, and Mr. McLaren stayed with him at his London house during the early months of more than one session. At other times, he and Mrs. McLaren were the guests in London and Brighton of Mr. and Mrs. Peter Taylor, at whose house he first met Mazzini. There he learned to appreciate the single-minded and unselfish character of the Italian patriot; and he regarded him, to use his own words, as "the most Christlike man he had ever met." He became associated with those in England who lent their assistance to the cause of Italian unity, and on more than one occasion the Italian friends of the exiled Mazzini availed themselves of his address in Edinburgh as their only safe means of corresponding with their chief. Mr. Peter Taylor, then Member for Leicester, was the son of an old colleague in the Anti-Corn-Law work, and was himself well known as an Advanced Radical in the House of Commons. Everything that could promote social and legislative reform of the laws affecting women was warmly and actively supported by Mrs. Pennington and Mrs. Peter Taylor, as well as by Mrs. Thomas Taylor of Aston Rowant, in Oxfordshire ; and Mr. McLaren's interest in these questions, in which Mrs. McLaren took an equally active part, enabled him to sympathise with and appreciate the success which the efforts of these ladies, and others of their circle, achieved. For Mr. and Mrs. Thomas Taylor he entertained the warmest regard, and he enjoyed his visits to their country-house in the richly-timbered slopes of the Chilterns with a zest which only a lover of Nature condemned to the hard labours of a session at Westminster can understand.

Amongst his other more intimate friends associated with him in Parliament were John Stuart Mill, John Benjamin Smith (a veteran reformer, whose political life began at the massacre of " Peterloo "), Mr. James Stansfeld, and Mr. H. D. Pochin, in whose homes he was a welcome guest ; and by the marriage of his son Charles with Mr. Pochin's only daughter a connection between the two families was formed.

A visit in 1867 to the old family home at Dalmally seemed to revive his early attachment to the North. The subjoined letter from Mrs. McLaren, giving an account of this Dalmally trip to Mr. McLaren's sisters in Edinburgh, shows how keenly she sympathised with her husband in visiting the scenes of his boyhood :—

Manor House, Oban, September 9, 1867.

My dear Sisters,—I hope Aunt Janet is still making progress, and that she will soon be able to prosecute her journey. We thought often, on our way here, that if she could have seen the beautiful scenes we saw, they would have done her far more good than all the doctors in Edinburgh. I have wished each day to write to you about the spots dear to you from early associations, but I did not feel well enough to attempt the task, as all the particulars I wished to give would involve a long letter. Will you please send this on to Agnes to read, and she can either keep it or you can preserve it, so that I may have it again as a memorandum of our delightful visit to dear Dalmally.

We found Glasgow depressing, but the fresh air of Loch Lomond had a very reviving effect. The lake and its surroundings did not present such an appearance of beauty as I should have liked for the sake of Helen and Walter. There were no shadows, and the water was not calm and peaceful-looking. Still the scene was very fine when we reached Luss, and Inversnaid waterfall was grand; and as nearly all the passengers left the boat there, we could enjoy more fully the view at the head of the lake. We spent the night at Inverarnan, a charming little hotel with cottage windows. It was a sweet rural spot, far nicer than Oban, in my opinion. We had a capital lunch—so good that the young folk made it their dinner, and only papa and I went down at five to a little *table-d'hôte*, when four gentlemen besides ourselves formed the company. The boys went out for a walk, and we followed. The views along the road were exquisite.

Next morning, the 16th, we started in a carriage and pair for Tyndrum. We had a very communicative and intelligent driver. He seemed aware of his powers of pleasing, and his rich Scotch accent added a charm to his information. He pointed out a farm of the old style, where, he said, he often went on winter evenings to sit round the fire in the middle of the room, over which hung the *pot*. A widow, whose memory went back to other days, held the farm. She always gave her guests the best she had, and told stories of times gone by, contrasting them with the present. The Marquis (Breadalbane) wished to build her a better house, but she preferred this old home with all its associations.

Old times came vividly back to papa's mind as we drove along; for he too could contrast the present with past times, when, a youth of seventeen, he crossed the hills alone from Dalmally to Loch Lomond without seeing an individual or a house for miles. Assisted by the knowledge of the mountain passes possessed by

our nice driver, many things came back to his remembrance
connected with the locality which had been lying dormant for
years, and I longed very much that we could have retraced the
very paths he trod. This could not be, except in imagination;
but I liked to witness old thoughts and feelings stirred up again.
It was a beautiful drive along Glen Falloch, the scenery becoming
less interesting at Tyndrum, where we changed our carriage and
horses, and parted with our choice guide and driver, who deserved
much credit in answering all our questions, seeing he had a
most painful whitlow on his finger, which had undergone an
operation too soon—much in accordance with the ways of doctors
—and he had in prospect another operation next day.

Heights and depths are our regular experience through life,
and now we made a sad descent, so to speak, in our driver. This
one would scarcely answer a question. His voice was as a feeble
squeak from the poorest penny-trumpet. So we contented ourselves with our own observations, and our admiration went on
increasing as the road opened out into the wide valley of Glenorchy, which took us into Dalmally, passing the Free Church and
the minister's house before reaching the town. We got very nice
rooms and ordered dinner, which was sent up so cold that papa,
who can bear many a more important trial with more philosophy
than cold viands which ought to be hot, gave the waiter a strong
reprimand, which seemed to cool his interest in us, until papa
asked him several questions about the neighbourhood, viz., is
there a village near here called Edandonich? and is there one
called Shainmealachan? and is there not a house that they call
Tulloch not far off? But the waiter expressed his ignorance. Still
papa looked out of the window as though trying to recognise the
faces of vanished friends. By and bye the waiter came back with
a manner betokening much more interest in us, and told us that
one below had said these places all existed, and he tried to point
out their localities. After dinner we sallied forth, and as Aunt
Janet said the house they were all born in was still there and
stood near the church, we thought we could not miss it. And we
fancied we saw it, yet did not think we were right either, and so
walked on and on along a beautiful road, when we saw an elderly

man with a bowed figure. "This will be the postman," said papa; "we will question him." Papa repeated his inquiries about the old places. The man said he would guide us to any objects of interest we might wish to see, and added, "You must have been well acquainted with this country some time, sir. The waiter told me there was a gentleman making inquiries about the place, and his name was McLaren. Are you the Lord Provost of Edinburgh? for he came from this place, and we are all very proud of him." Papa put him off and said he was not the Provost. "Well, well," said our guide, "but I'll take you to where Mr. McLaren stopped at a cousin's house. The cousin was called Hugh McLellan." And he went on to describe the family, and how there was a school-house a little on the other side of the road by the river-side, pointing out the very spot on which it stood. "He was counted a very wise boy—always a wise boy. There was none other like him. And when others would play, he would be at his lessons. Nothing could keep *him* back from the school. He was the cleverest boy there. But there came a letter from a Mr. McIntyre" (and here he related his connection with the family) "from Dunbar, asking for a suitable boy as an apprentice," &c., &c., going on to tell how the boy went to fill this place, and how well he did there, until he was made a partner and married a rich lady, and went on from one success to another, until he became Lord Provost of Edinburgh. "And I've been told," he added, "that he is now Member of Parliament." And so beguiling the way, which was a long one, he reached the very spot where the ruined cottage stands, on a hill overlooking one of the most exquisite of views; hills covered with beautiful light and shadows to the right, and Loch Awe and Kilchurn Castle to the left. It might have satisfied a monarch for the grandeur of its position. But that little ruined cottage felt more to me than Balmoral with all its associations and surroundings of royalty, especially when I looked to where the little school stood. It seemed more like a dream than a reality as I pictured in imagination the boy who, more than fifty years ago, trod and re-trod the path between that humble dwelling and the equally humble school-house amid such glorious scenery. And yet his soul was not fired by the sense of the natural beauty which surrounded him ; it was animated rather by a prosaic sense of duty, which has led him on ever since through many a dull routine, and borne him up to heights which he did not dream of then. But there have always been depths of poetic feeling within his heart, though these could only be reached by the hand of obedience faithful to the claim of the hour ; and whether this might lead to deeds of gentlest love and charity, or to those of high and heroic daring, it was all the same—his heart could always be moved at the shrine of duty.

Walter and Helen brought away some little relics from this spot of deepest interest. As we retraced our way to the inn— two miles and a half—heavy rain set in. But we were still interested in our guide's remarks, one of which struck me from the feeling with which he expressed it—that it was well for a man to be wise in his youth. We were pretty well drenched ere we reached the inn. We had hoped to have enjoyed our little excursion again over a snug tea by a peat-fire, but were disappointed. I went to bed at once to get rid of wet clothes, and papa, still following on where duty led, looked after the wet garments of the rest. Next morning our guide came at half-past nine to take us to the cottage where papa's parents had lived, and where his brothers and sisters were born. It was a pretty spot, but not so romantic as where cousin Hugh McLellan had lived, and yet one the heart might well love. A widow lives there with beautiful children. There was a spinning-wheel, telling of old-fashioned industry, and everything to make Highland cottage-life perfect except the " gude-man," who had gone to his rest some ten years ago. We lingered over the place, regretting to leave it ; but the postman had his duties to attend to, and so had we. Papa and the boys and Helen went afterwards to visit a distant relative named James McNicol, but I was too tired to venture farther. Before twelve we were off again on our journey, regretting much to leave Dalmally. The old postman took care to be on the roadside to give another look at papa. His eyes did not rest on any of us, but drank in all they could of him whom he considered the hero of the place. We felt rather disappointed with our drive along Loch Awe ; indeed, nothing felt very interesting to me since we left Dalmally. I should like to have stayed there. We lunched at a dreary place called Taynuilt, and reached Oban about five, finding Manor House very nice and comfortable. I trust the " leap in the dark " made by the House of Commons last session may be as successful as this one has been, for we took the house without having seen it. But papa is mostly always right.

I forgot to mention that we informed the postman-guide who papa was, and then put him right where he was wrong in his history, especially as to the fable of the " rich wife." We have been to call on Professor and Mrs. Blackie. I am glad to hear of you, through Agnes, a good report. With our united dear love to yourselves and Henrietta, I am, your affectionate sister,

Priscilla McLaren.

1867

" During the summer of 1871," his son Walter writes, " my sister Agnes and I had been to Ober-Ammergau, in Bavaria, to see the Passion Play, and we were so much charmed with it that we persuaded my father and mother to see it in the autumn of the same year. Mrs. Pennington and her daughter went with them, and they were joined by my brother Charles, who had been studying at Heidelberg. In spite of the heat, and the crowd, and the primitive accommodation which the place afforded, my father was deeply interested by this singular festival and its surroundings. The reverential and dignified presentation of the Passion Play probably jarred less upon his feelings than if he had been a frequenter of the ordinary secular drama ; but there is no doubt that to his mind, trained in the Puritanical spirit of his own country, the spectacle of Bavarian peasants enacting the life of Christ was not altogether congenial. From Munich my father and mother went on to Italy. Venice and Rome were the cities my father most wished to see. As regards Venice, this wish was gratified. The old-world city, with its water streets and swift silent gondolas, charmed

A Continental tour.

him beyond his expectations, whilst his love of architecture, stimulated by the study of Ruskin, made the stately rows of mediæval palaces an unceasing delight. In honour of a visit from the King of Italy the city was illuminated, and the contrast between the solemn dignity of a long-past grandeur and the lively brilliance of this nineteenth century festival touched his deepest feelings. Unfortunately he was here overtaken by a severe illness, due to the unwholesome state of the canals, from which he only fully recovered in the Riviera. I quote the following extract from one of my mother's letters :—

" ' At Bologna my husband's illness returned, and acting on the advice of our friend Lyon Playfair, who, with his wife, were at our hotel, and to whose kind help and sympathy we owed much, we turned our faces homewards. At Avignon we visited John Stuart Mill. . . . Before reaching his house we came to the cemetery in which his wife lies buried. It felt to me like classic ground. The grave was covered and surrounded by flowers of rare and exquisite beauty, and formed a contrast, the reverse of what we usually see, to the living home of the husband, which had a sombre and cheerless look as we approached it by a shaded avenue. But the warm reception given to us soon made everything feel bright; and in the drawing-room, which opened through French windows upon a sort of terrace-balcony—"all planned by my daughter," as Mr. Mill proudly explained to us—a fine view burst upon us of the distant mountains, with the summit of Mont Ventoux veiled in snow.

" ' The visit was delightful to us, and when conversing with Mr. Mill I was reminded, not for the first time, of the words, "The letter killeth, but the spirit giveth life;" for whatever may be the views of Christian doctrine held by this distinguished man, his spirit is imbued with that love for his fellow-creatures and that love of justice towards all which Christ came to teach.'

" After the session of 1872 we travelled for some time on

the Continent to give my father the rest and change he much
needed after his hard parliamentary work. Most of our
time was spent on the shores of the Swiss Lakes, in whose
calm beauty, brilliant colouring, and bright sunshine he delighted ; while the intense heat, so trying to many, always
seemed to give him new strength. A somewhat curious
trait, at which we often smiled among ourselves, was his
great dislike in travelling to use the public rooms in hotels.
We could seldom persuade him to remain long in any place
where these were the only accommodation ; but when we
could get a private sitting-room with a balcony commanding a beautiful view, we always knew that we could stay in
that place as long as any of the party wished it. The Court
of Arbitration on the Alabama claim was then sitting, and
we happened to be at Geneva when the award was given.
The decision was heard with great satisfaction by my father,
who had always believed the British Government to have been
in the wrong, and who had followed all the proceedings with
lively interest. He was present at the dinner given to the
arbitrators by the State Council of Geneva. We stayed a
good while at Chamounix, making many excursions, in which
my father, then seventy-two years of age, was really the
most vigorous of the party, walking and riding all day
without fatigue, and taking upon himself all the trouble of
arranging everything. His pleasure in again seeing Mont
Blanc and crossing the Mer-de-Glace was as keen as it had
been twenty-seven years previously, when he had visited at
Chamounix with my brother John. In crossing the Tête-
Noire, I remember we met a very lively old lady of seventy,
who made a yearly ascent of Mont Blanc, and who told us
that every night of her life she ended her prayers by a petition that she might again be permitted to see the view from
the top of her favourite mountain ! "

1867

In the later years of his life, however, it was in the Highlands of Scotland that Mr. McLaren found most enjoyment in the autumn months.

A holiday in the Highlands. Highland character.

During a residence with his family at Pitlochry in 1874, he and his wife visited the David Ainsworths at their shooting-lodge at Loch Rannoch. Referring to this visit, Mrs. McLaren writes: " He was always deeply touched by any trait which showed the depth of feeling in the Scottish character. While resting at the Rannoch Hotel, he was much interested in the conversation of the widowed landlady, who had brought up a large family under difficult circumstances; but she said, ' When my eldest daughter married, I cannot tell you what I suffered that night when I locked my door, and felt that I had locked one child out.' ' Ah !' he said, ' how different from those fashionable women who are glad when they get one daughter " off!" ' Another little trait of Scottish independence of character greatly pleased him. In taking a walk along the moor, we came to a cottage in a most desolate place inhabited by a poor old woman. He said to her in a tone of pity, ' You must be very lonely here in the winter time.' ' Lonely,' the old woman replied, ' I'm nae lonely. I have for company my clock, my cat, and my kettle !' On our return to Pitlochry, while taking some refreshment at the Bridge of Tummel, a farmer near, hearing of us, came, as he said, ' to pay his homage to Mr. McLaren,' and then alluding to John Bright, said, ' I have a great love for these warriors.' "

At Inverness and Strathpeffer.

The autumn of 1879 was spent at Inverness, at Dunain Park, and his attachment to the capital of the Highlands was strengthened by the Town Council conferring on him the freedom of the Burgh. His stay here was prolonged by severe illness. His anxiety to take part in Mr. Gladstone's meetings during what is known as the first Midlothian campaign induced him to hasten back as soon as he was able to travel, but his strength did not permit him to be present. In 1884 he spent some months at Strathpeffer, enjoying the beautiful scenery of this neighbourhood and driving more than once to Glen Carron Lodge, the residence of his eldest son, and also to Loch Maree and Lochinver. During this visit a bye-election took place for Ross-shire, on the retirement of Sir Alexander Mathieson of Ardross. The Tory candidate was Mr. McKenzie the younger of Kintail, while Mr. Munro-Fergusson of Novar championed the Liberal cause. This election was memorable from the fact that Dr. Roderick Macdonald (who subsequently under the extended franchise defeated Novar, and now sits for the county) came forward as a crofter candidate. At that time the Land League in Ireland was, from the attitude of the Irish party in Parliament, highly unpopular in Scotland and England, and the Highland Land Law Association, of which Dr. Macdonald was the representative, to some extent suffered in the public estimation from the supposed similarity of their aims to those of their Irish friends. The contest in Ross-shire was regarded as one between a good Liberal and Tory on the issue of the extension of the county franchise, and the introduction of Dr. Macdonald seemed unnecessary and likely to lead to a Tory success. Mr. McLaren espoused the cause of Novar, and at eighty-four years of age he addressed more than one meeting in his favour. It is only fair, however, to add that he sympathised with the aims of Dr. Macdonald, and no one rejoiced more than he did when the Doctor and five other crofter members were returned at the general election of 1885.

Early in January 1885 he suffered much anxiety owing to a severe illness which for six months prostrated the strength of Mrs. McLaren. One of the family writes: " It

1885

was on his birthday, the 12th of January, my brother-in-law and sister came over from Bradford on hearing of my mother's serious illness. In reply to their congratulations on the day, as my father met them at the door, he said, ' Ah! it is the saddest birthday I ever had in my life.' The skill of Dr. Rabagliati on that first visit averted immediate danger. During her long illness no loving thought or attention was spared by any member of the family, but to the unselfish devotion of my sister Helen, who left her home and nursed her for four months, we owed much. The nightly prayers offered at the bedside of my mother by my father were very touching. One day when she was very ill, he came to her and said, ' Now, my dear, I have had a strong and unmistakable feeling that you are going to recover ; when I kneel with you I must now use words of thanksgiving. You will recover, and will be raised up to do some things on which your heart is set.' Whether it was the strong faith she, along with the rest of us, had in my father, I know not, but recovery began ; and in August my father, encouraged by her valued medical attendant, Dr. Playfair, thought she might be removed to Highland air. Forgetful of his weight of years, he took long journeys to find a suitable house. It was not easy to do this so late in the season. It was with difficulty he could be persuaded to let any one accompany him on these journeys, and it was only on the plea that it would be a great treat to an American cousin who was staying with us that he consented to have a companion ; so difficult was it for him to recognise any diminution of physical power.

" When she was convalescent, my father brought a large bundle of letters, neatly tied up, which had cheered him through her illness, and gave them to my mother, saying, ' When you are able you will like to read these ; they contain the most touching expressions of sympathy for me and loving admiration for you which I ever read.' I give these particulars that the friends who penned those letters, should they read this memoir, may know in what estimation they were held, and what comfort they gave."

Two months were passed with great advantage at Grantown, where they were helped and cheered by the companionship of their daughter, Dr. Agnes McLaren, and by visits from their son Charles, with his wife and their eldest boy, also from Mr. Bright, who enjoyed driving to his old quarters at Tulchan Lodge, where he had so often indulged in his favourite sport of salmon-fishing. His daughter writes :—"A little incident occurred here which greatly pleased my father, who loved to recognise heart virtues in his children. His grandmamma had given little Harry, on setting out for a walk, some coppers in case he met any footsore pedestrians on the way. On his return he said he had not seen any poor people, ' but might he save the money to give to a poor woman who sold flowers in South Kensington when he went home again, as she used to sit for warmth at the grating of a druggist's shop, and the policeman had ordered her away to another place where it was very cold ?' My father, who knew what it was to carry the burdens of the poor on his own heart, welcomed this trait of loving sympathy in that of his grandchild."

" It was whilst at Grantown," Mrs. McLaren writes, " that Adam Black's Life came out. My husband read it with intense interest, and I could see that it rekindled so much life in past events, that he began to be a little shaken in the strong feeling he always had expressed, when appealed to by many friends that he should leave some reminiscences of his own life, that the questions he had fought for were of too dry and uninteresting a nature to be of any interest for the present generation." On leaving Grantown, Mr. and Mrs. McLaren once more visited Inverness, joining there their youngest son, Walter, then a candidate for the Inverness Burghs. Mr. McLaren was deeply interested in his son's championship of the principles of Advanced Liberalism. The contest was fought almost entirely on the Disestablishment question, and he attributed his son's defeat, and also the reverse sustained by the Advanced Liberal party at this election in Edinburgh and other Scotch constituencies, largely to the influence of Mr. Gladstone's speech in the Free Assembly Hall, Edinburgh, excluding Scottish Disestablishment from the authorised programme of the Liberal party. He, however, never felt himself bound to limit his aims to a programme authorised by party leaders, and was always eager to press forward his own more advanced views. A noteworthy opportunity for doing so occurred while he was at Inverness. When Mr. Chamberlain visited the town, and delivered a powerful speech on the Crofter question to an audience of over four thousand persons, he, at the request of the Liberal Association, followed him by a speech advocating Radical principles with all the vigour of his earlier days. He also spoke at several of his son's election meetings on the subject of Church Rates and Disestablishment. These were the last political meetings he ever attended, excepting that held in Edinburgh on Disestablishment a few weeks before his death.

Speaks at Mr. Chamberlain's meeting.

During his residence in Inverness, and especially during the electoral contest of 1885, he was brought into closer intimacy with his nephew, the Rev. George Robson, minister of the United Presbyterian Church. How highly Mr. Robson prized this confidential and affectionate relationship may be gathered from the letter he sent Mrs. McLaren after his uncle's death :—

" I would like to say that I feel very thankful for all the intercourse I have had with Uncle McLaren during these last twelve months. I have learned for myself the sterling splendour of his character, and have had something like a personal acquaintance, in some measure, with the disinterested devotion of his life to the public good. To have had this intercourse with him has lent to my own life a feeling of being richer and stronger, and by so much I feel the poorer, as countless friends will feel the poorer, that his presence is withdrawn from us. We hardly know the full worth of such men till they are gone from us; it needs the stroke of death to set their life forth round and complete, their character in its true proportions. I do hope that the story of his career will be told in a form which will set before the youth of Scotland, for many a day to come, the stimulus of what is to my mind a unique example of the very best qualities of the Scotch character, and of the honour and success they achieve in the warfare of life. I like to think of his untiring labour for the good of the people, for it always seemed to me to rest upon a loyal faith in God. His purity of aim and transparent integrity of manner and spirit could not have been otherwise so steadfastly maintained. One of the vivid recollections of my boyhood is hearing him explain the tenth chapter of John at Peebles to Helen when she was but a child; it charmed me then, and I have never forgotten the impression made by the simple, direct translation into our life and circumstances of the likeness of the Good Shepherd and the sheep. It came back to me again when you told me at Dunain Park how he had said, in reference to my little sermons to children, that he thought them as convincing to adults as to children. It was quite in keeping that, in his relations to the kingdom of God, he loved to feel and think as a little child."

1885

The sketches of Duncan McLaren's personal and family life presented in these three chapters will, it is hoped, have helped towards a just appreciation of his character, and a sympathetic interest in the record of the fifty years' public life and work, to which the remaining chapters of this book must be devoted.

CHAPTER IV.

THE REFORMED TOWN COUNCIL.

TRUE patriotism is not merely love for one's country. It 1833 includes the practical expression of that love in the form of disinterested service—work undertaken for the benefit of the State, independently of private aims and ambitions, and in recognition of the supreme claims of the commonwealth in matters temporal. In different ages and in different ways this claim has been advocated and honoured by the pure-minded and courageous, most frequently in the department of arms, sometimes in the affairs of civil administration, sometimes in the sacrifice of worldly goods and comfort—solidifying and ennobling national life while the impulse lasted, carrying forward the human family through successive stages towards the ideal of human life, and transmitting to succeeding generations a stimulating influence that never dies. With new times come new methods and new laws; and when the spirit of the age developed in Scotland an irresistible demand for local self-government as the highest condition of human freedom, an opportunity was presented in the reform of the municipal institutions in 1833 for the exercise of patriotism of the severest and purest kind. The old close Corporations, rotten and wasteful as well as secret, were abolished, and the public service was opened to all, subject to the safeguard that he who desired to enter it must be elected by the public, and must perform his duties under the gaze and the criticism of those to whom at the end of his term of office he must give an account of his stewardship.

The patriotic sentiment, in the sense just explained, then beat strong in Scotland ; and in Edinburgh, as in other towns, many public-spirited citizens volunteered for service under the novel and hard conditions imposed. Duncan McLaren was not among these volunteers. He was an ardent Liberal, and his loyalty to the cause of the people made him anxiously concerned for the successful working of the new popular institution set up in the midst of the community ; but he would not compete for a share in municipal administration with men who for many years had been fighting the battles of civil and religious liberty, and whom he was willing and proud to regard as his leaders, without aspiring to be their associate and coadjutor. Though then thirty-three years of age, he had not hitherto been identified with public work. Seven years previously he had joined the Merchant Company, but simply as a business man. He had entered as burgess and guild brother ; and according to the compulsory laws then in force, the fees claimed by the unreformed Town Council for this privilege of citizenship amounted to nearly £25. His business, after nine years' gradual development, still required close personal supervision, and imposed on him duties sufficiently onerous to have fully occupied his time. But while his own thoughts and inclinations were not at this particular time turned towards municipal service, those who knew and appreciated his character and talents marked him out as eminently qualified for the kind of work required ; and as, many years afterwards, Richard Cobden urged John Bright to seek relief from domestic sorrow in public cares, so his friends advised him to undertake the new and exacting duties of a Town

Councillor as a means of rousing him from the depression
of spirits caused by the death of his wife and child. Thus
advised, he consented to be nominated a very short time
before the election, and on the polling day the £10 householders ratified the action of his friends by placing him
among the six citizens elected as the representatives of the
Second Ward.

In his letter to the electors intimating acceptance, he
said :—

GENTLEMEN,—Being unfettered by any pledge, and indebted
to no exclusive party for my return, I esteem the honour the
more highly, and while I remain one of your representatives
I shall endeavour to merit the confidence you have reposed in
me by an assiduous and conscientious discharge of the duties of
the office.

Every question that comes before the Council I shall carefully
consider, and will give an independent vote without reference to
party politics. In filling vacant offices, I shall consider it my
duty to advocate the most rigid economy, and in every case to
vote for the candidate that appears to me best qualified to perform the duties.

I feel highly gratified by the flattering support afforded me as
indicated by the state of the poll, having consented to allow myself to be named as a candidate only the day before the election.

I am, gentlemen, your very obedient servant,

DUNCAN McLAREN.

Of all his colleagues in the Town Council, he felt most
drawn to Adam Black. As a young man he had conceived
a great admiration for this doughty champion of Reform in
pre-Reform days, and this admiration, strengthened subsequently by years of close and friendly co-operation, remained
with him, notwithstanding later differences, till the day of
his death.

In a letter to Mr. Black's sons, written from Grantown-on-Spey on 8th October 1885, after a perusal of the Memoirs,[1] he gave affectionate expression to the time-tested estimate of his early friend. "In the reformed Town Council," he wrote, "I became acquainted with your father. I was a member of his committee, and my seat was next his at the Council-room. He was sixteen years my senior, and had far more experience of the world than I, who up to that time had lived a very retired, obscure life. I greatly admired Mr. Black's talents and sound judgment, and generally followed his lead in voting with him about municipal affairs ; but in politics I was more Radical in my notions than he was, and this difference of opinion gradually increased as I became mixed up with the Anti-Corn-Law agitation and acquainted with its leaders. . . . I can truly say that, for your father personally, I never ceased to have the greatest respect to the day of his death, although our intimacy ceased many years earlier in consequence of political differences of opinion and action."

These reformed and reforming Town Councils had laborious and delicate tasks before them. As successors to the close Corporations that had wasted the public patrimony and incurred enormous debts, they were required to clear public faith "from the shameful brand of public fraud," and the operation excited against them many keen and bitter enmities. Perhaps nowhere was more angry criticism encountered than in Edinburgh. The new Council was persistently vilified by the friends of the dispossessed oligarchies and the foes of free popular government. A local Tory journal represented the "course of business" at the people's Council

---

[1] "Memoirs of Adam Black." Edited by Alexander Nicholson, LL.D. Edinburgh Adam and Charles Black.

as " one of continual uproar, mixed up with brawling, laugh- 1833
ing, groaning, grinning, hooting, hissing, ruffing, and every
other indication of *good breeding* usually exhibited in the
galleries of the lowest minor theatres ; " but the published
reports of the proceedings suggest nothing, and even the
illustrated specimens of misconduct quoted by this irate
censor contain nothing to justify this sweeping condemna-
tion.   The chief ground of complaint or dislike was evidently
the representative character of the assembly, and its fidelity
to popular interests.   For the Tory censor proceeds :—
" Business is not what these persons want to discuss, but to
give utterance to wild theories, rabid Radicalism, wretched
wit, and disgusting buffoonery.   The Council is regularly
divided into Whig, Radical, and Independent.   The Whigs
sit at the upper part of the hall, and the Radicals cluster at
the lower. . . . Truly these councillors are beginning to
find out, from the progress of public business in their hands,
that they are not fit to manage our concerns, as they are
ashamed of the disorderly nature of their meetings, which
are verily full of sound and fury, signifying nothing.   We
must watch these unruly spirits." [1]

But wholesale vituperation of this kind, while it may
be accepted as indicative of the irreconcilably unfriendly
attitude of a section of the population to the new municipal
administrators,[2] was harmless compared with the efforts of

The new
Council
vilified.

Ecclesi-
astical in-
tolerance.

---

[1] *Edinburgh Evening Post*, October 1834.

[2] The following note, kindly furnished by Mr. David McLaren, now of
Putney, shows that humbler officials, as well as servants, conspired to dis-
credit and defeat the new system of government, and tells the story of their
complete discomfiture in Heriot's Hospital:—" There was nothing more
characteristic of Mr. McLaren than the readiness with which he turned to
figures in support of any position which he took up. An amusing instance
of this took place in connection with the measures promoted by the Governors of Heriot's Hospital after the members of the reformed Town Council

the representatives of "vested interests" to introduce their claims and their defenders into the municipal parliament. Mr. McLaren, as an increasingly influential Dissenter, early became the object of their antipathy. At the election of 1834 he was opposed, not on the ground of anything he had done, although his active connection with twenty-two special and ordinary committees, including nearly all the most laborious, might have afforded a watchful enemy some cause of offence capable of public statement, but simply and solely because, being a conscientious Voluntary, he was "not a proper person to elect to represent the ward in the Town Council," and because, "in all our civic

---

took their place at the Board of that Institution. Great abuses had arisen in the home management; the waste of provisions was said to be extraordinary. A new dietary was ordered, ample but not extravagant. As might have been expected, it was extremely unpopular among the old employés. They stirred up the boys against it, alleging that they were being starved. A large Newfoundland dog belonging to the Hospital—a great favourite—died suddenly. The servants told the inmates it had succumbed to the new dietary. In order to see that justice was being done to their regulations, the Governors determined that for a time two or three of the House Committee should be present every day at the dinner-hour. One day it fell to Mr. McLaren, with two others, to attend. Broth or soup was brought in. It certainly did not look very attractive. It seemed very doubtful whether the full quantity of ingredients ordered had been put in. The peas especially seemed absurdly defective. The two other members could only shake their heads and doubt. Mr. McLaren ordered the cook to be sent for. 'Are you sure you put in all the quantities which were ordered by the Committee?' 'Quite sure, sir,' was the reply. 'There were eleven pounds of peas ordered; did you put in that quantity?' 'Yes, sir.' 'You are sure? Ah! There are 180 boys in the Hospital. We shall suppose there are four in the sick-room, or absent somehow. That will leave 176 to dine here. That is the exact number of ounces in eleven pounds. Do these three peas in this plate weigh an ounce? Does that pea in the other plate weigh an ounce?' The cook was dismissed, and the whole establishment with her, if I remember rightly. My informant, one of the members present, was Councillor Gifford, father of the late Lord Gifford and of the present Master of the Merchant Company."

elections it should now be Churchman or Voluntary." It
was admitted that he had proved " an active and efficient
councillor," but he was a Voluntary, and the able and
chosen champion of those who advocate liberal opinions,
and therefore he should be relegated to private life. Mr.
McLaren, in his address, while thanking the electors for
the honour they had conferred on him in the preceding
year, by returning him when he was comparatively little
known, although put in nomination only the day before
the election, very sharply rebuked the bigotry that refused
the rights of citizenship to Voluntaries. While he declined
to canvas, and warned the electors that he could not continue to render the same amount of service as he had done,
his constituents gratefully and heartily reappointed him
as their representative on his own conditions. But these
conditions he himself set aside. He was a willing horse
in the public service, and new burdens were being constantly laid upon him. He was soon promoted to the
Magistracy. Two years afterwards he surrendered his
Bailieship to assume the more congenial duties of the
Treasurership, in succession to his friend Mr. Black. With
each change his duties became more onerous and his influence increased. Within four years the unassuming High
Street merchant, who had hitherto lived a very retired life,
had, by his industry and his acknowledged single-hearted-
ness and purity of motive, become the leading member of
the metropolitan Town Council.

At that time this was no small distinction. The first reformed Town Council was composed of men conspicuous alike
for their talents and for their devotion to the public good.
An examination of the municipal annals of this period dis-
closes abundant proof of the ability, energy, and fidelity of the
councillors. The more important of the reports prepared by

committees and their conveners were printed in order to facilitate careful study on the part of all the members, and they cannot now be read without admiration, characterised as they are by originality of research and thoroughness of treatment, whatever may be the subject under discussion. One of the earliest of these reports, bearing the signatures of Councillor Grainger, the convener, the four Bailies Thomson, McFarlane, Donaldson, and McLaren, Deacon-Convener Banks, and Councillor R. H. Jameson, and dated February 1835, treats of " the eligibility of this city and its environs for manufacturing establishments." These early councillors recognised that it was their duty to study the economic conditions which tend to increase the wealth and material prosperity of the city, and they thought that such results could be best attained, not by the development of schemes of municipal socialism,—indeed, if such a remedy ever occurred to them, the impoverished state of the city finances must have forbidden any attempt to give it practical effect,—but by the encouragement of commercial enterprise. The committee evidently thought that Edinburgh might and ought to be made a great industrial centre, possessed as it was of those five natural aids to mercantile activity, viz., 1st, an abundant supply of cheap fuel of good quality ; 2nd, an abundant supply of water at a moderate expense ; 3rd, a populous district in its immediate neighbourhood, where young operatives of both sexes may be always obtained at moderate wages ; 4th, a seaport in its immediate vicinity, and facilities of internal communication for the convenient importation of raw material and for the exportation of manufactured goods to home and foreign markets ; and, 5th, abundance of good building materials. " The committee thought it prudent that, in the interests of Edinburgh, these facts should be made known through the medium of their report, and they recommended (not as a Corporation scheme, but as a distinctively commercial speculation outside of the Corporation) the formation of an ' Association for the Encouragement of Manufactures,' in so far as is necessary for providing buildings and machinery, and these only to be let on lease to enterprising and responsible individuals."

A still bulkier document, extending to seventy-four pages of large pamphlet size, issued during the same year, illustrates unity of aim with diversity of opinion—hearty co-operation in the defence of the rights of the Corporation along with independent individual effort. It is the municipal reply to the report of the Burgh Commissioners, which threatened the Council's patronage in the University and its interests in the port of Leith. The reply embraces an able statement by Bailie Donaldson relative to the Council's patronage and management of the University, a report on the same subject by Bailie McFarlane, who was formally thanked " for the ability, the propriety, and the dignity with which he had performed the task," along with a report by Treasurer Black and a speech by Bailie McLaren on " The Revenues of Leith and the Interest of the Corporation of Edinburgh in these revenues." Mr. Black was at this time the leading authority in the city on the subject of the ecclesiastical revenues, and a careful, painstaking report which he prepared, including a financial investigation dating back to the beginning of the century, laid the foundation for the future Anti-Annuity-Tax agitation. With commendable discretion and firmness, Bailie Sawers managed the relations of the Town Council with the Royal Infirmary, pointing out, when the right of municipal interference was challenged in 1837, that the Council " cannot consider any of the great institutions of the city as a matter of indifference to the representatives of the community, and least of all the Royal Infirmary, of whose management two of the Council must always form a part, and which annually derives the sum of £2000 (being more than one-third of the yearly revenue) from the attendance of students, in consequence of the regulations of a course of study sanctioned by the Town Council as patrons of the University."

About this time also the practice of examining parliamentary bills affecting municipal or Scottish interests was begun, and the reports submitted were generally masterly and elaborate. Referring to this period of exceptional municipal activity, Mr. McLaren at a later date named Sir James Spittal, the first Lord Provost of the reformed Town Council, as one of the inspiring forces, remarking that "there never was a man who more devoted himself heart and soul to the duties of the office, and gave his whole time and thoughts to it than he did." But the most cursory examination of the municipal history reveals Mr. McLaren himself as the chief centre of activity, initiating an administrative policy as pure and economical as the old close system was jobbing and wasteful, and at the same time expounding and defending it in exhaustive reports. His paper on "The best means of obtaining immediate accommodation for pauper lunatics," was one of the first steps taken in the direction of that humane treatment of the insane which happily now prevails universally throughout Scotland. His scheme for the reduction of the dues payable on the admission of burgesses, carried in 1837, was a fitting preliminary to his bill, passed by the Imperial Legislature in 1876, for the extension of the status and rights of burgess-ship to all ratepaying householders. Referring to Mr. McLaren's work and place in the first reformed Town Council, Mr. James

Aytoun, one of his colleagues at this early period, in a speech in support of his candidature for the Lord Provostship in 1851, said :—

"I recollect well when he took his place amongst us, with his pale, contemplative face. We were all untried, at least had never worked together, and almost from the very outset Mr. McLaren acquired, as if by a species of instinct, that leading position among his colleagues which he has retained ever since with all those among whom he acts. Every one of us soon perceived, and with astonishment, his judgment, his tact, and his persevering industry. He soon became an excellent speaker and writer, and in a very few months he was acknowledged by general consent by far the ablest man in the Town Council."

CHAPTER V.

SETTLEMENT OF THE CITY AFFAIRS.

In this position of acknowledged though unclaimed pre-eminence, Duncan McLaren was called upon to undertake a work which had baffled the skill of his accomplished predecessor in the Treasurership—namely, the extrication of the city finances from a position of impending bank-ruptcy.

In 1836 Mr. Black and Mr. Donaldson, deputies from the Council, wrote long private letters to Mr. McLaren from London, lamenting the little progress which was being made in the negotiations with the city creditors, calling attention to an attempt to complicate the question by a simultaneous settlement of the Annuity-Tax difficulty,[1] and telling him he must join them in London. Mr. Black wrote : " We found both Abercromby and Campbell (the city Members) set on mixing up the Annuity question with the general settlement. To us it appeared the sure way to ruin the whole scheme, for there was no prospect of Government furnishing the means of paying the clergy. There was less prospect of their abolishing the tax without providing a substitute. Therefore, if they relieved one class they must proportionally burden another, who would unquestionably oppose any such arrangement ; or, if they merely changed the name of the tax, then

---

[1] The Annuity-tax was a rate levied in aid of the stipends of ministers of the Established Church, and was bitterly opposed by the Voluntaries.

the whole affair would only be considered as humbug and
excite indignation; in which circumstances the whole measure was in imminent danger of being shipwrecked." Mr.
Donaldson was even more despondent of a satisfactory issue.
He wrote: "The drift of some of the people here (I mean
of the Edinburgh people) is to starve the Corporation."
On January 25, 1838, Sir John Campbell also wrote Mr.
McLaren in a most discouraging tone. "I am obliged," he
said, "to you for the copy of your able speech. The subject
is so beset with difficulties that what is to be done I know
not." But the successful completion of this work was urgently
necessary for the establishment of the conditions of freedom
and independence, without which the new municipal system
could not have a fair trial. In beginning his attempt to
arrange the financial affairs of the city, Mr. McLaren was
conscious that the magnitude and difficulties of the task
would withdraw his attention unduly from the management
of his own business, but he was equally conscious that an
early and satisfactory settlement was essential to the well-
being of the community; that postponement simply meant
the multiplication of complications, the increasing exas-
peration of all the parties concerned, and the growth of
the financial burden, already threatening to overwhelm
the municipal life of the city. Accordingly he resolved to
make what, for him at the time, was the very serious
sacrifice of almost complete withdrawal from his own
private business to promote the interests of the community
in a department of service for which he possessed a special
aptitude, and it might be said of him as of the old Roman
purist, that he "neglected his own concerns and rose before
day to find those of the public." In a private memorandum,
written a few months before his death, he thus described
the financial situation with which fifty years previously

the city was confronted, and the way in which it was
met :—

"The city affairs having become sadly involved by the
extravagance of the former Tory Town Councils, and in
later years chiefly by the building of three churches in the
New Town—St. George's, St. Stephen's, St. Mary's—which
together cost upwards of £80,000, the Town Council was
unable to meet its engagements, to pay interest on its debt
or its bonds as they became due. Its ordinary debts
amounted to nearly £400,000. The magnitude of these
debts and the complication of the affairs involved, including
an additional debt to Government of about a quarter of a
million, secured on the harbour and docks of Leith, which
financially were the property of the city of Edinburgh,
induced the Government of the day, on the advice and with
the consent of local parties, to pass a public Act of Parliament sequestrating the revenues and properties of the city,
so far as these might be found available for the benefit
of its creditors, and appointing trustees for the creditors
named in the Act, viz., Lord Rosebery, Lord Melville, Mr.
James Gibson-Craig, Mr. Learmonth of Dean, Mr. Richard
Mackenzie, W.S., and Mr. W. McHutchen, a large creditor.
This Act was passed in 1832, and the new Town Council,
which came into office in November 1833, had the great
responsibility of endeavouring to effect an arrangement
which would be satisfactory both to the trustees and the
creditors, whose assent was required to the Act, and also
to the Government and to parties connected with various
institutions having pecuniary interests involved, such as the
University, the High School, and many more private trusts.
The Treasurer, of course, had a large share of the responsibility of negotiating with all the parties interested, and
Mr. Black did a great deal to remove difficulties, but when

he retired there was no immediate prospect of a settlement. I followed his example in doing all I could to arrange matters, but the difficulties seemed overwhelming, there were so many interests involved, in addition to those of the ordinary creditors of the city. At length a basis of arrangement was suggested by me, which was ultimately carried through by a public Act, ' The Edinburgh and Leith Agreement Act,' passed in 1838."

But this transaction, thus modestly and summarily described, was not easily effected. The municipal boat did not reach smooth water and a safe anchorage the moment Mr. M°Laren appeared at the helm. It encountered for a time a persistent succession of storms, stirred up largely by the factious and intolerant spirit of the Anti-Reform party, Churchmen as well as Tories, who had no affection for the new system of government, and were only too willing to see it discredited. Mr. M°Laren, however, instead of being discouraged by this opposition, displayed increasing firmness in maintaining the interests of the city. His starting-point was that the offers of compromise formerly made by the Council and rejected by the creditors were too favourable and could not be repeated; and he was strengthened in this position by the withdrawal of Lord Rosebery, Lord Melville, Sir James Gibson-Craig, and Mr. Richard Mackenzie, W.S., from the trust because of what they considered the unreasonableness and unwisdom of the majority of the creditors. Further, he showed to the Council means by which, under the operation of what were called Ale Duty Acts, they could exercise some compulsion on the creditors and their trustees in guiding them " to adopt a more conciliatory course of conduct towards the Town Council, and to agree to a reasonable compromise." Later, the possibility of the assertion of claims against some of the creditors as creators of the debt was raised. Apparently as a diplomatic stroke for the purpose of compelling the creditors and their friends to a more conciliatory disposition, rather than with any serious intention of prosecuting the suit, the Treasurer quoted unrepealed Acts of Parliament " to show that the old Tory Town Councils of Edinburgh were prohibited by law to borrow from private parties above a certain amount ; or in other words, that the debts of the city were never to exceed £100,000." And the following formidable list of debts incurred during the government of successive Provosts since the year 1813 was compiled :—

				£ s. d.
1813.	Provost Creech, .	.	.	£22,566 10 7
1814–5.	Provost Marjoribanks,		.	10,822 16 10
1816–7.	Provost Arbuthnot,	.	.	20,174 17 9
1818–9.	Provost McKenzie,	.	.	7,105 13 6
1820–1.	Provost Manderston,	.	.	11,490 16 6
1822–3.	Provost Arbuthnot,	.	.	29,561 14 6
1824–5.	Provost Henderson,	.	.	19,480 16 9
1826–7.	Provost Trotter,	.	.	44,894 8 0
1828–9.	Provost Brown,	.	.	48,519 3 9
1830–1.	Provost Allan, .	.	.	44,951 12 11
1832–3.	Provost Learmonth, .		.	5,026 8 8

Total debt in twenty-one years, £264,595 19 9

" Such," remarked the *Edinburgh Chronicle*, a paper friendly to the Corporation and the Reform party, " is the splendid sum for which the creditors have evidently a claim ! and what a pretty specimen of Tory extravagance does it exhibit ! The debt incurred during Mr. Learmonth's Provostship would have been much greater, had not part of the Leith revenues, which should have been applied towards the payment of the instalments due to Government, been applied in payment of the ordinary expenditure of the burgh. We hope the creditors will look sharply after their interest, and thus both serve themselves and relieve the burdens of the city. Certain of the creditors, who are old corporators, will perhaps now regret, when too late, that they did not accept of the offer of a settlement made by the Town Council and by Government."

In a series of letters addressed to the municipal electors of the city in October and November 1837, Mr. McLaren explained that self-defence, and not vindictiveness, prompted the adoption of this monitory attitude. He had found that in their correspondence with the Town Council, and more especially in their rejection of the offers of settlement made during Mr. Black's Treasurership, the trustees for the creditors always assumed " high ground," and had exhibited an " utter disregard of every interest but that of their constituents ; " and he therefore was induced " to look carefully into all the Acts of Parliament regarding the affairs of the city, in the hope of being able to discover some effective means of defence against the encroachments." That hope was realised. The investigation he made satisfied him " that the old Town Councils were expressly prohibited by various Acts of Parliament from contracting additional debt ; that for three-fourths of the existing debt neither the funds of the city nor the property of the burgesses is liable ; and that the creditors are only entitled to claim repayment from those members of Council by whom it was contracted."

These conclusions he supported by a long series of quotations. He pointed out, too, that one or two faithful Abdiels had protested against the incurring of these debts in violation of the law, and that, in spite of their recorded protests, the administration became increasingly extravagant and profligate. He showed that during the concluding years of the close *regime*, from 1818 to 1833, more debt was incurred (viz., £209,472) than during the whole previous period of

1838

Letters to the electors.

the existence of the Corporation. He added, "The *proportionate* increase of the National Debt was never nearly equal to this; and it may well be doubted whether the annals of any Corporation in Britain afford a similar instance of reckless extravagance." With this weapon of offence in his hand, Mr. McLaren was not disposed to let the interests of the city be sacrificed, nor the representatives of the city browbeaten by the trustees for the creditors. He gave warning that if the policy of intimidation were continued, he would " carry the war into the enemy's camp" with the watchword of " No quarter ; " that if no reasonable compromise were agreed to —by which he meant a compromise more favourable to the city than the one the creditors had formerly rejected—he would advise that " steps should be taken to fasten the responsibility on those parties by whom the debt was contracted," and the Corporation, which ought to have been one of the most flourishing in the kingdom, overwhelmed by the shame and ruin of bankruptcy. As the controversy proceeded his indignation increased, and he concluded another letter in these words :—

" If the burgesses would compel the old corporators to refund to the extent of their delinquencies during this period of fifteen years, there would be ample funds and to spare with which to pay the creditors in full, even after construing all the acts of the Council in the most liberal manner, and allowing them to get credit for £42,000 expended during this period in the erection of St. Stephen's and St. Mary's Churches, which yield a fair return. Even if £150,000 could be recovered from the old spendthrifts, there would remain ample funds with which to pay the creditors and carry on the business of the city, without having recourse to any new assessment on the inhabitants."

His hopes. Sir John Campbell, writing Mr. McLaren on November 20, 1837, said, " I cannot refrain from expressing to you the extreme pleasure with which I have perused your letters to the municipal electors of Edinburgh. The legal argument, even, you put with great perspicuity, acuteness, and force. I do trust that a final settlement is now at hand, and I am convinced it is mainly to be ascribed to your exertions."

But while thus exhibiting towards his opponents a resolute front, sustained by a knowledge of the financial and legal difficulties greater than had hitherto been displayed by the city representatives, Mr. McLaren was preparing a basis of arrangement, as though he believed the settlement was within measurable distance of accomplishment. In his negotiations with all the parties concerned he was greatly assisted by the advice and action of Mr. Rutherfurd, then Solicitor-General, and who afterwards filled with conspicuous ability the offices of Lord Advocate and judge in the Court of Session. But all the elaborate financial calculations were his own, and these alone demanded from him an amount of labour greater perhaps than had ever before, or has since, been rendered by a lay Town Councillor without professional assistance.[1]

---

[1] At a banquet given to Sir James Spittal, the Lord Provost, Mr. J. T. Gordon, afterwards Sheriff of Midlothian, in proposing " Mr. Duncan McLaren and prosperity to the finances of Edinburgh," made the most complimentary recognition of the labours of the devoted and public-spirited Treasurer. Mr. Gordon said, " It is to the credit of Mr. McLaren that his friends are justly proud—that a party in the State are thankful for the assistance of his extensive learning, singular acuteness, and indomitable industry. But it is surely far more to his credit that, without touching forbidden ground—without uttering anything unbecoming in me to speak, or disagreeable for this meeting to hear—I can now call upon a mixed assemblage of his fellow-citizens to acknowledge how all the information, and talent, and assiduity for which Mr. McLaren is distinguished have been beneficially directed by him of late to the service of the most precious interests of the city. (Hear, hear, and great cheers.) Occupied with the

But it was after the basis of arrangement elaborated by Mr. McLaren had been tentatively accepted in Edinburgh, and the field of negotiation or of conflict for final adjustment had been transferred to London, that the most trying, if not also the most arduous, part of the work began. Before leaving Edinburgh, he had conscientiously and unreservedly informed his colleagues of all his plans and proposals, and having obtained their approval, he went to London as their plenipotentiary. The words of his commission (dated 24th April 1838) were :—" They (the Town Council) authorise Treasurer McLaren forthwith to proceed to London, with full powers on the part of the Lord Provost, Magistrates, and Council to act for them in completing the general arrangement with the creditors, and otherwise giving and granting to him full power and authority for them, and in their name to sign and present any memorials that may be necessary to Her Majesty's Government, or any petitions to either House of Parliament that may be required, or any other documents whatever." He went single-handed, without the aid of Town Clerk or other official, except the town's

---

cares of a large and flourishing business—engaged in the performance of many public functions—and, allow me to say, subjected not unfrequently to attacks which are, perhaps, the necessary lot of men of his eminence— with all those objects to direct his eye and fill his hands, it is yet impossible for me to speak of the whole extent of ability, research, and perseverance brought to bear by Mr. McLaren upon the most delicate and difficult questions in the settlement of the city affairs. It was but this forenoon that a worthy colleague of his showed me a paper of many folio pages, and said, ' There is a report by Treasurer McLaren, which probably few accountants in Edinburgh would have drawn up under a few hundred guineas.' This Mr. McLaren did in the simple conscientious discharge of his duty (cheers) ; and I am sure that Mr. McLaren feels himself to be better paid in the continued and increasing approbation of his fellow-citizens than he ever could have been if paid by gold."

London agent, and with the privilege of consulting with Sir John (afterwards Lord Chancellor) Campbell, the Attorney-General, then one of the Members for Edinburgh, if at any time this busy professional man could be caught. In starting, he was thrown entirely upon his own resources, and he felt the responsibility to be heavy. First he had an audience with Sir William Rae, ex-Lord Advocate, and chief representative of the creditors, a man of great talent and wide experience, and with Mr. Robert Philips, the conscientious representative of the town and harbour of Leith. By the consent of the Government to discharge one-half of the debt incurred by loans for the building of Leith docks, and to postpone the payment of principal and interest on the other half until all other claims should be satisfied, the negotiators had an advantageous starting-point; and ultimately they adjusted the terms of agreement among themselves in a manner which proved highly satisfactory to all.[1] It was not, however, an easy matter to effect this. Protracted conferences took place with the Select Committee of the House of Commons appointed to consider the matter. The Committee consisted of Mr. Labouchere (chairman), Mr. Stewart, M.P. for the Haddington Burghs, Sir James Graham (whose courtesy and helpfulness made an abiding impression of gratitude on Mr. McLaren's mind), Mr. Hawkins, Sir George Clerk, the Chancellor of the Exchequer (Mr. Spring Rice), Mr. W. Gibson-Craig, Mr. Warburton, and Sir W. Rae. For the character and ability of Mr. Labouchere (who was afterwards created Lord Taunton), Mr. McLaren retained a great respect, and he

---

[1] For the information of those who desire to see in full the terms agreed upon, they are given on page 127.

was wont to tell with approbation, as an illustration of public spirit and integrity, how Lord Taunton, having received
£80,000 from a railway company in compensation for a
passage through his Somersetshire property, returned the
money in later years on account of the increased value
his estate had derived from the construction of the line.
In his intercourse with the Committee, Mr. McLaren displayed a candour which won confidence, and a knowledge
which commanded deference, and thus gained influential
friends for the scheme.

In a letter to his wife, dated 4th July, he said, " I
expect to get *justice* for Edinburgh, which you know is
all I want from any one.   But most assuredly justice would
not have been obtained unless I had come."   Two days
afterwards he wrote, announcing that the justice he desired
had been obtained :—

" On seeing Sir James Graham half an hour before the Committee met, he mentioned accidentally that the Lord Advocate
(Mr. Murray, then Member for Leith), who is not a member of
Committee, was to be present on the part of Leith to conduct
the case along with Mr. Philips.   I said there must be some mistake in this, for Sir John Campbell had told me they had both
agreed not to interfere.   Sir James replied that the Advocate was
certainly to be there, for he had been invited by Mr. Warburton,
who had told him so, and he advised me to try to get the Attorney-
General immediately.   However, I thought, as he knew nothing
about the matter, I would lose as much by having him as I was
likely to gain, since I had not had an opportunity of priming him
beforehand.   When I mentioned the suggestion to Sir William
Rae about Sir John, and added that I did not like to have to
contend with the Advocate as well as Philips single-handed, he
said there was no fear of me, that he would back me against
the Advocate on the subject any day, and Mr. Spottiswoode also
advised me to proceed alone.   I went accordingly and debated

the different points at great length, and gained nearly every one of the least importance that I thought worth pressing ; *but you must not say this till the bill is passed.* The Committee always paid great attention to what I said, and seemed disposed to make allowances for my deficiencies. We were all desired to retire, according to custom, when they were about to divide on the most important point, and the Advocate also. Shortly afterwards they sent for me alone to ask my opinion as to what I thought of a compromise, and what sum would be fair. I had never thought of the contingency, but gave them an honest offhand opinion, and they all seemed to feel that it was so. I retired, and was again called in by name to get my opinion on the conditions of the compromise, and again retired. We were afterwards all called in and informed, to the amazement of the Advocate and evident mortification of Philips, that the Committee had agreed to a compromise, which was the very compromise and sum which I had suggested. The Advocate and others were all in the lobby while I was called in, and when I came out I never said a word to them about what had passed. I am very well pleased with the result."

But he never relaxed his personal vigilance and energies. He remained at his post till the measure had passed both Houses of Parliament. Had it been otherwise, it is almost certain the scheme of settlement would once more have been upset. Several surprise oppositions were started. One of these proceeded from the Duke of Buccleuch. The story of his Grace's opposition, and of the city plenipotentiary's successful dealing with it, is thus told. Writing in July to his wife, Mr. McLaren said :—

The Duke of Buccleuch.

"When engaged writing one day in the office of Messrs. Spottiswoode & Robertson, the London solicitors for the city, a gentleman passed through the room whom I did not notice. Shortly afterwards Mr. Robertson came to me, asking me to come in to explain to the Duke of Buccleuch, who had called about clauses in the bill which the Duke thought affected his

1838

properties at Granton, by including them within the burgh of Leith. It was a most intricate and difficult question about boundaries and rights of jurisdiction. . . . The Duke was greatly alarmed, having had letters from his agent in Edinburgh that his rights were affected, and he said he had already asked Lord Camperdown to delay the bill. I knew all about the difficulties, and turned up the Acts on the subject, and gave him a satisfactory explanation, which occupied three-quarters of an hour. He said he did not think he could be affected, and he was to state to Lord Camperdown that he would offer no opposition. If I had not been here great mischief would have followed, as his Grace has much influence in the House. Mr. Robertson said after he left, that it was a mercy I was here and in at the time, for neither he nor any other person in London could have removed the objections."

The Duke of Buccleuch afterwards formally intimated withdrawal of his opposition, and the accidental interview which had so satisfactory a termination proved the beginning of an acquaintance between the Duke and Mr. McLaren which, in spite of differences of political opinion, was maintained, and with growing respect on both sides, until the Duke's death in 1884. When it was proposed to erect the monument in honour of the Duke of Buccleuch which now faces the west door of St. Giles's Church, Mr. McLaren was one of the earliest and heartiest supporters of the scheme.

The city clergy.

A surprise opposition of another kind caused keen irritation. It proceeded from the city clergy. In a letter to the citizens, dated 17th July 1838, Mr. McLaren thus explains the circumstances :—" Yesterday a new opposition was started, Sir William Rae having left on Saturday for Scotland, thinking all safe. The Church, as usual, is the opponent of this, as of every other good measure. A petition from the Presbytery of Edinburgh to both Houses of Parliament was sent up, and that to the House of Commons was presented last night by Sir Robert Inglis, the Member for the University of Oxford, perhaps the Highest Churchman in the House. It was to the effect that the claim of the Presbytery for a *preferable* right to get funds to build new churches should be reserved to them. This is in opposition to the principle of the bill. I told their agent yesterday that I would never admit or reserve any right of *preference ;* that I would oppose it to the uttermost, and rather allow the bill to be thrown out in the Lords than submit to such a condition. I wrote to Sir William Rae strongly to the same effect last night, and sent a copy of my letter to the Council, telling them that such was my fixed resolution, and that if they did not get the Presbytery to withdraw their opposition by return of post, they might consider that this would be the result, as their agent said he would get some of the Bishops to move and carry the clause in the Lords. You know that in the Lords the Church can and will do anything, but I will give the Presbytery the odium of *throwing out* the bill rather than of defeating it by a side wind. It will be read in the Commons a third time this evening, and carried to the Lords and read a first time there, and finished, I think, one way or other, on Friday. I called on Sir Robert Inglis to-day, and gave him a full explanation of the case, and I am sure it is *too bad* for him. I don't think he will move in the matter."

In his active efforts to defeat this device, Mr. McLaren called on many other influential members besides Sir Robert Inglis. He sought and obtained interviews with the Speaker, Mr. Labouchere, and Mr. Stewart, and intimated his resolution to oppose " the trick " out and out. He was then asked by Sir James Graham, " a very High Churchman," to call for him at his house next morning.

"I called," says Mr. McLaren in another letter, "and found he was strongly imbued with notions in favour of the claims of the clergy. I argued the point with him fully in presence of his lady while they were at breakfast, and at last got him to say that it was right to abolish the whole thing, and that he would not interfere by proposing any amendment in the House. The House was to meet at twelve to-day, and he was breakfasting at half-past eleven! Accordingly the bill came on and passed without a word on the subject. . . . I called with Mr. Philips (Member for Leith) afterwards on the Earl of Camperdown, to get him to take charge of the bill. We had letters of introduction from Mr. Stewart and the Lord Advocate. He received us cordially, and is to take it in hand. Lord Melville has gone, and Lord Rosebery has not returned from the country."

Fortunately little further trouble was experienced, and the bill shortly afterwards became an Act of Parliament.

The Act was literally a *magnum opus*. It consisted of no fewer than eighty-three clauses. It secured for the creditors of the city three per cent. annuities on their debts, amounting to £400,000, but it dealt besides with interests affecting the Government, the port and burgh of Leith, the University, and the city clergy; and it satisfied them all. If ever, in a moment of self-complacency produced by the consciousness of having striven his best to hold the balance even through the multitudinous contentions and complications that obstructed his path, Mr. McLaren, as the chief author of the scheme of settlement, ventured to anticipate the reward of public approval, the appreciation actually shown must have greatly exceeded his most sanguine expectations. At a meet-

ing of the Council held on 31st July 1838, the Treasurer gave a full and lucid account of his stewardship, clearly described the provisions of the Act, and their relations to the several parties implicated, and acknowledged the help he had received from Mr. Rutherfurd and Sir James Graham, the

immense amount of trouble taken by Sir W. Rae, the
exertions of Mr. Stewart and of Lord Camperdown in
conducting the bill through Parliament, and the liberality
of the Government, which surrendered a debt of £200,000.
He had blame to cast on no one; and when asked as to
the nature and amount of aid he had received from the
city Members, he explained that Mr. Abercromby, from his
position as Speaker, was precluded from interfering, while
if Sir John Campbell had not given much assistance, it
was because it was not needed. " He (said the Treasurer)
saw Sir John Campbell the very first day he was in London,
and he stated that he would be happy to do everything
in his power, and be ready to make any sacrifice for the
purpose of promoting the interests of the city. Sir John
Campbell stated this in a manner so frank, that he had no
doubt Sir John would not have felt it a trouble if he had
seen it necessary to call upon him; but he had never been
placed in a position that rendered it necessary that he
should avail himself of his very handsome offer. The city
had given him full powers to act for them, and he had
always acted according to the best of his own judgment,
without consulting Sir John on any point." As regards
the general result, he believed the settlement would prove
of great benefit, not only to the creditors, but also to Edinburgh and Leith, reviving both " from the state of languor
in which they had been for some years, and would ultimately be the means of producing the most important
benefits to both communities." He further explained that
the University was placed in a more favourable position
financially by £2500 than it had ever been before, " which
was a matter of great importance to the prosperity of the
city;" while, as regards the city clergy, from whom he
differed in principle, he mentioned that he had not acted

in a paltry spirit, because "the only error he had discovered in the bill in its passage through Parliament was one in their favour, and though the slightest mention of it to the Committee would have got it altered, he had spoken of it to no one but their own agent."

When he had finished his long statement, Mr. McLaren found he had no critics in the Council. His colleagues did not conceal their feeling that their Treasurer, as their plenipotentiary, had acquitted himself with a distinction beyond their expectations, and had rendered the community a service greater than they had believed possible. Their speeches were full of laudation of Mr. McLaren and of self-congratulation that " Edinburgh had in its midst a person capable of conducting matters of such importance," and that for the first time they were in reality " a free Town Council." On the motion of Bailie Crooks, seconded by Bailie Sawers, the following notice was adopted and formally communicated to the Treasurer by Sir James Forrest of Comiston, the Lord Provost :—

" That the best thanks of the Council and the community are due to the Treasurer for his valuable services in London, as Commissioner for the Council, during the time when the bill was in course of preparation and passing through Parliament ; that it is the unanimous feeling of the Council that it was owing to these services that complete success has attended the measure ; and that the Lord Provost be requested to convey the thanks of the Council to the Treasurer from the chair."

But the expression of appreciation was not confined to the Council ; it was repeated by the press of the city, and endorsed by the general verdict of the community. Mr. McLaren having, on the 10th August, issued an address to the municipal electors of the city pointing to the provisions of the Act which fulfilled his promise that the settlement

which he arranged would be more advantageous for the
Corporation than the offers they had rejected, a controversy
arose as to which of the parties had most profited. Referring to this contention subsequently, he happily remarked,
"The only difference of opinion I have heard of is a good-
humoured dispute as to which of the parties has got the
best bargain. Our Leith friends insist that they have
got the best, the creditors contend that the best lot has
fallen to them, while the city think they have not got the
worst."

"The community of Edinburgh," said the *Edinburgh
Observer* of the time, "owe Mr. McLaren a debt of gratitude
which probably they will never be able to repay. All parties
being satisfied with the measure is proof strong as holy
writ that the work as a whole has been well executed."

But one point on which nearly all the parties concerned
were agreed was, that for the settlement which pleased them
all they were chiefly indebted to Mr. McLaren. They knew
that but for his rare talent for figures, his clearness and
calmness of judgment, and his unexampled devotion to
public duty, their extrication from the pit of financial confusion and ruin, dug by the extravagances of pre-Reform
administrators, would have been an impossibility. They
knew, moreover, that the work had been achieved at no
small personal sacrifice to their Treasurer, who, while lavish
of his own service to the community, was severely scrupulous
as regards the acceptance of payment or reward for the public
work he rendered. He rigidly limited his charges while in
London to his own modest personal expenses, determined
that beyond these he would take nothing from the Corporation, his wish being to serve the city, not to enrich himself.

It was not to be wondered at, therefore, that a public
testimonial should have been suggested as an expression of

gratitude for a great work done, and of appreciation of the spirit in which it was carried through. The proposal was formally submitted to a meeting of the principal inhabitants of Edinburgh and Leith, held in the Council Chamber on October 3, 1838, under the presidency of Sir James Forrest, Lord Provost, and attended, among others, by the Attorney-General, Sir John Campbell, M.P., Sir J. Gibson-Craig, Sir J. Graham Dalzell, Provost White of Leith, Mr. John Craig of Great King Street, and several of the magistrates and councillors of the two Corporations. Time and reflection had strengthened the public sense of the value of the work which had been accomplished, and the speakers were even less reserved in their praise than the surprised and gratified Town-Councillors at their July meeting. The Lord Provost spoke of the devoted application of the energies of Mr. McLaren's powerful mind to the city's affairs, with results which promised the highest material benefits to the city through the revival of public confidence and commercial prosperity. Sir James Gibson-Craig certified that it would " be impossible to find any man who had acted in these affairs with more respect to himself and more utility to the community." Mr. Robert Cadell tellingly illustrated the benefits which had been conferred on the creditors. " A considerable portion of this sum (£400,000) was," he said, " held by ladies and women with small means, whose all was invested in what was considered at the time a safe deposit. Very many of their cases were extremely hard. Let them only think of these poor women—their bread-winners gone, and their necessities compelling them to sell to the cool, calculating holders of money, who purchased, or were ready to purchase, the debts below their value—a settlement was to these poor creatures saving them from starvation or the poorhouse."

But, he added, the citizens of Edinburgh had greatest cause for congratulation—" they ought to feel proud that the city's affairs were no longer bankrupt, that, in fact, Edinburgh was again in a position that the finger of scorn could not be pointed at her." As one who had had opportunity in London of knowing how much time and pains Mr. McLaren bestowed on the fulfiment of his mission, and how much his opinion was respected in the Select Committee, Mr. Cadell testified that " no point could be raised, no difficulty started, which Mr. McLaren was not instantly ready to meet with a full and perfect knowledge of the subject." Sir John Campbell, the future Lord Chancellor, was even more complimentary alike to the Treasurer, whom he described as " a great public benefactor," and to his work, which he regarded as of the highest importance, as affecting not merely the reputation of the city, but its future prosperity. Sir John thus proceeded :—

" When he first became connected with Edinburgh, he found that the insolvency of the Corporation, arising from causes which it would now be unprofitable to trace, had caused the greatest confusion and mischief. There was the utmost difficulty in conducting the municipal affairs of the city, and it was only a high degree of patriotism and public spirit which induced individuals of respectability to fill situations of public trust. The creditors of the city had no means of procuring payment of their debt or rendering their securities available. There was a general distrust among all orders of the community. Strangers even were prevented from settling here as they desired, from an apprehension of the unknown burthens which might be brought upon them. Property was depreciated—trade was paralysed. From the complicated nature of the disputes and the conflicting interests of the parties concerned, a satisfactory settlement long seemed impossible. On several occasions he himself had anxiously tried to assist in the negotiations which were going forward, but disappointment was always the result; and at last he saw nothing before him but sequestration and long litigation, which would have swallowed up the funds for which the parties were contending. Under these circumstances Mr. McLaren came forward and proposed a plan based on justice and equity, which was universally approved of; and by his zeal, intelligence, and perseverance that plan was sanctioned by the Legislature, and a long course of peace, harmony, and prosperity was opened to the citizens of Edinburgh."

A subscription was at once proposed. Sir James Spittal accepted the convenership of the committee, and Mr. Adam Black acted as treasurer. By February of the following year (1839) their work was completed, and on the 6th of the month the presentation was made in the Merchants' Hall, Hunter Square. The testimonial consisted of silver plate of the value of upwards of £500, on which was engraved the following inscription :—

The testimonial.

" Presented to Duncan McLaren, Esq., by his fellow-citizens, as a mark of their esteem for his personal worth and great talents, and of their gratitude for the invaluable services he has rendered to the community as City Treasurer and member of the Town Council of Edinburgh; especially for his able, laborious, and successful exertions in effecting a settlement of the affairs of the City.—Edinburgh, 1839."

The Solicitor-General's speech.

On the motion of Sir James Spittal, the Lord Provost was called to the chair, and the presentation was afterwards made in name of the subscribers by Solicitor-General Rutherfurd. No man knew better than he the nature of the difficulties which confronted Mr. McLaren, and which he surmounted, in carrying through the settlement of the city's affairs, and no man was better qualified to bear testimony to the value of the service thus rendered. Having referred to his remarkable business habits and capacity, and to the ungrudging sacrifice he had made of personal

1839

ease and comfort and attention to his mercantile duties, Mr. Rutherfurd spoke of his assiduous devotion to the affairs of the city, and to the perfect mastery he had acquired of all their complex and intricate details.   He then proceeded:—

" You all know the circumstances in which he found matters. Leith and Edinburgh regarded each other with distrust and jealousy, the funds of the College were non-existent, and the city was reduced to a most degraded and humiliating situation.   In consequence mainly of his exertions, all these have disappeared.   He leaves office with the creditors not only possessing a larger return for their debts than at one time they ever hoped to receive, but with the College also in the enjoyment of a revenue of £2500, being more than they ever before possessed, while Edinburgh is reinstated in the situation in which she ought to be as the metropolis of Scotland, and Leith is relieved from a dependency which was neither creditable nor useful to her.   (Cheers.)· Of course I do not mean that his own individual hand accomplished all these purposes.   Of course he had assistance and co-operation. Of course a great deal is due to the liberality of the Government in bringing about an arrangement by which they consented to waive a debt of £200,000.   But taking into account this concession on the part of the Government, estimating—and I assure you I was in a position to estimate the assistance received from other quarters—I speak no more than the truth when I say that my friend Mr. McLaren was the person to whom these arrangements were principally intrusted.   (Loud cheers.) . . . I know well that at the last hours, when other parties were in London, and all hopes of passing an Act of Parliament were nearly gone from some hitch or other, they were anxious to have his services ; and so fully impressed were parties on the other side with the conviction that without his hand the work could not be accomplished, that they made a point, and I was applied to to use my influence to persuade him in the first instance to go to London, and then to remain there till he saw the measure safe and secure. (Loud cheers.)   Under these circumstances, and looking at his possession of all those qualities which are required of a public man ; looking at his great integrity, his firmness and decision, his making himself acquainted, at all sacrifices, with the interests with which he had to deal, and, in addition to these, his remarkable sagacity, and—I know I hurt my friend in speaking thus of him in his presence, but there are occasions when men are bound to hear their own praise—his remarkably sound and practical business habits, added to his moral and intellectual qualities, in which he has few equals—in consequence of these things, it is that we have been led to come forward and prepare this testimonial. (Loud cheers.)"

Mr. McLaren, in his reply, acknowledged the loyal support he had received from his colleagues, and expressed his appreciation of " the most kind and cordial and effective co-operation " of Mr. Philips, representative of Leith. But as Mr. Rutherfurd's commendation was to him most acceptable because best informed, so his own public recognition of Mr. Rutherfurd's help was the heartiest. " I feel," he said, " all the delicacy of my position, and the awkwardness of having it supposed that I am returning compliment for compliment, but I speak only the feelings of my heart when I say, that but for the influence of the Solicitor-General, but for the way in which he conducted the correspondence with the trustees, putting us right and keeping us right, we might have worked for a settlement day and night as long as we pleased, but the thing would never have been accomplished."[1]

As regards his own connection with the transaction, Mr. McLaren said, " I regard this splendid token of your approbation as an invaluable return for my services to the city. These services were rendered—I am sure all who know me will believe—in the most disinterested manner, without the hope or the expectation, or even the thought,

---

[1] Mr. Rutherfurd was presented with the Freedom of the City in recognition of these services.

of any recompense. I was convinced in my own mind that
I was doing all in my power to promote the interests of my
fellow-citizens, and that was all the reward I expected. I
got so much into the middle of these arrangements, and
knowing of how much consequence it was in matters of
such magnitude, involving nearly half a million of money,
that they should be settled at once, and not by a succession
of persons, each doing a little, I became anxious to have
them brought to a conclusion; and for that purpose I
made sacrifices greater than I at first thought of doing.
I am happy that matters have turned out so well—that,
mainly by the liberality of Government and by the candid
spirit in which the arrangement was discussed in a Committee of the House of Commons, composed of men of
all political parties, we have got all fairly settled." He
concluded: "This testimonial will ever be appreciated with
gratitude while I live, and I am sure that those who come
after me will be exceedingly proud of it." The only other
speaker was the Lord Provost, who, in closing the pleasant
proceedings, added this high testimony to Mr. McLaren's
merits: "He had devoted himself to the interests of the
city with an energy which would have led an observer to
imagine that he had nothing else to do, and many of his
reports and calculations, drawn up for the use of the Town
Council, would have done credit to the most experienced
accountant in Edinburgh."

The public testimonial and the speeches delivered at its
presentation by no means exhausted the compliments Mr.
McLaren received. Many came to him in writing. One
of the earliest of these appreciatory epistles was from a
talented Scottish nobleman, who had formerly bestowed
much disinterested labour on the unravelment of the financial entanglement, but without the success he desired and

deserved. In a letter dated Dalmeny Park, August 17, 1838, Lord Rosebery wrote: "I am happy to embrace the present opportunity to express the great satisfaction which the late settlement of the city's affairs gave me. Though I lamented at the time that the offer, which was made when I was one of the trustees, was rejected by a majority of the creditors, I never hesitated in wishing that any arrangement more satisfactory to them and equitable to all parties should be carried into effect. With this sincere feeling I rejoiced that a plan was finally proposed and adopted, which I trust will be found in its operation to combine this principle with a liberal regard to all the great interests which were at stake on the question." Sir James Graham, in reply to a letter of thanks for his sympathy and aid during the arduous conferences and negotiations in London, wrote: "I endeavoured in the Edinburgh case strictly to discharge my duty, without favour or affection, and it is a gratifying circumstance when this conduct is so fortunate as to win the approbation of persons whom I respect so much as you." Mr. Labouchere wrote expressing himself "truly gratified." Sir John Graham Dalzell was also warmly complimentary:—"I speak," he said, "literally as I think. No one has proved of equal ability or has devoted equal time and attention to the city's affairs, and all without the smallest pretension or ostentation on your part. The citizens owe you a deep debt of gratitude." Nor were less welcome the hearty congratulations of an old and steadfast friend, expressed in the simple and direct language characteristic of the speech of the members of the Society of Friends:—"I wish thou mayest through life, and at the close of it, enjoy an approving mind in proportion to the services thou hast rendered thy fellow-citizens. Thy exertions too, in ecclesi-

astical matters, thy clear sound statements, thy straight-
forward, upright conduct on all occasions, have not been
esteemed higher by any one than by thy sincere friend,
JOHN WIGHAM, Junior."

Some may be disposed to think that this catalogue of
the praises of Mr. McLaren as the liberator of the city
of his adoption from financial collapse has been unduly
detailed and prolonged. But the performance thus cele-
brated was no ordinary service. At a trying period in the
history of free institutions it afforded a splendid vindication
of the municipal system, and it still takes rank as one of
the most notable achievements recorded in the municipal
annals of Great Britain. This distinction achieved by Mr.
McLaren at the threshold of his public life has been regarded with peculiar interest and gratification by thousands
of his political disciples, who in all parts of the country, at
different periods of his half-century of active service, have
been conscious of having received guidance from his instructions and example.

Mr. McLaren was not spoiled by all this approbation. He
set aside the flattering assurances of men competent by
experience and observation to express an opinion on the
subject that he was possessed of the qualities which fit for
senatorial service, and which would quickly win for him a
high position in Parliament, and he prepared to return to
his counting-house. His attention to business had been
seriously interfered with by the monopoly of energy claimed
by his public duties and by his prolonged detention in
London. Home claims, too, always strong and attractive,
but now made urgent by the declining strength of his
wife, interposed, and he began to arrange for a temporary
withdrawal from municipal work. Immediately after the
passing of the Act he revolutionised the system of keeping

the city accounts by introducing " the principle uniformly acted upon in every department of the national revenue— that of charging the whole of the expenses connected with the collection and management of each department against the gross sum annually collected, and, after providing for these charges, stating only the balance as the real amount of the revenue." He constructed a series of financial state- ments illustrative of the operation of the new system, and also conforming to the principle of the settlement with the city creditors.[1]

Having set agoing this new and better method of stating the city accounts, Mr. McLaren resigned the Treasurership in November 1838, preparatory to his withdrawal from the Town Council at the close of his term of office in November 1839.

Absence from the Council did not, however, bring Mr. McLaren entire relief from public duty. Further healing legislation was required, and his experience and talent as an honorary parliamentary agent were earnestly applied for.

An agitation had been carried on for some years by the traders of the city against the petty customs, which were most vexatious in their incidence and operation; and during his Treasurership Mr. McLaren had prepared a

---

[1] The following note is interesting, as coming from a very competent critic :—

15 St. Andrew Square, 8th November 1838.

My dear Sir,—I return you my thanks for the copy of your report which you have been so kind as to send me. I have no hesitation in stating it to be the clearest and the most able and practically useful docu- ment which exists regarding the situation of the city affairs. I would certainly avail myself of your invitation to point out errors in it if they were to be found; but I consider the document to be as remarkable for its correctness as for its ability. . . .

Robt. Christie.

scheme for their abolition, introducing a uniform rate of a penny per cartload on all goods, with a few exceptions, such as building materials, brought within the police boundaries. The negotiations were prolonged beyond the period of his councillorship. But his plan was not abandoned, and in 1840 the traders and farmers, having accepted it, requested him to proceed to London to take charge of the bill he had prepared. Under a strong sense of duty, though reluctantly, because of the pressure of home-ties, he complied with their request, again unattended by Town Clerk or any paid official, or even any Town Councillor. After having been examined by Committees of both Houses, he succeeded in carrying the measure through Parliament, to the great satisfaction of the parties interested. Associated with him in the work was Mr. William Gibson-Craig, then Member for the county. Lord Melville was also most helpful. Writing from Melville Castle on 8th March 1840, he said, " Many thanks for your very satisfactory communication of yesterday's date, and which is the more acceptable as I had not heard from any other quarter what progress was making in the Edinburgh Customs Bill, except what I observed in the votes and proceedings of the House of Commons. I am writing to-day to Lord Haddington, and shall mention the bill to him. I am sorry that you are to have the trouble of another journey to London."

The intimacy with Mr. Black survived this first municipal period ; but though neither knew it, or wished to know it, the parting of the ways was near. Attempts were made to put the two friends in competition for the Lord Provostship in 1840. Mr. McLaren discouraged these attempts so promptly and firmly, that no one could doubt his resolution to remain for a time out of the Council ; and thereupon the Churchmen began to applaud him, to the disparagement of

1840

Mr. Black, being anxious to have both the champions of civil and religious freedom out of the way. Some years previously Mr. McLaren had been opposed as a Town Councillor solely on the ground that he was a Voluntary. Mr. Black in his candidature for the Lord Provostship was opposed precisely on the same ground; only he was now, in 1840, represented as the more objectionable man of the two—" a dangerous person, and violent in his opinions," " while Mr. McLaren was a mild man." Mr. Black was defeated on this occasion, but his friends were not discouraged; and at a banquet given in his honour on 25th November they pledged themselves to prosecute with renewed vigour the cause of civil and religious liberty, in which their champion had sustained a temporary reverse. Mr. McLaren was chairman of the committee that organised this demonstration. The leaders of the Edinburgh Whig party (who afterwards became Mr. Black's chief political supporters) are said to

Whig strategy.

have absented themselves from this banquet. In his letter to Mr. Black's sons in October 1885, Mr. McLaren thus explained the cause :—" The general feeling at the time was that there were hopes on the part of the Whig leaders that Government would yield to such an extent to the claims of the Non-Intrusionists as would prevent any disruption, and would make that party supporters of the Liberal Government in all time coming. It was said that Fox Maule (afterwards Lord Dalhousie) and Mr. Rutherfurd (then Lord Advocate) were the chief negotiators in this matter, and that their influence kept away the leading Whigs from the dinner, lest their appearing in support of Mr. Black and the Dissenting interest might injure the negotiations. But this beautifully laid scheme went sadly agee."

Mr. Black's defeat was temporary, and indeed prepared the way for a greater triumph. In 1843 he was unanimously chosen for the civic chair, and it was as Lord Provost that he, in July 1845, presided at a banquet given to Mr. McLaren as a public welcome home on his return from Madeira. Lord Provost Black on this occasion proposed the toast of the evening, and among others who were present to testify their appreciation of Mr. McLaren's public services and their gratification at his safe return were Mr. Charles Maclaren, editor of the *Scotsman*, and Councillor Macfarlane, a future candidate for the Lord Provostship.

1843

A welcome home.

The following are the terms of the settlement of the city's affairs as adjusted by Mr. McLaren :—

1. That the whole debts due by the city, as on January 1, 1833, including those charged on the Ale Duty, shall be compounded by payment to the creditors (other than the life annuitants) of a perpetual annuity of three per centum, free of all deductions, and redeemable only on payment to the holder of one hundred pounds sterling for every three pounds of annuity.

2. That the life annuitants shall receive, during their lives, three-fourths of the annuities due to them, in terms of an arrangement made between them and the trustees for the creditors.

3. That these annuities shall be paid half-yearly, and shall be constituted by bonds, to the transference of which the greatest facilities shall be afforded.

4. That the city shall grant a valid preferable security for those annuities of the whole property, of whatever description, now belonging to the city, with the following exceptions :—

(1.) The common good of the city and liberties. But this

to form the security of an annual payment to the creditors of £1000.

(2.) The assessment of one per cent. in lieu of the import on wines.

(3.) The fees payable on the entry of burgesses and guild brethren.

(4.) The petty port customs of Edinburgh, which, to remove all doubt on the subject, are to be declared by the Act to have fallen.

5. The city, after granting this security, shall do nothing by which the subjects of it may be dilapidated or their value materially diminished.

6. In the event of the foresaid annuities not being duly paid, the creditors shall have power, on three months' notice, to take possession of the whole subjects in the security (with the exception of the common good, in regard to the security over which a special provision shall be made), and the said subjects shall be completely surrendered to the creditors, to be disposed of by them in such manner as they may deem best, without any liability to account to the city thereanent ; provided always that the Royal Exchange Buildings, the Meadows, Bruntsfield Links, Calton Hill, and Princes Street Gardens shall be retained by the city at a value to be fixed by Sir William Rae and Mr. Solicitor-General Rutherfurd, and, in the event of their differing, by an oversman to be appointed by them ; it being always understood that the Gaols and High Schools are subjects on which no valuation shall, in that event, be put. That in the event of the subjects forming the security to the creditors being made over to them, and of the trustees of the middle district having then made good a claim against the city on account of the repairs of the streets, such claim shall form a burden upon the revenue reserved from the security for behoof of the city, estimated at £4500, in so far as the free revenues made over to the creditors, after the deduction of all preferable burdens and expenses, shall not amount to £8500, including the sum of £480 payable from

the merk per ton, and exclusive of the sum of £2500 to be derived from the Leith revenues.

The nature of the original agreement regarding the interests of the city and creditors in the revenues of the port of Leith will be seen from the printed copy of the entire proposals of the agreement sent with this, but that agreement has subsequently been modified for the reasons stated in Mr. M'Laren's "Explanatory Remarks," and the following propositions have *now been adopted in lieu of the original articles in reference to the revenues of the port of Leith.*

(1.) To give the creditors £2500 from the Leith revenues in lieu of all claims which they have thereon.

(2.) To provide that £2000 per annum shall be made payable in lieu of the merk per ton to be abolished, and that the sum of £480 presently payable from the merk shall form a burden on the other revenues of Leith, and be perfectly secured in the same manner as the sum of £2500.

(3.) To provide that the debt due to the College of £13,119 shall be extinguished, as recommended in the reports of Mr. Labouchere and the Select Committee, and that the annual payments chargeable thereon, together with the other claims for the support of the University and public schools, shall form a burden on the sum of £2500 proposed to be given for educational purposes out of the revenues of Leith.

(4.) To provide that the bonds be free from stamp duties, and transferable by endorsation in terms of the reports above referred to.

Mr. McLaren next prepared for the satisfaction of the Chancellor of the Exchequer, but generally in the interests of the scheme of settlement he had outlined, a detailed statement of the case entitled "Explanatory Remarks," which was subsequently printed as a parliamentary paper by order of the House of Commons. In conformity with the modifications suggested in the "Explanatory Remarks," the parties subsequently agreed to introduce the subjoined propositions in their terms of agreement, in lieu of the original articles in reference to the revenues of the port of Leith :—

(5.) That the common good or market dues, customs, and imposts of whatever description leviable within the boundaries of the municipal burgh of Leith, together with the gaol buildings, shall be made over to the Magistrates and Town Council of Leith, they being bound in consideration thereof to relieve the trustees of the Middle District of the obligation incumbent upon them under the terms of the Act 5 and 6 Will. IV., c. 68, to uphold and maintain certain roads and streets within the town of Leith which it was formerly incumbent upon the Lord Provost, Magistrates, and Council of Edinburgh to keep up and support, and to free and relieve the said Lord Provost, Magistrates, and Council of Edinburgh of all claim of relief competent to the said trustees against them thereanent under the provisions of the said Act ; and further, that the said Town Council of Leith shall free and relieve the said Lord Provost, Magistrates, and Council of the city of Edinburgh from all claims on account of the municipal government of Leith ; declaring that the obligations incumbent on the Commissioners of the Docks and Harbour, and those presently or who may hereafter be vested with the administration of the revenues thereof in regard to the streets of Leith, shall not be lessened or affected by anything herein contained.

(6.) That power be given to the Town Council of Leith to purchase the superiority of Leith, and that at such price as shall be fixed by the two arbiters to be mutually chosen by the Lord Provost, Magistrates, and Council of Edinburgh, with concurrence of the Committee of Creditors, and the Provost, Magistrates, and Council of Leith, or, in case of difference of opinion, by an oversman to be chosen by such arbiters.

(7.) That the Links of Leith shall be made over to the Town Council of Leith, for behoof of the community of the burgh, for an annual payment to the Lord Provost, Magistrates, and Council of Edinburgh of £25 sterling, being the amount of the present annual rent thereof. The Town Council of Leith to have the power to purchase this annual payment at the rate of twenty-five years' purchase at any period : the Links to be preserved as an open area in all time coming for the use of the inhabitants : the price of this and of the subjects authorised to be sold to be applied to the extinction of the transferable bonds.

(8.) That the Town Council of Edinburgh shall within one year from the passing of the Act to be obtained for the settlement of these affairs be bound to pay from their current revenues to the Town Council of Leith the sum of £500 in lieu of all claims on account of the common good of Leith heretofore drawn by the city of Edinburgh, and which payment shall be held to be a full discharge of all such claims on the part of the Town Council and community of Leith.

For the accomplishment of the foregoing public objects, and also for the purpose of improving the public harbour of Leith and rendering it fit for the accommodation of the trade, it is humbly submitted that the propositions contained in the reports of the Select Committee and of Mr. Labouchere to abolish or limit the amount of the debt due to the Government should be adopted, and that an independent Commission should be created, invested with sufficient power for the improvement and proper management of the port.

More than forty years after the adoption of this arrangement a leading member of the Leith Dock Commission, whose acquaintance with the affairs of the port extended back to a period anterior to 1838, declared it was Mr. McLaren that had " made Leith "——meaning thereby that the abolition of the merk per ton effected the liberation of the commerce of the port, and thus permitted the remarkable development and prosperity witnessed in subsequent years. The annual payment of £2000 in substitution for the merk per ton continued down to 1870, when the Act abolishing the Annuity-Tax in Edinburgh and Montrose was passed. A clause was introduced into that Act authorising the Leith Dock Commission to redeem the £2000 a year by a payment of £40,000, which they did soon after the Act was passed ; and thus ended the merk per ton and its substitute. The debt to Government was discharged in 1860 by a payment of £50,000, but the Dock Commission still pays £5680 per annum to Edinburgh, being £3180 to the city creditors and £2500 to the College and schools.

CHAPTER VI.

ESTABLISHMENT OF HERIOT FREE SCHOOLS.

YEARS before the time when Mr. Bright, in his powerful speech delivered in Edinburgh after the passing of the Household Franchise Reform Bill, had pleaded that the helping hand of Christian justice and kindness should be " let down to moral depths deeper than the cable fathoms, to bring up from thence misery's sons and daughters, and the multitude who are ready to perish," Mr. McLaren was enabled to embody in practical statesmanship the principles so beautifully and urgently commended by the champion of reform. That was the originating aim of the Free School system which he linked to the Heriot Trust, and which subsequently became the most beneficent feature of its administration.

The greatest good of the greatest number was the foundation principle of his municipal as well as of his parliamentary policy, and in the increasing revenues of the Heriot Trust he found the means of giving the doctrine practical exemplification. He believed that free schools, though not expressly provided for by the will and statutes, were nevertheless in strict harmony with the design of the founder. But he also believed that the citizens had even a stronger claim to the surplus than the right of inheritance conferred by George Heriot's will. It was through the wisdom and carefulness of their representatives that the original bequest of £23,625, 16s. 3d. had not only built a handsome college and provided for all the requirements of the will, including the maintenance and education of 180 boys within the Hospital, the payment of apprentice fees for boys who had left the Hospital, and of ten £20 bursaries to students at the University of Edinburgh, but had been employed so as to yield in 1835 a revenue of £14,500, leaving a clear surplus of £3000 a year. He was jealous for the right of the citizens thus acquired, and he was also concerned for their welfare. He feared that if this surplus remained unemployed or unclaimed for any length of time, some means of dissipating it, not advantageous to the general public, would quickly be discovered; and he set to work at once to make it available in a way most beneficial to the city. He proposed a system of free schools, as the best and safest means of aiding the class most deserving of help; a boon certain to be prized by the common people, who knew that the absence of education meant the degradation of their children, and that help from a fund destined for them by bequest, and guarded in their interest by their municipal representatives, could in no sense be fairly regarded as a pauper's dole.

Having satisfied himself of the justice and general advantageousness of his policy, Mr. McLaren forwarded its adoption with characteristic vigour. He spared no effort to carry his colleagues with him, and to have his action fortified by an approving public opinion. On 13th May 1835 he proposed at a general meeting of the Trust, "that it be remitted to the committee to consider and report as to the propriety of applying part of the surplus revenue of the Hospital to the erection of one or more schools for the education of the sons of such burgesses as cannot be admitted into the Hospital." His motion was adopted, and the remit was made to the Committee on Superintendence of Schools, of which Bailie Macfarlane was convener. For the guidance of the committee Mr. McLaren prepared a statement judicial alike in structure as in tone, advocating his reform on financial, legal, and educational grounds. He showed that the increased and still increasing revenue of the Trust had provided a revenue far in excess of the requirements of the will; that it would be impossible ever to employ the surplus revenue in enlarging the present Hospital, or in building another for the benefit of the decreasing number of burgesses; while to admit the children of such burgesses as were sufficiently able to maintain them to all the benefits of an institution which the Governors were charged in the most solemn manner to administer only to relieve the poor, would be a far greater evil and a more flagrant violation of the spirit and letter of the will of the founder, and of the statutes of Dr. Balcanquil, his executor, than the proposed application of the funds for the purposes of education, even although the benefits of gratuitous instruction were extended to the destitute children of all classes and of both sexes.

He did not conceal his distrust of the hospital system of education, for he expressed the view " that £800 a year judiciously expended on schools would do more good than the £8000 which is expended in connection with the Hospital." It will thus be seen he was, in point of time, a generation in advance of the modern reformers, by whom the hospital system has been condemned; nor did he conceal in the year 1835 that he was prepared for something approaching to a complete system of free elementary education, for he indicated his belief that the surplus would soon prove sufficient to erect and maintain a George

Heriot school in each of the thirteen city parishes, "which would be amply sufficient to educate gratuitously all the poor children in Edinburgh, besides fulfilling in the most ample manner the liberal intentions of the founder respecting burgesses' children. Thus the revenues of the Hospital would become an inestimable blessing to the community."

Mr. McLaren's statement, which concluded with a proposal that an Act of Parliament should be procured to remove all doubt as to the legality of the proposed application of a part of the funds of the institution, commanded the general assent of the committee, and it was printed for distribution among the Governors in anticipation of a meeting convened for the 12th October. When the Governors met, they unanimously approved of Mr. McLaren's work and expressed sympathy with its object; but some cautious members were indisposed to accept the responsibility of an immediate settlement, and suggested a year's delay in the application to Parliament. Meanwhile opinion outside grew steadily in favour of the reform. The press generally supported it.

The *Scotsman* newspaper said :—

" We may now be able to congratulate our townsmen on the acquisition of a number of free schools adequate to the instruction of all the poor children in the city. We are satisfied that the Hospital at present yields no advantage to the town proportionate to the magnitude of the funds, and by a more strict observance of the statutes as to claims for admission we have no doubt that a much larger portion of its revenue than £3000 may by-and-bye be made applicable to the beneficial object recommended by the committee."

The *Edinburgh Patriot* wrote :—

" Edinburgh already owes much to the munificence of George Heriot, but if the worthy Bailie's (Mr. McLaren) philanthropic idea of thus distributing the surplus funds of the institution be carried into effect, her debt of gratitude will be vastly increased, nor will the citizens soon forget that it is to the spirited and patriotic exertions of Mr. McLaren that they will chiefly owe this lasting advantage."

Mr. McLaren likewise communicated his purposes to the county and city Members.   Sir George Clerk replied :—

" It does not appear to me that any more eligible application of a portion of the surplus revenue of the Hospital could be proposed, and as it further appears from the extracts from the will of the founder contained in your suggestions that such application is not inconsistent with his benevolent intentions, I think that few or no objections will be urged to this measure, the principle of which I approve.   Not having seen the bill which it is intended to bring into Parliament to remove any doubts that may exist as to the powers of the Governors to apply part of the surplus funds, I cannot pledge myself to support all the minor details of such a bill, but I shall always feel anxious, as far as it can be done in accordance with the intentions of the founder of the Hospital, to extend to the children of the poor in the city of Edinburgh the inestimable advantages of sound and religious education."

Sir J. Campbell, the city Member, wrote :—

" I have read your suggestions with great interest, and I entirely concur in your view of the subject.   There seems to me to be no doubt that the proposed application of the surplus is in conformity with the intention of the founder, and is the most expedient that could be devised.   I should think the bill is not likely to be at all opposed, but if it be, it shall have my strenuous support."

Encouraged by the favourable reception given to his scheme, and by the general demand for immediate action, Mr. McLaren, with characteristic courage and self-reliance, resolved to secure for the Governors the opportunity they had neglected on 12th October, and on his own responsibility, and in his own name, he gave the necessary parliamentary notice of the proposed bill in time for its presentation during the coming session of 1836. When the Governors again met on 16th November, they heartily endorsed Mr. McLaren's action, and accepted the notice he had given as their own. They instructed the committee to prepare the heads of the proposed bill, and they " directed the Treasurer to repay Councillor McLaren the expense he had been put to in giving the requisite notice of the proposed application to Parliament." No further interruption to the progress of the measure occurred. The petition for the bill was signed on the 15th of February 1836. The heads of the bill were finally approved on the 3rd of March, the measure passed both Houses of Parliament without opposition, and on the 14th of July it received the royal assent under the title of " An Act to Explain and Extend the Powers of the Governors of the Hospital in Edinburgh founded by George Heriot, Jeweller to King James the Sixth." The total expense of procuring the Act was £922. For nearly fifty years this remained the charter of the poor of Edinburgh to a system of education, wide-reaching, free, and unsectarian, such as no other community in the United Kingdom then enjoyed.

The Governors of the Hospital did not forget the service Mr. McLaren had rendered after success had been achieved. At the first meeting of the Governors held after the bill had become law, Bailie Donaldson moved, and Dr. Macaulay seconded, the following resolution :—" That the Governors feel it their duty to express their approbation of the eminent services of Councillor McLaren in having originated and greatly aided in bringing to a successful issue this important measure, and that this testimony of their approbation be entered on the records of the Hospital." Two years afterwards, at the meeting at which Mr. McLaren received a presentation in recognition of his settlement of the city's financial affairs, the Solicitor-General (Mr. Rutherfurd) paid a warm tribute alike to the author of the School Act and his work.   He said :—

"It is also of importance to recall another benefit to the cause of education which I believe my friend first originated, and which has since been confirmed by Act of Parliament, to extend the benefits of the institution of Heriot's Hospital by employing the funds in erecting schools and diffusing the blessings of education more extensively over the community."

Solicitor-General Rutherfurd's tribute.

But the most gratifying reward of this beneficent effort on behalf of the classes of the community most in need of help was the remarkable success of the free schools.   True, much preliminary work was necessary, but no time was lost with it.   By the 11th of October Mr. McLaren had obtained for his committee the authority of the Governors to proceed with the erection of the first outdoor school " on that waste area at the entrance to the Hospital grounds leading from the Grassmarket opposite the porter's lodge."   The foundation-stone was laid in April 1837, and sites for other free schools were purchased in October of the same year.   The first school was opened in October 1838, and the other free schools in October 1840.   By 1854 ten were in operation, three infant schools, containing 606 children, and seven juvenile ordinary elementary schools, accommodating 2217. The total cost of erection of these ten schools amounted to the very moderate sum of £22,015 ; and at the date mentioned the rate of maintenance, including salaries of teachers, books for the scholars, and all other incidents, was £1, 4s. 3d. per annum per child.   By-and-bye the benefits of this free elementary education were extended,

Success of the free schools.

until the roll included upwards of 5000 day-scholars and 1000 night-scholars.

But Mr. McLaren did not only help to secure an early start to the free outdoor schools and a wide diffusion of their benefits by means of economical administration. He remained a member of the Trust till 1839 ; he was *ex officio* chairman during his three years' Provostship, 1851–54 ; he served for another year in 1860–61. But whether a member or not, during the whole period of his public life, from 1832 till 1886, he kept himself cognisant of all the affairs of the Hospital ; and while he never obtruded his ideas or opinion, his influence was felt in, and to no small extent guided, the more important deliberations and decisions of the Trust during that long period of fifty-four years. His policy was uniform ; its objects were the extension of the benefits of the educational scheme of the Hospital to the widest possible limits, and the guardianship of the interests of the poor. During all that time the Governors were remarkably, indeed it may be said unflinchingly, loyal to that policy. When in 1839 the Dean of Guild, speaking in name of " several respectable burgesses" who did not wish their children to mingle with the children of the poorer classes, and at the same time desired for them more than the elementary education provided under the Act, proposed that one of the schools should be reserved exclusively for burgesses' children, the Governors seemed practically unanimous in deprecating any separation of classes. The old "use and wont" of the Scottish educational system was that the children of all classes, the sons of the laird, of the minister, and of the labourer, should meet on equal terms in the parish schoolroom and in the playground, and the Heriot Governors were not disposed to countenance any breach of the old social solidarity, as far as their schools were concerned. Mr. McLaren showed by a reference

to the Act of Parliament that the outdoor schools were open
only to three classes, viz., first, the children in poor circumstances of deceased burgesses, who had a preferable right;
second, the children of burgesses "whose parents may not
be sufficiently able to maintain them;" and lastly, "the
children of poor citizens or inhabitants of Edinburgh." The
Rev. Dr. Lee, afterwards Principal of the University, Lord
Provost Sir James Forrest, and others, concurred with Mr.
McLaren, and the Dean of Guild unconditionally withdrew
his motion.

"Use and wont" was maintained in another respect.
Practically this was the basis on which the religious difficulty was settled.   Indeed, it may be said that conformity
to the parish school arrangement, so far as religious instruction was concerned, and regard for the spirit of George
Heriot's will, kept the Governors free of the religious difficulty altogether.   In a letter published in 1854, during the
last year of his Lord Provostship, Mr. McLaren thus described the provision for religious instruction in the Heriot
schools, in refutation of the idea that parliamentary securities were necessary :—

"In each of the Heriot's schools there is a religious instruction
class for an hour daily, which all the children in the juvenile
schools willingly attend, being the first school hour (from nine to
ten A.M.).   There is also in each a Sabbath-school at the same
hour, which all the children are expected to attend whose parents
do not prefer sending them to some other Sabbath-school, connected with their own religious denomination, or one which may
be more convenient from its vicinity to their residence.   In such
cases the children are not expected to attend the Heriot's Sabbath-
schools, but very large numbers do attend, and the result is that
all the children of the various sects into which the great community of Edinburgh is divided (with the exception of the Roman
Catholics, who do not send their children to these schools at

all), acquire at the Heriot's day and Sabbath schools what their parents severally believe to be 'a sound religious education.' . . . Here a state of perfect peace and amity, as regards the religious education of nearly one half of the children of the poorer classes within the city of Edinburgh, is proved to exist beyond the possibility of cavil or dispute; and surely the same end might be attained in other cases by the employment of similar means."

ecta-admi-ration.

But in reference to the appointment of teachers the Governors took a step in advance of parish school " use and wont," and prepared the way for the more liberal terms of settlement embodied in the Education Act of 1872. From the beginning the Governors resolved that they would impose no test on the members of the teaching staff, either in the supposed interest of religious orthodoxy or of the Established Church. Considering the composition of the governing Trust, namely, the Town Council and the ministers of the Church of Scotland for the city of Edinburgh, and also considering the time in which the arrangement was made, between thirty and forty years before the same principle was embodied in a national Act of Parliament, the liberality displayed by the eighteen Established Church ministers and the intelligent prudence shown by the general body of the Governors seem equally entitled to commendation. In the letters of 1854, already quoted, Lord Provost McLaren wrote :—

"They imposed no test; they required no declaration of religious belief; they left it to the good sense of each Governor in all time coming to vote for such masters as he believed in his conscience would impart to the children a sound religious education, leaving it to the candidates to furnish evidence, by certificates or otherwise, of their fitness to impart religious instruction in the same manner as they provided evidence of their fitness to impart secular instruction."

The result was that in course of time Congregationalists, United Presbyterians, and Free Churchmen, as well as Established Churchmen, became Heriot teachers, with the best advantage to the character of the religious and secular instruction provided.

This plan of " no legislation on the subject," as Mr. McLaren described it, was carried out under the rules and regulations for the management of the schools which the Act of 1836 authorised the Governors to frame. It bore the impress of Mr. McLaren's liberal ideas, for which he was then earnestly contending, alike in the educational and political sphere. It was, though on a limited scale, yet in a double sense a triumph of the Voluntary principle, of which he was, even then, one of the most powerful champions in Scotland ; and it was a forerunner of the cognate legislation passed by the Imperial Parliament, with no little difficulty, and with much fear and trembling, in 1872. Yet these principles, which under Mr. McLaren's guidance the Governors of Heriot's Hospital were ready in 1838 to accept, and did accept, were for nearly forty years afterwards dreaded and denounced as revolutionary and infidel by many good and religious men and women. Thus Edinburgh, while setting an example which attracted the notice and commendation of men who, in other spheres, were regarded as pioneers in the cause of educational reform, enjoyed a boon denied to the country generally till the passing of Lord Advocate Young's Act of 1872.

Another portion of the rules in the preparation of which Mr. McLaren showed special concern was the system of inquiry which was instituted before admission to the outdoor schools could be granted to any applicant. The inquiries were designed to secure two objects, viz., the preservation of the benefits of the free outdoor schools for the

most needy of the deserving poor, and the development of a
kindly interest in those classes on the part of the well-to-do
neighbours and citizens. As regards applicants, the object
was to find out and give preference to the children of families
who had lost their father, or mother, or guardian; where
the bread-winner had been struck down by disease or acci-
dent; where the earnings were lowest in proportion to the
number of mouths to be fed, and where the struggle with
poverty was bravest; for receipt of parochial relief was
regarded as a bar to Heriot aid. On the other side, as
regards the opening up of a legitimate field of benevolence for dutiful citizens more abundantly blessed with
worldly prosperity, the employer was consulted as to the
rate of wages earned, the minister as to the character of
the family, and two respectable householders were asked
to certify to the general accuracy of the facts set forth
in the application form. All this meant inquiry; inquiry
excited interest, and this interest was in many cases
continued until the family, relieved at a critical moment
and put in the way of employment, had struggled back into
a condition of comparative comfort.

The immediate educational results were gratifying beyond
expectation. They effectually vindicated the free school
system, and prepared the public mind for a reform which
is now not far distant. The attendance of pupils was more
regular than in the best elementary schools where fees were
exacted, and the average standard of educational efficiency
attained was higher. The testimony given from time to
time as to both of these points was unequivocal. Mr. John
Gibson, whom Mr. McLaren, in his evidence before the
Endowed Institutions Commissioners in 1879, described as
" one of the ablest men who ever filled the office of inspector of schools," and who afterwards became proprietor of

Merchiston Castle School, spontaneously offered the following certificate.   He wrote :—

"In 1843 Mr. George Combe introduced to Mr. McLaren the Hon. Horace Mann, Massachusetts, and Dr. Howe of Boston, who had visited Edinburgh to inspect its educational institutions, and asked him to direct 'their attention to whatever is best worth seeing in our city schools or Heriot schools.' Mr. Mann also bore a letter of introduction from Mr. Joseph Hume. Indeed, it may be said that for many years every distinguished visitor to the city, who wished to learn what was most noteworthy about its institutions, was shown the free Heriot schools. Strangers are attracted towards them by the accounts which they hear of the immense good they are accomplishing, and the wonderful change which they promise to effect upon our poor population. Every one projecting the institution of schools for the poor in Edinburgh and the surrounding country looks to them as the best models. . . . It is not too much to say that these schools form by far the most valuable elementary educational machinery existing in this country."

And to the chief author of the Act and of the regulations which brought this educational machinery into operation Mr. Gibson, with equal spontaneity, paid a well-earned tribute.

"I cannot (he wrote) pass from the consideration of these schools without mentioning that it is chiefly to Mr. Duncan McLaren, of this city, that the inhabitants are indebted for these invaluable institutions. By him was the suggestion first made that the surplus income of the Hospital should be devoted to such an object. To his enlightened interest in the elevation and amelioration of the condition of the poor, and to his zeal, activity, and sagacity in conducting the negotiations and arrangements necessary to the completion and establishment of the scheme which he had originated, is the promptitude in carrying the suggestion into effect principally to be ascribed. The accomplishment of such a measure of philanthropy may well be to him a subject of self-gratulation, and secure for its author the warmest gratitude of every one interested in the religious and moral wealth of the population."

Mr. John Gordon, another Government inspector, bore testimony as strongly eulogistic. He spoke of the convenience of the situation of the schools for the class of children for whom they were intended, praised the accommodation provided, including "the ample supply of school-room requisites," and expressed approval of their leading characteristic—"the exemption of all from the payment of school-pence." He continued: "They constitute a class of schools second in general merit to none of the purely primary class throughout the district. Of 7371 presentations in the three subjects of reading, writing to dictation, and arithmetic, according to the requirements of the Revised Code, there were 97½ per cent. of passes." As regards comparative attendances, Mr. McLaren, in his evidence before the Commission already referred to, stated that for the seven months ending 1st May 1879, out of every 100 children attending elementary schools, the absences were :—In the Heriot schools, 8 ; in the Board schools, 16 ; in the new Board schools, 19 ; and in the Roman Catholic schools, 21 ; while the average absences of all Scotland were 24, for all England 29, and for all Ireland 30. In a speech delivered in the House of Commons ten years previously, he had given the explanation of the superiority of attendance in the Heriot schools. "If a boy was absent," he said, "the teachers made inquiry, and if he was absent three times without good reason, he was dismissed from the school. The privilege of getting an excellent education free of expense was so highly valued, that the pupils dared not stay away.

Whereas, when weekly fees had to be paid, parents were apt to keep their children back from school for a whole week when circumstances prevented or threatened to prevent their attendance on one or more days of the week."

1838
—

CHAPTER VII

JOURNALISTIC WORK.

Mr. McLaren was a voluminous writer. Few professional men of letters, even among the busy scribes connected with the daily newspapers, have produced more copy for the printers, and this prolificness is all the more remarkable because of the nature of Mr. McLaren's writings. They dealt largely with facts and figures. They were the records of original research and of skilful and accurate tabulations, representing the work of the historical student and accomplished statistician in combination with the journalist's ready adaptation of ascertained or accepted results to the illustration of present duty. It was not the desire of literary fame that inspired his pen, though in his later years the discovery of the survival and continued appreciation of some letter or pamphlet, the existence of which he had temporarily forgotten, would afford him genuine satisfaction. He did not despise literary excellence, but he sought to attain it for its immediate and direct practical advantages to him as a public teacher and counsellor. Nor was it as a professional *littérateur* that he laboured incessantly at his desk. His literary work he regarded as only a part, a fractional but necessary and important part, of the public service he rendered at the call of duty and of patriotism. His elaborate municipal reports, some of them on questions that seem now-a-days comparatively trivial, but which he, as a guardian of civic interests, felt could not be ignored or be-littled, would, if compiled and republished, form a small library. His literary work in connection with the Central Board of Dissenters, apart from its great value in inspiring and consolidating the Dissenting party in Scotland as a political power, was enormous in bulk. His pamphlets on the Annuity-Tax question, Heriot Trust and Fettes administrations, and the Corn-Law agitation, would of themselves constitute several large-sized volumes. His letters to newspapers on current controversial questions, alike in the social, municipal, ecclesiastical, and political spheres, sometimes extending to two or three columns in length, are legion. Where he felt he had any call to speak, or any information to communicate which he thought would be of public advantage, or would aid the cause of truth and justice in the thousand and one causes in which he was interested at different periods of his long and active life, he never concealed his opinions or withheld his contribution. The popularity and disfavour of the view or cause that claimed his aid never entered into his calculations. He knew well that truth and justice were not unfrequently with minorities, and he did not fear to act on the principle of his favourite quotation, that—

> " He is brave who dares to be
> In the right with two or three."

And it was not unfrequently as the champion of unpopular causes, but often also as the defender of principles and reforms he had helped to embody in legislative enactment, that he appeared as a writer in the correspondence columns of the *Times*, the *Morning Star*, the *Manchester Examiner*, and in the Edinburgh and Glasgow papers.

One of his contributions to the *Morning Star* was a graphic sketch of the dinner given to Lord Brougham in

Edinburgh in October 1859, in recognition of his eminent services as a statesman. In Mr. McLaren's opinion, it was a mistake that this demonstration was made non-political —an arrangement which, while it secured the presence of not a few prominent Scottish Tories, deprived his Lordship's Liberal friends of the opportunity of grateful reference to his political services, and hampered the freedom of the orator himself. Compared with former tributes of a similar kind given to the same statesman in 1824, when he was still a member of the House of Commons, and in 1834, in company with members of the Grey Cabinet, when he was still Lord Chancellor, the 1859 banquet was, in Mr. McLaren's judgment, a failure; for the " gathering had no soul; " " the animating principle for a successful meeting was wanting."

" Lord Brougham," he continued, " has undoubtedly been a distinguished character in all the departments which the speakers severally described, but he was a great man chiefly as a political character—as the man who fought, although then unsuccessfully, the battle of the people against the Lowther interest, when they had few friends, assisted by those whom he described as ' the honest grey-coats of Westmoreland.' He was great as the champion of the people when he wrested the representation of the largest county in England from the hands of a grasping aristocracy; he was great as the successful defender of the constitution, which was shamelessly sought to be trampled under foot in the person of Queen Caroline; and he was, if possible, still greater as the successful champion of the rights of the people in compelling, by the force of his withering eloquence, a reluctant House of Lords to pass the charter of our modern liberties—the Reform Bill. He fought the battle of the Reform Bill day after day during two sessions, not only on the great principles of the measure, but on all the details of the clauses, of which he had made himself master. Referring afterwards to this fearful struggle, to the numbers and influence arrayed against him, and the spirit by which his opponents were animated, the noble Lord compared the contest to a struggle for seven months 'in a den of thieves.' Probably the Duke of Argyll, when bespattering his order with so much praise, forgot these passages of arms between the nobility of descent and one of Nature's nobility. But to return from this digression ; all these really great services of Lord Brougham were ignored, except one which was most handsomely referred to by a political opponent, Professor Aytoun, who, with singular felicity of language and good taste, noticed Brougham's superhuman efforts in defence of Queen Caroline. The effect of this mal-arrangement was to destroy all enthusiasm in the meeting—to make it ' flat, stale, and unprofitable.' It was performing the play of 'Hamlet' with the part of Hamlet left out. It was such a scene as might have been witnessed had a dinner been given to the Duke of Wellington at which all reference to his battles was by agreement omitted, and his praises sounded as a distinguished literary character, the proof being the composition of his admirable despatches."

Mr. McLaren was disappointed with the company as well as with the speaking.

"There was," he said, "only one man on that platform who ever moved a hand in this city to assist Lord Brougham in fighting the battles of the people. That exception was Mr. Adam Black, now Member for the city, and his speech, not very well heard in many parts of the hall, was the only one which appeared to breathe the same spirit of freedom which was so often and so effectively heard in Edinburgh during the period of the Reform agitation, and for some years thereafter."

Frequently Mr. McLaren's communications appeared in the form of editorials, and in his early public life in no journal more often than in the *Scotsman.* During the editorship of Mr. Charles Maclaren (an intimate friend, but not a relative), he was a constant contributor. The *Scotsman* was at that time in sympathy with Mr. McLaren's public work, and cordially supported it. Between the editor and the contributor a warm friendship arose. They had many mental and moral characteristics as well as public interests in common. Both were men of finely balanced minds, both were purists as regards public service, and both laboured whole-heartedly and devotedly to ensure the success of the popular representative systems of municipal and parliamentary government which had recently been inaugurated. In conducting his municipal work, Mr. MᶜLaren found it advantageous to make use of the columns of the *Scotsman*, and he was heartily and repeatedly invited by the editor to do so. But he did not by any means confine his communications to strictly municipal topics. He discussed the public questions of the day in the leading columns of the Liberal journal, and it was probably in large measure due to his influence and work that the *Scotsman* became for the time the trusted champion of the Voluntary party, and the opponent of the aggressive policy of the Established Church. Such was Mr. Charles Maclaren's sympathy with the views of his literary associate, that he was in the habit of passing his manuscript to the printer without the usual editorial revision. Grateful as well as appreciative, he sent many a complimentary epistle to his correspondent. Such of Mr. Charles Maclaren's notes as survive are for the most part undated. Here are a few illustrations:—

My DEAR SIR,—I went to Glasgow on Wednesday with Mrs. M., and on my return to-day found your note awaiting me. You might have taken for granted that I would never think of refusing you any space you may require for the purpose you have in view, or for any purpose which may lead you to communicate your sentiments to the public through a newspaper.— I am, my dear sir, yours faithfully,　　　　CHAS. MACLAREN.

Friday, 2 o'clock.

And again—

"Your communications are always most welcome.   I shall be happy to receive the letter you propose."

"Your article in yesterday's paper is excellent.   It shows up the pretended Liberal admirably, and has the force of demon·stration.

"Will Mrs. McLaren and you favour me with your company to tea and supper next Wednesday evening at seven?"

"I get so many good things from you, that I seldom think of thanking you for them singly, but I cannot pass over your article of Saturday in silence.   It has your best qualities as a writer—exact method, scrupulous accuracy, perfect disinterestedness, and practical ability.   It does credit to the paper, and will do much good.   There are very few persons in Edinburgh who could have written it."

Of course the articles referred to cannot now be identified, nor can even their subjects be named.   Subjoined is one dated letter showing more substantial appreciation of service :—

SCOTSMAN OFFICE, 17*th October* 1836.

Mr. Ritchie and I request your acceptance of a set of the *Edinburgh Review* from the commencement, as a slight acknowledgment of the obligations you have laid us under by your valuable communications to the *Scotsman.*

The book was selected as one likely to suit your taste and your habits of reading.   I know no single work which contains so large a mass of matter calculated to prove interesting and useful to a reflecting man, and the two ample indexes render the whole of its contents as accessible as those of an encyclopædia.

With best wishes for your health and happiness, in which Mr. Ritchie joins me, I am, my dear sir, yours most faithfully.

The book will be delivered at your house some time this evening.

Duncan M'Laren, Esq.

1833

This token of appreciation afforded Mr. McLaren much gratification, and the work continued without interruption, and with apparent mutual satisfaction, for fifteen months longer. One morning Mr. McLaren was surprised by the following communication :—

Scotsman Office, *January* 25, 1838.

Payment offered.

My dear Sir,—Mr. Ritchie and I request your acceptance of the enclosed for your valuable communications to the *Scotsman* last year.

Our rule is to pay all who contribute articles to the paper at the rate of £1 per column. I do not speak of letters or communications intended to serve the interest of private parties, but of articles on subjects of general interest, such as the editor himself would write if he had leisure and information. Your articles are all of this description. By their invariable accuracy, the judicious manner in which they are cast, and the interest of the matter they contain, they are calculated to benefit the paper, and are such as we are willing and glad to pay for. . . .

We pay —— for every line he writes. We paid —— formerly in the same way, and no reason exists why you should not accept a very moderate remuneration for the labour which puts money in our pockets. Had your articles been connected with some event or business which was to lose its interest in a few months, we would have presented you with a piece of plate or something similar, but it is our wish and hope that they may be continued for years, and we are therefore anxious to place them on a business footing. The sum enclosed is by no means adequate to the value of your communications to us; and I trust therefore you will have no hesitation in accepting it, along with the cordial thanks of Mr. Ritchie and myself.—I am, my dear sir, very truly yours,　　　　　　　　　　　　　　Chas. Maclaren.

£50.

Notwithstanding the friendly tone of this letter, Mr. McLaren interpreted it as an intimation that the proprietor and editor desired his relations as a perfectly free and

DUNCAN McLAREN

From a Portrait painted by Colvin Smith, R.S.A., in 1838.

independent contributor to cease. Hitherto he had written and worked in the interests of the public, and not as a professional journalist; hence he felt himself precluded from accepting literary remuneration. His first impulse was to return the cheque, and to express his willingness to continue his assistance on the old footing ; but further reflection suggested to him, perhaps causelessly, that differences of opinion —a desire to recover for the editor the supervision of the communicated " editorials," which he had practically surrendered—might have been the cause of alteration of the relationship intimated to him ; and recognising the right of the editor to claim entire responsibility and unfettered freedom in the management of his own journal, Mr. McLaren made up his mind to sever the connection, which, so long as it caused no embarrassment to Mr. Charles Maclaren, had afforded himself unqualified enjoyment. He accepted the cheque and the accompanying letter as a termination of the old arrangement, and as he did not wish to write for money, he shortly afterwards resolved to offer no more editorial communications. It may be interesting to note that this cheque was applied towards the payment of the portrait of himself by Colvin Smith, R.S.A., a photograph of which appears in this volume.

The letter intimating the resolution to decline any relation to the literary staff of the *Scotsman*, other than that of a voluntary and honorary contributor, caused Mr. Charles Maclaren "a good deal of pain." But he found himself unable to continue to accept unpaid service, evidently regarding such an arrangement as not only placing an undue strain upon private friendship, but also as inconsistent with his ideas of independent journalism. Accordingly, he asked Mr. McLaren to think over the subject once more, remarking in his closing sentence, " I would consider it no small misfortune to lose your counsel and assistance, and a still greater one to lose your friendship."

Mr. McLaren's resolution was not changed by this appeal, but this did not interfere with the relations of private friendship between him and the editor, which subsisted for many years unbroken. For a time, at least, Mr. Charles Maclaren followed the public career of his old literary colleague with the keenest interest and sympathy. When the Treasurer was preparing to leave Edinburgh on his mission to London as the Council's plenipotentiary for the settlement of the city affairs, Mr. Charles Maclaren gave evidence of his interest in this ecclesiastico-political work by volunteering the subjoined note of introduction to the editor of the *Morning Chronicle* in London :—

Scotsman Office, Edinburgh,
26th April 1838.

My dear Sir,—My friend, Mr. Duncan McLaren, Treasurer to the city of Edinburgh, is now in London on the town's business. He will deliver this note to you personally or leave it with his address.

My object in introducing him to you is this: Doctors McLeod, Chalmers, & Co., who are now in London, have been publishing special pleadings and garbled statements in the *Times* on the subject of our Kirk. Now, the articles on these subjects in the *Scotsman* have, with few exceptions, been written by my friend the Treasurer. The long one you copied ten days ago was his. The shorter one, copied into the *Chronicle* of Saturday 21st, was his also. Previous and elaborate articles on Funds and on the Scottish School Bill were his too, with most of those on the pretended *religious destitution* of Edinburgh and Glasgow, on our Annuity or Stipend Tax here, and similar subjects. There is no man living who has so complete a hold of the *facts* on these matters, and he is equally unrivalled in the minute accuracy with which he treats whatever topic he touches. If, therefore, he should see occasion to attack or reply to any article in the *Times*, he will send it to you, and you may rely on its correctness with the most entire confidence.

All his articles in the *Scotsman* go in as editorials, but on this point you will, of course, do as you think best. I may add that my friend is a man of sterling principle, and has one of the clearest and soundest heads I ever met with.—I am, my dear sir, very truly yours, CHAS. MACLAREN.

Estrangement from the *Scotsman*, however, increased. Mutual friends, especially Mr. George Combe and Lord Dunfermline, strove to stop the growing breach, and each of the principals evidently put a willing restraint upon himself to prevent misunderstanding. A letter from the editor, in reply to a mild remonstrance on the subject of some journalistic animadversion which Mr. McLaren had considered scarcely called for, illustrates this mutual reluctance to separate :—

"Your note (wrote Mr. Charles Maclaren) was most considerate and also most generous, but it was not necessary. I know your firmness of purpose, and thought that it took a wrong direction on Thursday ; but I know also your fearless adherence to the dictates of your conscience, and, like all men of well-poised minds, who make the approbation of the internal monitor their sheet-anchor, you are little disturbed by censures delivered in good faith, as mine would have been had I written any. But when I find it necessary to point out an error on the part of a friend, I never impeach his motives, thinking it sufficient to give my reasons for holding him to have committed an error of judgment. I would have done this to any friend, but I feel it to be doubly due to you, whose unswerving rectitude of purpose I know so thoroughly."

And still adhering to the old trustful relationship, he added :—

"I send you three small publications of mine, which fell into

1838

Growing estrangement.

my hands yesterday in rearranging my papers, a task which has loaded me with labour for a week past."

But in spite of private feeling, differences of opinion on public questions continued to emerge. Mr. McLaren's Liberalism broadened and ripened with his growing experience and with the development of the political power of the people. It welcomed the liberation of the Evangelical party from state control, and appreciated the impulse to reform, operating first on social questions, which the Free Church brought with it into the civic and national life. It received stimulus from contact with the robust and aggressive Liberalism that originated and sustained the Anti-Corn-Law agitation. "My impression is," wrote Mr. McLaren in a letter to the sons of Adam Black (referred to in another chapter), "that your father did not materially advance towards Radicalism during this period." Nor did the party in Edinburgh with which Mr. Black was associated. This party became more concerned for the unattainable idea of the "unity of the Liberal party" than for the immediate advancement of the principles of free trade and religious equality. Mr. McLaren cared very little for the cry of "Liberal unity," which he regarded as meaning nothing more than keeping Liberal statesmen in office by sacrifices of principle. He was intensely interested in the assertion of Voluntary principles, in the promotion of Temperance legislation, and in the propagation of the doctrine of Free Trade,—certainly much more so than the party known as the "Parliament House Whigs;" and in gradually separating himself from them, he also fell out of sympathy with the conductors of the *Scotsman*, as did a large and influential section of the Liberal party.

In 1847 he was asked to assist in the establishment of a new Edinburgh paper, the *Scottish Press*, with a view "to enable Scottish Dissenters to carry forward to the best advantage their various plans for promoting justice, liberty, religion, and happiness, both within and beyond their pale." The *Scotsman*, which had been originally regarded by Dissenters as a fair and friendly organ, was considered by them to have lately changed its attitude and tone towards the Nonconformist Churches. Former friends and supporters connected with these Churches became dissatisfied. Hence the movement for the *Scottish Press*. Mr. McLaren, as a prominent Dissenter, enjoying in a high degree the confidence of the party, was, of course, cognisant of the proposal on foot, but anxious to regain his old friend, or at all events unwilling to go into opposition without notice or warning, he addressed a letter to the proprietor of the *Scotsman*. He frankly told him that it was proposed to start a new paper, to be published twice a week, in order to represent especially the Dissenters, who had been much annoyed by the attitude of the *Scotsman* on the Sunday question and on other matters. He said he was anxious to prevent any misconception as to his own share in the matter, and explained that he had taken no part in organising the paper, but had given a subscription towards the expense of starting it, and his aim was, by a friendly warning, to induce the *Scotsman* to modify its policy, so that it might not be necessary to have a rival in the field who might possibly damage it. He concluded the letter by the following interesting statement of his own views:—

"To prevent any misconception as to what I mean by the conduct of the *Scotsman* on the Sunday question, I may state that my own opinions as to what *ought to be done* are the same as those of the *Scotsman*—that the trains should run twice on Sunday, and each man who uses them be responsible only to his Maker for his conduct; and I believe three-fourths of all the people of Edinburgh and Glasgow, if polled, would give the same deliverance.   But supposing there are 1100 ministers of the Established Church, 650 of the Free, and 1000 of all other denominations, or 2750 in all, I do not believe 250 hold my own opinions, and I believe 2500 hold my opinions to be wrong, and diametrically opposed to the Word of God.   Now, the *Scotsman*, in *tone and spirit*, holds all these ministers to be fools, and fanatics, and bigots, and people not to be reasoned with, and assumes that only a mere handful of people hold their views.   My opinion is that a very considerable proportion of what are called 'religious people' hold these views, and think *us* wrong."

This letter, though kindly meant, did not produce the conciliatory effect desired.   The probability is that its influence was the reverse of conciliatory.   Its author, among the many qualities valuable and useful in public life which he undoubtedly possessed, sometimes showed himself deficient in that undefinable something which we call "tact." To the end of his life he never could understand that a plain reference to facts, unaccompanied by the usual conventional phrases, might give offence.   He could not see that the possessor of an "agricultural implement" should object to having it called a "spade."   In this case it is probable that his well-intentioned warnings, suggested by the old regard both for Mr. Charles Maclaren and Mr. Ritchie, provoked resentment.   At all events, this was the view he himself was afterwards compelled to take; for the tendency towards alienation increased on both sides. Charles Maclaren was joined (in the year 1845), and afterwards was succeeded, in the editorship by Alexander Russel. With Mr. Russel, while editor of the *Fife Herald*, Mr. McLaren had had amicable correspondence with reference to the Anti-Corn-Law question.   But the relationship had never been intimate, and Mr. Russel, in criticising the public conduct and policy of the founder and leader of the

Independent Liberal party in Edinburgh, was unrestrained by the friendly feelings and high opinion entertained by Mr. Charles Maclaren for his old contributor.   Mr. McLaren also drifted farther away from the *Scotsman.*   He actively aided first the *Scottish Press,* and at a later period the *Caledonian Mercury,* and therefore occupied to a certain extent a position of journalistic rivalry.   Political differences called this rivalry into full play, while they steadily widened both the personal and the public breach.   In the election of 1847, Mr. McLaren was an influential promoter of the opposition which ousted Macaulay (whom the *Scotsman* as resolutely supported), and which placed Charles Cowan at the head of the poll.   Five years afterwards, in 1852, when Mr. McLaren was a parliamentary candidate, and when Mr. Cowan and Mr. Macaulay were also in the field, the *Scotsman* taunted Mr. McLaren with the break-up of the coalition.   The hostile criticism continued after Mr. McLaren's defeat and Mr. Macaulay's success.   Matters came to a crisis at the election of 1856, when Adam Black was nominated by the Whigs, and Francis Brown Douglas by the Independent Liberals, to the vacant seat caused by Macaulay's elevation to the peerage.   The *Scotsman* became so reckless and abusive in its attacks, that Mr. McLaren deemed it necessary to apply to the Court of Session for redress.   Mr. Inglis, then Dean of the Faculty of Advocates, now Lord Justice-General, was Mr. McLaren's senior counsel in the libel trial which followed, and in a very able and temperate address to the jury he thus explained the object of the action :—

"It is perhaps very much to be regretted that, in this country, and indeed almost everywhere, there is no means of estimating such an injury except by the vulgar medium of pounds, shillings, and pence; but I tell you at once I do not come here with any greedy demand for money. That is not the object of this action. By no means. The only object Mr. McLaren has in view is to vindicate his character and set himself right in the eyes, not merely of the citizens of Edinburgh, but of that far more extended class to whose eyes these articles have come, and by whom they have been read, and who have no opportunity of understanding what is the malignant spirit that dictated these articles, and who are therefore almost bound, in justice to the newspaper, to draw the inference that there must be some good foundation for this, and set himself right in the eyes of his fellow-citizens here and his fellow-countrymen elsewhere. It is for that purpose alone that this action has been instituted."

The counsel for the defenders were Mr. Moncreiff, afterwards Lord Justice-Clerk, and Mr. Logan. The chief grounds of defence were that the case was one neither of private slander nor of calumnious ridicule, but of justifiable criticism; that Mr. McLaren was himself in the habit of using strong language in speaking of opponents; that "liberty of speech and writing in this free country were involved," and that the object of the action was not to vindicate character, but "to gratify vindictiveness" and "to vent want of success in spleen."

The judge and the jury, however, took a different view. Lord Justice-Clerk Hope's summing up was distinctly in favour of Mr. McLaren, and the jury awarded damages to the amount of £400. This money Mr. McLaren handed over to the Heriot Trust to provide good-conduct prizes for the children attending the Heriot outdoor schools. The prize was to be awarded by the votes of the scholars in each class.

The trial, which lasted two days, and which, as has been seen, engaged the foremost talent of the Scottish bar, excited, not only in Edinburgh, but throughout Scotland, a keen amount of interest. Both parties had warm sympathisers; but while the press generally took the side of the libelling journal, it was significant that Mr. McLaren's popularity in Edinburgh was greatly increased.[1]

An additional motive to that stated by Mr. Inglis prompted Mr. McLaren to bring this action. He knew that many good men were deterred from serving the public by the dread of journalistic criticism; though in his own conduct he showed that no criticism, however unsparing and unjust, could drive him from the path of duty. In the midst of many arduous labours, carried on frequently under the fiercest attacks of his watchful and relentless opponent, he was sustained by the confidence and esteem of his fellow-citizens and his fellow-countrymen, who with ever-increasing admiration and veneration followed him as an able and trusted leader. "Thrice is he armed who hath his quarrel just;" and secure in this triple armour, Mr. McLaren calmly held on his way as a leader and defender of the people. It is pleasant to be able to add that, many years after the libel case, and just after the election of 1874, in which the *Scotsman* had heartily supported Mr. McLaren, and powerfully aided in securing for him the sweeping majority by which he was returned, Mr. McLaren, seeing Mr. Russel in the lobby of the House of Commons, stepped forward and offered his hand. The genial editor heartily responded, and a

1856

Friendly meeting with Mr. Russel.

---

[1] "It is notorious that at this present moment Mr. McLaren is tenfold more popular and respected than ever he was before. Ever, in fact, since the date of his prosecution of the *Scotsman* for libel, his popularity has been steadily on the increase. We do not tender our bare assertion in proof of this. The reception accorded to Mr. McLaren at all meetings, but particularly at *public* meetings where he appears, proves it. On these occasions his reception is more than warm—it is enthusiastic. This is a notorious fact, familiar to every one."—*Daily Express*, December 27, 1856.

pleasant though short conversation ensued. Afterwards Mr. Russel expressed to mutual friends the great gratification which this meeting at Westminster afforded him. It was an interesting episode, bringing to an end the warfare of more than a quarter of a century,—illustrative of the truth that nobility of soul can be best tested when there is anything to forgive and forget.

Versatility as a writer.

As a newspaper contributor and correspondent, Mr. McLaren wrote on a great variety of subjects. Trade and commerce, banking and railway administration, were favourite questions, and his treatment of them always evinced careful preparatory investigation as well as fertility of suggestion. On all matters affecting municipal administration and local and national taxation, and the rights and wrongs of Scotland in relation thereto as compared with England and Ireland, he was an acknowledged authority; and his papers, whether published as letters to editors or as pamphlets, never failed to stir inquiry and debate.

Perhaps the most noteworthy of his impromptu journalistic contributions was an elaborate statistical paper, published in 1861, entitled, " Expenditure of United States compared with United Kingdom." His first series of tables brought out these comparative general conclusions :—

The United Kingdom and the United States.

" In Britain we have an annual expenditure of £69,619,266 for thirty millions of people, and on the other side of the Atlantic an expenditure of only £19,853,960 for thirty-two millions and a half of the same race ! But even this comparison," he continued, " does not do full justice to our American cousins. To make the comparison perfectly fair, we ought to deduct the American expenditure for payment of Members of Parliament, seeing that we pay nothing—at least nothing directly as an acknowledged matter of business—under that head. We must likewise deduct the expenditure for Post Office purposes above

the revenues received, as we have no similar expenditure in
the United Kingdom, in consequence of our small, densely-
peopled territory. Above all, we are bound to deduct the difference betwixt the expenditure for 'Common Schools' in the
United States and our 'Educational Grants'—the former being
£4,446,814, and the latter only £982,575, making a difference
of £3,464,239 in favour of America. When these three sums,
amounting to £5,044,430, are deducted, the fair comparison will
be as follows :—

1884

UNITED STATES.	UNITED KINGDOM.
Population, . . . 32,600,000.	Population, . . . 30,000,000.
Comparative expenditure, . . } £14,809,530.	Comparative expenditure, . . } £66,619,266."

The chief object of this investigation was to aid the cause
of national education at home, by showing the pre-eminence
accorded in the States to education as a Government business or department, and by describing the operation of the
" common schools" system, which not only made education
universal throughout the States, but welded into one vast
and loyal English-speaking community populations drawn
from all the nationalities of Europe.

Mr. McLaren retained to the close of his life the journalistic
instinct, seizing on current controversies or passing movements as texts for the illustration and enforcement of his
political faith. During the leisure of holiday seasons more
especially, he not unfrequently surprised his friends by the
publication of an occasional letter dealing with some question with which, so far as they were aware, he had never
closely occupied his mind. One of the latest of these fugitive
pieces was written during the autumn of 1884, when he was
residing at Strathpeffer, and its subject was the depreciation
of land as the consequence of the great decline in the value
of farm produce.

1884

He was a close and conscientious student of the contemporary history of his country for upwards of fifty years, whilst old historical documents, especially ancient municipal records, possessed for him a charm as great as many readers find in the modern novel. The knowledge thus gained he often brought to bear on the social and political controversies of his own day, and it contributed not a little to his sound judgment and sagacity in political matters. If, at the close of a life-long career of political activity, he found himself generally in accord with the views and aspirations of his fellow-countrymen, it may truly be said that differences were more often resolved by the majority of his party coming over to his views, than by the surrender of his own convictions for the sake of an ephemeral popularity.

CHAPTER VIII.

THE VOLUNTARY CONTROVERSY.

Why is Scotland Liberal? Cobden's famous dictum, endorsed lately by Mr. Gladstone, " The soul of Liberalism
is Dissent," supplies an answer. The influence of Dissent
was undoubtedly the most powerful motive in placing Scotland in the vanguard of British Liberalism, and, more than
any single man, Mr. McLaren organised Scottish Dissent as
a political force.

If any one doubts either of these assertions, let him study
the history of Scotland for the second quarter of this century.
The Dissenters of that period were necessarily men of great
force of character and strict conscientiousness, accepting in
the fullest sense the Protestant principle of personal responsibility to God in all the duties of life, and more especially
in relation to Church ordinances. If they had not been
men of this stamp they would not have remained Dissenters, because all material advantages, personal comfort, and
social position pointed to an easy-going religious conformity.
But regard for purity and freedom of worship brought their
fathers out of the Establishment. Taught in the same
religious school which recognised Melville's doctrines of the
two kings and two kingdoms in Scotland, they faithfully
maintained the testimony of their fathers in the face of
worldly allurements. Exposed to political and spiritual

injustice, inasmuch as they were required to support a
Church whose ministrations they could not accept, they
were taught an application of Melville's principle of far-
reaching influence and priceless value.   Claiming for themselves the freedom of worship or " spiritual independence,"
they were bound to acknowledge the right of others to
that which they themselves required ; in other words,
to demand the exclusion of the State from the sphere of
Church patronage, with all its attendant duties in relation
to pecuniary support, and all its attendant responsibilities
in the shape of civil control.   Wrong-bearing is often a
valuable schoolmaster.   Most gifted men cradled into poetry
by wrong have learnt in suffering what they have taught
in song ; and the Scotsmen most exacting in their sense
of religious duty were taught by the spiritual and political
injustice to which they were subjected in giving effect to
their most sacred convictions to demand universal toleration for all creeds and fair play for all Churches.   That
demand of a fair field and no favour, applied in the political
domain, is the foundation of Liberalism ; and as the Presbyterian order of Church government created a tendency to
political democracy, so Presbyterian Dissent, making the
additional claim of universal toleration as the only abiding
security for itself, communicated fresh activity and strength
to Liberalism, guiding and directing it in later years to
resist and defeat the " levelling-up " method of meeting the
irresistible claim of religious equality ; making the endowment of Roman Catholicism at Maynooth and the continuance of the *regium donum* in Protestant Ulster equally
impossible ; enforcing a policy of complete disestablishment in Ireland, and gradually winning for a free church
in a free state recognition as an essential plank of the
Liberal programme.   It is to Mr. McLaren's share, in

combination with the Scottish Dissenters, in promoting this
development of Liberal policy, that attention is now to be
directed.

As has formerly been noted, Mr. McLaren's entrance
into public life was contemporaneous with the new development in self-government which dated from the Enfranchise-
ment Act of 1832. Simultaneously with, if not even in
advance of, his efforts to direct the power conferred upon
the £10 householders to the promotion of municipal reform,
were his attempts to organise the voting power of the
Dissenting communities in the interests of ecclesiastical
reform. For he was an ardent Dissenter, and his close
personal contact with the prominent ministers of the
Secession Church in Edinburgh in his early manhood—
men of the mental calibre and self-sacrificing zeal of Dr.
John Brown, Dr. Ritchie, Mr. Kirkwood, Mr. French, Mr.
McGilchrist, and especially his own minister Dr. James
Peddie—conjoined with extensive reading in early life, had
prepared him for the forthcoming Voluntary controversy.
His persistent counsel to his fellow-Dissenters was:—" Make
use of the franchise ; show in politics the same independence
of judgment and action you have displayed at all hazards
in Church affairs, and organise for united effort." Such
advice, harmonising with their convictions and views of
duty, was almost universally acted on. The result was that
in nearly every Scottish constituency the Dissenters, recognising politics as the present duty of the " Church militant,"
at once stepped to the front as leaders of the people towards
the realisation of their democratic aspirations.

Dissenters at this time were a minority of the population, in many districts despised by the aristocracy, in others
persecuted ; but what they lacked in numbers and social
influence, they made up in activity and independence, in

earnestness of purpose and definiteness of aim. Thus they came to be "the backbone of Liberalism" and a dominating factor in Scottish politics. Hitherto the tendency of Dissent had been towards further division; the tendency was now changed to reunion. State or civil authority in the Presbyterian Church had been the original cause of disruption, and the one common effort, begun in the sphere of political action, brought the scattered fragments of Presbyterian Dissent together, manfully supported by Independents and Baptists. This now united Dissenting party Mr. McLaren by pen and speech greatly helped to rally, and in an early stage of its two-sided conflict with Established Church aggression and Tory obstructiveness, he became its most prominent lay representative.

The Voluntary Church Association, of which the venerable Dr. James Peddie was president, with his eldest son, Mr. James Peddie, W.S., and the Rev. Dr. John Brown as secretaries, and Mr. James Duncan, W.S., as treasurer, gave place in 1834 to the Scottish Central Board of Dissenters, of which Mr. McLaren was made chairman, with Mr. James Peddie as secretary, and Mr. Archibald Smith as treasurer. This Central Board originated in a meeting held in Rose Street Church, under the presidency of Mr. McLaren, at which it was resolved that the grievances of Dissenters could only be redressed by "an immediate, total, and eternal separation of Church and State." It speedily became the head of a federation of Voluntary or Dissenting societies, and the members of the executive found that their offices were no sinecures. The Board placed itself in direct antagonism to the church extension scheme, then promoted with unexampled vigour by the Evangelical party in the Established Church, under the leadership of Dr. Chalmers. The principle on which that church extension scheme rested was that accommodation and religious instruction in connection with the Establishment should be provided by the State for the whole population, as a national duty, irrespective of the means of religious instruction existing outside the pale of the National Church. The demand obviously implied the formation of a league between Church and State for the obliteration of Dissent, and the institution of an all-embracing State Church uniformity. By this time the Presbyterian Dissenters, in harmony with their Baptist and Independent allies, while sympathising with the Evangelical opinions of Dr. Chalmers's party, in contradistinction to the principles of Moderatism, had fully and firmly accepted the Voluntary principle, as affording the best security for Evangelical teaching on the one hand, and popular rights on the other. They did not feel themselves called on to acquiesce tamely in a measure designed to strengthen Church Establishments, much less to submit to denominational extinction. Very ably and resolutely did the Central Board vindicate their rights. They met pamphlet with pamphlet, petition with counter-petition, statistical claims with masterly analysis and exposure ; and while the clerical members were actively engaged lecturing and publishing, masses of statistical work and of correspondence were done by Mr. McLaren, assisted mainly by Dr. Peddie's sons, whose filial devotion maintained their father's authority and influence as a pillar and ornament of Dissent long after the decay of his physical powers would have unfitted him for active leadership. In their first report the Central Board thus described their work :—

" As soon as it was understood that a general plan had been formed for getting up petitions to Parliament in support of this measure (the Church Extension Scheme, including the applications for endowments for chapels of ease), founded on very erroneous statistics, circulated by the Assembly's Committee, and when the subject was alluded to in Her Majesty's speech as a measure for the consideration of Parliament, the Board, by correspondence with the proper quarters, procured as accurate accounts as possible of the existing accommodation, both in Established and Dissenting churches, in all the different places alleged to be deficient in that respect. They then drew up and printed a Statement containing the results of their returns, in which they think it was satisfactorily shown that the measure was both unnecessary and unjust. Copies of the Statement were sent to most of the Dissenting ministers in Scotland, accompanied with a circular urging on them the necessity of counter-petitions against the grant being sent from every district; and in order to diffuse correct information on the subject as widely as possible, the Statement itself was sold at rather less than cost price. The Board also transmitted a copy of it to every Member of the House of Commons, from a very considerable number of whom prompt and decided intimations of their resolution to oppose the grant were received. The Statement, the Board have reason to think, has been productive of much benefit in opening the eyes of many to the injustice and sectarian character of the scheme, and of arousing such opposition to it as to render it extremely improbable that any Ministry that consults the opinions of the people will give it their support."

The State Church's claim.

The Statement contained a calculation showing that compliance with the Church's claim would involve a cost to the imperial exchequer of £7,000,000; and the principles on which it rested its opposition to the claim and its refutation of the Assembly's " erroneous statistics " were these :—
" That as Dissenters are included in the population, their church accommodation should also be included; that accommodation for 100 out of every 216 of the population is sufficient for the whole, as proved by Dr. Chalmers's investigations; that it is unfair to single out one parish of a populous town or district without regard to the surplus accommodation in the immediate neighbourhood; and that

the Voluntary system, under which the chapels of ease arose
and have prospered, is sufficient for their future support.
Mr. MᶜLaren further, as a member of the committee that
prepared the analysis of the denominational statistics for
the whole country, gave evidence before the Religious Instruction Commission, and the report of his evidence occu-
pies a third part of what they thought needful to publish
in their first report. The Dissenters, thus brought into
line over the whole country, thus unified as a political force,
in spite of the absence of quick and certain communication
(for these were the days of mail-coaches and dear postage),
and thus fortified by arguments and statistics, succeeded in
controlling the political situation against the Evangelical
party, powerful as it was in numbers, influence, and talent,
until the final conflict with the State which resulted in the
disruption of the National Church. It was because of the
part he took as the champion of the Dissenters in their
stubborn resistance of the claims of the Church Extension
party, and of their efforts to nationalise the Establishment
on the principle of absolute independence of the State, that
Mr. MᶜLaren was in after years described by Mr. Hugh
Miller as the " author of the Disruption."

Brave men engaged in a successful battle do not always
see the progress they are making, and a fear that they are
losing rather than gaining ground sometimes stimulates to
increased energy. With a powerful and energetic combination arrayed against him, and with statesmen in office so
friendly to the Established Church that they were willing
to grant Dr. Chalmers and his friends almost anything
short of complete spiritual independence, it is not wonderful
that Mr. MᶜLaren occasionally felt the influence of such an
apprehension. And it was well for the cause of the Dissenters that their courage and resolution were thus tried.

In 1841 the Scottish Dissenters had abundant cause for concern. The Ministers of the Crown, in constituting the Bible Board, proposed that Church membership should be a condition of office, thus in a manner affirming that a Dissenter was not fit to be intrusted with the revision of the text of the Bible—a proceeding which Mr. McLaren denounced as practically tantamount to a re-enactment, so far as the Bible Board was concerned, of the Test and Corporation Acts. Further, a clause was inserted in the Prisons Act by which no Dissenter was eligible to the office of prison chaplain, and under the operation of this retrograde legislation a chaplain in Edinburgh actually lost his situation. Again, an Act was passed establishing forty Highland schools, whose teachers were to be maintained, not by the heritors, but out of the public funds. In order to put these schools completely under the control of the Established Church, Government consented to the imposition on the schoolmasters appointed under the Act, of the Confession of Faith in the form in which it was subscribed by Established Churchmen, and without the modifications under which it could be subscribed by Protestant Dissenters. More recently Government gave the Church a controlling power in the appointment of the inspectors of schools. Speaking at a public meeting of Dissenters held to consider and protest against these encroachments, Mr. McLaren said, " My friend Mr. Gillon, at my request, moved for a copy of the correspondence between the Privy Council and the Committee of the Assembly. It has been printed by order of the House, and has come to Edinburgh only within the last four or five days, and a more truckling document to the Church, a more discreditable correspondence on the part of Ministers prostituting the powers of the Privy Council and Crown, and laying them at the feet of the General

Assembly, I never read." These and similar illustrations of the submissiveness of the Government to the demands of the Church on minor points, irrespective of the claims and rights of Dissenters, convinced the advocates of civil and religious equality that more than statements, and petitions, and public demonstrations were required at their hands. They brought them to the conclusion that a special representative of their views was needed in Parliament, and the meeting of Dissenters held in Edinburgh in 1841, elsewhere referred to, on the motion of Mr. M°Laren, adopted the following resolution :—" That the Dissenters of Edinburgh, . . . viewing with alarm the recent encroachments on their civil rights, many of which might have been prevented if their opinions had been properly represented in Parliament, and forming, as they do, a large portion of the Liberal constituency, consider themselves justified in requiring that one of the city Members, in addition to being well qualified in other respects, should possess that intimate knowledge of their principles and tried attachment to their cause which will secure their entire confidence, and entitle them to expect that he will constantly exert himself to prevent the occurrence of similar aggressions." The speech in which he supported this resolution was a masterly and effective exposition of the irritating wrongs to which the Dissenting communities were being subjected, through the agency of a Government eager, by minor concessions, to entrap the Church into some compromise of her essential and fundamental claims. He took pains, however, to make it evident that something more than sectarian service was necessary. He wished, indeed, a Member " who shall watch over and defend our rights—who will always be on the alert when any aggression is attempted—who will be prepared, for example, to go to Lord John Russell in such a case as the

1841

Parliamentary representation needed.

1841   Bible Board, and prove to him that he was about to impose on the Dissenters of Scotland the shackles which he removed from the Dissenters of England in 1829, and from which their Scottish brethren had been relieved since 1689." But at the same time he wished a Member who would be otherwise well qualified for parliamentary duties, and who would be a thorough all-round Liberal. "I for one," he concluded, "would never agree to put forward a man for whom I could not hold up my face and say that, in addition to being well qualified to defend our rights, he was trust-worthy in other respects; that he was a true friend of the people, and one who would not consent to legislate or carry on the Government of the country for the benefit of any one sect or party." The ideal Member thus sketched the Dissenters of Edinburgh never obtained until Mr. McLaren himself was returned in 1865. But at the time at which this sketch was drawn, a seat in Parliament was, in fact, unattainable by the ordinary citizen.[1]

Mr. McLaren named.   The Rev. Mr. McGilchrist, who spoke after Mr. McLaren, did indeed point to the proposer of the motion as the coming man, as "an individual who would be alike acceptable to Churchmen and Dissenters, who had no other object in view than the real interests of this metropolis—the great ends of good government, the enactment and administration of impartial laws, the extended commerce and growing prosperity of the Empire." But Mr. McLaren at once interposed and declined nomination, saying "he certainly could not but feel flattered by what had fallen from Mr. McGilchrist, and by the manner in which his name had been received by the meeting,

---

[1] According to our ancient constitution, Parliament was supposed to consist of commissioners of shires and "burgesses."

but he trusted that no person present would believe for
a moment that if he had known that, in any sense or
shape, he would have been proposed as a candidate, he
would have been there to take any part in the proceedings."

CHAPTER IX.

THE ANNUITY-TAX.

1833 FOR the information of readers whose personal acquaintance with Edinburgh politics is of recent date, it may be necessary to state what the Annuity-Tax was. It was, in brief, a personal tax of six per cent. levied on the occupiers of houses and warehouses to provide salaries for the city clergy. The tax was of some antiquity, having been first imposed in the time of King Charles I. It was regarded by most Dissenters in the present century as a badge of servitude to a Church to which they owed no allegiance, and by not a few its payment was felt to be inconsistent with their religious professions as dissenters from the principle of an Established Church depending on the State for patronage and support. The tax, besides being objectionable in principle, was rendered odious by the numerous exemptions which the law recognised. Incredible as it may appear, these exemptions included the entire legal profession, from judges to solicitors and advocates' clerks. The exemption was, in fact, claimed, with cynical indifference to public opinion, by a body who were more or less concerned in the enforcement of the statutory obligation against other classes of the community.

To understand the origin of the Annuity-Tax agitation, it is necessary to go back to the year 1834, the time when the philosophic and large-hearted Chalmers sought to engage the sympathies of the Christian world in a veritable new crusade—a scheme of Church Extension, whose primary aim was the "excavation of the heathen" at home, amongst whom Dr. Chalmers doubtless included a due proportion of the "scribes and lawyers," and "indifferent" upper classes, as well as that substratum of the "poor" which the existing Church organisation had failed to reach.

As an opponent of the then aggressive policy of the Established Church, Mr. McLaren, while admiring Dr. Chalmers as a Churchman in the large sense, felt constrained to offer opposition to his Church Extension scheme, and notably to the proposal to erect a city parish church in or near the Cowgate, in furtherance of his benevolent "excavation" or social reclamation designs.   Dr. Chalmers's proposal in its main aspect supplies a most suggestive illustration of what in those days even the best and most public-spirited of Established Church laymen considered liberality.   Thirty of these laymen, under the liberalising influence of the Doctor's teaching, agreed to subscribe £100 each for the erection of a church capable of holding 1000 sitters, and to meet the expected wants of a new parish to be restricted to 2500 souls, on this remarkable condition, that they should at no time receive from the Town Council (who were invited to take over the new church and parish) "more than four per cent. for the outlay of their money" until the advance should be repaid, and that they (the subscribers) should also retain the patronage and management in their own hands for ten years.   It is needless to say that this Cowgate Church scheme was not fitted to withstand the scathing criticism passed on it by the Dissenters.   Mr. McLaren pointed out that four per cent. was fair interest on the contributions, and that even apart from the rights of patronage and management reserved, these "lenders to the Lord" were, if not literally making the temple a house of merchandise, seeking

1834

The Church question in the Council.

Dr. Chalmers and the Cowgate.

to utilise it as a safe and profitable investment. He further pointed out that the concession of Dr. Chalmers's claim that a parish should not consist of more than 2500 souls, implied that fifty-four city parishes should be created in Edinburgh, with fifty-four city ministers, each receiving a salary of £600.

In a letter written from " Chapter Coffee-House," London, dated April 18, 1835, in reply to some reflections by Dr. Welsh on the magistrates for refusing another proposal, that Dr. Chalmers and his friends should offer to pay the rent of one of the city churches for a couple of years, and offer the seats to the poor, Mr. McLaren remarked :—

"The Joint Stock Church Building Company proposed by Dr. Chalmers was to keep up the fabric of the churches and pay all other incidental expenses out of the seat-rents, besides paying four per cent. to the stock-holders out of the remainder, if the sum realised were sufficient for the purpose; which would certainly have been the case *with any one church* let so much cheaper than all the others. Now, if Dr. Chalmers and his friends will offer to the Town Council the rent of £120 for each of their Old Town churches, taking all the other expenses on themselves, as proposed by the Joint Stock Company, and paying at the same time a reasonable feu-duty for the ground on which the churches are erected, as they must have done with the Cowgate church, I have not the least doubt that the Town Council will most readily agree to the proposal, *as these churches have never yielded nearly £120 each, free of all expenses.*"

But neither was this counter-offer accepted, although the old city churches cost from two to three times more than the outlay proposed to be expended on the Cowgate church.

The incident referred to may be regarded as the starting-point of the Annuity-Tax agitation, which terminated in

the abolition of the hateful impost, after a struggle extending over a period of nearly forty years.

Mr. McLaren was connected with the movement from
its beginning. As early as 1836, when a highly respected
citizen, Thomas Russell (afterwards a Magistrate of Edinburgh), was confined in the Debtors' Prison because of his
refusal, on conscientious grounds, to pay the Annuity-Tax,
Mr. McLaren placed himself in the front of the movement
by the publication of a pamphlet entitled " History of the
Resistance to the Annuity-Tax under each of the four
Church Establishments for which it has been levied, with
a Statement of its Annual Produce since 1690." [1] This pamphlet, extending to ninety-eight closely printed pages, and
embracing the results of painstaking original investigations
in historical byways hitherto almost untrodden, rapidly
obtained a large circulation. It became a Dissenter's text-
book, and indeed a standard of reference for disputants on
the question.[2]

In various other ways, through the arrangement regarding seat-rents, but more especially the Annuity-Tax, the
Council, as guardians of the public interests, were constantly
brought into conflict with the city ministers, the represen-

---

[1] Edinburgh : Adam & Charles Black.

[2] Among numerous letters expressing high appreciation of his services
was the following from the Rev. Dr. John Brown (father of John Brown,
M.D., and Professor Crum Brown) :—

16th July 1836.

MY DEAR SIR,—Many thanks for the present of your " History of the
Resistance to the Annuity-Tax." I had procured it immediately on its
publication, and have read it with great satisfaction. It must have cost
you a great deal of labour, but I trust it will not be lost labour. I hope
the legality of the exaction will soon become a subject of investigation
before the Court of Session. With kind regards to Mrs. McLaren, I am,
my dear sir, yours faithfully, JOHN BROWN.

tatives of privilege and monopoly. At the same meeting of Council at which Dr. Chalmers's Cowgate Church scheme was submitted, a committee reported that during 1833, 846 persons had been prosecuted for the non-payment of the Annuity-Tax; that the several sums of assessment prosecuted for amounted to £4707, 4s. 3d., that the several sums of expenses on 1st January 1834 amounted to £1127, 3s. 1d.; that the sums recovered were: of assessment, £1658, 15s. 1d.; of expenses, £70, 14s. 3¾d., leaving still unrecovered of assessment, £3048, 9s. 2d.; of expenses, £1051, 8s. 9¼d.,— total unrecovered, £4099, 17s. 11¼d. The committee recommended "That something should shortly be accomplished whereby the Annuity-Tax might be done away with, and the clergy provided for in some other way."

At a subsequent meeting, Mr. McLaren seconded a resolution proposed by Mr. Adam Black, then Treasurer, to the effect, "That the Town Council consider the Annuity-Tax, and all other compulsory assessments for support of the city clergy, unjust in principle, adverse to the interests of true religion, and oppressive to the inhabitants, and are therefore willing to concur in any lawful measures by which the support of the clergy may be placed upon a proper footing, without infringing the rights of present incumbents." This resolution was lost by twenty-two votes to nine.

The chief object of the pamphlet was to prove that from the date of its first imposition the tax was regarded as an injustice, and that the people of Edinburgh consistently maintained their protest against it. The Act of the Privy Council establishing the tax in 1634, in the face of the opposition of magistrates and people, represented that it was founded on the principle that all "who hear the Word and participate in the benefits of the Church ought to pay for the

same;" while it was notorious that the original object of
the tax was to provide for the sustenance of the Episcopal
clergy, whom the people would not hear.   Mr. McLaren very
effectively exposed this inconsistency as deceit, and likewise called special attention to the shameless selfishness, if
not the immorality, of the judges of the Court of Session
in 1687, in passing a judgment exempting themselves, and
all the members of the Faculty of Advocates, and all writers
—the wealthier professional classes—from liability for this
ecclesiastical tax.   But the chief point on which he founded
was the "smuggled clause" in the Act of 1809, by which
the clergy furtively obtained an enlargement of the assessment to provide for the salaries of eighteen instead of six
ministers—in other words, tripled the pecuniary liability
of the citizens for the support of the State clergy.   "Every
one knows (wrote Mr. McLaren) that when any local Act
is to be applied for, it is necessary, in compliance with the
standing orders of the House of Commons, for parties who
intend to introduce the bill to publish notices in the newspapers and on the church-doors, distinctly specifying all
the objects to be embraced in the bill, and that any clause
beyond the notices which finds its way into a bill is considered a fraud upon Parliament, and is instantly expunged
on the discovery being made, if the bill is not at once
thrown out."   The notice of the Act of 1809 simply intimated a desire for the extension of the royalty of the
city over certain grounds.   It was manifestly incompetent
under this notice, Mr. McLaren proceeded, " to introduce
any clause making a change in the property of the tax,
or any claim increasing the sum formerly authorised to be
raised, or any claim authorising it from being limited to the
payment of the stipends of six ministers to be applied in
payment of the stipends of all the seventeen existing

ministers, together with such additional number as might
be added for the two new churches authorised by the Act to
be built ; all these matters being clearly beyond the notice.
Yet a clause framed by the ministers which effected all
these changes was at their urgent entreaty smuggled into
the Act without the knowledge of the ratepayers. The
ministers obtained the consent of the Town Council to the
introduction of the clause in consequence of a threat that
they would oppose the bill unless their request was complied with. That all these changes followed from the inser-
tion of the clause was afterwards distinctly proved by the
opposite decisions of the Court in the cases of Edinburgh
and Montrose under circumstances precisely similar, with
the exception of the one party having the advantage of the
smuggled clause, and the other having no such auxiliary."
Mr. McLaren's historical studies confirmed his own and the
ratepayers' antipathy to the tax. " The history is a history
of frauds," exclaimed one newspaper critic of the tract ; and
the opposition to the collection continued to increase in
intensity and to extend in area. Poindings, sales of furniture and goods, and arrestments and other modes of legal
oppression, continued to be used for the enforcement of payment from an unwilling community. Eventually the friends
of that religion claimed a settlement of the question on the
lines laid down in Mr. Black's rejected resolution as a necessity for civic peace, and in the interests of the Established
Church itself, as well as on the grounds of justice.

The Disruption of 1843, which caused a pause in the
Disestablishment agitation so vigorously carried on by the
Voluntaries, likewise brought a temporary abatement of
the agitation on the Annuity-Tax grievance in Edinburgh.
People had to find their bearings politically and ecclesias-
tically under the new conditions created by the startling

ecclesiastical revolution. But it quickly became evident that, so far as the Annuity-Tax was concerned, no lengthened pause in the demand for reform could be possible. "It was tolerably certain," one writer remarked, "that two-thirds of the individuals for whose benefit the tax is in future to be levied will preach to almost empty pews." The Free Church exodus was in Edinburgh almost complete, and several of the city churches were almost entirely denuded of congregations. The injustice and indefensibility of the tax were thus made increasingly palpable ; and, in obedience to a very general demand for some attempt at legislative settlement, Sir George Grey, then Home Secretary, sent Mr. J. G. Shaw-Lefevre to make a thorough investigation of the whole question in Edinburgh. Mr. Lefevre, an able and impartial official, arrived in Edinburgh in October 1848 ; and in April 1849 he presented to the Government of the day an exhaustive and masterly report, in which he stated that he had refrained from holding a public inquiry, because he "was aware that the evils of the existing state of things were patent and notorious," and because he feared a public inquiry would interfere with an amicable adjustment. His leading recommendation was that in lieu of the Annuity-Tax a commutation grant should be settled by Parliament on the ministers of the ancient and extended royalties of Edinburgh of £8800, whereof £6250 should be permanent, and £2550 temporary, and subject to gradual diminution. Among various other suggestions were these :—that the College of Justice should be invited to waive their exemption ; that the stipends of the then ministers should be £600 per annum, but that the stipends of their successors should be fixed at £550, and that the number of the ministers should be reduced gradually from eighteen to fifteen. The practical advantages of this arrangement were thus described : " When the commutation annuity is finally reduced to £6250, an important pecuniary relief will have been afforded, for £6250, with the expenses of collection, would be 3½ per cent. upon the present valuation of property for the Annuity-Tax, and little more than 3 per cent. when the privileges of the College of Justice cease. The burden will thus be 3 per cent. instead of the present liability to 6 per cent." He admitted, however, that his scheme would not meet the objections " felt by many which are directed against an endowed Church, or to the support by general or local taxes of an Established National Church." Two years later the opponents of the tax obtained the appointment of a Select Committee of the House of Commons. To this Committee the Town Council held forth that the last-mentioned ground of objection was fatal to a peaceable settlement, " because by all the plans which met with any large share of public attention, the tax, although intended to be lessened in amount, and to be levied in a less direct form as an ecclesiastical impost, would in effect be continued."

A fatal objection.

Mr. McLaren, who continued to be identified with the opposition to the Annuity-Tax, went to London to be examined before the Select Committee of 1851, and during his absence he was re-elected a member of the Town Council, as a popular manifestation of the confidence with which he was regarded by his fellow-citizens. While, therefore, he did not in 1851 appear before the House of Commons Committee as the plenipotentiary of the Council, as he did when negotiating the settlement of the city's affairs in 1838, he nevertheless held a position of scarcely less authority as the spontaneously chosen representative of the ratepayers. Naturally he was examined at great length, as the man best informed on the whole question, and possessed of great influ-

Evidence before Parliamentary Committee.

ence with the citizens. But the interest of his examination centred in the revelation he made regarding what has already been described as the " smuggled clause " of the Act of 1809. He showed that if that clause had not been put into operation, and if the magistrates had levied no more than they had formerly levied, viz., a sufficiency for the stipends of six ministers instead of eighteen, the Annuity-Tax would have been reduced from six to two per cent., as in the case of Montrose. He re-told the story narrated in his " History of the Resistance to the Annuity-Tax," and maintained his contention in the face of prolonged cross-examination. At length the chairman, the Right Hon. Henry Tufnel, interposed and said, " I understand you to be of opinion that if Section 17 had not been introduced into the Act of 1809, the only law in Edinburgh on this subject would have been that of 1661, which limited the number of ministers to be paid out of the Annuity-Tax to six." Mr. McLaren at once replied, " Yes ; and I am glad you have put the question. If this Committee would just pass an Act repealing Section 17 of the Act of 1809, the inhabitants of Edinburgh would never trouble you again ; they would not ask for a grant from Government for anybody else. The repeal of Section 17 of the Act we feel satisfied will put us in the same position as we were in before the Act of 1809 passed, and you will never hear a complaint from the inhabitants of Edinburgh again."

But Mr. McLaren did not really expect so summary a mode of settlement. He was willing, as a compromise, to agree to nine ministers instead of six, but beyond this he would not move. Sir William Gibson-Craig pressed him to make a further concession. " Supposing," Sir William asked, " the Committee felt that that was a measure which it was impossible to propose to Parliament, what other arrangement do you conceive would be proper?" But Mr. MᶜLaren replied, "None occurs to me except that which I have stated. If the Committee think they cannot carry a reduction through Parliament of less than thirteen, I think they ought to find the ways and means of providing the additional funds from the bishops' teinds, which we think we have a claim to."

This introduction of the disposal of the bishops' teinds into the controversy gave rise to a very smart passage at arms between his friend Mr. J. B. Smith, one of the members of the Committee, and the witness. Mr. MᶜLaren had carefully studied the bishops' teinds question in its relation to Edinburgh; he had both written and spoken much on the subject; he had satisfied himself that the teinds were an Edinburgh endowment, and he had brought himself to the conclusion that while justice required the restoration of these teinds, their application to the ministers' fund in relief of the ratepayers might facilitate an amicable settlement of the complicated and perplexing Annuity-Tax question. But the doctrine shocked the less-informed but sensitive mind of a Voluntary purist like Mr. John Benjamin Smith.

" *Mr. J. B. Smith.*—You, as a Voluntary, object to the grant to Maynooth and to the *regium donum ;* how then can you sanction a grant of public money to the Established Church in Edinburgh?—I have already said that I do not think this can be considered a grant to Edinburgh.

" It goes out of the public purse?—But it got into the public purse when it ought not to have got there.

" Supposing a grant were made to the Established Church of Scotland, would it not be necessary to raise an amount of taxation equal to that?—It would, unless you reduce the expenditure of the Commissioners of Woods and Forests. I see that they dispose of 12s. in the pound of all they collect without accounting to Parliament for it.

"*Mr. J. B. Smith.*—You are opposed to the grant to Maynooth
in Ireland, and to all grants for religious purposes in England,
and yet you are in favour of a grant to the Church of Scotland;
do you think that compounding of your principles is likely to
secure the respect or the confidence of Parliament in those who
profess the Voluntary principle?—I do not admit that I am compounding my principles. I have stated that I see no ground for
considering it in that light. Honourable Members of course
have a right to form their own opinion. If Honourable Members
think my views inconsistent, I am willing to bear their displea-
sure in whatever way it may be shown, but it does not affect my
conscience; I see no inconsistency in it.

"*Mr. J. B. Smith.*—Do you think the Voluntaries, generally
speaking, throughout Edinburgh, would be willing to support the
grant of public money in the way you suggest?—Yes; as I before
said, I do not call it grant of public money. I must adhere to my
own explanation of it.

"Do you think it a just principle to shift the burden from the
Voluntaries in Edinburgh to the Voluntaries in England?—No;
I deny that interpretation of it. Scotland provides £200,000
public money from the teinds for other parishes; it provides
nothing for Edinburgh. We should have as good a right to our
share of that £200,000, if it were to be allocated to-day, as any
other parish. We find that the Crown has in its hands a certain
portion of that which has not been appropriated, and we say
to the Crown, Do us the justice that you have done to other
parishes."

Mr. Smith pressed hard for the withdrawal of the concession of nine in place of six churches, and showed that
Mr. McLaren's own figures proved six to be sufficient. Mr.
McLaren replied that, as an arithmetical question, six would
be more than sufficient, as matters then stood; but he looked
to the future, and he agreed with the evidence given by a
preceding witness, that if the Annuity-Tax, which interfered with the usefulness of the ministers very materially,

were abolished, the Established Church would have a better chance of attracting adherents. He wished to put himself in the shoes of an Established Churchman, and looking at the question as dispassionately as he could, he thought the proposal to fix the number of ministers at nine fair and reasonable.

Mr. Smith, returning to the charge, asked—

"Do you think the clergy are likely to assent to any diminution of their number?—I do not. I never knew clergymen assent to anything of the kind, however reasonable, when it was proposed.

"You never, in your reading, knew of a Church reforming itself?—No; they have always said, 'Give, give;' that has been the constant course for the last two centuries.

"If you ask for such a change as is just and reasonable, do you think that you ought to have more than six churches to meet the present wants of the people attached to the Established Church? —I have already stated that, if you regard it as an arithmetical question as to the present wants of those who are attached to the Established Church, it is more than sufficient; but if you look at the arrangement of the Established Church as a large question, if I were a Churchman I should object to such an arrangement."

Sir William Gibson-Craig reminded the witness that he had not alluded to the exemption of the College of Justice as one of the grievances of the Annuity-Tax. "No," Mr. McLaren rejoined; "I cannot characterise that exemption in terms sufficiently strong to express my own opinion upon it; it is a nefarious exemption, because it was the College of Justice deciding for itself the question." He continued—

"Incidentally the exemption of the College of Justice is one of the greatest grievances, when you trace its operation; for it comes to this: in Edinburgh the aristocracy are the lawyers; they occupy the highest-rented houses, and they are exempted; they are the parties who chiefly remain in the Established

Church. The poor, and what we call the shopocracy, have
almost all left the Church. The effect therefore is, that the
Annuity-Tax is levied in Edinburgh on the poor for the support
of an Establishment for the rich. The poor man living in a £20
house, and paying £20 a year for the rent of his shop (take the
case of a grocer, or a shoemaker, or a spirit dealer), has to pay
Annuity-Tax on his house and his shop, and in fact on everything
that he has, in order that the rich gentlemen may receive the
benefit of religious instruction from the Established Church at
his expense. That is the operation of the tax in Edinburgh."

The report of the Select Committee fell very far short
of the minimum requirements stated by Mr. M\ :sup:`c`\ Laren. It
proposed the reduction of the number of stipendiary ministers from eighteen to fifteen, by the gradual discontinuance
of double charges in the High, the Tron, and St. Andrew's
Churches, and it accepted the rate of stipend proposed by
Mr. Lefevre. Its recommendation caused great disappointment. It increased the popular irritation against the tax,
and the popular determination to effect its abolition. The
result of the next municipal election was the return of a
decided majority of Town Councillors opposed to the tax,
and favourable to the appointment of Mr. M\ :sup:`c`\ Laren as Lord
Provost, with the view of hastening a settlement on conditions acceptable to the citizens. The scene of action was
now transferred from the constituency to Parliament. A
series of bills were introduced and successively failed :—
Lord Dalhousie's bill in 1851; Lord Advocate Inglis's bill
in 1852; Lord Advocate Moncrieff's bill in 1853, framed
after consultation with Lord Provost M\ :sup:`c`\ Laren and Mr.
Macaulay,[1] and supported by the Voluntary party, but suc-

----

[1] ALBANY, LONDON, *March* 17, 1853.

MY LORD,—The Annuity-Tax Bill has been drawn as we agreed that it
should be, and yesterday the Lord Advocate mentioned the subject to

1860

cessfully opposed by the Conservatives ; another bill by Lord
Advocate Moncreiff in 1857, and Mr. Black's bills in 1858
and 1859. The latter were supported by the Town Council,
and the bill of 1859 passed the second reading in the House
of Commons by a majority of fifty-four. These various measures failed to obtain the assent of both Houses of Parliament; and in 1860 Lord Advocate Moncreiff, who in the
preceding year had become one of the city Members, introduced a scheme of compromise, with the view of putting
an end to the civic strife and division of the Liberals of
Edinburgh.

The Lord Advocate's object was laudable. In the interests of all parties—the city of Edinburgh, the Established
Church, and the Dissenting community—a settlement was
urgently required. The grievances of the conscientious opponents of the tax were sufficiently real. They were not limited
to the seizure of goods, but included cases of imprisonment.
" Some of the best citizens of Edinburgh," proceeds a State-

Popular
hostility
to tax.

Lord Aberdeen. Lord Aberdeen seems disposed to do everything that we
could wish, always, however, under one reservation. He and the Chancellor of the Exchequer will not consent to lay any charge in any event on
the general revenues of the kingdom for the support of the ministers
of Edinburgh. The matter has not yet been mentioned in Cabinet,
and therefore we must not consider the Government as irrevocably bound,
though I hope there is little danger in that quarter. I should have
thought it desirable that the Lord Advocate should take charge of the
bill. I find, however, that he, and, if I understand him rightly, Lord
Aberdeen, would much rather that I should bring it in. I am perfectly
willing to do so, if, on a full consideration, that shall be thought the best
course. The difficulty about the standing orders remains as it was ; and
whether we shall be able to get over it seems to be very doubtful. I have
had the honour of receiving a letter from your Lordship on the subject of
probates and letters of administration. I need hardly say that I entirely
agree with the Town Council as to that matter.—I have the honour to be,
my Lord, your Lordship's faithful servant,   T. B. MACAULAY.

The Lord Provost, &c.

ment from the ratepayers, " clerical and lay, had suffered 1850
in the cause. In 1849 companies of infantry and cavalry
were called out to enable a sale of the goods of Dissenters
to be accomplished. Among others who suffered in 1850
was the late Mr. John Tod, an engraver. For refusing to
pay the tax he was sent to prison, where he remained eight
weeks. Such was the indignation felt at his treatment, that
a subscription was raised in pennies to pay his fine, and he
was, while in prison, elected a member of the Town Council.
On his release he was escorted in a carriage and four from
the prison to take his seat in the Council-chamber.

" In 1851 a petition was sent to Parliament, signed by
49,000 persons, asking for a complete abolition of the rate.
. . . In 1857, the clergy having obtained warrants against
a great number of citizens, proceeded to put them in force.
In the early part of August four were arrested, one of whom
was thrown down in his own house, manacles were attempted
to be put on his wrists, his clothes were torn, and he was
conveyed to jail at midnight, contrary to the rule of law which
forbids arrest for debt between sunset and sunrise. In the
beginning of September two citizens were lodged in jail, and
a third, on being conveyed from his shop in a cab with manacles on his hands, excited such feelings on the part of the
assembled crowd that the warrant could not be executed. A
criminal trial for deforcement ensued before the High Court
of Justiciary, but the jury found the accused not guilty."

It is not wonderful that in these circumstances Mr. Mon- Mr. Moncreiff, as the chief representative of the Government in creiff's
com-
Scotland, as well as one of the Members for the city, should promise
scheme.
have resumed his efforts to end the quarrel. Undoubtedly
he took great pains to ensure the success of his measure.
He negotiated with the Conservatives; he studied how best
to meet the objections of former Liberal opponents, who

were unwilling that Edinburgh should enjoy any special relief; and he was assiduous in his endeavours to secure the assent of the Council to his ideal compromise. But the bill he produced, after many communings, oral and verbal, proved extremely unsatisfactory to the citizens. Mr. McLaren condemned it as the worst measure that had yet been offered; and though Mr. Black acquiesced in it in the interests of peace, his own more drastic measures, and many of his suggestive declarations as to the essential principles of a settlement, were quoted against him as a supporter of the Lord Advocate's arrangement. One of the strong points of the bill was the abolition of the " unconstitutional exemption " of the members of the College of Justice. Unfortunately it proposed that the tax should be levied to the extent of one penny per pound beyond the bounds of the royalty, contrary to one of the clauses of a recent Municipal Extension Act. It assessed the value of the seat-rents at the paltry sum of £1600, the sum obtained when the fortunes of the Established Church were at their lowest; while Mr. McLaren, whose consent to the compromise was desired, had at a public meeting, in presence of Mr. Moncreiff, stated that he would wash his hands of any scheme that assessed the seat-rents at less than £2500 per annum. The bill transferred the administration of the churches and seat-rents from the Town Council to Ecclesiastical Commissioners; and fixing the minimum payment at £7800 (stipends of £600 each for thirteen ministers), minus the £2000 due by the Leith Dock Commission, and the £1600 supplied by seat-rents, it left £4200 to be provided by taxation to be levied in combination with the police rates. But, most objectionable of all (though this condition was strenuously insisted on by the Lord Advocate), it placed the whole city property under a mortgage in security of the clerical annuities to the amount of this £4200.

Mr. McLaren was not left alone in his opposition to the bill. The Town Council, the Merchant Company, the Chamber of Commerce, the inhabitants of the southern districts, the heritors of the West Kirk parish, the citizens through public meetings and petitions—one of which bore 15,000 signatures—joined in a protest. Mr. McLaren vigorously encouraged and supported the opposition by speeches in public as opportunity offered, but more especially by letters and articles in Edinburgh and London newspapers he strove to convince the Legislature, wearied of the prolonged strife and willing now to accept any measure, that the Lord Advocate's bill would only make matters worse. Nevertheless the bill passed the House of Commons, as observed at the time, " with the opposition of the smallest fraction of Scotch members, and with the almost unanimous support of the House of Commons," and became law.

The bill did not in reality settle the question. Mr. Moncreiff certified that the Annuity-Tax was as dead as a door-nail, and predicted that the Act of 1860 would never be repealed ; but the agitation was renewed with increased vigour. The tax received the nickname of " Clerico-Police Tax," because the assessment for the ministers was mixed up with the police rate, and the old difficulty as to collection was revived. The Rev. Dr. Peter Davidson, one of the most scholarly and peace-loving of the ministers of the United Presbyterian Church, at the request of his Dissenting brethren, addressed an open letter to the Lord Advocate, entitled "Conscience and the New Police Rate ;" and afterwards the Rev. Dr. George Johnston, whose goods were seized by the tax-collector, further enforced the protest in a series of letters. Various other Anti-Annuity-Tax manifestations occurred. In the Council an unsuccessful attempt was made to arrest the operation of the Act.   The Treasurer signed the bonds in favour of the Ecclesiastical Commissioners under protest, and a deputation of ratepayers presented a memorial describing the Act as unjust and as tending to disturb the peace of the city, and entreating the Council " to use all lawful and constitutional means to obtain the entire repeal of said Act."   Ex-Bailie Fyfe, Mr. McLaren's right-hand municipal ally, offered, and for a time effectively, opposition.   He

raised an action in the Court of Session challenging the legality of the whole assessment ; and the Lord Advocate, as the defender of the 1860 arrangement, responded by introducing and carrying again, in the face of the opposition of the Council, another bill " to declare the limits within which increased assessments are authorised to be raised under the provisions of the previous Act."   Mr. McLaren, who was in London when this bill was introduced, at once wrote to the Council, objecting to the measure as " unexampled in the legislation of the United Kingdom, its object being to legislate respecting an action now pending in a court of law ;" and the Council, on the motion

of Lord Provost Brown Douglas, petitioned Parliament against the supplementary bill on this ground, adding a declaration of opinion " that no amendment of the Annuity-Tax Act will be generally satisfactory which does not secure a more equitable arrangement for the ratepayers than that made under the Act of last session."   The declaratory Act, however, passed, and under it a decision was given against

Mr. Fyfe.   This result was certainly discouraging to the Dissenters of Edinburgh and to the Advanced Liberal party. A number of their leaders retired from the Town Council, and on the expiry of Lord Provost Brown Douglas's term of office, the combined Whig and Tory forces obtained a majority in the municipal parliament in favour of the finality of Mr. Moncreiff's Act. But the reaction was nearer than was imagined.

The chief factor in convincing the citizens that the Lord Advocate's "final settlement" could not stand was the unflinching opposition of a large section of the ratepayers, including several ministers of religion, to the payment of the new police tax, on which the stipends were chargeable. They were confronted with the terror of the law, but remained unappalled. They were sneered at as martyrs by mistake, and as sham heroes, seeking fame at little cost; but they answered scorn with scorn. The social war steadily increased, alike in extent and intensity. The Act of 1860, which was heralded by its author as the certain cure for the civic ailment, introduced into the community not peace but a sword; and at times it seemed as though the whole municipal administration would be brought to a dead-lock. For ten years previous to the passing of the Lord Advocate's measure, no sales of furniture had been necessary to enforce the recovery of arrears of the police taxes, but after 1860 sales at the Town Cross became alarmingly frequent. The arrears of police rate increased from £9515 to £19,924; and in one year no fewer than 3475 summary warrants were put into the hands of sheriff-officers for collection.

"So strong was the feeling of hostility, that the Town Council were unable to procure the services of an auctioneer to sell the effects of those who conscientiously objected to pay the clerical portion of the police taxes, and they were consequently forced to make a special arrangement with a sheriff's officer, by which, to induce him to undertake the disagreeable task, they provided him for two years with an auctioneer's license from the police funds. In March 1865 it was found necessary to enter into another arrangement with the officer, by which the Council had to pay him $12\frac{1}{2}$ per cent. on all arrears, including the police,

1865

prison, and registration rates, as well as the clerical tax; and he receives this percentage whether the sums are recovered by himself or paid direct to the police collector, and that over and above all the expenses he recovers from the recusants. But this is not all. The Council were unable to hire a cart or vehicle from any of the citizens, and it was found necessary to purchase a lorry, and to provide all the necessary apparatus and assistance for enforcing payment of the arrears. All this machinery, which owes its existence entirely to the Clerico-Police Act, involves a wasteful expenditure of city funds, induces a chronic state of irritation in the minds of the citizens, and is felt to be a gross violation of the principles of civil and religious liberty." [1]

Thus the efforts of the Lord Advocate as an exorcist completely failed. His attempt to allay the evil spirit of the Annuity-Tax unfortunately increased its mischievousness, and his conspicuous want of success weakened his political position. The Dissenters, on the other hand, quickly recovered from their despondency. Convinced of the necessity of trustworthy parliamentary assistance in carrying their struggle to a successful issue, they rallied round Mr. McLaren, and in 1865 placed him in the honourable position of senior elected Member for Edinburgh. During that contest Mr. McLaren warned them of the difficulty, if not the impossibility, of a private Member overturning, after so short an interval as five years, an Act carried by the Government of the day, and he declined to give any pledge as to new legislation. His view of the difficulty in the way of repeal was increased when he found that Lord Advocate Moncreiff was his colleague in the representation of the city.

Mr. McLaren, however, resolved to make the best of his case, as opportunity offered. Experienced in parliamentary

Independent Liberalism.

<hr>

[1] Statement of facts handed to Select Committee of 1866 by Mr. McLaren.

tactics, though a new Member of the House, he first looked about for an advantageous starting-point, some special *locus standi* which might explain his demand for the repeal of a Government Act five years after its introduction. He sought first to find this advantage in the practical admission of the Lord Advocate that his Act was a failure, and in a conditional promise he made on the hustings after the election to assist Mr. McLaren if he attempted an amendment. Referring to the Annuity-Tax Mr. Moncreiff had said, " Mr. McLaren first introduced me to that subject in 1853. I have now done my best with it, and I now return it to him from whom it came. If he thinks he can, with the consent of the community and of Parliament, do anything better than what I have done, he may depend upon it that, as far as my assistance and co-operation go in anything that is just and equitable, they shall not be found wanting. If he can satisfy the community, and satisfy those who have interests concerned in the question, I shall be very glad indeed to give him any assistance I can." In a speech delivered eleven days afterwards at a large meeting held in the Music Hall in celebration of his return, Mr. McLaren declared that for himself, a new Member of Parliament, at once to propose the repeal of an Act passed with the authority of Her Majesty's Government, would be held to be a piece of impertinence. He was a practical man, fully alive to what was practicable and proper and the reverse ; and therefore he declined the Lord Advocate's offer, unless it meant that Mr. Moncreiff would consent to the reintroduction of what was generally called Mr. Black's bill, but in the preparation of which Mr. McLaren himself had a large share. If, however, the Lord Advocate himself would attempt the needed reform, he promised to undertake any amount of labour with the accounts, and otherwise to assist and facili-

1865

tate his efforts. He stipulated for one condition, viz., the separation of ecclesiastical imposts from the police tax. "Of all the multitude of bills," he said, "that ever were introduced to settle the Annuity-Tax question, there were none that connected it with the police tax except the Lord Advocate's, and he connected it by his own sovereign will and pleasure, not only without the consent of the Town Council, but against their most urgent remonstrances."

Nothing, however, came of this negotiation, and the next attempt to secure united action, in conformity with the wishes of the general body of the electors, and more especially the Liberal party in the city, when an influential deputation from the Anti-Annuity-Tax Association waited on the Lord Advocate and Mr. McLaren in the official chambers in Parliament Square, was equally unsuccessful. Mr. Moncreiff even declined to promise to support the appointment of a Commission of Inquiry as to the operation of the tax recommended by Mr. McLaren; and sturdy, single-hearted George Laing plainly told the Lord Advocate in parting with him that there could be no compromise with principle. On the religious side of the question, he said, the objectors to the Act recognised a higher authority than man, and they would not obey the laws of man when they were in conflict with that higher authority.

An appeal from electors.

Nevertheless progress was made. The inquiry which Mr. Moncreiff discouraged was ordered. Accompanied by his old friend Mr. Murray Dunlop, Mr. McLaren and a deputation from the city went to Sir George Grey, then Secretary of State, who, after hearing their case, at once issued the Commission. Mr. McLaren and Mr. Moncreiff were appointed members, and Mr. Bouverie, the Member for the Kilmarnock Burghs, was chosen chairman. Both parties were fully heard,

Parliamentary inquiry.

and Mr. McLaren and Mr. Moncreiff submitted their respective versions of the state of affairs to the committee. The testimony offered by the citizens concurred by prearrangement on these four points:—" (1.) That the greatest dissatisfaction exists with the Lord Advocate's Act of 1860. (2.) That it is essential to the peace and prosperity of the city that the Annuity-Tax should be finally and for ever abolished, always saving existing life-interests. (3.) That looking to the state of several of the city churches, and the undue proportion that the number of ministers bears to the population compared with other burghs, the number of clergymen should be reduced to ten. (4.) That while the citizens are willing to provide for the life-interests of the existing incumbents, they agree in addition that the Established Church should receive the £2000 annuity from Leith, the whole of the seat-rents, valued at £4000, and the church-door collections —a sum which would give £600 yearly to ten ministers, and admit of the church-door collections being applied to the upholding of the fabrics and the supplementing of the ministers." But the evidence on which Mr. McLaren most relied for the time being was that bearing on the unsatisfactory operation of the Act of 1860. He wished to provide justification for amending legislation which Parliament could not dispute, and as he considered the evidence reported to the House amply supplied that necessary justification, he was well satisfied with the result. Accordingly, though still conscious of the weakness of his position, arising from the presence of Mr. Moncreiff as his parliamentary colleague, he, early in the session of 1867, introduced his bill. The second reading was moved on February 21, 1867, and its chief opponent was Mr. Moncreiff. " While my colleague," said Mr. McLaren afterwards in speaking to his constituents, " was absent during the rest of the session,

1866

Mr. McLaren's Bills.

1867

the only thing he did in the way of the promised assistance was to go expressly to London for the purpose of speaking and voting against the bill which I had been induced to prepare and introduce." The second reading was lost by 107 votes against 74. But Mr. McLaren was far from discouraged. His bill had obtained the approval of the Town Council, of a public meeting of the citizens, of a majority of the Select Committee of Inquiry, of several members of the late Liberal Government, and of " many of the most distinguished men in the House." It was defeated by the Tories and Conservative Whigs; and as he confidently expected that the coming election would considerably weaken this obstructive coalition, he regarded the rejection of his measure as only a temporary check. Indeed, the first-fruits of victory were reaped even before the election. In his speech on the second reading he made out a case as regards the Canongate so strong that even the Tory Government could not deny redress; and on the death of one of the two ministers of the Canongate, Lord Advocate Gordon introduced and carried a measure for one of the objects of Mr. McLaren's bill—the reduction of the burden of the Annuity-Tax in Canongate by the cost of one minister. But the Member for Edinburgh gave notice at the time to all concerned, that while " an aiding party to the reduction of a burden, he could not be held precluded from getting the other half of the burden removed as soon as he possibly could." As an earnest of this determination, he reintroduced his bill in the session of 1868, though he did not look for success, and in a thin House it was rejected by 86 votes against 59.

Second reading carried.

In 1869 the conditions Mr. McLaren had desired as essential to success—the presence of a colleague from Edinburgh supporting his views and a working Liberal majority in the

House of Commons—were provided, and the second reading
of his bill was carried by 151 votes against 142. The Liberal
Government over which Mr. Gladstone presided felt that, in
a House of Commons based on household suffrage, opposition
to the repeal of the Act of 1860 could not be continued;
and Lord Advocate Moncreiff (who now sat for Glasgow and
Aberdeen Universities) changed his attitude so far as to
say that the compromise he had made in 1860 could not be
held binding on a new Parliament; and that though he
himself had not been prepared to disturb that settlement,
and had in consequence withdrawn from the representation
of Edinburgh, he would not oppose the second reading of
the bill. In a letter written shortly after the division Mr.
McLaren describes the extraordinary efforts made by the
Tories, who got " one of their most important leaders " (Mr.
Hardy) to oppose the bill most vehemently; the fidelity of
the Government and of many Liberal members, headed by
Mr. Gladstone, who made themselves late for the Lord Mayor's
dinner rather than let the measure be defeated by their
absence from the division; that but for the dinner the bill
would probably have obtained thirty additional votes; and
that of the Scotch members twenty-five Liberals had voted
for the second reading, while only five Liberals and seven
Tories had voted against it.

But the end, though even in sight, was not yet reached.
Negotiations ensued, in which the late Lord Advocate, who
by this time was Lord Justice-Clerk, Sir Graham Montgomery, the city clergy, Lord Provost Law, all figured
along with Mr. McLaren, and a basis of arrangement was
framed, under which the city clergy were to receive an
immediate payment of £53,000, to be advanced by the
Government, and repaid in ten years by the Council. These
negotiations failed chiefly through want of support from

the city clergy. Accordingly, in the subsequent session of 1870, Mr. McLaren reverted to his own bill and plan, proposing, in place of the £4200 raised by taxation along with the police rate, to give the whole pew-rents, now amounting to £4300 a year, but which previous to the Disruption yielded upwards of £7520, the Leith annuity of £2000, and £1200 a year for miscellaneous purposes from the collections, which, by Act of Parliament, were devoted to the support of the poor-rates. The financial bearing of his proposals he exhibited in these two tabular statements :—

First View.

Income.

From seat-rents	£4333
From Leith property belonging to City of Edinburgh, commuted into an annual payment	2000
Restricted amount under the bill . . .	2050
Additional annuity for nine ministers at £50 each	450
	£8853

Payments Preferably Secured.

Nine stipends at £600	£5400
Four stipends at £550	2200
To the minister of Canongate in part of his stipend	250
	£7850
Surplus available for other purposes . .	983
Of which required for church expenses (in addition to the £1200 from collections) .	600
General surplus not at present required for any purpose	383

SECOND VIEW, *when three of the Ministers now receiving £600 a year of Stipend have Died or demitted their Charges.*

Income.

Seat-rents	£4333
City property in Leith commuted . . .	2000
Restricted annuity (assuming that the Canon-gate minister is still living) . . .	250
Additional annuity for six ministers at £50 each	300
	£6883

Payments Preferably Secured.

Six stipends at £600	£3600
Four stipends at £550	2200
Minister of Canongate, in part of his stipend .	250
	£6050

Surplus available for other purposes . .	833
As the expenses connected with three churches will then be saved in £514 (three-thir-teenths of £1800), the deduction for church expenses (other than the £1200 from collections) will be only . . .	86
Leaving a general surplus not required for any purpose of	£747

Government intervention.

Mr. Young, the successor of Lord Advocate Moncreiff, now interposed, and secured an adjournment of the debate, in order to introduce a Government measure, framed on the lines of the arrangement sketched out in the previous written negotiations. Four days afterwards he presented his measure, which proved more favourable to the clergy than even the rejected basis of arrangement. It proposed to place in the hands of the Ecclesiastical Commissioners, in addition to the Leith £2000 as a substitute for the clerical tax, the produce of the pew-rents, the interest of a capital sum of £60,000 and the half of the church-door collections. This financial settlement was at once opposed both by the Council and a public meeting of the citizens, and a memorial was addressed to Mr. Gladstone by the Annuity-Tax Abolition Association, representing—"That the main provision of the bill, granting £60,000 as compensation for life-interests, is one strenuously resisted by the Town Council, and is much larger in amount than was approved of by the Home Secretary Mr. Bruce, the late Lord Advocate Moncreiff, and several members of Parliament, friends of the Church." Ultimately, after some excited meetings and a somewhat bitter controversy, in which Bailie Lewis distinguished himself by his eloquent championship of the claims of the Dissenters, and Lord Provost Law earnestly and prudently acted as mediator, the sum of £56,500 was substituted for £60,000, and general agreement was arrived at by all parties—the Government, the Council, the city clergy, and the citizens. Mr. McLaren met his friends in the saloon of the Royal Hotel on 28th April, and having reported the result, practically took leave of the question. He said :—

"Now that both the Council and the citizens have agreed to this arrangement, and it has been also approved of by the clergy, I feel as if a great load were removed from my shoulders for the future. Many of you know that I never made the non-payment of the tax a matter of conscience, as very many of my brethren have done. I believe that, as Dissenters, they acted more consistently in refusing than I did in paying. (Hear, hear.) But the fact remains that I have paid the tax for forty-six years without resistance, either legal or passive. I cannot therefore claim the merit of having made any great sacrifice in the cause. It has been well said that the blood of the martyrs is the seed of the Church, and it may with equal truth be said that the martyrs in this cause—those who suffered imprisonment and the spoiling of their goods—were the men who have settled this Annuity-Tax question—(applause)—and not any Lord Advocate, or Lord Provost, or Members of Parliament. Among those who suffered imprisonment, I may name my much-venerated friend, Bailie Thomas Russell, who has long since passed to his reward; and my no less excellent friend Bailie Stott, who still survives, but with seriously shattered health, brought on solely by his exertions to promote our cause. Those who suffered from arrestments, and poindings, and the sale of their goods at the Market Cross may be counted by hundreds; therefore I forbear to single out any of that band of martyrs by name. But you know them, and bear their labours in grateful remembrance. (Applause.) Many of you know that I have written pamphlets, and letters, and articles in newspapers, and made speeches, I do not know how many times, against this odious tax, and I believe there is no one in the city who feels more relief than I do at my labours in this department being ended, as I hope they soon will be. But the clauses of the bill are still to adjust between the Town Council and the Presbytery, and I hope no new ground of difference will arise out of this adjustment. . . . By the agreement now unanimously made the bill is to be imperative, the same as my bill of last session was. Even the single original idea in this bill of £60,000 has been changed to £56,500. I daresay you all remember a jocular remark by a distinguished nobleman in this neighbourhood, 'that the word "whereas" was the only part of Mr. Disraeli's Reform Bill which had not been changed.' I suspect, when this bill is licked into proper shape, every part of it will be in substance my bill of last year, except the sum mentioned, and that sum, as I have said, is not original."

In answer to an elector, Mr. McLaren explained the mode of operation agreed upon for the last ten years of the existence of the tax :—

"The tax will be continued for ten years, and during those ten years the whole amount of the assessment, the whole amount of the threepence, will be paid to pay off the sum of £56,500, which has now to be borrowed. The whole sum of threepence is not now required to pay the annuity of £4200 a year, so that during those ten years you will not only pay all you are now paying, but you will pay a little more, inasmuch as threepence now produces more than the £4200. The Act of 1860 requires that threepence to be laid on as part of the police assessment, and not to be distinct in the police assessment; and in the future the police collector just hands over the £4200 to the Magistrates or to the Church. Supposing £5000 is collected, £800 remains in the hands of the collector of police, and it goes for police purposes. In place of remaining in his hands, it will go to the creditor who lends the £56,500. I believe, from a close calculation, that the tax will expire in about nine years; but although that may be the case, nobody would lend money upon a closely fitting calculation. There must be a clause declaring that the tax shall be leviable until the sum borrowed is paid off. Without such a clause no sensible man would ever lend you a shilling. As I have said, I believe the tax will be paid off in less than ten years; and by my bill of last year it would also have been paid off in less than ten years. (Applause.)"

The real hero.

Thus ended the battle of the Annuity-Tax. Lord Advocate Young was nominally the author of the Abolition Act, but the real champion of the struggle was Mr. McLaren, and in popular estimation nearly all the prestige accruing from the successful issue of the protracted contest fell to him. In the earlier stages of the parliamentary conflict, he assisted both Liberal and Tory Lord Advocates in devising legislative settlements; he drafted the greater part of Mr. Black's bill, which in successive years held the confidence of the Council and the citizens; and he was the chief agent in ripening public opinion, both within and without Parliament, for the abolition of the tax. As a contemporary writer remarked when the end was in sight, Mr. McLaren from first to last was the active force of the opposition.

"If the abolition of the Annuity-Tax," said this writer, "had been his sole object, instead of merely one of the aims of a busy life, it could not have had bestowed upon it more sustained and unwearying attention. As to the judgment with which, under Mr. McLaren's guidance, the agitation has been managed, we need say nothing. The world is generally content to judge by results. Let it do so in this case. The test is often a fallible one, but in this instance it is safe. The end not only crowns the work, but it also indicates the character of the work done. Having set his face to the task, Mr. McLaren has never looked back; and after long years of apparently hopeless effort, embittered by the most envenomed abuse and the most unscrupulous calumny, he will have had the satisfaction of bringing about the only possible permanent settlement of the Annuity Tax—its abolition."

1870

This more than thirty years' war was not a mere "local squabble," as some critics chose to represent it. Leal-hearted Dissenters in all parts of Scotland regarded the battle as theirs. They followed every movement of the conflict with the keenest interest, and they regarded Mr. McLaren with grateful admiration. In the towns, villages, and hamlets of Scotland, wherever Dissent was known as a living force, Mr. McLaren's name became a household word, and fathers and mothers transmitted to their children a feeling of confidence in and veneration for the courageous and talented Edinburgh citizen who successfully withstood the oppression and aggression of a powerful and ambitious Church Establishment, and, undeterred by obloquy and opposition, asserted the civil rights of the Dissenting communities. It was then that Mr. McLaren gained that wonderful hold on the hearts and minds of the Voluntary party, by virtue of

Gratitude of the Dissenters.

1870   which he held their political leadership, and they under that
leadership became the backbone of Liberalism in Scotland.

> " The friends thou hast, and their adoption tried,
> Grapple them to thy soul with hoops of steel."

And because of his unflinching fidelity as a Voluntary,
Mr. McLaren was loved and valued as a proved friend by
thousands of his countrymen and country-women who never
saw his face.

CHAPTER X.

EARLY CORRESPONDENCE WITH MR. MACAULAY.

It was as the champion of the Scotch Dissenters that Mr. McLaren first came into conflict with Mr. Macaulay. He hoped to find the distinguished city Member an advocate of religious equality and friend of the Dissenters, and to induce him to use his influence and talents, if not for the enforcement of the political claims of the Nonconformists, at least for protection against Established Church aggression. Observant of the keen controversy then being waged between the Church and the civil authority, Mr. McLaren, as a Dissenter and a Liberal, resented the disposition of the Government of the day, and of English statesmen generally, to make concessions of principle with the view of conciliating the powerful Evangelical party in the Church of Scotland, and inducing them to forego their claim to spiritual independence. In this frame of mind Mr. McLaren wrote to Macaulay a long statement of the case from his point of view. This proved the starting-point of a most interesting correspondence, conducted on both sides with marked ability, though we can only gather the purport of Mr. McLaren's letters from Mr. Macaulay's replies. In a letter dated January 4, 1840, Mr. Macaulay assured Mr. McLaren that he had spared, and should spare, no exertions to prevent Dissenters from being aggrieved and to restrain the violence of extravagant High Churchmen. He continued :—" I will

Appeal to Mr. Macaulay.

only notice that part of your letter which relates to a personal matter. I suggested that the wisest and most honest man may, without knowing it, become heated in dispute, and may really act from passion while he fully believes that he is acting from principle. This is only what I shall readily admit of myself, and of much better persons than myself. You seem to think that I was led to make this suggestion by some remark which I had heard respecting you. I assure you, on my honour, that it was not so. I have not heard nor read, since the beginning of this unhappy dispute, a single word, directly or indirectly, reflecting on your character or conduct. My observation was founded solely on the papers which you sent to me, and which seemed to me to indicate a feeling on the part of the Dissenters such as was not justified by any provocation which they had received. Nor was my observation intended to apply particularly to you. I really think that the whole party with whom you act is open to it. The merits of that party I gladly acknowledge. For their kindness to myself I am most grateful. But I should be a mere flatterer if I did not say that I think their present temper a little punctilious and resentful, and that I am afraid of their being hurried by angry feelings into courses which will not raise their credit or give them satisfaction in the retrospect. You will see, I am sure, that though I say this, I by no means arrogate to myself any superiority over so many good and able men, except the superiority which necessarily arises from the circumstance that in the present unhappy disputes I am impartial, and that they cannot be so."

In another letter, dated June 15, Mr. Macaulay strove to gain Mr. McLaren's adhesion to the doctrine that Government may justifiably " humour those on whom they could not depend at the expense of those on whom they could depend." Mr. Macaulay proceeded :—" I will put you a case. Suppose that you knew that you could not have carried your City Customs Bill unless both the Attorney-General and the Lord Advocate supported it. The Advocate and the Attorney differ about one clause. The Advocate says that unless the clause be passed to suit his views, he will oppose the whole bill. The Attorney, though attached to his own view, yet says that he will in any case support the bill. What would you do? I have no doubt that although you might agree in opinion with the Attorney, you would adopt the Lord Advocate's clause precisely because he was a less thoroughgoing friend of your bill than the Attorney.

1840
Concessions to opponents.

" The education question is of just the same kind. The Dissenting body both in Scotland and England are staunch friends to national education. There is much hostility to national education in both the Established Churches. To maintain such a system against the opposition of both these Churches would be impossible. Is it not wise then and right in the Government to humour these Churches in matters not essential, even at the expense of the Dissenters? The consequence may be that a few unreasonable, irritable, or greedy Dissenters may desert us. I do not believe this of the body. It would give me the deepest pain to believe it. I am ready for my own part to quit office and Parliament later on. I am sick of both. But I should be sorry that the blow came from the Scottish Dissenters."

Feeling that nearly all the public interests he held dear were the objects of Established Church intolerance, Mr. McLaren was not disposed to accept these philosophic political discourses on compromise as embodying the essence of practical wisdom in statesmanship, and he felt that Mr. Macaulay's personal indifference was due to the absence of personal experience. The outbreak of the conflict over the nomination of Mr. Adam Black for the Lord Provostship furnished a local illustration which he thought Mr. Macaulay would appreciate; and in writing in October to the city Member on public business (the subject being the provision of an adequate salary for the Principal of the University), he took occasion to inform Mr. Macaulay that Mr. Black's election was being opposed by Whigs as well as Tories, on the sole ground of his being a Dissenter. Mr. Macaulay was at the time much occupied with Ministerial duties; he, however, wrote this brief but friendly reply :—

The Churchmen and Mr. Black.

LONDON, October 12, 1840.

DEAR MR. MCLAREN,—I have been a good deal vexed about the turn which things have taken respecting Dr. Lee's case. I will make another attempt to have the thing put on a right footing. But as you guess, we are so much occupied with matters of life and death that it is difficult to get a hearing on any other subject.

I have been greatly concerned about the Provostship. I should have been at Edinburgh before now but for the schism between two portions of the Liberal party. In November, when the election is over, I hope to be among you, and to talk freely and fairly with you over some of the important matters to which your letter refers.—Ever yours truly, T. B. MACAULAY.

Another appeal to Mr. Macaulay.

Mr. Black lost his election, and the disappointment of the Dissenters was intensified by the feeling that the political party whom they had helped to place in power had lent their influence to opponents. In a letter dated November 16th of the same year, Mr. Macaulay incidentally referred to the battle for the Lord Provostship, assuring Mr. McLaren that in this case his sympathies were with the Dissenters, and remarking, " Rely on it that no man will suffer in my opinion for having supported Black, since, had I had a vote, I should undoubtedly have done so myself." Mr. McLaren responded, inviting Mr. Macaulay to take Mr. Black's side publicly with the Dissenters, and to let it be known that he disapproved of the conduct of local Whig supporters, who had opposed Mr. Black's election on sectarian grounds. At the same time he recited the various grievances from which the Dissenters were suffering at the hands of the Whig Government, and warned him of the growth of a feeling of resentment and alienation on the part of the Scottish Nonconformists that might prove disastrous to the Whig party at future elections. Subjoined is Mr. Macaulay's reply, containing a handsome recognition of Mr. McLaren's statesmanlike qualities, but also an earnest and able remonstrance against the uncompromising policy of the Voluntary party :—

A friendly remonstrance.

LONDON, December 5, 1840.

DEAR MR. MCLAREN,—I am much obliged to you for the information and advice which are contained in your last letter. It would not have been proper in me to take a part in your municipal proceedings; still less would it have been proper to send a reprimand to the Town Council after they had made their choice. But I have never disguised my opinion, and perhaps have stated it more strongly to Mr. Dunlop, the only supporter of the Lord Provost with whom I have had any communication, than to anybody else. I think the conduct of the Whigs who opposed Black most highly censurable. Indeed, I must eat all the words that I ever uttered in my life on the subject of religious liberty if I were to admit that, because a man is a Dissenter, or even a Voluntary, he is to be considered as unfit for civil office.

At the same time I must say that I do not approve of the spirit which shows itself in a part of the Dissenting body. I observe that almost every Dissenter with whom I correspond— and I have the happiness of corresponding with several whom I greatly respect—disclaims for himself the sentiments which he describes as common among the class to which he belongs. The speech of Mr. Alexander [1] is, however, if I understand it rightly, a distinct avowal of what I must consider as very unreasonable sentiments and very unjustifiable purposes. To you I speak quite explicitly; for, without flattery, I may say that I have seldom found among men employed in the highest functions, and accustomed to the management of great affairs, a mind more statesmanlike than yours. Consider then for a moment what the interests are which are staked on the event of the contest between the great parties in this country. Consider how nicely balanced those parties are. Consider that it is in the power of the Scotch Dissenters to bring in a Tory Government with a decisive majority in the House of Commons. Consider how serious a trust the election franchise is. Consider that it is a power given to be used for the general good, and not for the gratification of private or natural feelings, either of an interested or of a vindictive kind. Consider then to what the provocations enumerated by Mr. Alexander amount. Some trifling matters of punctilio—some little slight about the printing of the Bible, or about the appointment of school inspectors. Are these things seriously to be maintained as aggressions on religious liberty? Look backwards to your own youth, and consider how gladly you would have compounded for one half of the progress which since that time religious liberty has made under the fostering care of Whig statesmen. I do not defend what was done about the Bible or about the inspectors. I tried to remove both grounds of discontent; and as to the first, I thought that I had succeeded. But say that the grievances were ten times as great as they are, would they justify the Dissenting body of Scotland in taking the course which we are told they mean to take? I am familiar, I am sorry to say, and so are all men in office, with the low selfishness of mankind. One man gives you to understand that unless his earldom is turned into a marquisate he cannot continue to support the Government. Another stays away from the House of Commons on an important division because his father is not made Lord-Lieutenant. Your precious townsman

---

[1] Afterwards well known as the Rev. Dr. Lindsay Alexander.

———— (but this is between ourselves) tells me that he shall withdraw his support from me because I have positively refused to ask Lord Melbourne to make him a Grand Cross of the Bath. These things are pitiable, but I am used to them. I do hope, however, that the whole Dissenting body of Scotland is not about to lower itself to the level of such people as I have mentioned. Only imagine a great party, containing as much intelligence as any equal portion of the British nation, and distinguished during many years by manly sense and zeal for the common government, addressing a Government thus :—" We believe your continuance in office to be for the advantage of the Empire. We believe that your fall would be a public calamity. But you have not treated us in some matters of precedence with sufficient respect. You have, indeed, given us an immense power in the State and in the local government of towns, such as we never possessed before. You have done more than all the Administrations that ever existed for those principles of civil and religious liberty to which we are devoted. But you have, in order to conciliate other parties whose support in your arduous situation was necessary to you, denied us twice or thrice some mark of respect, some mere feather in the cap ; and therefore we will be revenged, though our revenge be fatal to the whole Empire. We will have you out, cost what it may." What is the plain meaning of these threats ? I do not believe that they will ever be carried into effect. If they are, I shall grieve most deeply, not for the loss of my office and my seat—for I am sick of both—but for the irreparable infamy which will be brought on the very name of Scotch Dissenter. I must not run on any longer. I have not time even to read over what I have scrawled. It may be incorrectly expressed. But it is, I assure you, both honestly and kindly meant. And I leave it with perfect confidence to your candour and good sense.—Ever yours truly,

T. B. MACAULAY.

It was obviously a pain to Mr. Macaulay to differ with Mr. McLaren on a question of Liberal policy. He highly appreciated his personal talents, recognising that he had

1840

seldom found, even " among men employed in the highest functions, and accustomed to the management of great affairs, a more statesmanlike mind." He was conscious, too, that in his case great political capacity was strengthened and ennobled by uprightness of character and the absence of self-seeking motives. He further recognised his correspondent as the trusted representative of a political party powerful in numbers, and still more powerful from their intelligence and their devotion to the cause of Reform. Mr. Macaulay wished to stand well with Mr. McLaren and his political friends. On the other hand, Mr. McLaren wished to gain Mr. Macaulay as the advocate of the Scottish Nonconformist party, and he was disappointed to find that, though he believed his parliamentary representative was at heart with the Dissenters, he, under the benumbing and fettering influence of Ministerial position and party connection, set himself to be-little their grievances, and to induce them, in the interests of Whig supremacy, to acquiesce in a policy inconsistent with their ecclesiastical position and their convictions. Accordingly he once more put Mr. Macaulay on his defence, and again he elicited an extremely able but unconvincing reply :—

LONDON, *December* 11, 1840.

MY DEAR SIR,—I assure you that I give the fullest credit to your declaration that wounded pride and vindictive feeling are not the motives by which you are actuated. At the same time you will, I doubt not, allow me to suggest that the best and wisest men may, unconsciously, attach to their own pretensions an exaggerated importance, and feel undue resentment for slight injuries offered to themselves. And I own that, after reading the very able paper which you have sent me, I cannot, as an impartial man, doubt that this is the case with the Dissenting body of Scotland.

I am indeed glad to learn that you do not find in anything

that has been done a sufficient ground for withholding your
support from the Government. That the Government should
so grossly misconduct itself towards the Dissenters as to forfeit
all title to support, I do not credit. That it has as yet done
so, you do not contend. So far we are quite agreed.

But when I look at your list of grievances, I must own I am
a little astonished. It is a list which proves to me only how
little ground you really have to complain. I know something
about one of your charges, that respecting the printing of the
Bible. I went myself with Mr. Gillon and others to the Home
Office to plead your cause. I was spokesman on your behalf.
I obtained from Lord John Russell an assurance that your
representations should be considered. I was subsequently in
communication with your delegates. I was positively and repeatedly assured by one of them that the arrangement which
was finally made was perfectly satisfactory. Now, after all
this, how great must be my surprise to see it asserted that on
this occasion "the remonstrances of the Dissenters were dis-
regarded." Can you be surprised if I feel a little inclined to
suspect there is, in some of my Dissenting friends, a punctilious
disposition—a disposition, not perhaps suspected by themselves,
to make the most of small injuries and to remember them long?
Of your other grievances I know little, and can therefore say
little; but surely, even as stated by yourselves, they do not
bear out your conclusions. As to the prisons, for example, I
perfectly agree with you that Dissenting teachers ought not to
have been excluded. The Government did not intend to exclude
them. In the House of Lords, where the opposition is more than
two to one, the excluding clause was inserted. Probably, for I
really was not aware of the circumstances, the Minister of the
Home Department thought that he must either drop the bill
altogether or take it with this objectionable clause.

It was then his business to compare the inconveniences of the
two courses. The bill was, I believe, good, and indeed necessary.
In your paper it is mentioned with general praise. The excluding clause was exceptionable. So are many hundreds of clauses
for which I have voted in my time in order to secure the passing

of good bills. There are bad clauses, **very bad clauses, in** the Reform Bill, **in** the bill for abolishing slavery, in all the best bills of my time. The question is one of comparison. Does the measure on the whole do more good or harm? I really do not think that a candid Dissenter would **say that in this** case **the** Government decided wrongly. But I may be in the wrong here; **for, as I** tell you, I am but very imperfectly acquainted with the **facts.** Of this, **however, I am sure, that there was no ground for serious offence.**

About the inspectors of schools I really think the Committee of Council judged wisely. Consider the whole question together, and not merely that corner of it which relates to the precedency of Churchmen **or** Dissenters. **A** system of national education is essential **to the virtue,** peace, and prosperity of the nation. It is an object for which the greatest sacrifices ought to be made. It is an object which eighteen months ago seemed almost **un-attainable. It now seems** attainable. **The mass of prejudice which was opposed to us has yielded.** The clamour which **seemed likely to unseat the Government** has died **away.** How has this been brought **about? Chiefly, I believe,** by making some concessions—not, I admit, in themselves desirable, but a very small price **for a very** great benefit—to the bishops in England and **to the** General Assembly in Scotland. If you are determined to look at every question merely as Dissenters, **you may resent this.** But **you are not only Dissenters—you are also citizens. As citizens,** you must feel **that there may be evils even greater than the** giving to the Kirk a **feather in her** cap, which I acknowledge to be something more than **her due.** That millions **of** children should grow up with **as** little moral or intellectual training as the Hottentot,—that while **we** are squabbling about Intrusion and Non-Intrusion, multitudes of youth should, **in** every great city of the **realm,** be ripening for the brothel and the treadmill,— **this is, I do** think, as serious **a** public calamity as can well be imagined—a **much** more serious one than any that **is** set forth in your paper. The etiquette between Scotch sects is not the only thing that a Government has to **look to. It is** charged with the care of the physical and moral interests **of a** vast community. **It** may well happen that, in times like these, it may be impossible to carry some measure of vital importance to the great whole without the help of persons who insist on conditions open to just objection. I am sorry for this; but what am I to do? Even what I did in order to obtain the Reform Bill, the abolition of slavery, the abolition of the East India monopoly—voted for many things which I disliked, but which were necessary to the passing of those valuable measures.

These are my views as to the grievances of which you complain. As to Black's defeat, I am sure that no member of the Government had anything to do with it; nor have I heard one among them speak of it but with deep regret. As to the disputes between the Kirk and the civil power, I must make a distinction. Of course the Legislature is supreme. Any pretension to the contrary on the part of the Establishment I regard much as you do. But what the Legislature in the exercise of its supreme power ought to do is quite another question. I think that, if it chooses to maintain the Kirk, it ought to put the Kirk on the footing, whatever that may be, which may make the Kirk, while it exists, most useful to the country. I will not enter on the question of the Veto, about which I admit that there is much indeed to be said on both sides. I only mean to say I should discuss it just as I should discuss the question whether there should be a popular veto on the appointment of Commissioners of Supply or colonels of militia. I should examine in what way the public was likely to be on the whole best served, and should decide accordingly. You will, I think, admit that these principles are sound, supposing that we are to have a Church.

I have little more to say, except that as to tests, pledges, or whatever else you may call them, my mind has long been made up, and has often been publicly declared. My opinions, except where secrets of State are concerned, may be known to anybody for the asking. But I will never, while I live, give any promise as to any particular vote. I never did so, when an obscure and needy young barrister, to the Marquis of Lansdowne. I never did so to Leeds. I have never done so to the people of Edinburgh. If a life, during which I never, to the best of my belief,

wrote, or said, or did anything inconsistent with an honest attachment to the principles of religious liberty, is not a sufficient security to the Dissenters, I have no other to give them.

I have written ten times as much as I intended to write. I
hope I have expressed myself good-humouredly. I am certain
that neither to yourself nor to the great body of Scotch Dissenters
do I bear any other feeling than kindness and respect. Indeed,
I can assure you that, if you were to see my letters to High
Churchmen, you would find that they are in a very different tone
from this.—Ever yours truly,   T. B. Macaulay.

It is much to be regretted that the letters written by
Mr. McLaren, to which this and the others previously quoted
were a reply, have been destroyed, but Mr. Macaulay never
kept any letters, and therefore we can only gather Mr.
McLaren's arguments from Mr. Macaulay's answers to them,
which naturally place the former at a considerable disadvan-
tage. Nevertheless, it is clear, even from the few instances
chosen for reply, that the Dissenters had substantial grievances of which to complain; and while, taken singly, it was
easy to make each one appear trifling, yet taken altogether,
they showed that the Whig Government were overriding the
legitimate claims of the Dissenters on every occasion, and
perpetually sacrificing their rights to the necessity, real or
assumed, of conciliating the Church and Tory party in order
to pass some bill. It was this combination of small wrongs
which embittered the Dissenters, and made them feel that
the settled policy of the Whigs was to sacrifice them to
conciliate powerful opponents. For this Mr. Macaulay was
not responsible, but it was inevitable that in his constituency he had to bear the sins of his leaders. And when
charged with them, he naturally made an able defence, and
tried to show that the complaints were due to the Dissenters attaching an exaggerated importance to their
own pretensions.

Mr. McLaren, however, did not give up his attempt to win Mr. Macaulay to the direct and active service of the Dissenters. In continuance of his own work as the opponent of Established Church aggression, he wrote a controversial pamphlet in the beginning of 1841, and a copy sent to Mr. Macaulay produced a reply which satisfied him that, if the Liberal Member for the city would not act in entire harmony with the views and wishes of the majority of his political supporters, he was directly hostile to the claims of the Non-Intrusionists.

LONDON, January 30, 1841.

MY DEAR SIR,—Thanks for the tract. It is clear and able. Indeed, as to the particular point at which it runs, it is unanswerable.

I conceive that I am not inconsistent in saying that I do not think it necessarily wrong to have an Established Church,—that such an Established Church, being in some sense a civil institution, must be under the civil power, but that the civil power ought to regulate the Church, so as to make it in the highest degree efficient and respectable,—and that if a popular veto on ministers would conduce to the efficiency and respectability of the Church, the civil power may and ought to permit such a veto.

But the high Non-Intrusionists consider this as a low worldly view of the question. They are not content even to receive the veto as an improvement made by the State in the constitution of the Church. Nor will they even discuss the question whether lay patronage may, under certain modifications, be harmless or useful. They deny the right of the State to do anything with respect to the Church, except to give it money and to imprison Dissenters who refuse to pay rates. The civil magistrate in their system is nothing more than a bum-bailiff to the priest. Much is to be said in favour of Church Establishments, and much also in favour of the Voluntary system; but nothing at all, so far as I can see, in favour of the ecclesiastical polity which Mr. Guthrie and his brethren would give us.   We would have all the evils of an Establishment and all the evils that have ever been imputed to the Voluntary system together.

While the State and the Church are connected, the State must control the Church.   It ought indeed to exercise its powers in such a way as to make the Church in the highest degree useful to the people.   But it must control.   And I will never put the State under the feet of that Church which it feeds out of the common funds of the Empire.   To establish the supremacy of law seems to me to be now the first object.   To reform the law where the law requires reformation is the second.

You will have seen by the report of the proceedings of the Lords that Government means to do nothing at present except carrying into effect the law as the law now stands.—Very truly yours,   T. B. MACAULAY.

Unsatisfactory result of correspondence.

The correspondence thus ended was probably not altogether satisfactory either to Mr. McLaren and the Dissenting body which he represented, or to Mr. Macaulay and the Whigs. But the two men retained their respect for each other ; and for some time after, their friendly and confidential intercourse was maintained.   In April 1841 Mr. Macaulay wrote with great frankness on the subject of his relations with his Ministerial colleagues, especially of those connected with the administration of Scottish affairs, adding that " he would not speak so plainly to any other person," but that " your discretion and honour deserve this confidence."   " I wish that everybody were as scrupulous."   It was not till the Corn-Law controversy arose that the friends separated.

CHAPTER XI.

THE CORN-LAWS.

THE Corn-Law agitation of 1840–46 found Mr. McLaren in 1840 the maturity of his powers, or, it might be more correct to say, afforded scope for their further development, and an arena for their exercise greater than he had yet enjoyed. He was early associated with the movement, which had its headquarters at Manchester; indeed, he might not unfairly be described, though a Scotsman, as one of the founders of the Manchester School of politics. At the end of August 1840, Mr. Cobden presented to Mr. McLaren in Edinburgh the following note from the Rev. Dr. Heugh, a gifted and liberal-minded minister of the Secession Church and public-spirited citizen of Glasgow :—

GLASGOW, August 29, 1840.

MY DEAR SIR,—Allow me to introduce to you Mr. Cobden of Manchester, of whom, and whose talents and just influence, I am aware you must have heard, particularly in connection with the movement of the Anti-Corn-Law League. His conversation is full of intelligence, and his manners distinguished by their gentleness and urbanity. I am sure he will find in you a willing and zealous Anti-Corn-Law auxiliary, which will greatly delight him.— Believe me, my dear sir, yours with esteem,

H. HEUGH.

D. McLaren, Esq.

Mr. Cobden was agreeably surprised to find that Mr. McLaren was much more than a sympathetic listener; that

1840

he had carefully studied the question, and was able to give as well as willing to receive instruction, and that he was heart and soul with the newly-formed League. At this interview he supplied Mr. Cobden with information as to the effect of the Corn-laws on the prices of provisions in Edinburgh, which was afterwards used with much success in speeches delivered both in England and Scotland for the purpose of popularising the principles of the League. Sympathy of feeling and conviction, and a common devotion to a work which both foresaw would be arduous, but both knew to be necessary, quickly brought the two men near to each other, awakening a sense of companionship and producing a friendship which never wavered or weakened, but grew in trustfulness and affection till death intervened.

A lasting friendship.

Willing to engage in the work, and already known and highly appreciated in Manchester as a merchant and politician, Mr. McLaren was almost immediately appointed a member of the Council of the Anti-Corn-Law League, and in this capacity he was brought into intimate association with Mr. Bright as well as Mr. Cobden, and with a band of able and devoted coadjutors. In this society, peculiarly congenial to his political convictions and aspirations, he formed many highly prized and enduring friendships. His thorough mastery of the politico-economical questions involved in the controversy, his rare business capacity, and his unwearied personal services, quickly placed and throughout kept him in the front rank of the movement. This was exemplified by the confidence shown in his judgment on the occasion of the great Conference of the Anti-Corn-Law delegates which met in London in February 1842. There was so much difference of opinion amongst the delegates as to what was the most advisable course to pursue, that

Intimacy with Mr. Bright.

The London Conference.

it appeared as though no good results would accrue from
the Conference.   Mr. M°Laren, in a private memorandum,
gives a much more modest account of the matter than the
friends who witnessed the proceedings.   He writes :—
" When the meeting was called, there were two parties
among the friends of abolition.   One was the old Whig
party, who would be content with a fixed duty.   The
other section, and the stronger, was in favour of total
and immediate repeal.   It was because it was known that
I was firm on this point, and could not be talked over,
that I was selected by Joseph Sturge and other influential
local members of the deputation to be proposed as the
first chairman, in order to set matters fairly afoot.   It
was feared there might be a kind of split on the subject ;
but there was not.   The Whig section came in good force
from about Leeds : Mr. Edward Baines was one of them,
and Mr. Hamer Stansfeld another.   The Conference lasted
for six days.   I was chosen to act as chairman for the first
three days, and was succeeded by Mr. Taylor, father of P. A.
Taylor, late M.P.   I don't think there was any opposition
to my election or to Mr. Taylor's ; we were both in the
same boat."

The second day on which the Conference met was a
notable one in the history of the struggle, for in the
evening Sir Robert Peel brought forward his scheme in
the House of Commons for altering the sliding scale, so
that the duty should be at the maximum of 20s. when the
price of corn was under 51s., and should gradually go
down to 1s. when the price of corn was 75s.   In anticipation of the Ministerial statement, the members of the
Conference, to the number of 600, left the " Crown and
Anchor," where they had held their meeting, and, with
Mr. M°Laren, as chairman, at their head, marched down to

1842

the House of Commons. The treatment they received there was described next day by Colonel Perronet Thompson. He said, " Only one hundred gained admittance, the rest were locked out. It was within his memory that the last time Sir F. Burdett was elected, his Tory mob, horse and foot, went in procession to the House of Commons, and when he (Colonel Thompson), who was a member of that House, arrived there, he found the lobby filled with his infantry, who wore his colours in their hats. On that occasion the House had no objection to allow a mob with election colours to enter within its walls; but when six hundred gentlemen, the representatives of the oppressed country, went to the House of Commons, they were treated uncourteously; they were treated unhandsomely; indecency was thrust in the face of each of them, and that House had declared itself to be what they had found it, what they would find it, and what it would always remain till they had altered it."

The hundred who were admitted remained, however, till the close of Sir R. Peel's speech, when they adjourned to Brown's Coffee-house, and unanimously passed the following resolution, signed by Duncan McLaren, chairman :—

"That in the opinion of this meeting, the measure announced by Her Majesty's Government on the subject of the Corn-laws, so far from holding out the slightest prospect of any relief of the distress of the country, is an insult to a patient and suffering people; and the deputies view such a proposal as an indication that the landed aristocracy of this country are destitute of all sympathy for the poor, and are resolved, if permitted by an outraged people, to persist in a course of selfish policy which will involve the destruction of every interest in the country."

This very strong resolution was submitted to the Conference the next day, and was adopted as the opinion of the whole of the members. Thus the Government and the country were warned that nothing short of total and immediate repeal would satisfy the League.

1842

To the education of the country in the principles of Free Trade, and the final conflict with landlord influence and monopoly, it is well known that the Scottish Liberals largely contributed. A prize-essay written and a series of speeches delivered by George Hope of Fentonbarns exerted a powerful educational influence on the tenant-farmers. Mr. McLaren's sphere of work was more general and practical. He was the business man of the League. He planned the lecturing tours, and arranged all their meetings in Scotland. Cobden and Bright, when they visited Edinburgh, were always his guests; and the first in counsel, he was also the most abundant in labours. Among the most characteristic of these labours was his collections for the League funds—his appeals for the free-will offerings of the people for the provision of the sinews of war. "One year," he states in his private memorandum, "I sent a circular by my own clerks to every elector in the city, asking a subscription to be sent me for the League, and got between £1100 and £1200. Another year I sent circulars to every name in the 'Edinburgh Directory,' also addressed by my own clerks, and got above £1800." A portion of this, however, came from sympathisers in different districts of Scotland. In referring to this successful undertaking, the *Glasgow Argus* took notice of the presence in the subscription list of the poor man's mite and the handsome donation of his more wealthy fellow-citizen, and remarked :—"By the prevalence of such determined spirit did aristocratic Auld Reekie make her proud appearance in this righteous cause; but it must not be forgotten that the management of this matter was in the hands of that man who on so many occasions has distinguished himself in the cause of truth and justice—Mr. Duncan McLaren." It was not unusual for the contributors to make grateful acknowledgment of the stimulus and guidance in political study they received from the chief organiser of the fund, and sometimes this admiring gratitude was expressed in rhyme, of which one sample may be given. The lines accompanied an offering of 2s. 6d. from a working man :—

> Though my mite is but small, my heart's in the cause,
> To expose and suppress the odious Corn-laws.
> Staunch Cobden, press onward ; in the fight never fag
> Till " Free Trade Triumphant " emblazons our flag !
> With support of good Bright, and such stars of the nation,
> And Auld Reekie's true friend—honest Duncan McLaren.

The following letter from Cobden to Mr. McLaren, alluding to some manifestation of unfriendliness on the part of the Whig leaders, gives an amusing instance of the way in which subscriptions were obtained and the excitement kept up :—

MANCHESTER, *December* 8, 1842.

MY DEAR SIR,—I have been running "to and fro," and have only just got your letter. Your dilemma with your old Whig leaders is one that I have so often encountered in other places, that it only brings smiles into my face at the thoughts of the prevalence of the foolish subserviency to cliques in this country. Don't fancy for a moment that I am personally annoyed. I'll come to Edinburgh to convince you to the contrary. I should not have accepted a *personal* compliment had it been offered. In reply to the Glasgow invitation, I agreed to come only on condition that the demonstration was for Free Trade, and *not* for myself personally. I cannot come to Scotland till the beginning of next month. Consult with the Glasgow people as to time. Bright will come, and I hope we may bring Colonel Thompson.

Since you cannot catch the Whig *leaders*, the only plan is to carry off their *rank and file*.   Therefore make your arrangements for the largest meeting possible in the largest place you can get, whether temporary or not.   Let it be an unmixed and unqualified Free Trade and Anti-Corn-Law meeting, without the slightest alloy of the principle.

Last night I witnessed an extraordinary meeting in Rochdale, where £1300 was subscribed to the great League fund in the room in sums from £2 to £100.   The bidding (for it was really an auction) was continued till midnight.   It was a tea-party,[1] at which Bowring, Bright, Buckingham,[2] and I attended, and after our addresses the subscriptions commenced, led off by the chairman, Mr. Fenton, the late Member for the borough, with £100. It was a most amusing and interesting scene.   The gallery was filled with operatives, who called out the names of the leading men on the platform, and prompted them in the sums they were to give, amidst roars of laughter.   The good-humour, life, and liberality of the meeting were perfectly intoxicating to the friends of Repeal.—Believe me yours very truly,   RICHARD COBDEN.

Many other notes of encouragement and expressions of gratitude came from the headquarters of the League, and more especially from Mr. Bright, who actively superintended both the financial and literary business.   Mr. Bright became enthusiastic over Mr. McLaren's success.   " Your subscriptions are of appalling length," he sometimes observed, when oppressed with the difficulty of finding space for their acknowledgment in the *League Journal.* " You are a glorious people, notwithstanding your peculiarities," he wrote on another occasion.   Keenly interested in the work in Scotland, he ventured to give a hint of an apparently neglected field.   " I hope some of the Free Church people," he wrote on the last day of 1843, " will

---

[1] A public tea-party held in the theatre.
[2] James Silk Buckingham.

1842

come out now for us and give us a help. This district has done much for them. Rochdale, I think, has given them near £400." When Mr. McLaren had explained that Free Churchmen were for the time too fully occupied with the pressing claims of their Church to be able to aid the League much, Mr. Bright rejoined, with excellent taste and feeling :—" It may be that I have spoken too unfavourably of your Free Church people (in relation to the League). I don't forget, when comparing their subscriptions with yours, that they have had many calls upon them of late, and that now and for some time to come they must be chiefly occupied with their own question. Time will show what they will become. I trust that they may rival your body (the Secession Church)."

But the most important service rendered by Mr. McLaren to the cause of the League was his masterly array on its side of the Nonconformist Churches. Acting in harmony with his Dissenting friends in Edinburgh, and assisted by a committee consisting of the Revs. John McGilchrist, A. Fraser, W. Peddie, and James Robertson, Messrs. John Wigham, junior, James McLaren, John Grey, Thomas Russell, and John Howieson, he in 1841 instituted an inquiry as to the effect of the operation of the Corn-laws.

From upwards of four hundred ministers he received answers condemning the laws on account of their injustice and immoral tendency. A meeting of Dissenters, held in Broughton Place Session-house, to whom these answers were submitted, certified that they were " nearly unanimous in regarding the corn and provision laws as unjust in principle, vexatious and oppressive in their operation, and the main cause of all the distresses of the country, and in advocating their total repeal and the establishing an entirely free trade in corn ;" and that the ministers " condemn these laws as being alike opposed to the principles of religion and the precepts of morality." The preparation of these answers could not fail of itself to stimulate political inquiry and activity in every district of the country in which the inquiry was conscientiously conducted by the ministers and their elders. It was equally apparent that the publication of this great body of opinion in an orderly and intelligent form could not fail to exert a guiding and bracing influence on the Liberal party as a whole, and more especially on its leaders and parliamentary representatives. Mr. McLaren was requested to undertake their publication in abstract, and this delicate and responsible work he successfully performed. The publication of the pamphlet was a fit preparation for the great Conference which was afterwards held in South College Street Church on the 11th, 12th, and 13th of January 1842.[1]

---

[1] At this period of his life Mr. McLaren's extensive personal acquaintance among the Dissenting clergy of Scotland had ripened into many valued friendships, amongst which the most noticeable was the affectionate intimacy which bound together the Rev. Henry Renton of Kelso and himself. They were brothers-in-law, but they were far more. They were typical men in their spheres of life, Mr. Renton as a minister, and Mr. McLaren as a layman; the one the most unworldly of men, a ripe scholar, a cultured gentleman; the other skilled in the management of worldly affairs, unsparing in his public services, dignifying the title of merchant-citizen;—both at once austere and chivalrous, grasping clearly and tenaciously the same principles of life and duty, and resolved to follow them out regardless of the cost to personal comfort or popularity. During many heated and arduous controversies regarding Church and State, Education, Free Trade, and the policy of the Peace Society, the two men stood together, helping and stimulating each other, as their example helped and stimulated hundreds and thousands more. Mr. Renton accompanied Mr. McLaren to London as a delegate to the great Anti-Corn-Law Conference held in 1842. In a note to Mr. McLaren, in which he expresses himself strongly against any compromise with Whig officialism, Mr. Renton remarked to his friend that he was "working double tides" in order that his congregation might not suffer during his prospective temporary absence

A more purpose-like gathering had, perhaps, never before assembled in Edinburgh than that Conference of ministers and representatives of congregations. Great pains had been taken to make it thoroughly representative of the Dissenting denominations, and to induce the delegates to furnish themselves with facts and arguments collected and endorsed by their constituents ; and these efforts were rewarded with a success which surpassed the most sanguine anticipations. In the first place, the attendance was much larger than had been looked for : 976 invitation circulars were issued to Dissenting ministers ; 712 delegates promised attendance, but the actual number who came with the necessary authorisation was 801. The statistics of the sederunt were thus summarised :—

	Promised Attendance.	Actual Attendance.
Secession Church . . .	384	429
Relief Church . . .	130	156
Independent Church . .	110	109
Baptist Church . . .	52	60
Smaller sects	36	42
Deputations	0	5
Totals . .	712	801

In addition to the 801 members of Conference who alone took part in the proceedings, 150 tickets of admission were issued to friends to witness the proceedings and subscribe to defray the expenses, and about 500 family tickets of admission were presented to those families who were hospitably lodging and entertaining ministers and members who had come from a distance. Thus there were from 1400 to 1600 persons constantly present, and the Conference lasted three days.

" Assuming," Mr. McLaren afterwards remarked, " that

on the business of the Anti-Corn-Law League, for he never allowed the public work in which he interested himself to interfere with the conscientious and punctilious discharge of his duties as a minister.

the opinions of 500 congregations were fairly represented by the meeting, and that on an average each congregation consisted of only 200 families of the usual size, the Conference, even at this very reduced calculation, would truly represent a population of half a million of souls. The importance of the opinions promulgated by such a meeting, based as they are, in the words of their address to the people, on a conviction of the 'sinfulness and injustice of these laws, as being alike opposed to the revealed will and providence of God,' can hardly be over-estimated by the Legislature and Government of the country." The character of the speakers and of the speeches added to the significance and impressiveness of the demonstration. The order of business, the speakers, and the subjects had all been definitely arranged beforehand, in the full knowledge and with the aid of the delegates themselves; and while the movers and supporters of resolutions came fully prepared with local information, and as nearly as possible first-hand facts, a definiteness of purpose ran through the whole proceedings, with perfect freedom of discussion. Mr. McLaren, in his introduction to the report of the speeches afterwards published, recorded his opinion that the meeting was perhaps the most interesting and successful ever held in the city. "This," he added, "is admitted by all who witnessed its proceedings, and those who had an opportunity of conversing with the ministers and members from a distance are all strongly impressed with the conviction that they left the Conference for their respective localities with the fixed resolution never to cease denouncing the wickedness of the Corn-laws until every shred of them shall be erased from the statute-book, until the means employed shall be effective to convince the Legislature that 'he that withholdeth corn, the people shall curse him, but blessings shall be upon the head of him that selleth it,' and that it is the path of duty and safety 'to do justice and love mercy.' "

Unfortunately the chief organiser of this remarkable demonstration of public opinion and resoluteness of aim was unable to be present at the meetings. He was detained at home, prostrated by the effects of the fatiguing preliminary work he had been conducting for weeks. The resolutions and the whole order of procedure bear, however, the impress of his well-informed convictions and practical genius, while his compilation of the reports previously sent in by the five hundred ministers was the text-book of the speakers. John Wigham, who presided at the opening meeting, expressed the general sentiment when he said, "To Duncan McLaren the friends of Free Trade and justice to *all* are indebted chiefly for the constitution and the arrangements connected with this meeting, and not least to the labour he has bestowed in carrying them so far into effect. While we are deprived of this gentleman's services, I trust this meeting will be so conducted as to answer the important end his disinterested mind contemplated."

Mr. Cobden, in a letter excusing his absence on account of a sudden attack of cold with slight inflammation, made grateful acknowledgment of Mr. McLaren's "able and energetic efforts in promoting the Conference." Towards the close of the proceedings, Rev. James Robertson, Edinburgh, moved, "That the heartfelt thanks of the Conference be returned to Duncan McLaren, Esq., and the other gentlemen with whom this Conference originated, and by whom the preliminary arrangement was made. Of Mr. McLaren he begged leave to say that he knew no man of greater capacity of mind, of greater integrity of character, of greater modesty of disposition, and whose energy was more disinterestedly and cordially devoted to the public good." He was

appointed convener of the committee chosen to superintend
the printing and circulation of the address to the people of
Scotland adopted by the Conference, and under his personal
direction practical effect was given to all the resolutions, so
far as these bore on the future conduct of the agitation.

As a citizen, Mr. M[c]Laren endeavoured to carry his
fellow-electors along with him in the support given to the
League, and as Edinburgh, then represented by Mr. Macaulay, was one of the keys which controlled the direction
of the Liberal party, this local work was one of great importance. Mr. Macaulay's support was earnestly coveted
by the Free Traders. And as this influential statesman
and thinker, unlike some of his Whig colleagues, cordially
and unreservedly accepted the Free Trade doctrine, Mr.
M[c]Laren made it his care to fortify him in his position
of economist and Free Trader against the subtle devices
of social influence and party by the constant pressure of his
constituents in favour of " total and immediate repeal." In
these efforts Mr. M[c]Laren was less successful than in his
more public labours on behalf of Free Trade. For a time
all went well. The Member and his Liberal supporters,
now organised into an Anti-Corn-Law Association, of which
Mr. Wigham was chairman and Mr. W. Miller, S.S.C.,
secretary, and in which the " Parliament House " was well
represented, seemed completely united in conviction and
desire. Mr. M[c]Laren attended a banquet given to Macaulay in 1840, and in proposing the toast of " Freedom
of Trade and the Abolition of the Corn-Laws," expressed
sentiments which apparently commanded universal acceptance. As a plea for the repeal of the restrictive laws the
speech was apt and effective. It brought home to his
fellow-citizens a conviction of the nature and extent of the
burden the Corn-laws placed upon them. By a few figures

1842

and calculations it was shown that "Protection" to the agricultural classes, as sanctioned and maintained by Parliament, entailed on each of the 30,000 families comprising the population of the city a bread-tax amounting to fifteen pence per week, or £3, 5s. per year; a total assessment on the city of £97,000 per annum, or £27,000 more than was extracted from the taxpayers by all the other local taxes, including the police-tax, the annuity-tax, the road-money, the poor-money, water-duty, improvement-tax, &c. It is important also to note that at this early stage of the agitation in the company of Mr. Macaulay and his friends, and apparently with their hearty approval, Mr. McLaren clearly and definitely pronounced for total abolition.

"It has been said," he concluded, "we should petition, not for the total abolition of the Corn-laws, but for a fixed duty. A fixed duty would, no doubt, be a great improvement on the present system, which is one of speculation and gambling; but if we believe that any system of duties would be a system of injustice, we are bound honestly to express our opinions, and to petition only for a total repeal. As friends of the slave, we did not petition for a transition state of apprenticeship, but for the total abolition of slavery. The transition state was originally suggested by the opponents of immediate abolition, and ultimately tolerated only as a compromise by the friends of the slave. Let us pursue the same honest course of policy with the Corn-laws. Let us petition for the total abolition of a system of injustice, and leave it to our opponents to offer terms of capitulation. If they shall offer a transition state of fixed duties, to terminate in seven years, it will then be for the friends of abolition to consider the proposal in a spirit of conciliation. But the toast is in favour of freedom of trade in all other articles as well as in corn. When we refuse any protection to the landowners, we ask none for the manufacturers. We seek no protection for our cottons or woollens, for our cutlery, or silks, or gloves. We seek equal justice for all classes of the community. Let Parliament impose such taxes as they may think best for the purposes of national revenue, but they should impose no tax for the purpose of protecting any interest, whether agricultural or manufacturing; and this feeling has been strongly expressed in petitions emanating from the mercantile and manufacturing interests of all parts of the kingdom."

It will here be noted that Mr. M°Laren in this, as in other reforms with which he was associated, did not commit himself to the doctrine of unpractical extremists, that a part must be refused when the whole is unattainable. When he thought public opinion or party organisation was not sufficiently strong to carry a complete measure of reform, he was in general willing to accept an instalment, but without abatement of the original claim, founded on justice and public right. But being a courageous, resolute man, he was often disposed to form a more hopeful estimate of the possibilities of reform than associates who appalled themselves with visions of difficulties, and always saw the conventional " lion in the way." In the following year, as chairman of a meeting of Dissenters held to consider the representation of the city, Mr. M°Laren carried a motion for a " petition to Parliament in favour of the measure recently introduced by Government relative to the sugar, timber, and corn duties ; the petition to state that although in the opinion of the meeting justice and sound policy alike require the total abolition of the Corn-laws, they consider the plan now proposed by Government of a fixed duty a great improvement on the present system." But as the movement for the total abolition advanced and grew in strength with the progress of the times, partly under the educational influence of the League's propagandism, and still more under the pressure of industrial distress, Mr.

McLaren also advanced, and he was not by any means inclined to halt, or to go back to suit the opportunism of his more cautious allies.

In support of the forward policy of the League, Mr. McLaren unhesitatingly employed all the political influence he possessed. In connection with municipal, ecclesiastical, and city election business he had many opportunities of forming acquaintanceships among the leaders and officials of the political parties; and in the interests of justice he for some time actively exerted himself to induce the political representatives of the old Reform party to adopt the Anti-Corn-Law platform. An instance of a similar effort in a different direction may here be given. Acknowledging receipt of a pamphlet sent him by Mr. McLaren in the autumn of 1841, Sir James Graham at once wrote:—" I shall read it with the respect and attention due to whatever you recommend to my notice; " and five months afterwards, in reply to an earnest expostulation, Mr. McLaren received another letter from the then Home Secretary, dignified in tone and apparently fatal to the hope of relief from the Peel Government, which was nevertheless eventually to take the decisive step in the settlement of this great question. The letter is as follows:—

WHITEHALL, *January* 31, 1842.

DEAR SIR,—I have received your letter denouncing the Corn-laws in no measured terms.

I give you full credit for the sincerity of your opinions and for your frankness in declaring them to me.

I am the last man to undervalue or disregard the deliberate judgment of the middle classes; and when it has been formed on sound reasoning and is distinctly pronounced, it will never fail to overpower all opposition. But you must not mistake the views of public meetings in cities for the voice of the community; and I suspect that Free Trade in foreign corn has stronger and more numerous opponents than you may be prepared to admit.

I will not, however, argue the matter adversely with you. I believe it was your honest wish to convey to me information which you thought it was important I should possess; and I answer your letter, as written to me, in a friendly spirit.—I am, yours very faithfully, JAS. GRAHAM.

D. McLaren, Esq.

Never was a public movement more frowned upon in its earlier days by statesmen than the Anti-Corn-Law agitation. In the House of Peers Lord Melbourne said " he had heard of many mad things in his life, but before God, the idea of repealing the Corn-laws was the maddest he had ever heard of;" and afterwards, replying to a deputation from the League's London Conference, over which Mr. McLaren presided, his Lordship said, " Why, gentlemen, you might as well talk of abolishing the throne !"—an observation which provoked from Mr. Rawson, the treasurer of the League fund, the startling retort, " Well, my Lord, these laws must be abolished, even if the throne should go." On another occasion, Sir James Graham interrupted Mr. John Brooks of Manchester with the exclamation, " Why, you are a Chartist ;" and when Mr. Henry Ashworth was speaking he accused him of being " a leveller." At an earlier stage Lord John Russell had advised the House of Commons to refuse to hear evidence on the operation of the Corn-laws ; while the Conservative leaders, the Duke of Wellington, Lord Stanley, and Sir Robert Peel, were, if possible, more pronouncedly hostile.

In the face of opposition such as this the League had a hard battle to fight. The whole strength of the aristocracy was used against it for the most selfish reasons ; hence the League was compelled to declare, in the words of the

resolution of 1842, previously quoted, that the landed aristocracy were destitute of all sympathy for the poor, and were
pursuing a policy which would involve the destruction of
every interest in the country. The *Times* was against it.
But the League was composed of men resolute and able.
They had first-class talent and first-class character on their
side; facts and arguments and experience were all with
them; and when the great subscription of £50,000 was
raised in support of the agitation, the *Times*, then in the
zenith of its influence, was among the first to discern the
inevitable result. It saw the nation was in earnest, and in
a leading article which has become historical, it proclaimed
the League "a great fact!" It more strongly recognised
this when a further subscription of £100,000 was raised,
which, when proposed at a public meeting by Mr. Cobden,
served only to rouse the enthusiasm of the people to the
highest pitch. There was another scene, which baffles
description, when in December 1845, at a meeting held in
the Town Hall in Manchester, composed of bankers, merchants, manufacturers, and others, a resolution was proposed
to raise another great fund of £250,000, of which £60,000
was subscribed before the meeting separated. The Liberal
leaders began to waver; then compromise was offered and
rejected. In 1846, after meetings and conferences, addressed
by the first orators of the day, had been held everywhere
throughout the kingdom—four years after the protest of the
London Conference, signed by Mr. McLaren as chairman—
Sir Robert Peel was converted, and Free Trade was carried.
It will be remembered, as characteristic of the candid and
high-minded English statesman, that he gave the credit of
this great reform to "the unadorned eloquence of Richard
Cobden."

When the end came suddenly in sight, the parliamentary

chiefs of the League, who had, in frequent conference with Mr. McLaren during the progress of the struggle, learned to trust his sagacity and knowledge as well as to admire his readiness of resource, at once consulted him as to the acceptability of the Government's proposals. Mr. Bright, in reporting them, did not conceal his own favourable opinion. Writing on 25th January 1846 he said :—

London, *January 25, 1846.*

My DEAR FRIEND,—I have your letter of the 19th inst., and your remarks on the meeting and the speakers are interesting. The old Whig leaven seems a something which no experience can eradicate, and in truth I have no hope of any great good from this generation of the subordinates of the party. . . .

Peel has made a clean breast of it; at least, he is finally committed to Free Trade, and I believe will give complete liberty to our commerce before he has done with it. His measure will be total—we are not sure it will be immediate—but I confess I think it not unlikely. Beyond three years no one expects any delay. Cheese and butter are to share a like fate, and we have reason to believe that a really great measure is in contemplation, by which a large number of articles will be entirely freed from duty, and our import duties be levied from a very few of the most important articles. We are on the eve of great changes, and they will not all be confined to commercial matters. The Lords and squires are savage enough, but there are symptoms of cooling down, although the subordinates of the Government seem oppressed with a sense of the insecurity of their position, and talk of the almost certainty of another resignation or a dissolution.

Mr. McLaren in his reply expressed the opinion that the battle was over, and advised a prompt and hearty support of the Peel Ministry in their Free Trade policy. Mr. Cobden then penned the subjoined note, which tells, without a word of boastfulness or self-commendation, the sacrifices he had made, illustrates his vigilance and fidelity as a leader, and touchingly anticipates his restoration to peaceful home life :—

MANCHESTER, *February* 2, 1846.

MY DEAR SIR,—Your view of the Peel measure is precisely that which Villiers, Bright, Gibson, and myself took of it, and I find our friends here acquiescing in the same opinion, though at first they were rather disposed to go into opposition to Peel. *It is a great measure,* and would have been a complete one if Peel, Graham, and Aberdeen could have induced the Duke and the rest of the Cabinet to have agreed to total and immediate. As it is, I don't quite despair of making it *immediate* with the consent of the agricultural party, when they reflect upon the obvious injury which a gradual repeal will inflict upon the farmers. But we shall not endanger the measure in the House by our opposition. Villiers will take a vote upon his old principle in such a way as will preclude the Protectionists from giving us a cross vote, and, failing this, we shall lend our support to Peel. Out of doors we must stick to our principles, for it is not certain that the measure will pass the Lords, and in case of a general election we shall want our old watchword and bond of union, *total and immediate repeal.*

You may well believe I look forward with joy to the prospect of my emancipation from a vortex of agitation, in which, for nearly seven years, I have neglected almost every private claim and domestic duty, almost to the forgetfulness of my own identity.

Believe me truly yours,   RICHARD COBDEN.

D. McLaren, Esq.

The Government accepted the amendments which the League desired, and the bill was passed without a Ministerial defeat, without a collision with the House of Lords, and without a dissolution of Parliament.

This agitation, like that which preceded it and which resulted in the freedom of the slave, had its roots in every household ; it was a domestic question though fought with political weapons, and women came forward instinctively to join their husbands, fathers, and brothers in these two great struggles. They attended the Anti-Corn-Law meetings in great numbers, and gave substantial aid to the funds of the League. They held a great bazaar in Manchester. In those days (upwards of forty years ago) large bazaars were less common than now, and it was a great work to realise £10,000; but the ladies handed this sum to the League Fund, as the proceeds of their patriotic labours. On the 15th of May 1845 they held another bazaar of greater magnitude in the Covent Garden Theatre, London, which lasted for three weeks, and realised upwards of £25,000. This was the ladies' contribution towards the fund of £100,000. Edinburgh, Glasgow, Dundee, Paisley, and Dunfermline furnished stalls which for value and beauty were comparable with the contributions of the larger English towns. The chief inspirers of this Scottish manifestation of interest and zeal were undoubtedly Mrs. Renton (Mr. McLaren's mother-in-law) and Miss Eliza Wigham; while Mr. McLaren's future wife, Miss Bright, presided, at both bazaars, over the stalls furnished by the ladies of Rochdale and its neighbourhood.[1]

---

[1] Whilst we are becoming accustomed to women taking part in all moral and political movements, it may be interesting to quote from an article in the *Times*, written at the conclusion of the Anti-Corn-Law Bazaar, to show how much influence that great agitation had in bringing women to the front in all patriotic and beneficent work.

The bazaar, " regarded simply as a spectacle, was one of the most gorgeous ever beheld in London, but which, as a manifestation of moral power, is without a parallel in the world's history. There were aggregated there ladies who, for seventeen days, had devoted their time, their toil, and, we fear their health, with unwonted assiduity to advance the great cause of humanity and justice—ladies who had manifested an intelligence, tact, and spirit of self-sacrifice which cannot be too highly estimated or too gratefully remembered. They were not conscious of the capabilities they possessed until **they found them developed in action by the force of cir-**cumstance. . . . Collected together from **all** parts of the British Islands, those who had never seen or heard of each other in their lives found themselves encircled by friends though surrounded by strangers, community **of** feeling becoming **the basis** for community **of affection.** . . . No one could gaze for hours together, as we have done, on the continuous stream in which the crowd flowed through the hall, without being deeply impressed by the order, the forbearance, and the conciliatory demeanour of every **individual in the** vast multitude ; women went about fearless of insult, and children without danger **of** injury. It was a striking evidence of **the im-**proved culture and higher tone **of** moral feeling which **the** discussions and instructions of the League had infused into the public mind. It was a **manifestation of the intellectual and ethical character** which a **great** political **movement assumes when kept free from the** exacerbations of party."

CHAPTER XII.

CONTROVERSY WITH MR. MACAULAY.

As a party to Mr. Macaulay's election, as a public man, and a "Leaguer" deeply impressed with a sense of the evil influences of the Corn-laws, Mr. McLaren felt himself bound to endeavour to prevent a misrepresentation of his views and of the views of the electors in Parliament. With this object he entered into correspondence with Mr. Macaulay on the subject of the motion annually submitted to Parliament by Mr. Villiers, which was to the effect " that all duties on the importation of corn shall *now* cease and determine." At first the attitude assumed by the distinguished representative of the city was not discouraging. On 8th May 1841 Mr. Macaulay wrote :—

" We are not likely to come to the discussion of our Corn-law plan for some time. We shall be beaten on Lord Sandon's motion by a league of landed gentlemen and old slave-drivers, mingled with two or three honest but mistaken enemies of slavery. We shall then, of course, either resign or dissolve. My own opinion, though not absolutely made up, leans at present towards resignation. I am quite satisfied that the measures which we have proposed will in no long time be carried, and I shall not be surprised if they should be carried by the very men who now lead the Opposition. I am afraid you will think the 8s. duty too high. I am convinced that it is the lowest which there is any chance of obtaining for a long time to come ; and, for my own part, I would very much rather have a fixed duty of 10s. than the present system."

Macaulay's forecast was justified by events. The Whigs were defeated both in Parliament and at the poll, and in September Sir Robert Peel became Prime Minister. But freedom from the restraints of office was not followed by the acceptance of Free Trade principles. The policy of the Whig party was to temporise on the question, and Mr. McLaren's suspicion of Mr. Macaulay's reliability as a supporter of the League received unexpected confirmation from a speech delivered by the right honourable gentleman against Villiers' motion in the House of Commons in February 1842. In this speech Mr. Macaulay declared that in the then existing circumstances he was not in favour of the total and immediate repeal of the Corn-laws, though he would not carry his opposition to the extent of voting against the parliamentary champion of the cause. Mr. McLaren, indeed, was not unprepared for this answer. In a letter written some time afterwards, giving an account of his relations with Macaulay at this period, he said :—

" Shortly before that date (February 21, 1842, when the speech against Mr. Villiers' motion was delivered), a petition in favour of the total and immediate repeal of the Corn-laws had been signed in Edinburgh by 27,000 inhabitants. It was sent up to London by the Association, with a request that Mr. James Aytoun and myself, then in London as Anti-Corn-Law delegates, would wait on Mr. Macaulay officially as a deputation from the Association, and request him to present it to the House, on the single condition that he would support its prayer by voting for Mr. Villiers' motion. We accordingly waited on him (having made a previous appointment for that purpose) at his residence in the Albany. We stated the object of our mission, and explained what we believed to be the state of public feeling on the question in Edinburgh. He received us with great courtesy, but at the same time told us that he could not present the petition on these terms, and that he could not vote for Mr. Villiers' motion, because he was favourable to a fixed duty. We stated that, in these circumstances, our instructions were to give the petition to some other Member who would support its prayer. He assented to the propriety of this course, situated as we were, and accordingly the petition was handed to Mr. Ewart, and presented by him. Again, in 1843 a petition, signed by upwards of 30,000 inhabitants, praying for total and immediate repeal, was sent to the Hon. Fox Maule, and presented by him, because neither of our Members would support its prayer, as we had ascertained from their answers to our letters. And I may mention here that this course met with the unanimous approval of Mr. Moncreiff (the present Lord Moncreiff), Mr. Craufurd (afterwards Lord Ardmillan), Mr. Montgomery Bell, and the other learned gentlemen who now differ with us on some other points."

Before the presentation of this second petition, Macaulay had written a letter to John Wigham, which was interpreted as a retrogression on the question of Free Trade, and as a direct defiance of the opinions of his constituents :—

" In speculation," he said, " my opinion is that all protecting duties whatever are bad—that protecting duties on the necessaries of life are of all protecting duties the worst, and that a protecting duty raised on foreign corn according to a sliding scale is a protecting duty of the worst sort, raised in the worst way. But I do not, even in speculation, pronounce all duties on foreign corn to be indefensible; for I conceive that there are cases in which such duties, when levied in good faith, solely for the purpose of revenue, may be justified. When I come from the speculative to the practical question, I am met by great difficulties. I am firmly convinced that the total and immediate repeal of the Corn-laws, whether desirable or not, is unattainable; and that the only effect of demanding such repeal, in the way in which some of my friends demand it, and of rejecting all fellowship with the supporters of a moderate fixed duty, will be to prevent all change for the better, and to prolong the existence of the sliding scale."

And he added, "Thinking thus, I will not pledge myself to vote for total and immediate repeal, *and I am perfectly ready to take the consequences.*" Nevertheless Macaulay, in spite of this refusal to consider himself pledged, had, in the same session in which he delivered an adverse speech and withheld his vote, supported another amendment moved by Villiers and directed against the Peel Government in favour of total repeal. It was in this speech that Mr. Macaulay denounced the Peel tariff in vigorous phrases, which have passed into the stock-in-trade of the hack orator of our day. He described Sir Robert Peel's plan as "a measure which unsettles everything and settles nothing; a measure which pleases nobody; a measure which nobody asks for; a measure which will neither extend trade nor relieve distress." And again in 1843 and 1844 he voted with Mr. Villiers. His position was this: he was in favour of Free Trade in principle, subject to duties "levied in good faith solely for the purposes of revenue;" but he did not believe that Free Trade, with the modifications which he considered necessary, could then be carried, and as a party man he was unwilling to make the repeal of the Corn-laws a vital principle of policy.

This view Mr. Macaulay elaborated and reiterated in a long correspondence which he conducted with Mr. McLaren, in which each sought to gain the other over to his position —Mr. McLaren labouring to induce a parliamentary representative whose talents he admired to accept the policy as well as the platform of the League; Mr. Macaulay devoting many hours of a busy life, with other urgent claims upon his time and energies, to earnest efforts to win from the League and for the Whig party a constituent whose probity and capacity he held in equal respect. Evidently a common ground of argument could only be reached by

the conversion of one or the other; and as the controversy 1842
proceeded the impossibility of agreement became increasingly
evident.   By and by Mr. Macaulay's sensitiveness and Mr.
McLaren's views of duty brought the two allies, though
really not far apart, into stern conflict.   Even in the first
letter of the series, which merely acknowledges receipt of
some Anti-Corn-Law literature, the city Member marked
out the difference which made ultimate agreement impossible.
It was the root difference between the Ministerialist and the
Radical—the man of expediency and "the man in earnest."

ALBANY, LONDON, January 29, 1842.

MY DEAR SIR,—I have to thank you for several very interesting documents.   It is hardly necessary for me to tell you that
my views as to the corn question agree with yours, except perhaps that my hopes of success are less sanguine, and my disposition to accept any tolerable compromise consequently greater.
Of any tolerable compromise there is, I fear me, not the smallest
chance, and we may therefore adjourn, I am sorry to say, to a
distant period the discussion of the question whether it would
be right to accept a large instalment of what is our due and to
waive our claim to the rest.—Ever yours very truly,

T. B. MACAULAY.

The following letter, evidently in reply to one suggesting Urgency admitted, but aboli-tion im-possible.
an advance along the line in support of Free Trade, is
specially interesting because of the accuracy with which
the writer forecasted the public policy of the Non-Intrusion
party in the event of disruption from the State Church:—

ALBANY, LONDON, April 13, 1842.

MY DEAR SIR,— . . . I agree with you in thinking that the
Corn-laws, as the worst of all commercial abuses, ought to go
first; then perhaps the sugar-duties ought to follow.   But we
cannot effect this at present, and when we shall effect it is quite
in the dark.   Are we, therefore, to prop up all other monopolies?

Far from it. I do not think we are beginning our inroad on this system at the right end. But, after all, the whole system hangs together, while at whatever end we effect a breach, the whole is in danger of ruin. Hitherto the landlords have pointed to the protection enjoyed by various trades. Every trade, as soon as its protection is menaced, has pointed to the great monopoly of the landlords. One abuse has been made the plea for another, and we have gone on in what Lord John well called a circle of false reasoning. "Why is bread to have protection?" "Because shoes, cork, &c., have protection." "Why are shoes and cork to be protected?" "Because bread is protected." It would be best to reform the whole system together. It would be next best to begin with the greatest evil, the corn monopoly. But it is a good thing to begin to reform anywhere. And I have no doubt that just as your High Churchmen, if they lose their benefices, will all turn Voluntaries before long, so will all the small protected interests, as soon as they lose their protection, fall with zeal never before known on the great interest which still retains an undue protection. On these grounds I intend, in the main, to support with all my power the new tariff; and I trust that you will think that I act rightly. If we choose to join with the Tories to oppose it, we shall certainly throw it out and unseat the Government. But I should think a change of Ministry at present a great public calamity. We cannot at present carry any really good measure. We can only maintain good principles, and those principles we shall maintain with more freedom and effect in opposition.—Yours very truly, T. B. MACAULAY.

The progress of events illustrated only too painfully and conclusively the soundness of Mr. McLaren's view as to the urgency of the question. Trade was depressed; wages were low and bread was dear; famine stalked through the land, and a dangerous social agitation was threatened. Writing from Rochdale in August 1842, Mr. Bright said:—"Our prophecies are being fulfilled. The people are all out or are ceasing to work. They refuse to work until they have their rights. Wages and food they demand. The towns in this district are nearly all in the hands of vast bodies of workmen and women. Has the revolution commenced? It looks very probable. The authorities are powerless. Troops cannot be had for every body of turnouts. We are truly in a strange and fearful position. All are peaceable as to person and property, but hunger in a few days must overturn good resolutions. What will Peel, Graham, and Co. say?"

Conscious of the danger to public order caused by the increasing popular distress, fortified by evidences of local opinion in favour of the policy of total and immediate repeal, and strongly advised by his English friends to use all his influence to gain Mr. Macaulay, and with him the Whig party, to the platform of the League, Mr. McLaren continued the correspondence with his parliamentary representative, traversing and retraversing all the ground of controversy, urging the claims of the electors to representation of their opinions in Parliament, citing proofs of popular sympathy with the League, answering the frequently-used excuse for delay, that though the cities were for repeal the counties were not, by pointing to the opinions of the intelligent Scotch farmers; and above all, claiming support for " total and immediate repeal," because justice, and therefore wise statesmanship, demanded the abolition of the Corn-laws. Mr. McLaren apparently had not made copies of his own letters, but so much may be gathered from the replies which follow.[1] Thus put on his defence, Mr. Macaulay wrote the series of able letters which follow :—

---

[1] This was in accordance with Mr. McLaren's usual practice. He appears not to have made copies of his letters, unless when he contemplated publication, either by his own desire or at the instance of his correspondent.

ALBANY, LONDON, *January 4, 1843.*

MY DEAR SIR,—I am not quite sure that I fully understand you; but if I do, I am afraid that I must differ from you. You seem to me to lay down this principle, that no revenue ought to be raised for the exigencies of the State by duties of customs on the importation of any article from abroad, unless an equivalent duty be imposed on the production of that article at home. I have not studied these questions very deeply, but I have a strong impression that no financier or political economist ever maintained such a proposition as this.

I hold the doctrines of Free Trade as strongly, I believe, as any person who has ever written about them; but I cannot admit that when a Government wants money, and is under the necessity of raising money by taxation, it ought to reject every tax which may interfere with the freedom of trade. That a tax interferes with the freedom of trade I admit is an objection, and a grave one. But there are, as you well know, objections to all taxes; and the business of the Legislature is to choose the least evil among the evils which present themselves. Though it is an evil that a tax should interfere with the freedom of trade, it may be a greater evil that a tax should be such as can only be levied by a most vexatious process or by means of a very costly machinery. The advantage which the customs have over other modes of taxation is this, that the collection causes scarcely any annoyance to the body of the people, and that the expense of agency is exceedingly small in comparison of the sum raised. Now this seems to me to be a sufficient reason for laying duties or customs on the importation of many articles, though the production of these articles at home is not taxed. Take timber, for example. I think a duty on the importation of timber defensible in a country which, like ours, requires a large revenue. The duty is got with very little deduction. So bulky an article is not likely to be smuggled. The payment is made at the port, and the body of the people never see the face of the collectors. But suppose that, in order to prevent any interference with the freedom of trade, we were to lay an equivalent tax on British timber, what vexation must inevitably follow, unless, indeed, the tax were to

be a mere dead-letter. An army of spies must be paid to fill all
our woods and parks, and to besiege the shops of the joiners and
builders. I therefore think it right to tax imported timber,
and yet not to tax British timber. This, you say, acts as a protection to the British timber. I admit it. I cannot help it. It
is not my object to protect British timber. My object is in good
faith to get revenue which must be got somewhere, and to get
it in the least vexatious and in the least chargeable way. If I
cannot do this without incidentally affecting the freedom of trade,
this is an evil. But still it may be the less of two evils.

I am persuaded that you will, on consideration, agree with me
that, in imposing taxes for purposes of revenue, freedom of trade
is only one of several important considerations by which the
policy of a Government ought to be guided, and that it may be
right to lay duties on the importation of an article from abroad
without taxing the production of that article at home.

Whether corn be an article which ought to be thus dealt
with is quite another question—a question respecting which I
have still much to learn, and on which I have not given, in Parliament or elsewhere, an opinion. I content myself with saying
that on the question of duty imposed for the purpose of protection, my mind is made up.

I should be glad to learn whether we differ as to the principles which I have laid down. To me—perhaps from not
having thought very much on financial science—they seem im-
pregnable.—Yours very truly, T. B. MACAULAY.

ALBANY, LONDON, *January* 12, 1843.

MY DEAR SIR,—I am glad to find that we do not differ on
any matter of principle. We both think duties imposed for the
purpose of protection indefensible. We both think that it may
sometimes be fit to impose duties on the importation of articles
the home production of which is not taxed. We both see that
such duties must to a certain extent operate as a protection.
But we think that, for the purposes of revenue, that evil must
sometimes be incurred. Whether any particular article is of such
a kind that it ought to be taxed when imported, and not taxed

when produced at home, is a question which must be determined, as we both agree, by many considerations of convenience. You think with me that timber, in the present state of our finances, is such an article. The question whether corn be such an article is not to me equally clear. You confidently pronounce that it is not; I must examine into that matter much more deeply before I pronounce.

As to the credit which I may gain or lose, it is the smallest part of my care. I will most willingly consent to be called a mere party man all my life, if by taking that name on myself I can promote the abolition, or even the mitigation, of the present system of monopoly.

I will not detain you longer, as you must be busy at this time. I wish you a good meeting, and unmolested by the Chartists.— Ever yours truly,   T. B. MACAULAY.

ALBANY, LONDON, February 24, 1843.

MY DEAR SIR,— . . . . The only question between us is one of fact. Is it the fact that a duty on home-grown corn could be collected with as little risk of evasion, as little charge of collection, and as little interference with the freedom and comfort of home life as a duty on foreign corn? If this be so, I at once admit that there ought to be no duty on foreign corn for purposes of revenue without a countervailing duty on home-grown corn. But as to this fact I feel considerable doubt. And that doubt is not removed by the circumstance that most versatile and unscrupulous debaters, whose great object is to defend the sliding scale, take the view contained in the speech which you have sent me.

I have been a little misunderstood by you if you think that I am friendly to a duty on corn for purposes of revenue. I have no decided opinion on the fiscal question. All that I say is this, the fiscal question and the commercial question are quite distinct, and must be decided on different principles. As to the commercial question, I have made up my mind fully. As to the fiscal question, I see very much to be said on both sides, and I will not give a decided opinion.

"As to the question of the Corn-laws generally, I wrote yesterday to Mr. Wigham. I daresay that my conduct will be much censured; but my mind is made up. I am certain that the great object of the Tory squires is to effect a complete breach between the fixed-duty men and the no-duty men. They have for a time succeeded. While that breach continues, the sliding scale is in perfect security. The experience of a very few months will, I hope, teach many of my friends that it is far better to take half, and only half, than to stickle for all and get nothing. But be this as it may, I shall leave with them the responsibility of throwing away what is attainable in the pursuit of what is unattainable, and of dissolving the alliance which at last general election seemed to be firmly established between all who are honestly desirous to give a large extension to the freedom of trade.—Ever yours truly,   T. B. MACAULAY.

1843

ALBANY, LONDON, *March* 1, 1843.

MY DEAR SIR,—It was quite unnecessary in you to assure me that you meant me no personal disrespect. Your expressions were quite within the limits of courteous discussion. Had it been otherwise, I know how to make allowance for a little controversial warmth. You will extend to me the same indulgence if I should happen to need it.

I repeat, I consider your proceedings as imprudent and your objects as unattainable; that I believe it to be utterly impossible to obtain at present a perfectly free trade in corn, and that, in my opinion, the only way in which you will be able to obtain any important mitigation of the existing evil is by joining with more moderate reformers to support a fixed duty. I do not say an 8s. duty, but the lowest upon which we can agree to co-operate— perhaps a 6s. duty, perhaps a 5s. duty.

At this you express great amazement, and say that either I must of late have been shut up from the world, or must fancy that you have been so shut up.

You are quite right. I do firmly believe that you have been so shut up. A man may be shut up from the world, in my sense, though he lives in a great city, though he reads much, speaks much, hears much, attends meetings of many thousands of people. In a society composed of many elements, he whose converse is with one element alone may properly be said to be subject to all the illusions of a recluse. I say this not of you alone. I have said so to other valuable men,—to my friend Adam Black, for example. You live in a great city, it is true; but great cities do not make up the whole of the United Kingdom. And you seem to me to be under a complete delusion on that subject. You talk of public opinion; but you mean only the public opinion of that portion of the nation which is crowded together by a hundred thousand to the square mile. I need no other proof of what I say than your letter, which is before me. You describe strongly, and I believe justly, the intense feeling about the Corn-laws which exists at Edinburgh and Glasgow; and this feeling seems to you to be the same thing with the national feeling. I am not, I assure you, so completely shut up from the world as not to be quite aware that a strong feeling in favour of a perfectly free corn trade exists in most towns of 10,000 inhabitants and upwards, and in none more than in Edinburgh. But is the whole rural population to go for nothing? You must admit, I think, that almost the whole strength of the party which is for perfectly free trade in corn lies in towns of 10,000 inhabitants and upwards. The inhabitants of the small market-towns are generally, as far as I have observed, more prejudiced in favour of agricultural protection than even the neighbouring farmers. Now, what proportion of the people of the United Kingdom lives in the towns of 10,000 inhabitants and upwards? In England, I think, not quite a third. In Scotland, certainly not a third. In Ireland, not a tenth.

I give you a great deal indeed if I give you seven or eight millions of the people, if told by the head. There remain about twenty millions. Are they with you? Of the counties of England which may be said to be purely agricultural, there are about thirty which have more inhabitants and more voters than Edinburgh. There are several, Devonshire, Kent, Somersetshire, Norfolk, which have more inhabitants and more voters than Edinburgh and Glasgow put together. You tell me of the strong feeling of Edinburgh and Glasgow against a fixed duty, as if that were to decide the question; and there is not one of the thirty counties of which I speak where a candidate who is not for an extravagant amount of protection dares to show his face. At this moment a division of Warwickshire, with more inhabitants than Edinburgh, is vacant. The Tories will walk over the course, I am told, because no gentleman who is even for a modification of the Corn-laws will have the least chance of support. All these circumstances you seem to me to overlook altogether; and you merely repeat, what I admit, that the Liberal electors of Edinburgh have a strong objection to any tax on corn. This is a decisive argument certainly, if the only object which you suppose me to have in view is the keeping of my seat for Edinburgh. But I am sure you think better of me, and that you would not address to me any reasonings grounded on interests merely selfish. Let us then quit all local considerations, and speak, not about my seat, which, God knows, I would gladly resign to-day if by so doing I could make the quarter loaf a farthing cheaper, but about the public interests.

I am certain you must mistake the cry of those who surround you, and with whose cry your own is mingled, for the voice of the nation. I know that yours is the stirring party and the noisy party; but I know that it is the weaker party—weaker in numbers, in wealth, in constitutional power, in physical power. What, then, ought to be your course? I should say to my friends, to consider all as with you who are not wholly against you; to be grateful to everybody who is disposed to assist you in getting half or a quarter of what you want. What is your course? To reject all allies who will not go the extreme length with you—to treat Lord John like Mr. Christopher,[1] and Lord Fitzwilliam like the Duke of Cleveland. If this policy answers, I am a very bad politician.

But, you say, it cannot be wise to support a fixed duty, for no great party is for a fixed duty. The Tories are not for it. The Anti-Corn-Law League are not for it. No public meeting clamours for it. No petition asks for it. A sliding scale has

---

[1] Protectionist Member for Lincoln.

friends; total repeal has friends; a fixed duty has no friends. Surely you are not the dupe of your own fallacy. Might not all this have been said of every compromise that ever took place in the world? Was ever a compromise made on the terms which either of the contending parties had demanded? Take the boundary dispute between England and the United States. " We have a right to all this territory," said England. " No; we have a right to it all," answers Jonathan. Neither the one nor the other proposed to halve the territory. At last, after years of bickering, extreme inconvenience and danger induce both to be content with what, at first, would have satisfied neither. Each is grumbling. Each thinks that too much has been ceded. But still the compromise is made. I think this a parallel case to your Corn-law controversy. I know that, at present, a fixed duty is equally detested by you and by the Tories; but I know also that they like it better than a perfectly free trade, and that you like it better than a sliding scale. . When the struggle has lasted a certain time, when you are afraid of getting nothing and they of losing everything, you will all, as has happened ten thousand times, be glad to take some intermediate measure. The effect of the course now taken by your party will be that you will have to wait for such an intermediate measure some years longer than is at all necessary.

These are my views as to the public. My seat at Edinburgh is not of the least value to me unless I can hold it with honour and independence. Nor shall I ever suffer any selfish considerations to guide my conduct as to a question which is so important to the welfare of the whole Empire.—Ever yours truly,

T. B. MACAULAY.

Mr. Macaulay's letters are evidence of the ability, the vigour, and the courtesy with which Duncan McLaren conducted the controversy. But the leaders of the League, while recognising the value of the service Mr. McLaren was rendering in trying to persuade Mr. Macaulay to more active effort, their own leanings were rather in the direction of taking public action against the Member whom they believed to be misrepresenting his constituents as well as his convic-

tions, and also against the ex-Minister whose obduracy was
the mainstay of the Whig policy of expediency.   Joseph
Sturge, in an appreciative letter, said, " I think T. Macaulay
will not find his standard of political expediency answer quite
so well in the long-run as he calculated upon."   In February
1843 Mr. Bright wrote : " Macaulay is a Total Repealer at
heart and in principle, and only holds back because he is an
attaché of the old Whig party.   Therefore I think it would
be perfectly just to turn him out if his constituents are
Total Repealers.   The wisdom of this course depends upon
the probability there is of sending a better man in his
place.   If he were to resign and stand again on *fixed-duty*
grounds, and be returned, we should be greatly injured.
If a Total Repealer could be got in, the reaction would be
all in our favour ; and I am persuaded that an election on
Total Repeal principles, if successful, would be an immense
advantage to the cause.   Now all depends on the temper
of your constituency.   If a large majority of Liberals are
staunch to the League faith, the experiment would be well
tried ; if not, I would not recommend it.   You can judge
probably better than any one else."   Whatever might be
the issue, Mr. McLaren was now convinced that further
letter controversy would be profitless, and that on the points
raised an appeal must be made to the public.   He appears
to have intimated as much to the city Member, at the same
time expressing his deep regret that a statesman so gifted
and high-minded should subordinate his own convictions of
what was right and just to the momentary exigencies of
party.   He solemnly referred him to the law and the testimony as the safe guide of conduct—" To him who knoweth
to do good and doeth it not, to him it is sin." [1]

---

[1] James iv. 17.

To this exhortation Mr. Macaulay at once replied:—

ALBANY, LONDON, *March 7, 1843.*

MY DEAR SIR,—I agree with you that it would not at present be of any use to continue our controversy.

I have given no distinct answer to the question about Villiers' motion, for this simple reason, that I do not know what the terms of the motion are to be.

I quite agree with you that "to him who knoweth to do good and doeth it not, to him it is sin." If I vote against Villiers' motion, it will be solely because I am convinced that by supporting it I should be doing not good, but harm.—Ever yours truly,   T. B. MACAULAY.

McLa-'s fide-

The temptation to Mr. McLaren to surrender was great, and if he had been a self-seeking man it would doubtless have been irresistible. The Whig party was powerful, and it had many gifts to bestow for such a man as the leader of the Liberalism of Edinburgh and of Scottish Dissent. It could smooth his way to a political career; it could elevate his social position; it could hold out the prospect of office and the patronage of offices; it could secure for him the association and the support of great political leaders, who believed with Mr. Macaulay that he possessed in an eminent degree the faculty for statesmanship, and anticipated for him, if he chose to become a partisan, high party rank and a bright political career. What had the League to offer as a counter-attraction? The sacrifice of time and money and friendships; arduous labour, of which the end was not in sight, ever becoming heavier and more exacting in its demands. His personal sense of fidelity to a great public cause was, however, strengthened by the consciousness of the confidence reposed in him by thousands of his countrymen, and by the example of his companions in the struggle. He knew he was associated with men who had left all at the call of national duty and in obedience to the inspiration of Christian patriotism,—business, money-making, personal and political friendships, sweet domestic comforts, aye, and domestic duties and responsibilities.

1843

Patriotism of League leaders.

At the bidding of the higher duty Cobden was letting his private business go to ruin, and, very shortly, domestic grief was added to his anxieties. In the latter end of May of this year (1843) he wrote his fellow-labourer in Edinburgh: "My little girl, six months old, was a week since in blooming health. Last night my boy called me out of the Bristol meeting to announce the melancholy intelligence that she had been seized with convulsions, and her innocent spirit had been called hence. This is my first trial as a parent. You can sympathise with me." In February Mr. Bright wrote: "Under pressure to go to Sheffield. My brother ill. My business, my friends, and my country!—what am I to decide for? Cobden says I *must* go and be returned, even if I stay at home half the session. The League must fight and win a battle." Such was the spirit of the men with whom Mr. McLaren was associated, and he was kin with them. He was not made of yielding stuff. Moreover, having faith in the invincibility of truth and justice, he was not afraid of the host encamped around him—the aristocracy, the monopolists, probably the majority of the electors, as yet not fully instructed, and the chiefs of the parties, who take their direction from electoral majorities. He believed the League was on the winning side. "We rise higher after every blow," reported Mr. Bright in reference to the attacks of Brougham, Roebuck, and Peel, which he said "have done us essential service." And this was Mr. McLaren's experience of the progress of events in Edinburgh and in Scotland. Public opinion was steadily growing in favour of "total and immediate repeal."

He saw that compromise, even though it were morally permissible, would be a tactical mistake, and he would not declare for compromise to retain the friendship of Mr. Macaulay or to purchase the favour of the Whig party.

Public meeting in Edinburgh.

But he made a further effort to put both right, this time by public speech, and not by private letter. At a meeting of the Anti-Corn-Law Association of Edinburgh he urged the right of constituencies to have their views represented in Parliament, and among other proofs adduced the fact that 1100 electors of the city had contributed to the League fund as evidence that Mr. Macaulay's constituents were in favour of the total and immediate abolition of the Corn-laws. Alluding apparently to a letter from Macaulay to the Anti-Corn-Law Association (which has not been found), he described Mr. Macaulay's argument in favour of a revenue duty as the greatest fallacy that could be stated, for there was no difference between a duty for protection and a duty for revenue; and he was surprised and amazed that a man of Mr. Macaulay's sagacity and talent should have had recourse to such a distinction. He did not, as Mr. Macaulay in his reply assumed, admit that the majority of the people and of the aristocracy were against the policy of the League. But his argument was this :—Supposing they were adverse, what does it matter? If the people are opposed to it, it is because they do not yet understand it; if the aristocratic classes are hostile, it is because they assume their interests are in danger. But ignorance and self-interest cannot long withstand truth and justice; and truth and justice are with the League; so is the logic of debate; so are the Liberal electors of Edinburgh. Proceeding next to deal with the objection that the chiefs of the parties were against the League, Mr. McLaren continued :—" He tells us, last of all—as if it were the most

important point in his estimation—that we are in a small
minority among the chiefs of parties. Let us tell him in
reply that the time has happily gone by when the enlightened public opinion of the middle classes can be turned
aside or controlled by the chiefs of parties. United, as in
the present case, we can succeed without their support, but
they can do nothing without ours. Our movement is not
directed for the purpose of interfering with the chiefs of
parties. If they shall think fit to place themselves at its
head, we will go forward, as we have hitherto done, with all
the power and energy which our principles, and our union,
and the sympathies of the enlightened portion of our fellow-
countrymen secure to us ; but if they shall place themselves
in our way to obstruct our progress, they need not be surprised if they are either trampled on in our progress or
thrown aside, that we may be enabled to proceed in our
onward course."

After the meeting Mr. McLaren at once wrote Mr.
Macaulay :—" You will see from the report in the *Scotsman*
of to-day (11th March 1843) that I have made a very easy
path for you to go forward, and that to go backward is impossible. In fact, every one expects you will go forward,
and that there can be no doubt about it." But Macaulay
refused to say he would go forward. He was irritated at
the pressure to which he was subjected, and refused to be
converted to belief in the practicability of the reform demanded by the League in the then existing state of public
opinion. He replied by return of post :—

ALBANY, LONDON, *March* 13, 1843.

MY DEAR SIR,—I do not at all complain of your speech, but
I do not agree with it. You have not touched my proposition
that a perfectly free trade in corn is unattainable, and therefore
you have in my opinion done nothing.

My facts you acknowledge. You own that we have against us the majority of the people told by the head, the majority of the 800,000 electors, in other words, of the middle class, and, lastly, a very large majority of the rich, the great, and the chiefs of the parties. Then you attack all these majorities in turn. You show that each has its faults and weaknesses, and you give instances in which each has been overpowered. You attack the multitude in the language of an aristocrat, and the rich in the language of a democrat. The people are not to be regarded because they are stupid. The great are not to be regarded because they are oppressors.

My answer is this. I know that there have been instances in which numerical majorities have been forced to yield to the upper and middle classes. The refusal of the Charter is an instance. There have been instances in which the majority of the middle and lower classes have been forced to yield to the firm union of all the chiefs of parties, as in the case of the Catholic Bill. There have been instances in which the upper class has been forced to yield to the majority of the middle class. Witness the Reform Bill. But my assertion, admitted, I think, by yourself, is this, that on the subject of the Corn-laws you have against you a majority of all the three classes, low, middle, and high. Now show me an instance of a measure carried against such an opposition, and you will have shaken my argument. But this I may safely defy you to do.

One word about the chiefs of parties. Perhaps it was unwise in me to mention them in my letter. I might have guessed that an Anti-Corn-Law Association would not feel the force of that argument. But people who know anything of the way in which this country is really governed know that there is in fact a certain small class of men who have a real veto on all public measures which they agree to oppose. There must be a Government. You cannot make a Government out of men without weight, talents, knowledge, or experience; and if you did, they would soon make themselves and everything that they took up odious and ridiculous. It is quite impossible that a Ministry composed of such men as Dr. Browning, Colonel Thompson, and Mr. Wil-

liams of Coventry can ever hold power. It would expose itself
to universal contempt within three days. Try to make a list of
a Cabinet of Total and Immediate Repealers. I will engage that
you will yourself burst out a-laughing at it. Now, that the Corn-
laws will not be repealed till a Ministry takes the matter up,
you will, I suppose, admit. You must also admit that among
the supporters of immediate and total repeal there is not one
whom you would not be surprised to see even in the second
rank of a Ministry. It is very easy to declaim about throwing
the chiefs of parties aside or trampling them down, but not
so easy to understand how affairs are to be managed with
Mr. Wallace[1] at the Colonial Office, Mr. Ewart[2] at the Foreign
Office, and Mr. Hume[3] made First Commissioner of the Trea-
sury, and sent to lead the House of Lords. Nothing except
an outbreak like that which overthrew the old monarchy and
aristocracy of France can produce such an effect. I conceive,
therefore, that the unanimous declaration of the chiefs of
parties against total and immediate repeal is a very grave circumstance, and deserves much more consideration than it has
received from you.

I have not time to proceed. I can say nothing about Villiers'
motion, for he himself seems to know neither what he shall
move nor when.—Yours very truly,

T. B. MACAULAY.

Notwithstanding this letter, Macaulay was really in
closer agreement with the principles of the League than
he was willing to admit. The debate on Villiers' motion
took place in May, and Mr. Bright, who was then Mr.
McLaren's chief London correspondent, was able to report,
" Macaulay has yielded to your pressure." But he yielded
ungracefully. He complained very bitterly of the pressure
put upon him by Mr. McLaren, and he actively co-operated

---

[1] Member for Greenock. [2] Member for Dumfries Burghs.
[3] Member for Montrose Burghs.

with the Whig party in the hope of checking the growing power of the League. His personal relations with the English leaders of the movement also became increasingly unfriendly, and the Council of the League began to perceive it would be necessary to treat him not as a friend, but as an opponent. In December 1843 Mr. Bright wrote Mr. McLaren : "As to Macaulay, he is the chief of Whig 'half-way-house men.' He is a waiter not on Providence, but on the fortunes of the party to which he has tied himself. You must cure him. The constituency pill is the only medicine for his complaint. Macaulay hates us cordially, and you will have to choose between him and our principle. Lord John, it is said, is balancing, and I should not be surprised at his taking another step. There is some scheme on foot to swamp us with a fixed duty ; some coalition of aristocratic parties to accomplish this is talked of. Our Covent Garden meeting gave it a great blow. . . . The papers are consternated ; 'the great fact' grows greater hourly ; and if we remain true to each other and our great principle, our triumph is not far off. Evidently the present law is given up by all parties, and it remains for us to extinguish all hope of a compromise." In the following month he wrote : "I am glad Macaulay is becoming unpopular with you. He has no claim to be a representative of *the people*. Office has raised him out of his senses and good feeling. The late meetings and all your printing must have saturated the Scotch mind with Free Trade doctrines. Next election will help us with you, I feel certain. . . . The M.P.'s begin to fear us greatly ; and I suspect Cobden and I will be no great favourites with many of them in the House." As to Mr. McLaren's own relations to Macaulay, and the course he should follow in taking public action against him because of his practical

unfaithfulness to the cause, Mr. Bright proffered his advice
as follows :—

1843

" I see the course the *Scotsman* has taken. The only valid
excuse for him is that your Members have either already voted
with Villiers or intend to do so on the next occasion. Fox Maule
is annoyed at your disturbance of Macaulay and Craig—so, of
course, are all the Whigs. Some of them do you the injustice
of charging you with a wish to get into Parliament by turning
one of your present Members out. Of course, to damage an
opponent is with them as good a thing as to prove his cause bad.
You will not regard this, especially seeing how much the proof
in your favour preponderates.

" Now, I take it that you don't want to dislodge Macaulay and
Craig *per se*, but to make them serve you well, and in the public
meeting it will be desirable to keep out any animus against them,
and to show a steady resolve that whoever sits for Edinburgh
must give a hearty support to Free Trade. I think you may
manage so as to secure your object without driving the more
timid of your party away. Put it this way : Macaulay is and
must be a Free Trader in sentiment ; he was a member of the
late, and hopes to be of the next Government ; he is Member for
Edinburgh, and ought to serve you. Which is his first duty ?
Certainly to his own opinions and to his constituents. A good
argument for your cause may be had thus : The small boroughs
are in fetters and can't speak out—the counties are in the hands
of landlords ; from Edinburgh, then, with its free constituency, a
powerful and steady and uncompromising expression of opinion
should go forth. You can't sacrifice a great principle from personal feelings to a particular man. If the case applied to some
other borough, would the *Scotsman* take the same course ? The
case requires able management, and in no other hands should I
feel it so safe as in yours.—Ever truly your friend,

" JOHN BRIGHT."

Mr. McLaren's view of the political situation was in complete agreement with Mr. Bright's, and quite different from

Mr. Macaulay's.   He thought the times were ripe for Free Trade legislation, and held the Member's irresolution a hindrance to the accomplishment of the desired reforms. He was now not at all disposed to take a lenient view of Macaulay's conduct.   He knew well that the Member was giving the Free Trade party among his constituents little encouragement, even denying them his countenance at the great meetings addressed by Cobden, Bright, Colonel Thompson, and others, and sending, in answer to an invitation to attend the Music Hall demonstration (January 1844), a note of declinature so curt that it elicited sounds of disapprobation from an audience composed of constituents who had hitherto been proud of their distinguished representative.

At a meeting of the Anti-Corn-Law Association held in Edinburgh on 22nd April 1844, Mr. McLaren said they were now prepared to tell their Members that unless they not only voted for Mr. Villiers' motion, but were prepared to give it a cordial and welcome support, the constituency must look out for other Members when their term of office expired.   He thought Mr. Gibson-Craig was with them already, and he hoped, or at least he wished, that Mr. Macaulay would take the same course.   " If he did not, their duty was to do the thing that was right, leaving him to do what he thought right. . . . With regard to what had been said by Bailie Gray as to Mr. Macaulay being fettered by his party, he thought that he (Bailie Gray) had hit the nail on the head.   If Mr. Macaulay had not been a member of the late Government, and if he did not expect to be a member of the next, he would now have been found fighting in the foremost ranks of Corn-law repeal; and this should be a lesson to them that, in looking to fill their Members' seats in case of a general election, they should neither look to men who were in place nor to those who were expecting places."

The Association unanimously passed a resolution expressing a hope that the city's representatives would support the immediate and entire abolition of all duties on the importation of foreign corn; and in particular, that they would be prepared to give their cordial and unqualified support to Mr. Villiers' motion for the immediate and entire abolition of these duties. By an overwhelming majority another resolution was carried recommending the timely selection of candidates for next general election holding views on the question of Free Trade in unison with the opinions of the great body of the electors.

The timely and effective action of the Edinburgh Association afforded the Council of the League great satisfaction. Mr. Bright wrote: " I rejoice at the result. Such a decisive demonstration cannot fail to have a powerful influence on the opinions and policy of the Whig party. They are an infatuated and imbecile party, and are every day working their own destruction. After all, I have no expectation Macaulay will resign. You may as well be prepared with a candidate in case he should try resigning and stand again to prove his hold on your electoral body. . . . I expect the Whigs would be consternated somewhat, for your city is regarded as their stronghold; but everywhere with a leader of tact and courage the mass of the voters are in favour of thoroughgoing principles." In another letter Mr. Bright remarked: " I know exactly what the lawyers (the Parliament House supporters of Mr. Macaulay) mean, but I can't see how you can act otherwise. It is no use holding up true principles unless we are prepared to urge the representatives to adopt them. And then Macaulay's refusal is doubtless caused by his connection with the Whigs, and the League is not a pleasant subject with them. . . . I hope the effect of your proceedings will be salutary upon waverers in other quarters."

Mr. Macaulay was greatly incensed. On 1st May 1844 he wrote a long letter in reply to the resolutions of the Association. In the first place he sought to establish the identity of his views with those of the Anti-Corn-Law Association. He wished, he said, to see the Corn-laws totally repealed, and he should vote in 1844, as he did in 1843, for Mr. Villiers' motion. " Of what do you complain ? " he asked. " Of my opinions respecting Free Trade ? They are your own. Of my votes ? They have been such as you requested me and are now requesting me to give. In what division on the Corn-laws have I been in a different lobby from Mr. Villiers and Mr. Cobden ? I remember none. My crime is simply this, that I have recommended union; that I have refused to concur in a policy which tends to divide against itself a force already too weak. As I have acted I will continue to act. When a motion is made for the total repeal of the Corn-laws, I think it right to mark my opinion by my vote. But I am certain that the total repeal will never take place till the views of a large part of the agricultural population have undergone a great change, and I apprehend that such a change in the views of such a population must be gradual." In short, he did not think the country ripe for a reform which he desired, and while in agreement with the Anti-Corn-Law Leaguers on the question of political economy, he was against them on the question of practical politics. " It is easy," he proceeded, " for the members of any Anti-Corn-Law League to deceive themselves about their strength. They are generally inhabitants of great towns. Everybody with whom they converse is for Free Trade. If they attend a meeting on the subject of the Corn-laws, they see every hand held up for total and immediate repeal. No supporter of the sliding scale, no supporter of a fixed duty, can obtain a hearing. It is not strange that even people so intelligent as my constituents should go home from such meetings with the conviction that the voice of the nation is the voice of the League, and that the good cause is on the point of triumphing. I am certain that you deceive yourselves. The House of Lords is against you almost to a man. But this is the smallest of the obstacles which lie in your way. If the House of Commons were with you, the Lords might find it necessary to yield. But you have against you a great majority of the House of Commons. If the constituent body were with you, you might hope to procure at the next election a House of Commons favourable to your views. But you have against you, I grieve to say, a majority of the constituent body."

But retaliation on the League was not the chief motive of Mr. Macaulay's elaborate epistle. Looking on Mr. McLaren as the mainspring of that organisation in Edinburgh, he determined, if possible, to crush his political influence; to hold him up to public reprobation as the utterer of " such counsels" as " have often brought gain to the demagogue who gives them," but " have never brought anything but disaster to the ignorant whom they have misled." Assuredly Mr. Macaulay must have been very angry when he penned the concluding paragraph, which too obviously recalls the prayer beginning, " I thank Thee, O Lord, that I am not as other men." " I see that one gentleman who harangued the late meeting favoured his hearers with new definitions of Toryism, of Liberalism, and of hypocrisy. According to this teacher of politics and morals, a Member of Parliament who does not submissively conform to the

voice of his constituents is essentially a Tory, and if he calls
himself a Liberal, is guilty of adding hypocrisy to Toryism.
My notions of right and wrong have been learned in a
different school.   I have been in the habit of considering a
man who injured his country in order to curry favour with
his constituents, not as a Liberal, but as a knave.   I do
not believe that Edinburgh will ever send to the House of
Commons a man abject enough to sit there on such terms;
at all events, I will not be that man.   If you wish to be so
represented, you can have no difficulty in finding an in-
triguing sycophant every way qualified for the purpose.   It
will be for you to consider whether your dearest rights can
be safely intrusted to the care of one who is destitute of
honesty, courage, and self-respect.   As for myself, while I
continue to be honoured with the confidence of the electors
of Edinburgh, I will attempt to show my gratitude not by
adulation and obsequiousness, but by manly rectitude; and
if they shall be pleased to dismiss me, I trust that though
I may lose their suffrages I shall retain their esteem."

Effect of
Mr. Mac-
aulay's
letter.

This letter did much to forfeit for Mr. Macaulay the suffrages and esteem of his constituents.   It did no harm to
Mr. McLaren.   In the Association Mr. Macaulay's friends
did not resist a motion containing a declaration that there
was much in his letter of which they disapproved; and
amid enthusiastic applause another resolution was unanimously carried expressing thanks to Mr. McLaren, and
assuring him of "the high confidence of the meeting in his
sincere and disinterested devotedness to the interests of the
Association, gratitude for his unwearied exertions in the
cause of Free Trade, and especially for his valuable services
in twice superintending the collection of the contributions
to the Anti-Corn-Law League, in which he gratuitously performed an immense amount of labour."

Mr. R. R. Blyth, in seconding this resolution, which was proposed by Mr. Archibald Thomson, interpreted it as "a practical refutation of the groundless insinuations contained in Mr. Macaulay's letter." On this episode the Edinburgh Whig party had the good sense to preserve a discreet silence. Mr. Prentice, editor of the *Manchester Times*, who happened to be present at the meeting, spontaneously certified that Mr. McLaren was considered by the Council of the League the most efficient auxiliary they had in the country; and the *Edinburgh Weekly Chronicle*, in commenting on the proceedings, lamented Mr. Macaulay's letter as the "betrayal of a pettiness unworthy of his high character;" adding, "The plain insinuation of sinister motives which he throws out against a citizen not more remarkable for intellectual eminence than for inflexible integrity, and more distinguished for both endowments than any other individual it would be easy to name, is contemptible in the last degree. Mr. Macaulay has mistaken his man."

If Mr. Macaulay forgot for the moment the ability as well as the character of the opponent against whom he directed his wrathful explosion, he was quickly reminded of both. Mr. McLaren answered for himself, and with powerful effect. He did not make use of offensive epithets, but he did not conceal the scorn he felt for the scorn of of his antagonist. He expressed his abhorrence for the sentiment imputed to him by Mr. Macaulay, that Members are bound to vote against their conscientious convictions, even to the injury of their country, to please their constituents, and challenged the production of anything he had said to justify the imputation to him of such a plea. He showed that Mr. Macaulay was not by any means the immaculate Corn-law abolitionist and supporter of the League he was ever anxious to make his constituents believe him to be. Out of his own mouth he condemned him, appealing to the declaration in favour of a duty for revenue contained in the letters written to Mr. Wigham in answer to the attempt, now studiously and carefully made, to convey the impression that he had never expressed opinions in favour of any duty or revenue, and that he had always opposed a fixed duty for protection. Nay, in that letter to Mr. Wigham, Mr. Macaulay had distinctly refused to promise to apply the principles which he now told the Association he had always supported, for he had explicitly and emphatically declared, " I will not pledge myself to support total and immediate repeal, and I am perfectly ready to take the consequences." Further, in the presence of Mr. Moncreiff, of Mr. Craufurd (afterwards Lord Ardmillan), and other Parliament House political chiefs, he quoted the testimony of Mr. Macaulay's most devoted adherents against himself. " Who," he asked, are the parties that argued incessantly that Mr. Macaulay was conscientiously opposed to a total and immediate repeal, and in favour of a small duty either for revenue or protection ? " He answered, " They were Mr. Macaulay's own friends and supporters ; " and pointing to chapter and verse in support of this answer, he did not meet a single denial. He repeated and justified his former contention that it was not scruple of conscience, but party connection, that made Mr. Macaulay oppose the voice of the great body of his constituents when he refused to present their petition in favour of total and immediate repeal, and spoke against Mr. Villiers' motion in February 1842 ; that " any man who might thus set the opinions of his constituents at defiance acted on Tory principles, and, if a professed Liberal, only added practical hypocrisy to Toryism ; " and that if party or other considerations prevented him or any other man similarly situated from truly representing the sentiments of those who elected him on the great public question of the day, justice and fairness required that he should resign his seat. In other words, he held that the Member of Parliament is chosen to advance the interests of his constituents and not his own, and that if personal interest or party connection require him to misrepresent the known views of his constituents, as Mr. Macaulay confessedly had done in his speech against Mr. Villiers' motion in 1842, he should resign his seat. In that speech Mr. Macaulay had objected to Mr. Villiers' motion because it contained the word *now*. "He had no objections, I daresay," Mr. McLaren continued, "to these laws being abolished next century, or after he had ceased to be Member for Edinburgh, or at any other time; but as to their being abolished *now*, he would have nothing to do with any such measure. And yet this is the man who wishes to persuade us that he has always held our opinions, and was always to be found in the same lobby with Messrs. Cobden and Villiers." Mr. Macaulay practically adopted as "an unanswerable argument" the stale fallacy of the country squires, that land would be thrown out of cultivation and that farmers would have to become shopkeepers if the Corn-laws were abolished. For he had said in his 1842 speech, "I am not disposed to take away at once all protection from the English farmer. I think that time should be allowed to enable him to transfer his capital from one branch of industry to another; and therefore I consider *now* in the honourable Member for Wolverhampton's motion objectionable;" and in 1843 he had written a letter affirming that his views were unchanged, and that he could give no pledge regarding future votes.

Nearly eighteen months previously Mr. McLaren had examined and satisfactorily answered this plea for delay on the ground of consideration for the farmer. At one of the meetings addressed by Mr. Bright and Mr. Cobden in Edinburgh in January 1843, Mr. McLaren showed that the interests of the farmers were far more likely to be injured than protected by a process of gradual abolition :—

"I have spoken with many farmers, and I know the opinion of others; and though they are certainly not all in favour of the entire abolition of the Corn-laws, I know of none who, if these laws were to be abolished at any rate, would not much rather that the question should be settled at once; and they gave good reasons for this opinion. If a fixed duty were once agreed to, on the plan of diminishing one shilling every year, when the farmer went to pay his rent and sought an abatement, his landlord would tell him, 'Oh, the duty's only reduced a shilling, and you have had an excellent crop; you have sustained no loss by the change; it is, therefore, not necessary for me to give you any abatement.' When he went back next year, although he had not a good crop, the landlord would have some other reason for withholding redress. He would perhaps say, 'Corn is now fetching a high price, although the quantity is not great; you are doing very well; I can give you nothing.' Another year he would refer to the high price of cattle, or sheep, or wool, as a reason for not listening to the farmer's claim. In short, he would always have some reason for not letting down the rent. (Cries of 'Hear, hear.') This is certainly the opinion of many farmers regarding the gradual abolition of the Corn-laws. In place of being in favour of the farmers—the farmers themselves being judges—the gradual abolition plan is of all plans the worst, and the one they most hate."

To his mind, therefore, the plea in which Mr. Macaulay sought justification for inaction was an exploded fallacy.

Mr. Macaulay naturally showed no abatement of resentment after the discussion in the Association, and the ready sympathy of the political friends who shared his mortification made him feel and act as a deeply wronged man. Mr. Bright reported, "The Whigs are more savage than ever against us. Fox Maule will not second Villiers' motion on account of the badgering—'bullying,' he calls it—to which Macaulay has been subjected." When Mr. Villiers' motion was brought before the House in June, both the Members voted for it, but Mr. Macaulay and his friends, in their anxiety to show they considered themselves ill-used, wronged themselves. Mr. Bright in his note to Mr. McLaren graphically described the relations of the Whig leaders to the League, and the scene in the House during the debate. "Doubtless the Whigs hate us. Nobody denies it. And yet what can be done that is not done? Most of their hatred is laid to the charge of the Leaguers of Edinburgh, because they bothered Craig and Macaulay; and yet I can see no wrong you did to goad on the shufflers. Macaulay came into the House the second night of the Corn-Law debate and lay down on a bench up in the gallery, and slept or appeared to sleep there I believe for hours. The front Opposition bench was wholly unoccupied during the whole night; and the whole question was treated by the Whigs, and by Macaulay among the rest, with the utmost contempt; and doubtless his vote was only secured by your compulsion."

Apart from the personal interests and questions involved in the controversy between Mr. Macaulay and the Edinburgh Leaguers, Mr. McLaren enunciated in the speech from which we have already quoted the principles of Independent Liberalism with which he was ever afterwards identified, and which the political party in Edinburgh and Scotland that accepted his leadership heartily endorsed. The Whig doctrine that the political principle professed in election addresses, and accepted by the electors, could be held in abeyance for an indefinite period in the supposed interests of the party, or at the bidding of a small section of it, he repudiated

1844

as fatal to all reform, and as practically Toryism plus hypocrisy. He maintained that Liberal Members of Parliament were bound to be in earnest about the business which they were elected to advance, and were faithless to the cause of Reform when they sought excuses for postponement instead of pressing for legislative settlement at the earliest possible moment. He saw that if all Corn-Law abolitionists in principle were like Mr. Macaulay—afraid to proceed to legislation lest they should temporarily injure a privileged class, or encounter opposition in the House of Lords, or endanger the possession of office by their party—the work of the League would never be accomplished. And so with all other reforms. Happily the League was composed of men of strong political fibre and great political prescience. They continued their work with ever-increasing firmness of purpose and rapidly growing public approval; and the day

The verdict of the nation.

of the great reform, of which in 1844 the Whig orator could only dimly discern the glimmering of the dawn, broke in fullest splendour within the brief period of two years. In 1846, with the consent and assistance of both parties, and in the certain conviction that the change would be to the advantage not merely of the general community, but also of the agricultural classes hitherto privileged, the Corn-laws were totally repealed. Parliament and the nation confirmed the verdict given by the Edinburgh Anti-Corn-Law Association against Mr. Macaulay.

Attacks by the *Scotsman.*

So far as regards personal consequences, the speech in the Anti-Corn-Law Association meeting proved disastrous to Mr. Macaulay, while it separated Mr. McLaren definitely and finally from his old newspaper friend the *Scotsman.* It clearly and distinctly laid down the grounds on which three years afterwards Mr. Macaulay was condemned and rejected by the electors of Edinburgh. It showed that not only had the right hon. gentleman rendered equivocal service to the cause of Free Trade, but that he was in conflict with his constituents on the subjects of Concurrent Endowment and Parliamentary Reform; that he was in favour of the endowment of Maynooth, and unfriendly to an extension of the suffrage; and in 1847 the Independent Liberals of the city ousted the Whig statesman from the representation, notwithstanding the charm of his oratory and his world-wide reputation as a man of letters.

The penalty paid by Mr. McLaren for his action was his breach with the *Scotsman*. In 1844, after three successive articles had been published containing violent attacks on the Anti-Corn-Law Association and its leading member on account of their treatment of Mr. Macaulay, Mr. McLaren, recognising that " all future co-operation between us in the public questions in which we had previously acted together " was now impossible, undertook his own defence. The tone of his letter, dated 14th May 1844, was courteous and temperate, but its argument was cogent and crushing. It was quite as masterly a performance as the speech on Mr. Macaulay's letter, which letter the journalistic critic charged him with having perverted and distorted. It maintained with fresh force the points against Mr. Macaulay elaborated in the speech, and passing from the defensive to the offensive, it proved to demonstration that the real perverter and distorter of the letter was Mr. Macaulay's newspaper apologist. So confident, and justly confident, was Mr. McLaren in the impregnability of his position, that he wrote to the editor :—

"I will agree to refer the matter to any six men in the city who have formed no opinion on either side of the question, allowing you to select them all; and if any one of the six shall take your view of the question, and think that my interpretation of the passage is not a fair and candid one, and that yours is not more justly chargeable with being a 'perversion' of its true meaning than mine is, I shall never complain of your remarks, or again use the same argument against Mr. Macaulay, even although the other five should all give a decision in my favour."

This offer was not accepted, and Mr. McLaren's interpretation and argument triumphantly held the field against all its adversaries, legal, parliamentary and journalistic.

Mr. McLaren did not enter into this controversy without great and frequent searchings of heart, and this disposition towards self-examination was quickened by the faithful words of a friend.   Mr. George Combe, the famous phrenologist and essayist, cherished a sincere regard both for Mr. McLaren, the public-spirited citizen, and Mr. Charles Maclaren, the high-minded editor of the *Scotsman ;* and as a friend of both, who nevertheless kept himself outside the sphere of political controversy, he observed with genuine concern the party separation, if not the personal alienation, that controversy was producing.   On 19th August 1844 he sent Mr. McLaren a copy of his " Notes on America," saying, " I beg as a favour to present you with one, as I have no other means of showing the high respect I entertain for your valuable exertions for the good of the human kind in every department open to your zeal."   This gift must have been acknowledged by return of post in a manner which enabled Mr. Combe to interpose a word of warning and counsel as a mediator, and he at once seized his opportunity :—

SOUTH CLERMISTON, CORSTORPHINE,
August 20, 1844.

MY DEAR SIR,—I regret exceedingly to hear that there is any misunderstanding, however slight, between you and Mr. Charles Maclaren.   You have often been coupled together as ornaments to the name, and as the ablest advocates of Liberal principles in

Edinburgh, and should continue united. I am glad to learn that personally you continue to be so, and hope ere long every cause of difference may be removed. . . .

I have read your article in answer to Sheriff Alison with the greatest interest and instruction. It is irresistible, and should be widely diffused. I confess, however, that it is not improved in my eyes by a certain tone of self-esteem and combativeness that occasionally leaks out in it; but I know how extremely difficult it is to avoid this in a controversy in which one is in dead earnest and full of the conviction of being in the right. I have had a world of literary controversies in my day, and in my early career fell into that tone irresistibly. But one effect of phrenology was to convince me that the direct effect of these faculties was to rouse the same faculties in the opposite party into corresponding activity, and thereby to increase the obstacles to my making an impression on their judgment and consciences. I therefore strove to suppress these, and to rely on reason, justice, and benevolence, and in so far as I have proceeded in this attempt, I have had occasion to know that I have in such instances best promoted my object. You know Sir William Hamilton's power and temper as a controversialist. When he was waging war against me with all the vigour of his intellect and the utmost bitterness of his destructiveness, and I was doing my best to reply to him, we sent our letters to each other amicably before publication; and on one occasion he willingly cancelled a portion of one, when I informed him that if he retained and printed it, I could no longer treat him as a friend. It is an excellent rule in controversy never to *pen* what you would not *say* to your opponent if you met him face to face before an impartial public. Excuse me for introducing these remarks; some expressions in your own letter led to them; and I entertain so high an estimate of your talents, activity, and attainments, that I should rejoice to see every particle of alloy withdrawn from the sterling metal of your composition. One of Mr. Macaulay's letters was disfigured, in my judgment, by a tone of self-esteem.

GEORGE COMBE.

Mr. McLaren acknowledged this letter in a grateful and friendly spirit, and Mr. Combe again wrote on the day following :—

" . . . When I get my house in order, I shall request the pleasure of your spending an evening with us, in order to discuss *viva voce* the questions how far one is justified in supporting a party or views which coincide to a certain extent with one's own, although not entirely, and also how far one is justified in a publication in withholding part of what one believes to be truth, but for which the public mind is obviously not prepared. On these points some of my best and wisest friends differ in opinion, and I acknowledge that I have never been able to see my way satisfactorily through them. My *inclination* is to act on principle and speak out truth, come what may, believing that the world is arranged in harmony with truth and principle *in the long run.* But then so many strong reasons are advanced to show that this is *not the best way of gaining the co-operation and conviction of other men,* without which nothing practical can be accomplished, that my reflective judgment differs from my inclination.

" I am quite prepared to believe that it will cost you no difficulty to lay aside every sort of sneering and contemptuous tone, and the reason why I took the liberty to allude to it was the conviction that it tended to diminish the admirable effect which your clear and vigorous intellect would produce without it. You make 'a person feel his misdeeds' most effectually when you place him out-and-out in the wrong, as you have done with Mr. Alison. The rest is a manifestation of your own conscious superiority in having been able to do this, and disposes not only the offender, but readers in general, to *resist* rather than yield to your argument, because they feel that, in doing the latter, they are also yielding to your superiority. Excuse me, my dear sir, for expounding the workings of the faculties in this manner ; but you know that I have made the study of mind my hobby, and have also some practical experience in controversy. . . .

"If you will excuse my using phrenological language, I will add that without a good natural endowment of the organs and faculties of combativeness and self-esteem you *could not have accomplished* what you have done. Great moral courage was necessary to enable you, in so many instances, to take your stand against prejudices, 'principalities and powers,' and these faculties give you boldness and self-reliance. But at that point their moral effect terminates. We all feel the great advantages which the moral tone gives to the communications of the excellent members of the Society of Friends who write in political controversy ; and I regard this as the result of the habitual restraint under which they keep their propensities."

Mr. Combe's intervention was of a kind which obviously could not, as it did not, arrest the political controversy, or even smooth the way to political reconciliation. But Mr. McLaren, willing to believe that "friendship by sweet reproof is shown," gratefully accepted the advice given in affection, as harmonising with the promptings of his own conscience ; and in this, as in all other controversies, strove to keep personal feeling under restraint, and to avoid indulgence in personal recrimination.

After reading the above letters from Mr. Combe, Mrs. McLaren writes to a friend :—

"I have been deeply interested in reading the valuable and beautiful letters written to my husband by his friend George Combe, as far back as 1844. I send you a copy of both. You will see how gently he reproves him for what I used to call, in stronger words, the rather sledge-hammer way in which he sometimes dealt with an opponent. You will notice Mr. Combe's phrenological use of the organs of *self-esteem* and combativeness, and that he says without these qualities Mr. McLaren could not have accomplished what he has done. 'Great moral courage,' he says, 'was necessary to enable you, in so many instances, to take your stand against prejudices, principalities and powers, and those faculties gave you boldness and self-reliance.'

"Now I believe, phrenologically speaking, my husband was deficient in self-esteem *per se*, which in its excess leads to arrogance and pride.

"I remember in 1864, when we were residing at Clifton, we visited a photographer there who is quite a character—a phrenologist and fond of mental philosophy. He looked earnestly at my husband, and turning to me said, 'I do not know the gentleman who is with you, but I am much struck with his head. Do you think he would allow me to examine it?' After he had done so, the photographer said, 'It is a remarkable head; the love of justice dominates every organ of the mind, whilst the phrenological organ of self-esteem is greatly deficient; but his great conscientiousness and combativeness and reverence for what is right compensate for this, and will give courage for moral action which most men would think the result of selfesteem. He could give no quarter where he thought there was injustice, and if he were a judge, I would not like to appear before him unless I had truth on my side.'

"A professional phrenologist once told him the same thing. It accounted for what I had frequently remarked in my husband's character—a shyness which, he often told me, he always had to struggle against. This caused him to have so little personal ambition, and often prevented him from doing things which might have been of advantage to himself and his family. . . . He espoused no principle or cause rashly. He was either firmly persuaded of its moral rectitude or he had tested its justice by the uncompromising testimony of facts and figures; and the strongest feature of his character, the basis of his strength, lay in his power courageously, pertinaciously, or, as some might call it, dogmatically to hold his ground; and in his earnest combat for what he believed to be the truth, he no doubt sometimes appeared to think as little of the feelings of his opponent as he did of his own popularity."

CHAPTER XIII.

THE LORD PROVOSTSHIP.

BEFORE his retirement from the Town Council in 1839 Mr.
McLaren had been marked by public though informal selec-
tion as a future Lord Provost, and if self-exaltation on the
easiest terms had been the object of his ambition, he could
have won his way to the civic chair.   But he ignored conciliatory arts as a means of self-advancement ; and out of office
he was as unsparing in his exposure of, and as uncompromising in his resistance to wrong-doing as when, a chosen
representative of the people, under obligation to be faithful
to their interests, he contended for administrative purity
and efficiency.   Much more sensitively affectionate in his
nature than was generally supposed, the severance of friendships cost him pain keener far than the virulent opposition
of monopolists or the cruel misrepresentation of baffled
critics.   But private friendships as well as personal interests he sacrificed at the call of public duty.   As years
and experience multiplied, and as his character developed
and strengthened, he felt with increasing force that he
must be faithful to his convictions, whatever might be the
cost.   He had within him the spirit of the true reformer :
" I am in the place where I am demanded of conscience
to speak the truth ; therefore the truth I speak—impugn it
who so list."

To Mr. McLaren, thus inspired with devotion to the

1842

public service, retirement from the Council brought little relief from public work. Over the proceedings of the Corporation more especially he kept a vigilant eye, and he continued to stand out prominently before his fellow-citizens as the best-informed man with respect to municipal affairs in their midst. It may be said without exaggeration that at every recurring election about this time the thoughts of the ratepayers, and more especially of the most public-spirited of the citizens, turned to the ex-Treasurer, and many attempts were made to induce him to re-enter the Council. In 1842 he received the following requisition:—

September 29, 1842.

Requisitions.

DEAR SIR,—We, the undersigned members of the Town Council, believing that your services would be of incalculable benefit to the community were you returned as a member to that board, earnestly entreat you to allow your name to be mentioned at the ensuing election. Satisfied that any constituency will be proud to return you as one of its representatives, we are, dear sir, yours very truly,　(Signed)　ARCHD. GEIKIE, Jun.

„　AD. BLACK.

„　JAS. GRAY.

„　D. J. THOMSON.

„　ANDW. WILKIE.

„　ANDW. DODDS.

„　JOHN DUNCAN.

„　JOHN ROBERTSON.

„　JOHN RICHARDSON.

Mr. Geikie accompanied the requisition with the following note:—

MY DEAR SIR,—I met one of the committee of the first ward this morning, who, in speaking of the difficulty of obtaining good men to represent the different wards, said that if you would only consent to your name being mentioned, the difficulty would disappear, as in such case able and excellent individuals would cheerfully come forward ; that possibly were a number of the members of Council to appeal to you, you might reconsider your expressed resolution. The remark struck me at the time, and having a little spare time this forenoon, I saw the several Councillors and Magistrates whose names are in the annexed paper. Had time allowed, I believe I could have obtained a great many more, and thereby have convinced you how much your valuable co-operation is desired. My anxiety must be my apology for intruding the matter on you. But no one who watches the progress of events, and witnesses the gradual declension of the Council, ought to hesitate in doing what he can to remedy the evil, and by endeavouring to obtain gentlemen of talents and reputation to stay the mischief. Allow me to crave your kindly consideration of the enclosed, and believe me to be, my dear sir, ever truly yours, ARCHD. GEIKIE, Jun.

NORTH BRIDGE, *Sept.* 29, 1842.

In a previous chapter reference was made to the contest for the Provostship in 1840, when Mr. Black lost his election through the defection of the Moderate Whigs and the active hostility of the Church party. Apparently the election had come to depend on the votes of one or two of the Councillors. When, on the eve of the election-day in November 1840, Mr. Black discovered that Dean of Guild Aitken had yielded to the Church party, he penned a hurried note to Mr. McLaren to this effect : " The game is up. The Dean says he is to vote against me because I am a Voluntary, and am just making way for you as my successor." This conjecture was eventually verified. Mr. Black became Lord Provost on the next occasion when he offered his services to the city, and after an interval was succeeded in the civic chair by Mr. McLaren. So early as the year 1843, friends of Mr. McLaren, who desired his assistance in the business of the Town Council, sought

1842

to strengthen their appeals to him for his return to the Council by promises of the Lord Provostship. In 1843 he mentioned the subject to his friend Mr. Bright, and also explained the difficulties in the way, the chief of which seemed to have been dislike of the pomp and circumstance attendant on the office of chief magistrate of the capital of Scotland. Mr. Bright, not then his brother-in-law, but a warm admirer of his character and worth, replied in a happy, playful letter, indicative of the personal gratification which the elevation of the most active and valuable ally of the Anti-Corn-Law League in Scotland would afford him.

Mr. Bright on the Lord Provostship.

" You are in the position of a man," wrote Mr. Bright, " having honours thrust upon him. I don't suspect you of looking out for a baronetcy, or else the birth of the next prince or princess might give you a chance. I understand the difficulty about the carriage and style, &c. Is it not possible to fill the office without making a fool of oneself? I think a man might make a good Lord Provost and yet maintain only his usual state. The citizens, knowing his circumstances and his usual mode of living, would prefer him, I suspect, as he is, rather than in the trappings and livery which his predecessors had worn."

A civic tribune.

But neither the entreaties of prominent fellow-citizens nor the gentle coaxings of a friend, who, sensible of his worth, wished for him the honours he had deserved, could induce Mr. McLaren at this time to withdraw from the position of independent private citizenship. He did not, however, shirk municipal work, though he determined for the time being to remain outside the Council. He was frequently consulted by its members, and by the higher officers of all the municipal departments; and sometimes, as in 1841, when some disagreement arose as to the constitution of the Royal Infirmary Board of Management, he was able to render

valuable aid to the Corporation.   His relation to the citizens
was that of a civic tribune, always within call to defend their
rights ; and perhaps the most noteworthy and effective municipal service he rendered about this time was his defence
of the interests of the ratepayers while the Water Company
Bill of 1843 was before Parliament—a commission undertaken at the request of the ratepayers, but at his own expense, the execution of which brought advantage to them,
but widened the alienation between himself and the city
Members, Mr. Macaulay and Mr. Gibson-Craig, whose " frigid
neutrality " he had found " greatly damaging to our cause,"
in contrast to the helpfulness of his old friend, Solicitor-
General Rutherfurd, then Member for Leith.   At the close of
this struggle Mr. McLaren compiled for the " Inhabitants'
Committee " a bulky report, extending to 112 double-column
pages, embracing the evidence taken before the Parliamentary
Committees, " with numerous notes and documents, including
the principal clauses of the new Act."   In a preface Mr.
McLaren showed the important advantages gained by the
ratepayers in the contest before the Committees, and made
special acknowledgment of the " untiring energy and perseverance " of Councillor Macfarlane, his future opponent in his
candidature for the Lord Provostship, and of Mr. Morton and
other colleagues.   From this time the Water Company in
all their legislative and other projects had to reckon with
Mr. McLaren as an uncompromising guardian of the ratepayers' interests, and the Council repeatedly availed itself of
the special experience and knowledge he had acquired of
the relations of the Company to the community, until in
1870 the whole business was transferred to the Corporation
to be managed as a municipal undertaking.   The official
reports of the Corporation, and the newspaper letters he
wrote in his contentions with the Company on behalf of the

1843

The Water
Company.

ratepayers between 1843 and 1870, would form a large volume, which would itself furnish no mean testimony to his industry, disinterestedness, and talent as a citizens' advocate.

The poet and the statistician.

Frequently during his public controversies Mr. McLaren was gratified and encouraged by spontaneous expressions of appreciation of his services, conveyed sometimes verbally, sometimes by letter. One of these valued communications came to him from Mr. Robert Gilfillan, the author of " Oh ! Why Left I my Hame ? " and many other popular Scottish songs. The poet wrote, " Accept my grateful thanks for your valuable tractate upon the water question ; it is indeed a *Vade mecum,* which no citizen of Edinburgh should be without. Of a surety what Bailie Nicol Jarvie said of Owen in ' Rob Roy ' may be said of you : ' He is a man of figures and a man of calculations, and when he speaks o' danger, ruin is no' far off ! ' The good folks of Auld Reekie owe you *another day at the harvest* for this labour of love."

He likewise gained the respect of many sturdy foes. One of these was the devoted manager of the Water Company, whose measures (in the interest of the ratepayers) Mr. McLaren had more than once been called to oppose. The Water Company, in his view, were under a statutory obligation to increase the supply of water concurrently with the extension of the city ; but the Company naturally preferred to increase its dividends and to put the inhabitants on short allowance of water. Eventually the ratepayers obtained from Parliament the desired guarantee that the Water Company should purchase and bring into the city certain additional springs and running streams from the Pentland Hills. Mr. Ramsey, the Company's manager, in accordance with the instructions of his directors, sent Mr. McLaren the share of fees due to him as a parliamentary witness. Mr. McLaren, however, politely returned the money; and Mr. Ramsey replied expressing regret, but acknowledging with appreciation the consistency and conscientiousness of his conduct.

But municipal questions were not the only subjects that kept Mr. McLaren in the arena of public conflict and controversy, and the discussion of which kindled against him new hostilities, while it made clearer and stronger his position as a champion of popular freedom and just laws. The Free Trade campaign, of which he was the chief director in Scotland, widened the breach in the ranks of the descendants of the old Reform party, and made still more urgent the separation of Liberals and Whigs which the Annuity-Tax agitation had previously demanded. By this time Mr. McLaren had, through his association with the Central Board of Dissenters, and by innumerable written as well as platform polemics, won recognition as the foremost lay Dissenter in Scotland, while his mastery of all the intricacies of the Annuity-Tax question made his advice and aid essential to the Council in their efforts to effect a settlement, as a necessity for civil peace. In 1851 he was asked by the Town Council to proceed to London to be examined before the Select Committee of the House of Commons, referred to in a previous chapter, which had been appointed on the motion of Sir W. Gibson-Craig, "to consider the operation of the Acts relating to the Annuity-Tax levied in Edinburgh, Canongate, and Montrose," and it was the struggle which then began that compelled Mr. McLaren to re-enter the Council. While he was absent in London, he was, without his knowledge or consent, nominated for the Second Ward, of which he had formerly been one of the representatives, and unwilling to disappoint or discourage his friends on the eve of what he knew would prove an arduous battle, he accepted nomination. It was as a man of war, therefore,

1851

The Annuity-Tax.

that he was again summoned to official service in the Corporation; but a man of war against his will, fighting for a righteous settlement of an irritating ecclesiastico-municipal conflict, as a necessity for an ultimate and an enduring peace.

Edinburgh perhaps never witnessed a more keenly contested municipal election than that which was fought in October 1851. Public opinion was strangely excited and divided. The disturbing influences of the Free Church Disruption had not yet spent their force; and while in political life they were still weakening the Tory party, as the natural defenders of Church Establishment, they were beginning to react on the disestablished Non-Intrusionists themselves, forcing them to recognise the Liberal tendencies of their own movement, and gradually drawing them into active co-operation with the Dissenters. One of the earliest and most influential pioneers of this approximation in public testimony and policy of the Free Church with the earlier Secession or disestablished communions was the late Mr. David Dickson, who found in the leader of the Dissenting party in Edinburgh the chief centre of attraction, and who about this time entered with Mr. McLaren into a close friendship, which lasted until his death in 1885.

The late Mr. Francis Brown Douglas, also a leading layman in the Free Church, assisted this transition. These laymen's hearty and active support of Mr. McLaren largely contributed to the defeat of the policy, then ably and earnestly advocated by Mr. Hugh Miller in the *Witness*, viz., that Free Church electors should vote solely for Free Church candidates. But the force of Mr. McLaren's character also proved a powerful factor operating in the same direction, and compelled the respect and admiration of his most resolute Free Church opponents. Hugh Miller's testimony as to the manner of man Mr. McLaren was between 1840 and 1851 is highly interesting and suggestive. In two editorial articles, strongly adverse to Mr. McLaren's candidature, the editor of the *Witness* made these two remarkable acknowledgments :—" In several important respects Duncan McLaren is the most remarkable man now in the field. We well remember when, in the year 1840, he was pointed out to us on the High Street of Edinburgh by a prominent member of the Evangelical party, and we looked for the first time, and not without interest, at the large-headed, broad-browed, thoughtful-looking man, whose name had been so familiar to us during the wars of the Voluntary controversy. ' That,' said our companion, ' is the most formidable opponent the Evangelical cause has at the present moment in Scotland. We shall get no measure from the Whigs that does not satisfy him ; and the measure that satisfies him will be of no use to us.' It is really highly creditable to the talents and peculiarly *Scotch* pertinacity of Mr. McLaren, that he who, as Carlyle says of Knox, was not one of the nobles of the land, but simply a subject born within the same—he, a retail dealer of woollens in the High Street of Edinburgh, could, through the influence which he exerted on the Whig Ministry as the lay leader of Voluntaryism, do more to thwart and prevent the right settlement of one of the most important questions Scotland ever saw, than profound talent such as that of Chalmers, and high political position such as that of the Marquis of Breadalbane and the Hon. Fox Maule, could do to secure it. He stands in the van of his party as their most energetic and zealous champion. He has struggled long and hard against the assertion of the Establishment principle, and at length sees as his reward the Evangelical portion of them disestablished for ever." The gifted editor of the *Witness* misjudged to some extent Mr. McLaren's relations to the Non-Intrusionist party and struggle, as he failed to comprehend or foresee the true destiny of the Free Church. But the distrustfulness and unfriendliness of his view of the lay leader of the Dissenting party makes his admission and description of Mr. McLaren's powerful influence alike in the ecclesiastical and political sphere all the more noteworthy.

Three candidates for the Lord Provostship were named in the wards—Mr. Grainger, C.E., nominated by the Tories and Churchmen; Mr. Macfarlane, brought forward by the Free Church party, encouraged by a section of the Whigs; and Mr. McLaren, who in the Second Ward was proposed by Mr. Law, who at a subsequent period became Lord Provost, and seconded by Mr. J. Johnstone, of the firm of Messrs. Johnstone & Hunter. All three were eminently deserving of municipal distinction. They all had served in the first reformed Town Council, and while Mr. Grainger had, outside the municipal sphere, attained a high reputation as an engineer, and was able to place at the disposal of the community professional services of a kind of which they at the time stood urgently in need, Mr. Macfarlane had, as already seen, distinguished himself while still in municipal service by the ability and fidelity with which he had defended the rights of the Corporation in connection with the University and the interests of the ratepayers as against the Water Company. Neither of them, however, as regards amount and value of, or capacity for, municipal service, in the words of Mr. James Aytoun (who also had sat in the first reformed Council), could " hold a candle " to Mr. McLaren, and neither of them was so well qualified for the unravelment of the Annuity-Tax complication. Indeed, it was Mr. McLaren's acknowledged special fitness for this work that was the chief animating cause of the bitter and determined opposition that was offered to his candidature for the civic chair. The election to the Town Council on the occasion was perhaps the most keenly contested of any that had taken place under the £10 franchise qualification. The excitement in the city was great. The question really submitted to the wards was, Shall Duncan McLaren be Lord Provost or not? The answer was in the affirmative. Of the twelve candidates elected, seven were pledged to vote for Mr. McLaren, four for Mr. Grainger, and one for Mr. Macfarlane; and Mr. Grainger only secured his own seat in the Town Council by a majority of one vote over Mr. David Dickson. The gross vote over the city showed 2925 for Mr. McLaren, 2346 for Mr. Grainger, and 457 for Mr. Macfarlane; and the Council recognised the popular verdict. At the first meeting held after the choice of Councillors, Bailie Fyfe proposed, and Mr. Francis Brown Douglas seconded, the election of Mr. McLaren to the Lord Provost's chair; and on a division this motion was carried by twenty votes against ten for Mr. Grainger. Mr. Macfarlane was not proposed, and at the next meeting his withdrawal from the Council was intimated. Shortly afterwards the Lord Provost's party in the Council was strengthened by the return of Mr. Dickson, Mr. Grainger having also withdrawn.

Mr. McLaren's success was welcomed throughout Scotland as a great Liberal victory, and it afforded much gratification to many friends in England. Numerous letters of congratulation were received, and among the earliest was one from his political friend, the veteran Reformer, Joseph Hume, who wrote, "I hope the result will be useful to the city and honourable to yourself. Much may be done by a public officer in your high station to influence the current of public events, and although it cannot be concealed that the settlement of the Annuity-Tax question (so long the cause of discontent and trouble) is to be the principal object of your ambition, yet I hope the cause of Reform, so essential for the future harmonious working of our Liberal institutions, will not be forgotten."   In a subsequent letter Mr. Hume enumerated his reasons for holding the opinion that the question of Church Establishment was one on which no Liberal could consent to a compromise.   Mr. Bright wrote, "I am delighted to find that you are elected in a manner so satisfactory and so flattering; it is a good sign of the feeling of the city to yourself and to great public questions."

CHAPTER XIV.

THE CIVIC REIGN.

EDINBURGH did not enjoy the questionable happiness of dull annals during Lord Provost McLaren's civic reign, which extended to the statutory limit of three years. Public life was intensely active; and the reforming zeal of the Chief Magistrate was the mainspring of this activity. The ecclesiastico-political movements connected with the Annuity-Tax struggle and the opposition to the election of Mr. Macaulay, in which Mr. McLaren was recognised as the champion of the Independent and Advanced Liberal party, not only of Edinburgh but of Scotland, have been recorded in previous chapters; and the multiplicity of the details connected with his searching and thorough local administration forbid anything more than a general sketch of his strictly municipal work. Mr. McLaren's exacting conscientiousness developed within him that infinite capacity for taking pains with small things as well as great, which wise men have declared to be true genius; and the minor affairs affecting the business of the city and lying at the root of efficient administration were certainly not neglected during the three years 1851–54. Mr. McLaren was a rigid economist, and he personally practised what he preached. He generally contrived to combine his municipal journeys to London with those which he took for his own business purposes; and to charge his business or private account with the heavier part of the expenses. As a Director of the York, Newcastle, and Berwick Railway (now the North-Eastern), he possessed a free pass over a considerable portion of the line between Edinburgh and London, and this privilege enabled him to still further limit his charges against the municipal exchequer.[1] In these days of lavish political expenditure it is worthy of note that the total amount of personal expenses charged by Mr. McLaren against the Corporation during his three years tenure of the office of Chief Magistrate, notwithstanding his prolonged visits to London, in connection more especially with the Annuity-Tax Bills in the sessions of 1852 and 1853, was only £81, 13s. 3d. As to the general effect of his economical administration, it is sufficient to say that while, according to the *Scotsman* of December 15, 1852, only in one year before Mr. McLaren's accession to office the Council seemed to have paid its way, the balances in the municipal accounts were now restored to the right side.

Another feature of his administration was his restoration of the powers of control of all the municipal departments from the officials to the Town Council. He insisted that the representatives of the ratepayers should be the masters, and that the paid officials should be the servants. No man was quicker to appreciate independence of judgment or

---

[1] Mr. McLaren justified this use of his Director's pass while engaged on municipal or public business by associating directorial duties with these journeys; but he scrupulously refused to take personal advantage from his connection with the Board of Management. On one occasion when he was staying at Harrogate, he was offered free tickets for himself and family to enable them to join the families of other Directors in going to see the Queen and the Royal Family as they travelled over the North-Eastern line. In declining the tickets he replied that he had not been appointed a Director to enable him to take his family journeys for nothing, but to manage the Company's affairs for the benefit of the shareholders.

honesty of opinion, and to listen to the advice of experienced officers when satisfied of their loyalty to the public interest. But he would brook no dictation ; and he claimed from the official that the authority of the Corporation should be regarded as absolute. His unbending fidelity to the public rights in this respect caused him to challenge the conduct of Dr. Glover, the police-surgeon, in communicating with the Board of Health in London, as with a superior department, without the knowledge or sanction of the Council, and in conflict with its drainage policy. This ultimately caused the termination of the offending official's connection with the service of the Corporation. The same sentiment brought Mr. McLaren into collision with Sheriff Jameson and Superintendent Linton as to the right of the Sheriff and the superintendent of police to send the city constables to Kelso at the request of the Duke of Buccleuch, who apprehended a riot, without the sanction of the municipal authorities. In his assertion of the powers of the Police Commissioners and " of the supremacy of the Lord Provost within the city and liberties," as " High Sheriff" and " King's Lieutenant," as well as Chief Magistrate, he was ably assisted by Bailie Fyfe and supported by Councillor Macknight, both of them accomplished lawyers as well as devoted public servants. Even a wakeful and wary Town Clerk may sometimes err ; but a transgression during Mr. McLaren's Lord Provostship was quickly corrected, as is illustrated by the following letter, written in answer to a note from Mr. Sinclair, the Town Clerk, intimating certain verbal amendments on minutes dictated in the Council Chambers :—

EDINBURGH, *January* 30, 1854.

DEAR SIR,—I have received your letter and draft of proposed minute this evening. The minute I have corrected and now return. I do not approve of your suggestion to alter the resolu-

1852

tion from the form in which it was proposed by Bailie Morrison
and adopted by the meeting, after it had been read over several
times publicly and handed about for inspection to all who wished
to see it. I do not think either the chairman or the clerk of
any meeting possesses such a power. For the same reason, I do
not approve of altering the form of the motion proposed by Mr.
Hill, or the order in which it was taken up in going through the
business. I have, therefore, made the minute exactly as the
meeting agreed it should stand.—I am, dear sir, yours truly,

D. McLaren.

John Sinclair, Esq., City Chambers.

Mr. McLaren was also a strenuous upholder of the dignity
of his office outside the Council Chamber. In a letter to
his wife, dated May 20, 1854, he wrote in reference to a
public meeting in favour of education that was to be held:
" I yesterday refused to take part in the proceedings, on the
ground that, as Lord Panmure is to be chairman, it would
be derogatory to my dignity to be present. It was adver-
tised as a public meeting of the inhabitants, and I hold that
the Lord Provost and Lord Lieutenant of the city should
never be present at such a meeting except in the character
of chairman. However, I said that as an *educationalist* I
would rather have Lord Panmure as chairman than have
the Lord Provost ; for if I were there as chairman, it would
be misrepresented as being a *Voluntary* meeting, and numbers would absent themselves."

In after years Mr. McLaren resented the submissiveness
of Town Council majorities to the dictum of the Town
Clerks that minorities are entitled to meet, and, in defiance of the law as to quorums and of the decisions of the
Councils themselves, issue commissions to Established
Church elders as municipal representatives in the Established Assembly. While sympathising with the feeling that

prompted refusal to elect representative elders as a protest against the claims and position of the privileged Church, his own view was that an election could be made in the exercise of a civil right without in any way compromising the Anti-Establishment attitude of the Voluntaries and other advocates of Disestablishment. At the first of these appointments made after his elevation to the civic chair, he took part in the proceedings, and supported as the Council's representative elders men who were pledged to vote for the abolition of tests in the Universities; a reform which at this period was being energetically advocated, and in support of which he in the following winter presided at an influential public meeting held in the Queen Street Hall, and addressed, among others, by Professor Maclagan, Drs. Cunningham and Cairns, Sheriff Craufurd (afterwards Lord Ardmillan), and Mr. Adam Black. In the following year he obtained the election of an elder opposed to the Annuity-tax as a colleague to the Anti-University Test representative. As an illustration of his view of the claims of another religious communion, it may here be mentioned, that when, in the spring of 1854, Bishop Terrot of the Scottish Episcopal Church called attention to some damage done to Episcopal property by the fall of a high stone wall in Leith Wynd, and asked that it might be repaired, the Lord Provost objected to entertain a request from any man in Scotland styling himself a bishop, and therefore claiming precedence and pre-eminence over other ministers. He had no desire to interfere with any religious body in the titles they conferred on their ministers, but he was unwilling to give municipal sanction to a designation unacknowledged by law, yet implying a claim to a status higher than that of ministers of other denominations. His views were endorsed by the Council, who, by 16 votes against 8, declined to entertain Dr. Terrot's application. Subsequently, as a Member of

1852

The representative elder.

Ecclesiastical titles.

Parliament, he repeated his testimony against the legalisation or recognition of assumed titles of superiority. He voted with a small minority against a motion for the repeal of the Ecclesiastical Titles Act of 1851. " I object," he said, " to the thrusting upon a Presbyterian community of sets of men who are to assume titles of superiority over other ministers in Scotland. . . . . Such an assumption of superiority in a Presbyterian country where Presbyterianism is enacted by law is altogether out of the question."

The attitude of Free Churchmen.

Attention has already been called to the gradual modification of the attitude of distrust and hostility which Free Churchmen, in memory of the old Voluntary controversies, continued to maintain towards the champion of the Dissenters for many years after the Disruption. During the Lord Provostship this process of approximation continued. On various questions, more especially those in which the moral and religious well-being of the people was directly concerned, he showed that co-operation was possible and advantageous, though the platforms occupied might not be precisely the same. For example, with respect to the grant of £30,000 to Maynooth Catholic College, he advocated opposition on the ground of objection to concurrent endowment, as well as on the old Voluntary ground of opposition to all state endowments. As an illustration of this unification of opinion amongst Presbyterian Dissenters, it may be noted that while on 9th December 1851 Mr. McLaren appeared on the platform of the Scottish Reformation Society, then exerting itself as a Protestant institution to secure the withdrawal of state support to the Roman Catholic college, he, on 3rd May 1855, wrote to Mr. A. Murray-Dunlop, M.P., then one of the most prominent laymen of the Free Church, alike as regards talent, service, and liberality of opinion : " I have read with great pleasure in the *Times* the report of your speech on the Maynooth grant. You have taken up the ground which I am satisfied is the one that will ultimately prevail, because it is the only ground really defensible in the present circumstances of the country. Most heartily do I wish you success in the cause; but there are many intolerant people who will not thank you for your advocacy on account of the grounds on which it was based." Mr. Murray-Dunlop saw at an early stage of the agitation that justice and true statesmanship required the withdrawal of the *Regium Donum* to the Ulster Presbyterians as well as of the Maynooth grant to the Roman Catholics, and that, too, as a preliminary to the disestablishment of all the Churches.

Another link of connection between Mr. McLaren and the Nonconformist Evangelical Society, which was then divided upon many political questions, was social reform. He and they were deeply concerned for the moral welfare of the community, and equally recognised that it is righteousness which exalts a nation. Accordingly, when, in the second year of his Lord Provostship, he proceeded to apply himself practically to the cure of Sunday-drunkenness in Edinburgh, he attracted to his side the friends of sobriety and morality in all the Churches; and many good men and patriotic citizens, strongly opposed to him in politics, and dreading him as a more dangerous Voluntary than even Mr. Black was supposed to be, were thankful they had a Lord Provost who was not afraid to combat what was perhaps the greatest public evil and scandal of the time.[1] Here is

---

[1] Mr. McLaren was himself a most abstemious man. He was a friend of temperance in practice as well as in precept; and for twelve years, including the period during which he was Lord Provost, he never tasted wine or spirits, though his sense of the duties of hospitality made him consider it right to place wine on his table for the use of his guests.

Mr. McLaren's own account of the evil, and of the steps he took to cure it, given before a Committee of the House of Commons in 1868 :—

"At the period to which I have referred, it was a matter of public notoriety that drunkenness prevailed to an enormous extent in Edinburgh, as it did in all the large towns of Scotland; and on Sundays it was particularly marked and offensive, by reason of the fact that well-behaved citizens on their way through the streets saw drunken people reeling about in large numbers, using bad language, and otherwise rendering themselves great nuisances. There was a great desire on the part of men of all classes to put an end to this enormous amount of drunkenness. I, with a view to do something in this direction, called a meeting of the acting Magistrates of the city and of the county of the city of Edinburgh, and I proposed certain matters to them. Then at a special licensing session for the city, resolutions were passed which formed the basis of legislation subsequently. The principle affirmed by the resolutions was, that in cases where publicans were charged with offences in contravention of their licenses, the fact of their keeping their houses open on Sunday should be regarded as an aggravation of the offence committed. The change that took place was almost instantaneous. A large proportion of the persons who had before kept open their houses on the Sunday closed them, and the drunkenness visibly decreased in all quarters of the city. I made it my business to walk through the lowest parts of the city on Sunday evenings, and I can say, as the result of personal experience so gained, that the effect was really startling. Those persons who were noticeable as objecting to what is called Sabbatarian legislation were equally ready with other people to admit the good result which had followed the action taken by the Magistrates."

But highly encouraging as the immediate results of this tentative reform, based on the voluntary co-operation of the better-class public-house-keepers, were shown to be, it was felt that something more than permissive local legislation was required. Public sentiment, not only in Edinburgh, but throughout Scotland, stimulated by the admittedly great advantages resulting from Sunday restriction in the capital, called for a general Act ; and on business grounds the publicans who sympathised with Sunday-closing supported this demand, because, " as some persons chose to keep open their houses on the Sunday, they took the customers of their neighbours who did so close, not only on the Sunday, but on the week-days also." Mr. McLaren, it will thus be seen, really initiated the restrictive legislation which has since been associated with the name of Mr. Forbes-Mackenzie. As the direct result of the Edinburgh experiment, a bill was framed making general and compulsory the principle embodied in the resolutions of the Edinburgh Magistrates, the application of which had hitherto been local and optional. The measure was brought into the House of Commons by Mr. Forbes-Mackenzie, formerly Member for Peeblesshire, but then Member for Liverpool, and into the House of Peers by Lord Kinnaird, and it was carried in a single session. Lord Kinnaird, writing on 27th July 1853 to Mr. McLaren, announced that he had " succeeded in passing the Public-House Bill, with all the amendments suggested by you and your brother Magistrates, including the one proposed by (I believe) Mr. Douglas, as to summary proceedings against persons selling without having taken out a certificate."

As no man had more contributed to the introduction and rapid passage of the new bill than Mr. McLaren, so no one watched the operation of the Act with keener attention or championed its policy with greater resolution and ability. He early satisfied himself, by a careful examination of the police-court returns, of the healthful influence of the new Act on the social and moral condition of the people. But he did not content himself with the evidence of statistical tables. He made personal investigation. In one of the earliest of the letters or reports he prepared, which was issued in pamphlet form by the Committee of the Edinburgh Total Abstinence Society, he wrote :—

" For the last thirty-five years I have spent the greater portion of my time in the Old Town, and therefore will not be thought presumptuous in saying that I know something of the character and habits of its population. On the last Sunday of July and the first Sunday of the present month (August) I spent an hour each day, from nine to ten o'clock at night, in walking through the low neighbourhoods along with a friend. Our course was down the Candlemaker Row, along the Grassmarket and West Port, back by the same course, and along the whole of the Cowgate and St. Mary's Wynd; down the Canongate midway, and back up the High Street to the Tron Church. During these perambulations I saw no person drunk, heard no swearing or obscene language, and saw no fighting or improper conduct, although we passed through numerous groups of the very lowest classes of the inhabitants. I have gone over the same ground on several other Sundays, about the same hour, within the last three years, and knowing what I do of the Old Town population, I can unhesitatingly state that the change for the better on Sundays is truly marvellous."

Let any one at the present day perambulate on a Saturday night the same districts as those visited by Mr. McLaren, and repeat his inspection on the Sunday night, and he will be able to form some conception of the " truly marvellous " improvement that delighted the heart of the Lord Provost and his friends in the summer of 1854.

By and by Mr. McLaren extended his examination of the results of the new Act over the whole of Scotland. Through the agency of Mr. Murray-Dunlop, Member for Greenock, he obtained a series of parliamentary returns

designed to illustrate the diminution of drunkenness and
crime which had followed the closing of public-houses on
Sundays, and to answer the misstatements and misunder-
standings of the hostile critics of the restrictive law. An
analysis of one of these returns, published in 1858, which he
incorporated in a masterly pamphlet, extending to forty-
eight pages, entitled " The Rise and Progress of Whisky-
Drinking in Scotland, and the Working of the Public-
Houses (Scotland) Act, commonly called the Forbes-Mackenzie Act,"[1] led him to the conclusion that " the number of
cases of drunkenness alone and drunkenness combined with
crime was 165 per cent. greater on Sundays under the old
law than under the new in the chief towns of Scotland, including a population exceeding a million." By lectures and
speeches, by letters to the *Times*[2] and nearly every other
important journal in the United Kingdom, by evidence
before a Parliamentary Committee and two Royal Commissions, and by a continuation of parliamentary returns
obtained by himself after his election to Parliament in
1865, he maintained his defence of the Forbes-Mackenzie
Act and his advocacy of a policy of restriction. Sometimes
he offered help and encouragement to the promoters of

---

[1] Published by the Scottish Temperance League, Glasgow.

[2] On 1st September 1854 Mr. McLaren received the following note:—
" The Secretary of the National Temperance Society, London, presents his
respectful compliments to the Lord Provost of Edinburgh, and on behalf
of the Committee would feel greatly obliged by learning whether his Lordship's permission can be granted to the reprinting of his recent letter to
the *Times*. It would be the object of the Committee to make this republi-
cation, if allowed, useful to the promotion of the movement for obtaining a
law closing public-houses, &c., in England during the whole of Sunday.
No pecuniary advantage would be regarded, and should the step taken
involve a charge on the Society's funds, this would be gladly borne for the
sake of the end desired." Of course the permission asked for was freely
granted.

Sunday-closing in Ireland, also in several of the English counties. At other times, acting on the defensive, he combated the view that any good effected by Sunday-closing in Scotland had been neutralised by the increase of she-beens,[1] or exposed mistakes, such as those into which even so expert a statistician as Mr. Leoni Levi fell in a paper he read before the British Association at its meeting in Dundee. Mr. Levi then stated that between 1857 and 1866 there was an increase in the consumption of spirits in Scotland of 23 per cent., whereas Mr. McLaren showed that there had been "a decreased consumption since 1854, when the Forbes-Mackenzie Act came into operation, of no less than 2,036,924 gallons per annum, being about 30 per cent.," irrespective of the increase of the population. He continued his interest in the question till the close of his life; and in a long letter he contributed to the *Daily Review* in 1884, he used the latest available statistics for the purpose of again illustrating the enormous social benefits produced by the Sunday-closing Act. In his closing sentence he pleaded for a large reduction in the number of spirit licenses in Edinburgh. He endorsed the language employed by the deputations who waited on the Magistrates, and in effect said to them, in the name of the poor wretched inebriates, and those having a tendency to become so, "Lead us not into temptation," by the large number of public-houses which you think "fit and convenient" (in the words of the Act) to establish in the city.

As a Member of Parliament, he cordially supported Sir Wilfrid Lawson's Permissive Bill and resolution, both within and without the House; and on his property of Mayfield, on the south side of Edinburgh, which he feued for building, he

---

[1] Unlicensed rooms where drink is secretly and illicitly retailed.

incorporated in his articles and conditions of feu the stipulation that " no feuar or his tenant shall erect, or open, or keep an hotel or a public-house, . . . or sell any excisable liquors, or allow the same to be used on his feu." From the days of his Lord Provostship, and indeed much earlier, Mr. McLaren was in the front rank of temperance and social reformers; and his influence and aid proved of incalculable advantage to the cause. He was one of the chief witnesses examined by the Royal Commission on grocers' licenses in 1877, of which Sir James Fergusson was chairman, and he gave effective evidence in favour of restriction, strongly urging that grocers should not be allowed to sell spirits at all, but should be confined as licensed liquor merchants to the sale of ale, beer, and wines.

Mr. McLaren's courage and success in dealing with the Sunday-drinking scandal won for him the grateful appreciation of not a few Established Churchmen and Episcopalians, interested in social reform, but widely and radically differing from him in general politics; and in subsequent years he was not unfrequently agreeably surprised to find such gentlemen giving him political support on personal or non-political grounds. Of course the reform he carried through aroused against him in certain quarters bitter and unrelenting hostility, and exposed him to much abuse; but his opponents and censors belonged to a class whose support he never valued or sought, and he felt himself abundantly rewarded by the vast benefits which visibly resulted from his work, and which many of the more respectable spirit-dealers frankly acknowledged.[1]

---

[1] Among other touching evidences of the good results of his labours, he was frequently thanked in the streets by poor women, the wives of workingmen, for the boon which Sunday-closing had proved to them; and some even, at times, took his hand and kissed it, blessing him as their benefactor.

The controversies which arose regarding the Trinity Hospital and Church were of a different kind. Trinity College Church, a splendid specimen of old Gothic architecture, built by Mary of Gueldres, and surrounded with many historical associations, was demolished by the North British Railway Company to make room for their Central Station, on payment of compensation. The struggles which followed turned upon the question whether the money thus acquired should be spent in rebuilding the old church in another part of the city, or whether a more suitable and less costly church should be built near the old site in the poorest part of the parish, and the remainder of the money devoted to the charitable purposes of Trinity Hospital. This brought him into acrimonious conflict with old friends, amongst whom was Mr. Adam Black, and with many of the professional and wealthier classes. Their motive was a desire to adorn the city out of this fund. Their distrust pained him, and their opposition he knew to be far more formidable, as it was infinitely more discouraging, than the hostility of a mere "interest" which he had deprived of a privilege injurious to the common weal. Many of his Trinity College critics—members of the Antiquarian Society, advocates, lawyers, men of letters and learned leisure, possessing immense social influence—wielded the pen with powerful effect, and were clever speakers as well as ready writers. But Mr. McLaren was undismayed; and in a speech delivered to the Town Council on 6th December 1853 (afterwards issued as a pamphlet in thirty-two pages) he proved more than a match for all his acute and merciless adversaries. He showed that the claim of the antiquarians and city beautifiers for the re-erection of the church according to the style and model, stone for stone, of the old building was justified neither by law nor public advantage; that the old church was the most comfortless in the city, and wholly unadapted for Protestant service ; and that what was wanted was a church suitable in respect of site and accommodation and structural design to the wants of the parish and the modern forms of worship—the surplus of the purchase-money received from the Railway Company being devoted to an extension of the beneficent designs of the Hospital, or, in other words, to an increase of the number of the beneficiaries.

"For ancient buildings and old ruins," he concluded, "he had always entertained the greatest veneration ; and he would not, without the most urgent necessity, be a party to the destruction of such relics of other times. It was in vain to say, as had been said, that all the beauty and all the original associations connected with this church would be restored by adopting the plan of re-building recommended by Mr. Bryce. No opinion could be more erroneous. Even in the case of existing ancient buildings, which, from necessity, have been partially rebuilt with stones newly dressed, there is a striking deterioration of effect as compared with the ancient time-worn portions which had not been renovated. He had often been forcibly struck with this difference in looking at the exterior of Westminster Abbey. The clean, nicely chiselled, new surface of the restored portions was, in his eyes, far less beautiful and far less interesting than the mouldering stones of the portions which had not been touched by the hands of the renovator. But when, as in this case, the whole of the exterior surface was to be renewed, and the new church to be merely a copy of the old church, with certain alleged improvements in the details, it was in vain to pretend that all the original pleasing associations, and all the original beauties belonging to the church erected by Mary of Gueldres, would be restored."

"Into the many-corridor'd complexities" of the dispute, which preceded and long outlived Mr. M\u1d9cLaren's Lord Provostship, raising questions of æsthetics as well as of law, involving the Railway Company and the Presbytery as well as the Corporation, discussed sometimes in public meetings and at other times in Parliament, but more frequently in courts of law, and producing a countless issue of letters and pamphlets, it would be profitless now to enter. It is sufficient to say that, unappalled by the denunciations of the antiquarians and of members of polite society in Edinburgh, who held him up to scorn as a Vandal, and by the desertion of trusted supporters in the Council, where, after the presentation of a memorial by an influential deputation headed by Mr. Black, he found himself in a minority of two, Mr. McLaren manfully held his ground.

He refused " in deference to mere clamour to remove a church from a poor parish to which it belongs, and also to rob a public charity of a portion of its funds in order to embellish the city by the erection of a church in or near the New Town, where none is required, and where the cost of a suitable site would swallow up the whole balance, which otherwise would go to the Trinity Hospital." He pleaded that the interests of the parishioners, that the policy of the Town Council during the earlier Provostship of Mr. Black himself, that the conditions of sale and purchase as settled in Parliament and interpreted by the Sheriff, and that public utility and common sense were all on his side. And so were the mass of the citizens, as a subsequent election proved. After many years, in which much bitterness of spirit was engendered, much public money was wasted, and the spiritual interests of the parish were neglected, Mr. McLaren's views were, in 1864, confirmed by a decision of the House of Lords, by which it was adjudged that the duty of the Corporation was confined to the erection of a suitable church, adapted to the wants of the parish, and that all the surplus of the price obtained from the Railway Company for the old church ought to be applied to the benefit of the Trinity Hospital Charity.

In a letter to Mrs. McLaren, dated 16th February 1864,

he wrote: "You will be delighted to hear that the Trinity Church case is decided in our favour, as I proposed when Provost. The Charity Fund will get £10,000 by the judgment, in place of spending it all on a church." It is very characteristic that at the moment when this long and angry controversy was decided in accordance with his views, there was no indication of any feeling of personal victory. A church suitable for the parish was accordingly built, and the surplus funds were applied to the original benevolent objects of the Hospital, in accordance with the opinion long previously given by Mr. Inglis, now Lord-Justice General, and Mr., now Lord, Young. At the time of the struggle, the higher scale of pension granted by the Hospital was £20 per annum, limited to forty-two persons, and the lower scale £6 per annum, enjoyed by eighty persons. After the settlement the higher scale of pension was increased to £25 for sixty, and the lower scale to £15 for a hundred beneficiaries; and the Trust remains a distinctly Edinburgh institution, under the management of the Town Council.

At the time he was being denounced as a Goth and a Vandal because of his refusal to undertake the impossible and undesirable task of rebuilding Trinity College Church stone for stone after the style and model of the old building, Mr. McLaren was labouring to promote artistic taste and scientific education in a far more effective way than by the reconstruction of a monument of Gothic architecture. He was employing his influence with the Government to induce them to utilise all the undisplayed stores of the University Museum by the erection of a great National Museum for Scotland, on an equal footing with the British Museum, and open to all persons free of expense. He took an active part with the deputation who waited upon the Government for the purpose of inducing them to begin the work, as some small instalment of justice to Scotland, and as a means of providing for the public inspection and use of the hidden treasures of the University collections. The deputation were successful so far, that a first grant of £3000 was inserted in the estimates, and actually voted by Parliament, when the outbreak of the Russian war caused the cancelling of this and similar obligations. Mr. McLaren immediately went up to London alone, called on Lord Aberdeen, then Prime Minister, and Mr. Gladstone, then Chancellor of the Exchequer, and induced them to restore the Museum grant as an exceptional vote. Thus was begun the splendid building which now forms the chief architectural feature in Chambers Street, and which has proved the most popular and instructive of all the Government institutions in Edinburgh. His interest in the Museum lasted long beyond the period of his Lord Provostship. As Member of Parliament he re-opened the negotiations which led to the extension and completion of the buildings by the Government's contribution to the city improvements which distinguished the civic reign of Lord Provost Chambers; and in December 1867 he was cordially thanked by the Council for his services. Nor did his vigilance relax after his retirement from Parliament. The probability is that but for his urgency as a private citizen in requiring the Government's fulfilment of their part of the contract, the extension buildings would not have been completed as they were in 1886—the year of his death.

Many other practical advantages were conferred on the citizens during his Lord Provostship. The Meadows were secured as a public park; and in order that the full benefit of this place of recreation might be obtained, and also that an additional access to the town from the south and west might be provided, Mr. McLaren, continuing his work in

co-operation with his successor, Sir John Melville, effected
an arrangement by which what was then part of a market-
garden was opened up as Brougham Street. The public
health and enjoyment were promoted, too, in another way.
The Corporation set an example of cleanliness ; and while
the streets were beautified, a large scheme of drainage was
undertaken. In his private memorandum Mr. McLaren
says :—" During my period of office I was *ex officio* a Commissioner of Police, and as chairman of the Drainage Committee of that body took a great deal of trouble in getting
drains formed on the south side of the town, where there
were very few, particularly to the east of Nicolson Street.
The Public Act authorised this to be done at the expense
of the owners, and we did it to a large extent. After my
Provostship was over, I consented to be returned as a Commissioner of Police to endeavour to finish our work, and resumed my duties as chairman of the committee for another
year."

The irksome duty of caring for small things Mr. McLaren
did not shirk, and his vigorous attention to these secured,
to a greater extent than was ever before known or has
since been seen in the municipal administration, the maximum of efficiency with the minimum of waste. But the
personal superintendence of administrative details did not
by any means monopolise his time and attention as Chief
Magistrate. Apart from Annuity-Tax and election struggles (elsewhere referred to), he discharged all the public non-
municipal work pertaining to the Chief Magistracy. As the
head of the community, he placed himself at the call of the
directors of charitable and philanthropic societies and the
promoters of social and political reforms ; and one of the
earliest public meetings over which he presided in his capacity as Lord Provost was that held in the Hopetoun Rooms,

1853

Drainage
schemes.

Multi-
farious
duties of
Chief Ma-
gistrate.

consequent on Sir John McNeill's report on the condition
of the Highlands, in favour of raising a fund to provide for
the voluntary emigration of 500 families from Skye. While
anxious to aid in practical efforts for the mitigation of
human suffering at home, he was ready to listen to the cry
for sympathy and help from over the sea. He followed with
the keenest interest the struggle for the abolition of slavery
in the United States; and as Lord Provost he gave a warm
welcome to Mrs. Beecher Stowe when that distinguished
lady visited the city to plead the cause of the emancipation
of the slaves. He arranged the more important meetings
addressed by Mrs. Stowe in Edinburgh, and presided at the
banquet given in her honour. Some time after her return
to her home across the Atlantic he received the subjoined
letter :—

ANDOVER, MASS., U.S.A.,
July 11, 1853.

RIGHT HON. LORD PROVOST,—Since my return to America, I
find a story very extensively circulated which is calculated strongly
to prejudice the people of this country against the good people
of Edinburgh, and to counteract any good influence which their
proceedings might have had.

It is this, to wit, that at the banquet in Edinburgh in honour
of Mrs. Stowe, over which your Lordship presided, the American
flag was exhibited, torn and mutilated, the stars without the
stripes, amid the shouts of the people.

The story, so far as I can learn, was first told in the Old School
Presbyterian newspaper in Philadelphia credited to the Edinburgh *Witness.* It has been confirmed by the following passage
in the *Guardian's* report of Dr. Guthrie's speech : "Look (pointing to the flags displayed in front of the platform) at these
stars there, though wanting the stripes. (Cheers.)" Now, my
recollection is very strong that in front of the platform were
displayed both the British and American flags equally honoured,
both new and entire. I have no remembrance, either at that or

any other meeting, of a mutilated American flag. On the contrary, the whole tone and spirit of the meetings, and of the
people whom I met in private, was altogether respectful and
kind towards America and American institutions. (Slavery I do
not recognise as an American institution.)

I have written to Dr. Guthrie, and hope to have a speedy
answer. But I am particularly desirous of having your
Lordship's testimony. You were chairman of the meeting,
and it was attended and patronised by the very best men
and women in Edinburgh, and indeed I may say in all Scotland.

Whenever anything effective is done against slavery, the
method here is to excite some prejudice, to bring in some side
issue, to destroy its influence for good.

Will you be so kind as to give us your help in this matter?
I shall always retain the most grateful remembrance of your
Lordship's attention to us while in your city. Nor can I ever
sufficiently express my gratitude to the citizens of Edinburgh
and the people of Scotland generally.

We are here in the midst of a terrible conflict, but the Lord
is our Helper.—Very respectfully yours,

C. E. Stowe.

The Lord Provost found little difficulty in removing the
misunderstanding which had arisen, and the incident closed
without any estrangement of feeling among Mrs. Stowe's
numerous Edinburgh friends.

In September 1853, Mr. McLaren, as Chief Magistrate,
was privileged to render a complimentary service of which
he was ever afterwards proud—to confer an honour which
itself reflected an honour on the city. Having induced the
Council to confer a free burgess-ticket on Mr. Gladstone,
then Chancellor of the Exchequer, he established the connection of citizenship between Edinburgh and a statesman
who now ranks as one of the most distinguished men of
his day.

1853

Mr. Glad-
stone and
the City
Freedom.

The Town Council having discussed Mr. Gladstone's Budget of 1853, the Lord Provost wrote to inform him of their approval of his financial policy.

Writing on May 4, Mr. Gladstone replied:—

My Lord,—I have not had the honour to receive the copy of the *Scottish Press* to which you refer in your letter of the 27th, nor, therefore, the advantage of perusing the report of the proceedings of the Town Council of Edinburgh on the subject of the financial measures of the Government.

I am unwilling, however, longer to postpone my acknowledgments for your very courteous letter, and the expression of my gratification on learning that a body of so much weight and intelligence as that over which your Lordship presides has declared almost unanimously its approval of the financial policy which, with my colleagues, I have recommended.

The approval of Parliament and of the country has already more than fulfilled all our wishes with regard to the broad outlines and leading principles of those measures, and I trust that, after such an interval as the discussion of subjects so important may demand, we shall see them securely embodied in the law.

I have the honour to be, my Lord, your very faithful and obedient servant,   W. E. GLADSTONE.

The Right Hon. the Lord Provost
   of Edinburgh.

After the Town Council had agreed to recognise in a still more substantial manner Mr. Gladstone's legislative services and eminence as a statesman by conferring on him the Freedom of the City, Mr. McLaren received the following letter, dated from the seat of the Duke of Buccleuch, Dumfriesshire :—

DRUMLANRIG CASTLE, THORNHILL,
September 30, 1853.

My Lord Provost,—I have had the honour to receive, at this place, where I have been spending to-day, your obliging letter of the 29th, in which you state that an official communication had been addressed to me at Dunrobin Castle, with the intelligence that the high honour of the Freedom of the City of Edinburgh had been unanimously voted to me. I have likewise read the report and correspondence on the same subject in the *Courant* yesterday.

I sincerely regret that you should have been put personally to so much trouble on my account. When I receive the official letter which has been addressed to me in the North, I shall better understand whether the vote of the Town Council of itself completes the act of giving me the Freedom, or whether it is in reality a preliminary proceeding only, which takes effect upon personal appearance and acceptance. I shall then form the best judgment in my power as to the terms in which I shall reply to it, or if I shall be favoured by any information in a further letter from your Lordship, I shall endeavour to profit by it. In the meantime, adverting to the feelings which have been expressed by some gentlemen, I less regret than I should otherwise have done that my having fixed my engagements for this week, at the time when I first heard from you, together with the pressure of public business for the next, shall have disabled me from doing what is always very agreeable to me, and would on this occasion have been peculiarly so, namely, paying a visit to Edinburgh.—I have the honour to be, my Lord Provost, your very faithful servant, W. E. GLADSTONE.

The Lord Provost of Edinburgh.

Mr. McLaren replied, supplying the information desired, and a few days after he reached London Mr. Gladstone again wrote :—

DOWNING STREET, *October* 9, 1853.

MY LORD,—I postponed for a couple of days my acknowledgment of the vote of the Town Council, partly under the pressure of business, and partly in the hope that I might be favoured with information from your Lordship which might serve to guide me. This I obtained in the letter you were kind enough to address to me on the 1st, but which did not come into my hands till the day before yesterday. I prepared yesterday evening too late for post the letter of thanks which I now transmit under another cover, and which I shall be obliged by your making known to the Magistrates and Council on Tuesday.

With respect to the gentleman whose religious opinions make him apprehensive of what he supposes to be mine, I fear it will be impossible for me to disarm or qualify his suspicions within the compass of a letter, but I have the hope that, if we were better acquainted, he might find me less formidable on that score than he imagines.

I am exceedingly obliged by the trouble your Lordship has taken in supplying me with useful information, as well as by the prominent and decided part which you have borne on this whole question, and I have the honour to remain, my Lord, your most faithful servant,   W. E. GLADSTONE.

The Right Hon. the Lord Provost
    of Edinburgh.

A reminiscence at Inverness.

Many years afterwards, in November 1879, when he himself received the Freedom of the Burgh of Inverness, Mr. McLaren pleasantly recalled this incident in answer to a cordial cheer elicited by his mention of Mr. Gladstone's name.

"It may be worth mentioning (he said), that at the time you made him a burgess of the capital of the Highlands, we, the citizens of Edinburgh, made him a burgess of Edinburgh. You were fortunate in having his presence; but we unfortunately missed him. He had to go back rapidly to London, and consequently did not go through Edinburgh; so we had to send him the burgess-ticket, and sacrifice the great pleasure of presenting it to him in person, and of hearing an address from him. I have always looked back with pride on that event; for I happened to be Lord Provost of Edinburgh at the time, and was the suggester of the resolution that the Freedom of the City should be presented to Mr. Gladstone."

Business tact.

Mr. McLaren, like most public men, learned to avoid controversy for its own sake. But it may safely be affirmed

that he never declined it when public interests forced it upon
him. Like John Knox, " he never feared the face of man,"
and his dauntless spirit was always ready to combat for
the truth and right, whatever were the odds arrayed against
him. But regard for public interests was equally operative in
causing him to study the things that make for peace. As
Lord Provost, he cultivated and maintained most cordial relations with the county neighbours of the city ; and though, by
this time, the determined opponent of the political influence
of Parliament House, he had many friends both at the Bar
and on the Bench. To Mr. Inglis (afterwards Lord President Inglis), then a leading counsel, he offered a Deputy-
Lieutenancy ; and Mr. Inglis, in intimating his acceptance
and appreciation, wrote :—" Permit me to add, that it is all
the more gratifying that this honour should come to me
through the hands of one with whom I have been so much
brought in contact as yourself in public affairs—an intercourse which to me, at least, and I hope to both of us, has
been productive of so much pleasure and satisfaction." With
Lord Advocate Moncreiff he was more frequently engaged
in the management of public business; and the following
little pleasantry, dated 1st November 1854, testifies to the
happy relations that then existed between the civic and
Government chiefs :—

My dear Lord Provost,—Papers are never *mislaid* in the
Lord Advocate's hands—only too successfully concealed sometimes. I shall do as you wish, but it must be in more formal
shape than you suggest.—Ever yours, J. Moncreiff.

Lord Rutherfurd (the Solicitor-General whose aid had been
given in settling the city affairs) proved a steadfast friend ;
and Lord Ivory shared his brother Judge's confidence in and
admiration for the Lord Provost. In the discharge of his

municipal duties Mr. McLaren was brought occasionally into contact with Lord Justice-Clerk Hope on questions of judicial administration, and the learned Judge formed a high estimate of his character and talents. In the spring of 1854, having learned that the Lord Provost was contemplating a journey to London in connection with municipal business, the Lord Justice-Clerk volunteered a letter of introduction to Lord Aberdeen, which led to friendly relations which Mr. McLaren valued. When the Lord Provost's term of office was approaching its close, the Judge earnestly advised Mr. McLaren's re-election; and when he found that at last retirement could not be avoided, he wrote: "I have for long thought, as I said to Lord Aberdeen in the letter I sent you last spring, that there was no one in Scotland who so well understood or could so well employ the powers, the duties, and usefulness, not only for local but public objects, of municipal government, and of the interests and classes it represents. And the state of the representation of this town makes your retirement a misfortune. It is most true that you have given way to no sect or party, and therefore various parties have not supported you." He concluded: "I ought not to say it, but I hope you will look forward to the representation of the town." In another letter his Lordship said, if he had not been a Judge, and as such precluded from taking part in public questions, he would have attended a public meeting, and, in proposing a vote of thanks to Lord Provost McLaren, would have deprecated his retirement as a misfortune for the city. Through Mr. McLaren the Lord Justice-Clerk was led to take a warm interest in the Heriot schools. The successful administration of these schools, where "for three thousand children education goes on without dispute or collision," supplied, in the opinion of the Lord Justice-Clerk, an *experimentum crucis* which was fitted to do more to advance the cause of educational reform than years of discussion. In the closing days of the Lord Provostship, Mr. McLaren, on the suggestion of Lord Justice-Clerk Hope, who pleaded for the benefit of his " vigorous management," opened in Edinburgh a Patriotic Fund for the benefit of the families of the soldiers engaged in the Crimea.

Before the end of the year 1854, a sum of £16,285 was raised by 11,440 contributors (of whom 2506 had been obtained by a servants' committee) from among a population of 220,000 in Leith, Edinburgh, Portobello, and Dalkeith. Mr. McLaren calculated that if London and the United Kingdom had contributed in the same proportion, the capital would have raised £200,000, and the United Kingdom £1,600,000, whereas the total fund only amounted to £400,000. In conducting this benevolent scheme, Mr. McLaren had many willing coadjutors; and in his speech recording the result at the beginning of 1855, he made special acknowledgment of the aid he had received from General Dyce, Colonel Hope, Sir R. K. Arbuthnot, and Mr. James Richardson.

At the termination of the work he received the following acknowledgment from the Secretary of War :—

WAR DEPARTMENT, January 6, 1855.

SIR,—I am desired by the Duke of Newcastle to acknowledge the receipt of your letter, and to thank you for the great and successful efforts which you have made in aid of the Patriotic Fund in Edinburgh, as also for your kindness in forwarding an account of your proceedings.—I remain, sir, yours obediently,

W. P. C. WINTON.

D. McLaren, Esq.

Mr. McLaren likewise informed Lord Aberdeen of the result of the fund, expressing at the same time his conviction of the existence of a general desire for a termination of the war. He received in reply the following autograph letter :—

DOWNING STREET, July 6, 1855.

DEAR SIR,—I beg to return you my sincere thanks for the interesting account of your exertions on behalf of the Patriotic Fund, to which must in great measure be attributed the contrast afforded by Edinburgh compared with other cities and towns in the United Kingdom.

I am obliged to you for the intimation you give me of the present state of public opinion, which, from the opportunities you possess of arriving at a just conclusion, entitle any statement made by you on the subject to be received with respect and confidence. —I have the honour to be, dear sir, very truly yours,

ABERDEEN.

D. McLaren, Esq.

About the time that Lord Justice-Clerk Hope induced Mr. McLaren to undertake the promotion and organisation of the Patriotic Fund, his fellow-Magistrates proposed to take action to secure for him some mark of royal recognition. Mr. McLaren courteously set aside the proposal the moment it was mooted to him. He announced his decision in the following letter :—

NEWINGTON HOUSE, EDINBURGH,
September 7, 1854.

[Confidential.]

MY DEAR SIR,—This morning I have been favoured with your letter of yesterday, communicating the kind intentions of yourself and the other Magistrates towards me; and I beg that you will accept for yourself, and convey to them, my very sincere thanks for this mark of confidence.

I will at once frankly state my views on the subject; for having understood that such an application had been made by the Magistrates on behalf of my predecessor, I thought it not improbable that they might about this time make a similar proposal to me, and therefore I have had the advantage of turning over the possible contingency in my mind.

1854

The opinion, then, to which I have come is, that an application of this kind might fairly be held to be, although indirectly, an application from myself; and with my views, I would not solicit any honour or reward in any quarter whatever. I make this last remark because I think it would not be difficult for me to find other quarters from which I might also, in the same indirect way, get such an application made.

At the same time, I do not wish, even by implication, to say that other men might not fairly hold and act on the opposite opinion.

When I consented to stand for the civic chair, I resolved, if elected, to act with strict impartiality to all, as if I had neither friends or opponents at the Council, and as if all sects and parties were alike to me. I also resolved to endeavour, as far as my influence would extend, to raise the respectability of the Council as a body by keeping down opposition to men of good talents and position, although they might hold opposite views to mine on many important questions, and to conduct the business of the Council so as to keep down the unpleasant scenes and contests which had often occurred in former times. I hoped also to be able to conduct the general business of the city in all other departments so as to benefit the inhabitants.

These were the objects at which I aimed, and which I have steadily kept in view; and the only honours and rewards I expected were the consciousness of having faithfully discharged the duties of my office, and the approbation of a large portion of my fellow-citizens. These honours and rewards I have obtained to at least as great an extent as ever I expected; and the accompanying amount of opposition, jealousy, and bad feeling has not been greater than I calculated upon; for the uncompromising course I resolved to follow led me to anticipate a large portion of these disagreeables, and I have not been far out of my reckoning.

Having thus obtained all the honours and rewards I ever desired, and being quite satisfied on that head, I have only again

to thank you and the other Magistrates for the great kindness
and honour intended towards me, and am, my dear sir, yours
very sincerely,   D. McLaren.

To Bailie Fyfe.

Mr. McLaren had no desire for a knighthood or a baronetcy.
He looked for his reward in the prosperity of the city and
the success of his work; and he did not look in vain.

" Si monumentum quæris, circumspice " :—

The financial equilibrium of a great Corporation established
as a corollary to its delivery from bankruptcy; the supremacy
of the Council in civic administration asserted; a deplorable
social scandal checked, and the practical ability and advantages of a prohibitory liquor law illustrated; the rights of the
poor and of the many maintained in the face of a powerful
oligarchical confederacy; the general health promoted by
the acquisition of a central public park, by the completion
of extensive drainage schemes, and by the introduction of
efficient sanitary arrangements; the sphere of the municipal parliament in relation to municipal life marked out and
occupied; and an example set of indomitable probity and
vigour in the conduct of public affairs which has long
exerted, and will continue to exert, a purifying and elevat-
ing influence on municipal administration.

In the Council Mr. McLaren encouraged the discussion
of non-partisan political measures bearing directly on the
well-being of the people, and in this way he was enabled
to give timely and influential encouragement to the movement for the introduction of a system of national education.
As the Lord Provost, too, he greatly aided, if he did not
actually start, an association for a political cause which he
afterwards made peculiarly his own—the National Association for the Vindication of Scottish Rights. His Lord Pro-

vostship was not merely a civic affair ; it was really a national concern, and it will remain for all time part of the national history.

The contemporaneous verdict passed by the *Edinburgh News*, just as Mr. McLaren was about to bid farewell to the Lord Provostship, is justified by the historical record :—

"He has been pre-eminently (says this journal) the civic head of the entire people, refusing steadily to sacrifice his own convictions to a fleeting popularity, or the principle of self-government and the city's rights either to the blandishments or frowns of imperial power; while his dignity as a magistrate and his deportment as a man have been an ever-present example and rebuke to many with whom office brought him into official contact. These have been more intolerable to some than his Lordship's unconcealed hatred of Whig chicanery or his resistance to Tory exclusiveness. Party will never forgive his tenacity to principles, far less will some of the heads of party forgive that rigid adherence to dignity of deportment and sobriety of life which have constituted the moral glories of his Lordship's civic reign. Without professing religion so loudly as his predecessors, he has refused to sully the official ermine by pandering to the dissipations of the rich, and despised popularity from fanning the delusions of the ill-informed poor; while no cause whose object was charity at home or liberty abroad, or whose aim was the moral elevation of any section of the world's peoples, but what has received from him, officially and personally, when sought, prompt and able support. He has offended palaverers by curt replies, and unmasked self-seeking to the mortification of many. Many more, stung with a sense of their own insignificance as they became dwarfed by his intellectual power, have been soured through envy or made enemies from being 'snubbed,' which meant that his Lordship extinguished by a sentence what they had wasted hours in uttering. Among civic weaklings and self-seekers and make-believes he has literally left no friends, and the entire tribe of political partisans, tax-eaters, and expectants, whether lay or clerical, hate him with a perfect hatred. But in spite of such sectional wrath he has accomplished much for the community, which is acknowledged by all but the entire people now, and which will ever be remembered with gratitude. This consolation his Lordship will have, his bitterest enemies being judges, that his reign has never seen civic rights sacrificed to gratify centralised ambition or cover the conveniences of party, nor by an easy facility has he deceived all with whom he came in contact. Men may differ from him in opinion, but his example as Chief Magistrate can never be cited as a justification of selfish shuffling or discreditable immoderation, while his ability, energy, and devoted application to the city's business have extorted admiration from the most personal and interested of his revilers. . . . He has secured the Meadows as a people's park and advanced the drainage of a large portion of the town where miasma was dispensing death ; he will leave the city 50 per cent. cleaner than he found it ; he has drained the Water of Leith, effected the removal of toll-bars ; he has secured for the community a constant supply of water, and given the inhabitants thirty public wells which the Water Company had long resisted or refused, and would have been refusing still to a more 'pliable' Lord Provost ; he has abolished the impost-tax, and seen another Heriot's school erected to his honour ; he has secured for the University a reading-room, and for Scotland a National Industrial Museum ; he has opened Holyrood to the people, and will also, we hope, before laying down the chain of office, secure the people access to the College Museum ; he has defended the honour of his office with courage from the ambition of Sheriffs and gracefully corrected the inadvertence of a Cabinet Minister ; he has given his intellect and the influence of his office to the defence of Scotland's right against the accumulated wrongs of generations, and has done that parliamentary business for the city which other constituencies have performed for them by their Members ; and having done all this useful and substantial work, he may doff the ermine with the conscious satisfaction that he has done much for which the public will more and more loudly thank him. . . . He has not been without his faults, and these we have freely challenged and opposed ; but as a Chief Magistrate, taking him all in all, he has exhibited a greater amount of both head and heart in action, if not in speech, for the benefit of the entire people than any man who has occupied the ' reformed ' chair before him, so far as our experience goes ; and the city will look long and earnestly before they see his like again guiding their civic counsels from the seat of the Chief Magistrate."

1854

END OF VOLUME I.